SATAN'S HEAD

A THRILLER

SIMON OLDMAN

iUniverse, Inc.
New York   Bloomington

Satan's Head

iUniverse books may be ordered through booksellers or by contacting:

iUniverse
1663 Liberty Drive
Bloomington, IN 47403
www.iuniverse.com
1-800-Authors (1-800-288-4677)

Because of the dynamic nature of the Internet, any Web addresses or links contained in this book may have changed since publication and may no longer be valid. The views expressed in this work are solely those of the author and do not necessarily reflect the views of the publisher, and the publisher hereby disclaims any responsibility for them.

ISBN: 978-1-4502-4250-9 (sc)
ISBN: 978-1-4502-4251-6 (dj)
ISBN: 978-1-4502-4252-3 (ebook)

Library of Congress Control Number: 2010909474

Printed in the United States of America

iUniverse rev. date: 07/19/2010

To my lifelong friend Richard Lock; whose enthusiasm and encouragement made me keep typing; and to my daughter-in-law Carol Schumacher whose computer knowledge and assistance kept me sane.

Let us never forget that government is ourselves and not an alien power over us. The ultimate rulers of our democracy are not a President and senators and congressmen and government officials, but the voters of this country.

Franklin D. Roosevelt

MID-EAST 1976

ENVISION THE TRIBAL lands of Pakistan near Peshawar. This rugged mountainous country- side is perfect for remaining hidden from all enemies and ideal for setting ambushes. Most consider it a lawless no-man's land inhabited mainly by thieves and smugglers. As home to the Khyber Pass, the reputation is well deserved. This rugged terrain consists of dusty trails winding through an arid inhospitable landscape. An equally rugged tribe of Jihadist Muslims named the Sword of Allah call this area home. Today their leader is accepting visitors.

*　　*　　*

As Ahmad paced nervously back and forth in the anteroom, he clutched the razor sharp dagger hidden beneath his kameez so hard his hand ached. The knife, given to him by his squad leader, was his pride and joy. Today it would taste blood for the first time.

Last night the elders had sighted the new lunar crescent. That meant *Ramadan*; the holiest season of the year began today. It was unusually hot, but 12-year-old Ahmad Abdullah Ali knew that fear, not temperature caused the sweat to run down his face and body. Surely, the sound of his heart pounding so frantically in his chest could be heard in the next room where Imam Muhammad Jamali awaited him. Ahmad worried. Did he truly have the courage to carry out his

1

resolution? Might his underweight body fail him when he needed it most to be strong?

Light skinned for a Pakistani, Ahmad was otherwise a typical tribal member with distinctive features. Thick dark hair and eyebrows accented his narrow face. His brown-bordering-on-black eyes were always serious. His thin nose was long enough to cast a shadow over his equally thin lips which, as usual, were pursed. However, Ahmad was neither typical nor average. As a descendant of *Ali, the son-in-law and rightful successor of Muhammad*, he believed he was destined to leave his mark on the world.

A fat Pakistani man wearing shalvar kameez (loose fitting shirt with baggy pants) and a turban came into the room. He had a long scar which ran from his cheek to his chin and then turned downward onto his throat. He had an Uzi slung casually over his left shoulder. Ahmad thought this man must have been close to death when he got that scar. It was the only thing he noticed about his face.

"The Imam has one more guest before you. He should be finished soon. Then I will allow you in," the guard's voice was strangely high pitched and totally out character for the image he projected. His voice should have been deep and raspy. He turned abruptly and went back into the room from which he had come.

The entranceway where Ahmad stood was ordinary; but to a boy of his rural upbringing it seemed magnificent. The furnishings, while sparse, were obviously durable and of good quality. And the colors! Gold's and reds mixed vibrantly with blues and greens. It all spoke of stature and importance. It was indeed a room worthy of the Imam.

The air had a dry over-used smell. A single shaft of sunlight snuck past the edge of a heavy curtain on a high window. Ahmad forced himself to stop his pacing. He then stared at the light beam and concentrated on the dust motes circling within it. Squaring his shoulders, he took a long slow breath. This had a calming effect and allowed him to reflect on his purpose. He believed that today his life would surely change forever. Just as surely, this night the tribal Members would talk of his courage and praise his submission to Allah's will. Then he heard his name called and his knees went weak. The scar-face man gestured for him to follow. Struggling to breathe, Ahmad choked down the gorge threatening to rise from his stomach and walked unsteadily, into the next room on shaky legs.

Imam Muhammad Jamali was feeling testy. The room was hot, the air still and the endless line of self-important self-serving idiots who had gained audience with him this morning, particularly annoying. Maybe he should re-consider air conditioning. The Imam was perched on a large comfortable chair on a platform, which kept him elevated and looking down upon all callers. Personal guards with Uzis slung over their shoulders stood to either side of him, as well as in each doorway and in each corner of the room.

He was a large man with a commanding presence. His penetrating black eyes had a glint of good humor in them. They lied. The man himself had no good will, only a total commitment to the will of Allah and he alone knew that. Bushy eyebrows accented his eyes while a full black and pre-maturely grey beard hid most of his face. He wore traditional shalvar kameez. A large turban obscured his hair. Thick cruel lips completed the visage of, arguably, the most dangerous man in Pakistan. At 34, he was very young to have reached his position of absolute authority in both secular and political matters.

He was Imam of The Sword of Allah, a fundamental Jihadist sect which was the law in this area. A Shia Muslim, Jamali attributed much of his rise to power to his willingness to do whatever was necessary to achieve Allah's sacred will; "acts of terrorism" the liberal Western media called them. The December 29 bomb at La Guardia in New York last year gave him particular pleasure. While only 11 were killed and 75 injured, he considered it a major victory because it took place on the Great Satan's home soil.

A young local trainee being ushered into the room interrupted his thoughts. He vaguely recalled the boys name as Achmed or Ahmed, or something like that. Most of the boys in the area were being prepared for Jihad. According to the squad leader's monthly reports, this one's progress had been notable.

Ahmad strode resolutely behind the guard who had brought him in while his eyes quickly scanned the room. The simple and stark décor surprised him. The walls were bare. A small low table with a pitcher of water and a single glass sat next to the Imam. A single naked light bulb suspended on its cord lit the area. The sole exception to austerity was a large intricately woven rug on the floor immediately in front of the platform. The guard pointed and left. Ahmad stepped onto the carpet and fell to his knees in front of the Holy One. Quickly, he salaamed.

He remained so until the Imam graciously told him to stand. The time had come.

Carefully keeping his head down, so as not to look directly at the Holy One, Ahmad took a few steps backward, off the rug. Where he now stood, a shaft of sunlight cut through the room as if to spotlight his performance. Slowly and deliberately, he recited the phrase he had carefully memorized in Pashto, Urdu and then English, "There is no God but Allah and Muhammad is his messenger. I surrender myself to Allah and to you. From this day forward, I ask to be called Ammar." Then he deftly brought out the hidden dagger with his right hand and raised it above his head.

Instantly, the guards started toward him, but a slight hand movement from the Imam stopped them. Seeing the approval in the Holy One's eyes, Ahmad found the will to continue. With his left hand, he held his left ear out and away from his head. Then, with one powerful stroke, he slashed downward with his razor-sharp knife and severed the ear. Searing pain engulfed him. A quick intake of breath from all the on-lookers and a hush fell over the room. Blood spurted out from the fresh wound. It flowed warmly down his neck, onto his shoulder and spattered the tiled floor. He broke out in a sweat and began to tremble uncontrollably. Unwanted tears welled up in his eyes and coursed down his cheeks. Ahmad dropped his dagger and stood looking at the strange little bloody fragment of himself in his left hand. How long he stood that way, he did not know, but it seemed very long as the pain worsened. Then a single sharp clap from the Imam's hands startled everyone back to reality.

Ahmad dared to look up at the Imam and saw his hand stretched out to him. The Imam made an encouraging gesture. Feeling light-headed, Ahmad found himself stepping as if in a trance toward the outstretched hand. As he did so, he automatically transferred the bloody piece of flesh to his right hand; his clean hand. Carefully, he placed his offering in the hand of his spiritual leader. The Imam smiled at him and said, "See to his wound."

Immediately, the fat guard on his right stepped forward and gently touched the boy on the shoulder. As he led the child away, the guard thanked Allah for allowing him to be present at this important event. Surely, this child was a chosen one. The Imam was obviously pleased with the boy. Tonight there would be much to talk about around the campfire and he had been an eye witness.

As Imam Jamali watched the boy being led away, he thought, this one is exceptional; I must verify his name and step up his training.

For Ahmad, whose name was now Ammar, life could not be better. He had touched the hand of Allah!

CHAPTER 1

FRIDAY JANUARY 18, 2013

U.S. SENATOR JOHN Franks, (Dem-WI) was acutely uncomfortable. He was sitting alone in a booth in a dimly lit area along the back wall of the Baltimore Falcon, a bar billed as the city's hottest leather/levi cruise scene. The booth was upholstered in fake denim. The purple, red and gold color scheme on the walls and carpeting made him feel like he was in an Asian bordello. He cast brief awkward glances at some of the other patrons who, fortunately, didn't seem to notice or were simply ignoring him. It was 12:05 pm and he had been here since 11:30 sipping on a single bottle of Rolling Rock and eating stale pretzels. He had a 3:30 flight home to Madison, and he had to be on it.

His wife Teri's face popped into his head and he could hear her admonishing him, "Don't miss your plane, John. Remember it's a 3:30 flight so be sure you leave in plenty of time." He took another sip and her face and voice went out of his head. Was that man over there looking at him? Was that his contact? Neil Diamond's *Rambling Rose* came on the jukebox. The man rose and asked another man to dance. False alarm, he thought.

He glanced out the window in the front part of the bar. It looked like it was starting to drizzle. Today was a dreary Friday and the small crowd was quiet, almost subdued. An occasional clink of a glass or a murmur of voices would carry to his far corner. He checked his watch for the umpteenth time and took another sip. The man he was to meet had stressed the urgency of his information; otherwise, he would have left at noon.

Dressed in his usual blue suit, white shirt and red tie, he knew he looked out of place. He studied the green bottle and contemplated his situation. It was not that he had anything against gays. He had known a few in his life, even been friends with a couple. In fact, he assured himself, he had rather enjoyed socializing with them.

This was different. He knew no one here. He felt like an intruder. He felt even worse because he had to pee and had been holding it for a good ten minutes now. Senator Franks crossed his legs. This gave him a brief respite from his dilemma, but then the urge returned two-fold. To hell with it! John stood and stepped quickly into the hall. After a seconds hesitation, he chose the door marked 'Kings' and strode purposefully into what thankfully turned out to be the men's room.

He was glad to see that he was alone and unzipped as he rushed to the nearest urinal. As he stood in front of the porcelain K of K gratefully relieving himself, John wondered again, what in the hell was he doing in a gay bar waiting to meet with someone he did not know. Not that he was a stranger to clandestine meetings. Any successful politician had to spend most of his working day in meetings. The most important meetings were with people who were (A) powerful (B) rich or (C) knew a valuable secret. Every so often, he would hit the jackpot and meet with an ABC: a wealthy supporter who had connections and could help him get his job done. This meeting was just about information.

John quickly finished his business and just as quickly zipped up. As he washed his hands, he checked his appearance in the wall length mirror by the sinks. It was then that he noticed the wall length mirror by the urinals on the other side of the room. His image was reflecting back and forth ad infinitum. It created a strange cozy effect, but at the same time, it seemed to expose you from all angles. It would be hard to ignore anyone.

The Senator admired his reflection. He knew he was handsome and he enjoyed viewing his tanned features. His strong chin and deep blue eyes, which lit up when he smiled, were assets he used to good effect. He had learned early in his political career that his good looks and his poise were powerful tools; and not just with women. He believed that many more ordinary looking men, even powerful men, just naturally accorded him a special degree of respect. John often thanked his lucky stars. Good grooming and 'choosing his genes carefully' had made life in the public eye a lot easier. He ran his hand through his reddish-brown hair and smiled at himself again. Many had told him he resembled JFK. Confident that he looked good, he returned to his table and his now warm beer. Once seated, John was relieved. He had felt very vulnerable at the urinal. He had feared that someone would come in and come on to him, someone with a knowing look and a friendly offer. Now, John grudgingly admitted to himself that he was in some weird way, disappointed that had not happened. Not that he was interested at all, no way.

"Are you ready?" A good-looking slender young man was standing at his table. John glanced up to see a man he could only describe as "pretty". He was thin with a Mediterranean looking face. He had pouty lips and ringlets of black curls cascading off his head. Then John saw he was wearing mascara and blue-green eye liner which really brought out his dark eyes. He was wearing a loose peasant blouse with a plunging neckline that revealed his hairless torso. John was startled. After quickly looking the man over he managed to choke out a response, "Ready?"

"Yes sir; would you like another Rolling Rock?" It was then that John saw the tray in the waiter's hand and said, "Ah, no thank you. I'm not quite done with this one." The waiter huffed off. How would he make any money if every customer sat and nursed every drink for an hour?

John was relieved that it had just been the waiter at his table. Still, he wondered, how long could a good-looking man like himself sit here before someone hit on him? Maybe he was too handsome. Maybe he was like Estelle, his gorgeous blonde secretary who was so breathtakingly beautiful few men could muster the courage to ask her out. She spent so many weekends alone it was a running joke at the office. It was not funny to her.

A man, also in a suit, standing next to his table interrupted John's ego trip. John looked up at the man and immediately formed a positive opinion. His custom-made suit, tailored shirt and impeccable tie gave him an air of respectability. His hair was close cropped, and his face clean-shaven. Sincere features defined him as trustworthy even before he opened his mouth to speak. When he did, his voice was a smooth baritone.

"Senator Thank you very much for coming." John, realizing that he wasn't being hit on smiled, stood and automatically offered his hand. As they shook, the man introduced himself, "In case you've forgotten, my name is Don Whitman. This is the second time we have met, but you probably don't remember the first time. You were doing a tour of our facility, and we were introduced."

"Sorry to say, but I don't remember. I meet so many..."

"No need to apologize, Senator," Whitman interrupted. I'm very appreciative that as busy as you are, you agreed to get together."

"Well, your message was very cryptic and I really am a sucker for mysteries," John replied.

"Thank God for that, because what I have to tell you may have incredible implications and you are just about my last hope," Whitman said.

"OK, OK, the plot thickens. I'm all ears," John smiled and leaned toward his messenger.

"I suggest we talk outside," Don said and turned to leave. The Senator grabbed his coat and followed him out the door. Whitman wore no coat. Two patrons sitting at the bar cast knowing glances in their direction as they left. They stepped out into a light drizzle. The temperature was in the mid-forties. All in all it was an unpleasant, uncomfortable day, but Whitman, dressed only in suit and tie seemed not to notice.

"Let me begin by explaining that I am with the NSB, the National Security Branch of the FBI. My title is Associate Director of the Joint Terrorist Task Force. You are probably more familiar with the acronym JTTF. I've been with the bureau ten years." Whitman handed him his identification badge. As he looked it over, Franks said, "Now your name rings a bell; I've seen your name on several reports."

"Reports that have been ignored," Whitman spat out. "That wasn't meant as an insult," he quickly added. There was a brief lull as Franks decided not to take offense.

"So, just what is it I've been ignoring?" the Senator asked mildly, as he handed the ID back to Whitman. Whitman didn't respond to that question; instead he asked, "Are you on American flight 27 out of Dulles?"

"Actually, I am. I'm heading home. How did you know?" Franks asked.

"I've been trying to think of a way I could talk with you personally.

Fortunately, you keep a pretty regular schedule, Senator. I thought if I could give you a lift to the airport, it'd give us a chance to talk," Whitman explained. With that, he hit a button on his keychain. His grey Acura beeped once, the lights flashed and he opened the front passenger door.

"Thank you," John Franks said as he sat. "I appreciate the offer." The moment Don Whitman was behind the wheel John turned to him and said, "Donald Whitman, I have a question eating at me. May I call you Don Mr. Whitman?"

"Of course Senator, I'd prefer it," Don replied.

"Well," Franks asked, "just why in the hell did we have to meet at a gay bar?"

Don laughed, and choked out, "Really, hah, really sorry about that, Senator. It's just that I've used gay bars as hook up points for a number of years. They're one of the few places where two men, apparent strangers, can meet and leave together without suspicion. We may have raised an eyebrow or two, but, I'm pretty confident no one looked at us as being anything more than two horny gay nellies."

"Humph," the Senator chuckled, "can't argue with that." During the ride to Dulles, agent Whitman outlined his findings and his suspicions. The longer he talked, the more concerned Senator John Franks, majority member of the Homeland Security Committee became. About half way to the airport Don pulled out a folder from a briefcase in his back seat and gave it to him. John read while Don drove and what he saw sent chills down his spine. They made it to the airport on time and when Senator Franks got out of the car he gave Whitman a look of extreme concern.

"Why wasn't I told about this sooner?" The Senator asked. Clearly, he was exasperated.

Whitman just cocked his head. Christ the Senator thought the Inauguration is only three days away. He couldn't wait to get to his seat on the airplane so he could study the report in detail. Yet, he was also dreading it.

CHAPTER 2

FRIDAY

MARGARET STOKOWSKI COULD not believe her ears. Her wedding was only two months away, yet Lorna-the-Bitch Jorgenson still wouldn't give her a definite commitment. Biting her tongue almost in two, Maggie paced the room and listened patiently as Lorna droned on and on about her incredibly full social schedule and all the important events she had coming up. So, my fucking wedding isn't that important, Maggie thought to herself. On the phone, she said sweetly, "Lorna, I appreciate your busy schedule. I really, really do. It's just that I'd be devastated if you weren't part of the most important day of my life."

Lorna droned on, and Maggie held the phone against her body as she silently cursed her mother for insisting that Lorna be a bridesmaid. Lorna took a breath and Maggie jumped in,   "Hey, I don't want to cut you off but I just heard the garage door. My mom must be back and we're going to a matinee of Jesus Christ Super Star at the Overture Center."

"Oh, you lucky," Lorna moaned. "I wanted to go to that."

"Yeah, well I wish we were going instead of me and my mother, puke, puke." Lorna giggled and said, "Have fun" and hung up.

"Bitch," Maggie muttered. She went downstairs to greet her mother.

"Hi sweetie, I'm home," Teri Stokowski-Franks yelled as she hurried to the bathroom off the entry way. She quickly peed and washed her

11

hands thoroughly with soap and water. She then ran a brush through her curly blonde hair, which she wore in a perky page boy. Her full eyebrows needed no attention and her mascara was fine too. Teri's deep blue eyes were her most stunning feature and she always made sure to show them to their best advantage. Teri Franks was what men describe as drop dead gorgeous. She touched up her lipstick and went to find her daughter.

Except for her longer hair and multi-color nails, Margaret Stokowski could pass as a younger version of her mother. Wherever they went together, they turned heads. They both enjoyed that. For Margaret, it was almost the only thing she liked about being with her mother. She was sitting on the second step from the bottom waiting.

"Hi, Mom, I'm ready," she said.

"Me too, I'm really excited about this," her mother said. "Give me a kiss and grab your coat. It's chilly out," she added.

"Can't wait," Margaret said as she pecked her mother on the cheek and headed for the front hall closet. "When is Dad due home?" she asked.

Teri paused, "He should get home about the same time we do; six or so."

"Sounds like a pizza night," Margaret lamented. How was she ever going to get back down to size 6 if they kept eating fast food all the time? They got in the car. Teri let Margaret get behind the wheel. Not that she felt OK about it, but it was Sunday and traffic was pretty light. She strapped in and tried not to show her disapproval as Maggie backed out of the garage a bit too quickly.

Teri Stokowski-Franks was in her late forties, but she had avoided middle age spread syndrome by running, working out and swimming regularly. She was justifiably proud of her trim figure. She wished she were a B cup instead of an A, other than that she was content. She was married to a U.S. Senator. She lived in a lovely two-story English Tudor home on a quiet street just off University Avenue in Madison, Wisconsin. It was a respectable house in a well-established upper middle class neighborhood. In short, it was the perfect house for someone who was successful and did not wish to appear ostentatious. Her beautiful daughter was getting married to an up and coming future president of a large paint manufacturing company and she was on her way to see JC

Superstar. Life was good. If Maggie would just slow down, she could actually enjoy the ride into town.

"Turn left here," Teri said.

"I know, mother. Why do you think I have my directional on?" Maggie snapped.

"It just seemed like you weren't paying attention, dear; that's all."

The day was dreary. It was overcast and drizzling a bit, but Maggie wasn't using her wipers. It was just one more little irritation. At least it was not snowing. Teri found her thoughts returning to the day she met her handsome successful husband.

*   *   *

They had been introduced at the FrostiBall in 2004 before he ran for U.S. Senator.

She had lost her husband two years previously as the result of a gruesome skiing accident. Tom Stokowski, the ever-youthful ever-childish daredevil, went skiing in an unauthorized area in Aspen and hit a tree. He had died instantly. This unpleasant recollection interrupted Teri's warm fuzzy trip down memory lane. She remembered coming home from Aspen alone and facing her daughter.

Maggie had not been with them on this trip. It was a get-away just for the two of them. Breaking the news to Margaret had been a heart-wrenching experience. Maggie had the kind of close relationship with her father every daughter wished for but few ever achieved. Teri had occasionally experienced a twinge of jealousy when she saw them together. She knew it was silly. She had the feeling anyway.

Tom's death put a strain on both of them. For a long while, they were like two feral cats forced to co-exist in a one-cat cage. Teri could not understand the cold stony silence her daughter had exhibited when she had given her the news. Did she not have a heart? Margaret deeply resented her mother for taking her father away on a trip and coming home without him. She knew the hatred she felt was irrational, but it persisted anyway. Neither was able to admit how deeply the loss affected them and neither was able to provide much solace to the other. Eventually, they reached an accommodation whereby they both tried to avoid issues known to be problematic. Both knew the situation was awkward. Each blamed the other for most of the difficulty. It only started to get better when John Franks came into their lives.

*   *   *

The annual FrostiBall in Madison was a prestigious formal event. Tuxedos and gowns of all styles and colors swirled about the room. Each man was handsome and every woman beautiful. Teri wore a simple black dress that emphasized her slim figure with a single strand of pearls, matching earrings and dinner ring. Her black stiletto heel shoes accented her shapely legs.

She was there as the guest of her future father-in-law, although neither of them knew it at the time. Edward Matzke, president and owner of a large paint company had invited her. His wife Betty hated formal events. In fact, she hated anything requiring her to be in public. Obviously, he shouldn't attend such an important social event alone, and he was pleased when the widowed daughter of his old friend agreed to go with him. He had called on January 2nd.

*   *   *

"Hello is this Teri?"

"Hello, yes it is." Teri answered politely. The voice was familiar.

"Oh good, Teri this is Ed Matzke. How are you doing?"

"Uncle Ed," Teri exclaimed delightedly. Ed and her father were long time friends and she had been to Ed and Betty's home many times over the years. They were her aunt and uncle by association, and she loved them both. "How are you doing?" She asked.

"I'm great," Ed replied. "Teri, the reason I called is I have two tickets to this year's Frosti Ball and, as usual, Betty doesn't want to go. You know how your aunt is right?"

"Oh yes, I know how Aunt Betty hates crowds and public places."

"Well then, would you be willing to accompany your old coot Uncle to the ball? I promise to not tie you up talking to other old coots."

"I'd love to go with you, Uncle Ed. When is it? I'll need to get a new dress and shoes and..." Ed cut her off with a cheerful chuckle.

"It's not for a couple weeks yet. I'll get back to you soon with details. And, Teri I want you to know you've made an old man very happy."

"I'm the one who has been made happy," she replied. "Thank you for thinking of me."

*   *   *

Even at his advanced age Ed thought it was nice to be seen with a lovely piece of eye candy. He carefully circulated around the room giving everyone an opportunity to see him squiring his beautiful companion. Then he spied his protégé near the front of the room and steered his date that way. John Franks was a popular State Representative who, with Ed Matzke's sponsorship was planning to run for U.S. Senator. When Matzke introduced John to his date, John immediately perked up. Being at this stuffy affair suddenly seemed a good idea. For his part, once introductions were over, Ed Matzke quickly saw he was a third wheel. He excused himself and left. Neither John nor Teri heard or saw him go.

Individually, John and Teri were gorgeous. Together, they were stunning, like a beacon shining in the night. Other attendees all dressed to the nines and looking as good as they were able gawked at them in awe and quickly turn away. Some would hurriedly whisper to others in their group to look. John looked Teri in the eye and she returned his gaze appreciatively. Each was aware of their effect on the other as they held eye contact and grasped each other's hand. They held hands much longer than necessary for a simple introduction. His hand was gentle and protective. Hers was small in his and warm.

Each knew that this moment was important. It was not just a casual encounter. This was not the time for superficial flirting or small talk. Each felt an immediate and special connection. It was a fragile, yet very tangible sense of togetherness. How could such an incredible feeling of oneness develop so quickly and so intensely? Neither of them understood it, but each knew the other was feeling it too.

"So Teri how do you spell your name, T-e-r-r-y?" John asked after introductions.

Teri spelled her name for him and then said, "And yours is J-o-h-n, right?" Her smile told him she was teasing.

"Ed called you <u>Ms.</u> Stokowski. So you're single?" John asked. Then he winced. Why had he been bold and impulsive? It was not like him at all.

"Actually, I'm a widow," Teri replied. "I have a teenage daughter." She liked his directness. "Let's sit," Teri said with a grimace.

"My feet are killing me. That's the price I pay for wearing spikes." They found a small round table with two chairs. During the next three hours they explored each other's histories and hopes. They talked candidly about their strengths and weaknesses.

Teri had a red flag pop up when John told her he was 'not a religious man', but she decided to let that rest until later. There was an awkward pause while he tried to think of something to say. Finally, feeling like he needed to say something, he started to talk at the same time she did. They both laughed and she closed her mouth. The silence persisted for another awkward moment.

"My wife used to tell me I was a procrastinator." He finally blurted. "In fact, she made me promise I'd join the Procrastinator's Club of America, but I just never quite got around to it."

They both chuckled at his humor and self deprecation.

"Maybe you're just one of those people who do their best work when they're under pressure from a deadline."

"Well, that could explain how I got 'A's' on my term papers which I usually started writing the day before they were due."

"One day?" She laughed.

The conversation meandered with a purpose; not idly. They shared past painful events and enjoyed each other's past triumphs and happy times. When John told her about the horrible way in which he had lost his wife and daughter, Teri was filled with sympathy. She actually cried as he told of how life had been savagely ripped from his little girl; how she had disintegrated before his eyes. She understood and shared the loss of his beloved life mate. She told him about her own loss and how it had affected her and Maggie.

She sympathized when he told of how his life had lost its purpose. She stiffened up when he described how booze had provided no real relief, yet he had turned to it to lessen his pain and his loneliness. That was strike two.

Brandy manhattans had been his nightly and often daily ritual. In his disoriented, depressed state, he barely managed to get an honorable discharge from the air force.

At last, when his enlistment was over, he returned to Madison. He did not go there with a purpose. He went because that was where his dad lived and he had nowhere else to go. At the time, he had thought wryly of Robert Frost's words, "Home is where, when you have to go there, they have to take you in." It was true. His father had welcomed him with open arms.

"Your father sounds like a good man. I was lucky too; my parents were great. They're both gone now." Teri was very sympathetic again when he told her that his mother had committed suicide when he was twelve.

"How awful for you and for your father," she said.

"Yes, Dad took it very hard; probably the worst thing was that he believed suicide was a mortal sin. It caused him unending grief to think that his wife was in hell. I tried to console him by telling him that hell was just a mythical place invented by religions to scare people and make them toe the line. He told me I was an idiot. Oh, I forgot to mention that my father is a Pastor."

"Your Dad is a minister and you don't believe in hell?" Teri gasped?

"We maintain an uneasy truce," John said with a grin. I tolerate his superstitions and he prays that someday I'll see the light." Teri winced at the word 'superstitions' but again elected to explore John's beliefs in more depth at a later date.

Teri admitted she had been lucky. She hadn't had too many significant hurts or joys in her life except for the loss of her husband. Prior to that, the worst tragedies in her life had been not being chosen prom queen and having to drop out of college because she was "a little bit preggers" with Maggie. He listened intently. John and Teri, absorbed in each other's stories, sat quietly talking until the ball was over. They did not dance a single dance, nor did they have a second glass of wine. Although they both urgently wanted to touch again, they did not.

When Ed Matzke came back to take Teri home, they politely exchanged cell phone numbers. Then, as Teri was leaving, John asked her what she was doing for dinner the next day. Teri exhaled. She had been very worried that he was just going to let her go.

"Nothing," she smiled.

"How about I take you and your daughter out for pizza? Margaret, isn't it?"

"It is and we'd be delighted. I know Maggie will want to meet you."

"All right; let's say about six then. I'll call you tomorrow to confirm."

"Thanks. Bye."

"Bye." Neither of them remembered their trip home that night.

CHAPTER 3

FRIDAY

THAT NIGHT, AFTER meeting the lovely
Teri Stokowski John was both exhilarated and depressed. He hadn't felt
this way about a woman in several years. Of course it was too soon to
start thinking seriously, but he was very excited by her. At the same time
he was bothered by a sense of guilt. Was he betraying the memory of
his deceased wife Marcia? No, of course not; that was nonsense. He had
been alone a long time now and no one could blame him for finding
a new love in his life. Still, when he went to bed he tossed and turned
and was unable to relax. The conversation with Teri had stirred some
long silent memories and he was wrestling with them now. Finally, he
fell asleep.

*   *   *

In an instant he was back at the airport in Rome Italy 1990. He
seemed to be floating in the air and watching the scene unfold. He
stared in fascination because he knew he was watching himself and yet
he was an observer at an event.

*It was 8:15 GMT on December 27. Second Lieutenant John Franks
USAF stood in line with his wife Marcia and daughter Brenda at the El
Al ticket counter at Leonardo da Vinci-Fiumicino airport. The airport
was crowded. The line was creeping slowly, and 3 year old Brenda was
complaining that she had to go to the bathroom. She only recently had
stopped wearing training pants. She was very proud of her new ability to use*

a toilet, and took every opportunity to demonstrate it. Marcia grabbed her left hand with an air of resignation and started toward the nearest ladies room. Brenda clutched her favorite doll under her right arm and smiled.

The first bullet struck precisely where Brenda's right arm joined into the socket of her shoulder, shattering nerves, muscles, tendons and bones. It severed her arm completely. Her doll went flying. Splinters of bone poked through the hole where the bullet had exited. The impact spun her rudely to the right. The third slug hit her left clavicle with a glancing blow, yet with enough force to snap this vulnerable bone as easily and as indifferently as an eggshell cracked on the rim of a bowl. Yet, it was the second bullet that did the job. This one caught her on the left side of her throat, sliced her left carotid artery, destroyed her larynx and exploded through the vertebrae in her neck. It almost decapitated her.

From the first to the third bullet, scarcely a heartbeat of time had passed. In that brief instant, Brenda Franks went from carefree toddler to gruesome corpse. Such is the power of a short burst of .223 caliber shells fired by an M-16 rifle set on automatic and spewing over 700 rounds per minute. Propelled by over-sized cartridges, the missiles tumble as they travel at a rate of 3200 feet per second. The tumbling maximizes damage on soft flesh. While these first three projectiles performed their gruesome task, four more found Marcia Franks with equally deadly effect. Her expression of horror at seeing her daughter torn apart, changed to one of agony as she was struck with lethal force simultaneously in her leg, groin, heart and shoulder. The impact sent her sprawling backward, her head cocked at an odd angle and her heart still defiantly beating and spraying her bright red blood onto fellow victims. In one shattering moment, Lieutenant Franks' world disintegrated before his eyes. He went from annoyance at the slow-moving line at the ticket counter to anguish and stunned disbelief.

Impossibly, his beautiful little girl appeared to come apart before his eyes, while his beloved wife reeled backward and hit the terrazzo floor. She too was clearly dead. The sound of automatic rifle fire registered with him only vaguely, as if it were merely some muted background noise accompanying the carnage. His mind was rejecting the tragic meaning of what his eyes and ears were telling him. The evidence beat insistently on the closed doors of his consciousness. As his mind rebelled, John's survival instincts kicked in and he dropped to the floor. Two bullets instantly tore through the space where he had been standing. A third grazed his elbow causing immediate pain.

"God damn it," he yelled as he focused his rage on the gunmen. "Who the hell are you? Why in the hell are you doing this?" As if in answer, yet another bullet whizzed by his head narrowly missing him and striking an elderly Jewish man just above his right knee. The old man's cries of pain added to the screams of the panicked and terrified travelers and the moans of the wounded and dying. The man crumpled to the floor, cruelly twisting his injured leg. The sharp pain caused his heart to begin beating erratically.

'Stay down," Lieutenant Franks said as he took a quick look at the man's knee. He could see that the wound was surely not fatal.

Others were not so lucky. Brenda and Marcia had the distinction of being the first two victims, but when the slaughter was over there would be sixteen fatalities and ninety-nine wounded. John rolled to his right and started to crawl out of range of the murderous gunfire. As his brain acknowledged the pain in his elbow, more sounds began to register on his consciousness: the angry crack, crack, crack of the rapid-fire weapons, the sickening thump as a bullet found flesh, the disappointed twang as one ricocheted off a wall, and the constant cries of pain mixed with wails of fear, some muted and stifled and others loud and piercing.

"Get down, everyone get down!" The El Al ticket agent was yelling and waving his arms up and down to his sides just as a bullet caught him in the side of his head. His arms stopped immediately and he dropped to the floor. In the very back of John's mind a thought surfaced: Marcia and Brenda were dead. They were both dead. He tried to suppress the thought, but in his heart he knew it was true. What he did not understand was, why.

John raised himself to a prone position on his good elbow. As he blinked his eyes his vision cleared and he saw three men standing not thirty feet away; each was calmly and methodically firing short bursts of automatic fire into the crowd. They were dressed like Americans in jeans, pullover sweatshirts, tennis shoes and baseball caps. The three butchers were obviously from some Middle Eastern country. They held their weapons at waist height and slowly turned their bodies from side to side as they randomly executed the group of strangers. Their faces exhibited malice and grim determination.

"Death to all infidels and Jews," screamed the nearest terrorist as he raised his rifle above his head. John spotted a fourth terrorist standing by the entrance. This one appeared to be serving as a lookout. He held his rifle at the ready, but was not firing. He seemed to be observing the operation and *nervously checking for airport security. His brown-bordering-on-black eyes were darting back and forth and his lips were pursed. He was not happy. Something might be wrong. Surely, John thought. The sounds had carried outside. Where was airport security? Where were the police? The man at the door must have been thinking along the same lines. He looked at his watch. John estimated no more than twenty seconds had elapsed since the first shot. The man raised his rifle above his head and shouted "Allahu Akbar!" The rest of the assassins repeated the phrase three times as the killing continued. Then the lookout yelled "Time!" while dropping his rifle, pulling the pin on a hand grenade and lobbing it into the crowd. The others followed suit and the group of four strode quickly out the door. Just before the hand grenades went off, John Franks realized what was wrong with the terrorist at the door. The disfigured son-of-a-bitch was missing his left ear. Then the concussion from the grenades caused him to lose consciousness.*

*   *   *

In his dream John looked down on his comatose body and surveyed the destruction and mayhem which the terrorists had caused. A strong sense of remorse engulfed him along with an even stronger thirst for revenge. It was the beginning of the healing process for getting over the loss of his beloved wife and daughter. He understood that he could and would love again when the time was right. It was also the start of a lifelong drive to find the one-eared asshole who had led the raid.

*   *   *

John awoke the next morning feeling very refreshed and eager to greet the day. He did not remember re-visiting the horrific 1990 scene at the airport in Rome. All he thought of was the gorgeous woman he had met last night at the Frosti Ball.

CHAPTER 4

FRIDAY

AMMAR ALI USED every bit of self-control
he had not to slap the insolent woman's spiteful face. He was sitting
at the counter in a small grungy diner called Chet's Place. It was just
around the corner from his small walk-up apartment and he found
himself eating here more often than he liked. He had respectfully
requested some packets of sugar for his milk. Americans drank cow's
milk, which was practically tasteless. He needed to travel clear across
town to a specialty store to get goats milk for home. Some sugar in the
restaurant milk helped make it drinkable.

The waitress had made it quite clear that she was not happy
about the extra trip to the other end of the counter. She shrugged her
shoulders and then she hunched them forward as she plodded over
to the condiments area. She shook her head back and forth, as she
plodded. Drama was the only joy her job gave her. When she returned
with the sugar packets, she slung them onto the counter and walked
away muttering under her breath about "damn sand niggers." In her
defense, she continued to serve Ammar whenever he came in and the
cheap SOB never left her more than a quarter.

Fortunately, Ammar did not hear her. Her attitude was enough
insolence for a woman. Had he heard the remark, she would have
needed to be disciplined publicly and soundly.   He finished his
lunch. Since he had drunk milk, he prayed softly to himself *"Allah
bless me with it and increase it for me."* Having also finished a meal, he

continued *"Praise be to Allah who fed me and gave me drink and made me Muslim."* Then he left. Today he would leave no tip.

Ammar had aged greatly over the years. He showed every one of his forty-nine years.

Some of it was due to the harsh sun and arid climate of his homeland, some to the stressful life he had chosen as a jihadist; but, much of his aged look had occurred in the last couple of years due to the anguish he experienced everyday in America. Living among the infidels was truly a test of one's commitment to doing Allah's will. Ammar had been here for almost three years. Now the end was so close he could taste it. He longed to be home among his own people. He missed the daily rituals of prayers with fellow believers, the familiar foods and smells, the sights and sounds, the common courtesies.

"Oh, what I'd give for the scent of lamb being roasted in an open pot; or just for the acrid smell of a small wood fire burning just hot enough to slowly cook the succulent meat." He realized suddenly that he had voiced his desires aloud. He looked around him and saw that no one appeared to have heard him. He ached for the comfort of being among people with similar features and skin tones. Mostly, he missed the reassurance of living in a land where people took their religion seriously. He hated America for its tolerance for any belief or lack of belief. How can anyone feel safe amidst such religious anarchy?

Perhaps the worst thing was how most people in this country viewed him. He could see it in their eyes. Their looks conveyed the message 'just another towel-head, probably a cab driver or a store clerk.' The people on the street who formed this bigoted opinion could not be more wrong. None of them had a clue that this quiet Arab looking man was going to change their lives forever.

"Watch it gramps!" A boy of about 15 on a skateboard almost knocked him over. He watched as the youth sped away and lamented the lack of respect for elders displayed by so many American children. He had been diligent in his efforts to fit into American society. He wore tee shirts with logos and a Washington Senators baseball cap. He had grown his hair out so that it covered the sides of his head. His badge of honor, his missing left ear, was too prominent. It drew attention to him needlessly, so he kept it covered. In his mind, he dressed like a typical middle-aged American male who had to work for a living. However, his swarthy complexion and mid-eastern features meant almost everyone he met immediately tagged him as Arabian. His actual heritage was of no consequence to most Americans. His looks classified him as 'Arab'. He was fluent in Urdu and English, both official languages of his native Pakistan. He also spoke a smattering of Pashto.

Try as he might, he could not mask his accent, the result of regional dialects and British influence. English had become an official language of his country during its years of occupation by the United Kingdom. His landlord had once told him he sounded like "Gunga Din trying to pass himself off as a Brit." He didn't know what that meant and had to have it explained. When he learned that it was a reference to an Indian, he was insulted. Pakistan and India were long-time bitter enemies. When anyone asked him where he was from, he kept his answer brief and truthful, "I am Pakistani", and then changed the subject to discourage any further inquiries. Today was Friday, his usual day off from his job at the Hotel Harrison. As he waited to catch the bus that would take him to the hotel, he noted the flurry of activity as more and more workers and tourists poured into town. Traffic was much heavier than usual. Horns beeped, drivers cursed and police blew whistles. Listening to the cacophony, he thought what a place this is. Only a madman would choose to live here. Then he chuckled to himself. Some might call *him* mad.

Of course, the frantic activity was due to the Inauguration Ceremony and Inaugural events, which were only two days away. Oh, blessed day, he smiled. He had decided earlier, right after morning prayers, that he would "check his locker" today. He knew everything would be fine, just as it had been every day for the past two months. Nonetheless, he would not rest easy if he did not see it with his own eyes. The police officer on the corner directing traffic blew his whistle and put up his hands to stop traffic.

"OK to cross now," he said looking at Ammar. He motioned impatiently when Ammar stood there not moving.

"No thank you, officer." Ammar said. "I'm waiting for the bus."

The officer gave him a disgusted look like he didn't belong on that corner if he wasn't planning on crossing the street. Just then the bus pulled into the stop and disgorged a load of riders. Ammar boarded it and took a seat in the rear where he would be less noticeable and where he could think with fewer interruptions.

As he had been doing all week, he reflected on the current month of *Rabi-ul-Awwal.* The third month of the Islamic calendar, he also considered it third in significance. It was a very holy time and a period of special meaning to all Shiites. Ammar, along with a strong minority of Shia Muslims, believed that yesterday, the 17th was the birthday of Muhammad. He had spent the day fasting and praying. Second in importance for Muslims, especially Shia Muslims, is the month of *Muharram.* It marks the anniversary of *The Battle of Karbala* in 680 AD. In the fighting, *Imam Husayn ibn Ali,* a grandson of *Muhammad the founder of Islam,* and a *Shia Imam,* died. Muslims everywhere honored Ammar's ancestor, *Imam Husayn ibn Ali* as a martyr.

Ammar wondered if he might be so honored one day. However, that was not his primary concern. Imam Jamali had assured him that it was his destiny to bring the Great Satan to its knees at this time. It would be a fitting tribute, an act of retribution in memory of the Prophet. Yet, as a diligent student of the *Quran* and *Al-Kafi Hadith,* Ammar was torn. There were guidelines for everything; how to eat, how to pray, how to treat women, how and when to fast, how to treat enemies, how to raise children, and on and on. The guidelines covered every aspect of life. Unfortunately, the teachings of the *Quran* and the meanings of the *Hadith* were sometimes subject to interpretation or were even in conflict. One chapter said one thing while another contradicted it. Ammar considered himself a man of faith, not a scholar, so, whenever he found himself caught in a quandary of conflicting beliefs, he prayed fervently until his questions went away.

"Hey, buddy. Are you all right?" The questioner was a younger man in his thirties. He was looking at him with concern. Ammar realized that he had been praying aloud, under his breath but loud enough that he had attracted the attention of those around him.

"Yes, yes I am good. I was just praying," he explained. The man smiled.

"Well, you better watch it partner. That can get you in trouble in this neighborhood."

He laughed to let Ammar know he was just kidding. Ammar smiled and nodded. Living among the hedonistic Americans had only served to convince Ammar more firmly that he was engaged in a Holy War against the great Satan. He was the one who had come up with this plan to strike fear into the hearts of all Americans.

Almost three and a half years ago, he had convinced his leaders to think big, to have patience, to deliver a knock-out blow instead of concentrating on a series of minor irritations like blowing up airplanes or sending individual suicide bombers to various minor targets. He had challenged them with a simple question.

"Why do you settle for being a mosquito biting an elephant on its behind, when you could be a lion biting off the serpent's head?"

Then he had proceeded to explain that once every four years for one or two days, the United States was extremely vulnerable. For this brief period, virtually every leader of the country was in Washington DC for the Inauguration of the President and Vice President. This ceremony took place at the White House. Why not send an entire squad of suicide bombers to attack during the ceremony?

His idea had caught the imaginations of his leaders, especially Imam Jamali and Hassan Habib. When Hassan confided that he had access to a nuclear weapon, their ambitions grew. The plan took on a life of its own and reached out to several Jihadist groups. Even rival Sunni sects were eager to be co-conspirators and willing to help finance the operation. Admiration and respect for the Sword of Allah soared along with the grandiose objectives. As the originator, Ammar would command the operation. Now, as the day drew near, Ammar was sleeping poorly and his stomach ached constantly. He was powerless to stop the mighty forces of destruction he had put in motion.

The sound of the bus's brakes interrupted his thoughts. He looked out, saw that he was already at his stop, and quickly got off. Now he wondered what excuse he would give for coming in on his day off. Ammar actually liked working at the Hotel Harrison. Being a bellman was relatively easy work and the tips were generally quite good. He needed the flexibility his job provided, and as a bellman in uniform, he was practically invisible.

The Hotel Harrison's claim to fame was that it had the longest record of continuous operation of any hotel in the city of Washington D.C. At one time, it was the largest. These days, guests enjoyed the antique feel of the place including a working mailbox installed in 1918. It used a chute and had a drop slot and a glass panel on every floor that allowed you to see all the mail falling to the ornate holding box in the lobby. Ammar had sought a job here for one reason.

It was dead center between the Whitehouse and the Capitol and about six blocks from each.

CHAPTER 5

FRIDAY

ADMIRAL LEON "MAC" MacKenzie picked up the metallic scale model of the U.S.S. Bertram off his desk. It had been a gift from his crew when he retired from active command. He turned it over in his hands and marveled at the detail. He found himself longing for the simpler life he had led in his days as a Fleet Admiral. Today everything was more complex. His intercom buzzed, "Admiral, your constituents are here for your meeting."

"Thank you, Grace. Please show them in, and bring a pitcher of water with four glasses."

"Yes sir." She answered.

He set the ship back down and turned to survey his office. Then he laughed at himself. After years of shipboard living where space was at a premium, he now had the luxury of plenty of wall space and a huge room for his office. He had taken the opportunity to fill his walls with photos of himself with various dignitaries, including two presidents, and mementoes of places he had been and awards he had won. Looks like a goddam cluttered museum he said aloud.

A moment later the door swung open and three men filed in followed by Grace with a pitcher of water and four glasses on a tray. She set the tray on the round meeting table and exited without a word. Admiral MacKenzie was the first to speak.

"Blackjack, Archie, Nate thank you for coming and for your promptness. Let me assure you, I had this office swept for listening devices earlier this morning and my personal microphones are turned off. The room is secure."

"Never a doubt in my mind," General of the Army Nate Grumwell said. General Grumwell was five foot ten inches tall and weighed 190 pounds. Try as he might, he could not prevent added pounds from accumulating on his body. He blamed it on his age and his desk job.

His wife Sarah said it was too much drinking and too many banquets. They were both right.

His rounded face was consistent with his sagging lips and narrow eyes. He had recently given up smoking cigars and it still bothered him. A fringe of black hair circled his bald pate.

"Of course," Vice Chairman of the Joint Chiefs General Jack "Blackjack" Carson of the U.S. Marine Corps said heartily and a bit too loudly. General Carson looked exactly like what everyone would expect the leader of the U.S. Marines to look. At six feet even, he stood rigidly erect and had a flat stomach and broad shoulders. His no-nonsense expression was enhanced by his square jaw and perfectly formed nose. His deep blue eyes looked both serious and, yet somehow, boyish. His ears stuck out boldly; a feature that was exaggerated by the close shaved haircut of a marine.

General of the Air Force Archibald Simmons nodded. Simmons was a beanpole. He stood six feet four inches on a slender frame and weighed in at a lean 180 pounds. His face was pinched and his nose, which was much too large for the rest of his face, ended in a slight hook.

He had a small mouth and when he spoke his teeth seemed too small. All in all, his facial expression said he had just tasted something that was way too sour. Large ears completed the awkward arrangement that constituted General Simmons' persnickety image.

"Gentlemen, please be seated," Mac said as he took a chair. It was a round table and there were no seats with any more rank than any other, yet each of the chiefs sat in exactly the same chair they always sat in for these meetings. This observation amused the admiral.

Admiral MacKenzie was a made-to-order role model of leadership. Average in height and slim of build, his handsome rugged good looks exuded competence and ability. His full head of snow white hair accented his pleasant features. If there was ever a recruiting poster needed for the Chairman of the Joint Chiefs of Staff, he would surely have been on it. Whenever he spoke, he smiled.

"Gentlemen, as always anything we say in this room is considered top secret and is not for repetition."

"Mac, we're not children here," Nate protested.

"No, but Archie was not among us when we did what we're about to discuss, Nate."

With that he turned to General Simmons and said, "Archie, I know where your heart is and so I've decided we need to let you in on some of the history of this office. He then addressed the other two. Nate, Blackjack, I believe Archie deserves to understand why we're all so concerned." They nodded their assents. He turned back to Simmons.

"Archie, in 1997 I had just been promoted to Chairman of the Joint Chiefs. Soon after, your predecessor and I, with the help and full agreement of these two fine officers seated here, arranged to steal a Nuclear Weapon from the U.S. arsenal."

"You did what?" General Simmons almost laughed then he sobered. "Why?"

"Well, we were all sick of the war in Afghanistan that the politicians had gotten us into. Every year we were sending more and more troops into that quagmire with no real plan for victory and no exit strategy. It was a waste of good men and equipment."

"And here we are now, thirteen years later and nothing has changed. We're still waging an unwinnable war and sacrificing Americans every day for no good reason," added Blackjack Carson. General Grumwell slid his chair back from the table and took a sip of water.

"If you knew the corrupt Afghan government we have had to deal with, you'd come to the same conclusion-the war has always been unwinnable, Archie."

"Gentlemen, I know my history. Please don't treat me as a freshman just because you've all been here longer than me."

"Not at all," Mac said quickly. But, you should know that we, with the help of General Wayne Armstrong did manage to secure a nuclear device."

"Then you better fill me in. What did you do with it? Do you still have it? What are your plans?" At this point General Carson jumped back in.

"Let me answer your questions in reverse order: one, we have no plan, two, we do not have it, and three, after we stole it, someone stole it from us."

"Good God," General Simmons gasped. "How in the hell…"

"Let me explain," Mac said. We wanted to detonate a large nuclear device in the SWAT valley where the Taliban was in hiding. We wanted to take the fight out of them."

"OK, I can follow that reasoning," Archie offered.

"So, Wayne had connections at Minot Air Force base. In fact, he had gotten the base commander, General Wiggins, his position. We arranged with Wiggins to have six Cruise Missiles flown to Barksdale Air Force Base."

"That's in Louisiana," Simmons stated.

"That's right, Nate said. "You see, this whole thing was mostly Wayne's idea. He knew the head psychiatrist at Barksdale. I think the shrink mostly treated soldiers for PTSD, but he also treated civilians who worked at the base."

"Yeah, what does this all have to do with stealing a nuke?" Simmons was getting irritated. It was too much detail.

"Well," Mac interjected in a calm voice, "we knew we couldn't just fire a Cruise Missile or drop a nuclear device from an airplane. Everyone would know it was a U.S attack. So, Wayne got the idea that we could remove a warhead from a missile, smuggle it to our target and then detonate it. No one would know who did it."

"You're shittin' me," Archie said. "Don't you people know that every nuclear device is traceable? A post-detonation forensics team could probably pinpoint where the fissionable material came from down to one or two possibilities." They all looked at each other. No one wanted to be the first to admit their ignorance.

"Anyway," Mac continued, "the shrink had told Wayne that one of his patients, a Mexican named Pedro or Pablo or whatever, was in a major state of depression and wanted desperately to go back to Mexico."

"Yes, and?" Archie was almost out of patience.

"The upshot is this Mexican was in charge of monitoring all nuclear devices on the base. We offered him $500,000 to remove the payload from a Cruise Missile." Mac explained.

"And, he did it," General Simmons concluded.

"Well, at first we weren't sure," General Grumwell said with a glum face.

"You were not sure of what?" Simmons almost choked.

"The missiles arrived at Barksdale on August 30 1997. A couple of days later the Mexican's body was found floating in a bayou. We didn't know for certain what had happened until the shipment was sent back to Minot and they discovered there was a missing payload." Admiral MacKenzie spoke dejectedly.

"And, of course all you master-minds have no idea where the weapon is." Simmons said disgustedly.

"Let's retain an air of decorum and respect." Mac said abruptly.

"Sorry, you're right. My apologies, gentlemen; my temper got the best of me," Simmons said sincerely. "I guess the best we can hope for is that it wasn't a uranium based weapon."

"Why do you say that?" Blackjack asked.

"Nuclear arms that use Uranium 238 and several other types have incredibly long shelf lives. If this stolen payload is of that type it is still dangerous. However, we have made many weapons with other fissionable materials that have much shorter shelf lives. With any luck, the stolen device has expired by now and is no longer a threat."

"Well, that's a happy thought to end this meeting on," MacKenzie exclaimed. "Now, the other reason I called this meeting is to ask that each of you arrange to be out of town over the next couple of days. I'm sure you're all aware of the rumors floating around about an Inauguration plot."

"Way ahead of you Mac," Grumwell said. "I'll be in Wyoming this time tomorrow, hunting elk."

General Carson told them he was scheduled for a ceremony at Camp Le Jeune.

"I've been meaning to do some things at Vandenberg Air Force Base in California. I think now is a good time to go." Simmons added.

"Well, I'm heading for the Nimitz this afternoon, so I guess that's that." The Admiral said with finality. He stood and the rest joined him

"Thank you all. Gentlemen, you're dismissed." Mac said with a smile. They all smiled at his military humor and left. Archie Simmons was silently cursing his predecessor Wayne Armstrong for leaving him with this mess. Generals Grumwell and Carson put most of the blame on Admiral MacKenzie. He and Armstrong had been the driving force for stealing the nuke. Mac too accepted the majority of the blame. It was the price of patriotism.

CHAPTER 6

FRIDAY

As HE DROVE away from Dulles Airport, Don Whitman congratulated himself. His bold move had been successful. Senator Franks had listened and had asked the right questions. Finally, he had gotten the attention he needed. The question remained, was he in time?

Whatever the outcome, at least he was no longer shouldering the worry alone. It was a great relief to have the Senator as an ally.

He continued east on highway 267 while giving himself a pat on the back for his accomplishment; it was a habit he had picked up years ago. In his line of work, compliments were rare. Drop the ball and your ass was on the carpet in an instant, save the world and your bosses took the credit. One way to live with the reality of life in the NSB was to acknowledge when you had done well and reward yourself for it.

Today, he had done well, and he was on his way to his reward before going home to his family and their never ending problems of *earth shaking* importance. Don loved his wife and his kids, but they tended to get on his nerves with their incessant whining and complaining over petty issues. His wife, Vera bitched all the time about his long hours. Don Jr. wanted to get his temps and start learning to drive. Wanda hated school and *needed* cooler clothes, so she could fit in better. Often he came home to all three waiting at the door, each trying to be the first to tell him their problems. He found himself coming home later and later.

"You're a wonderful husband, Don. Trouble is you're married to your goddam job and that's what get's all your attention." This was Vera's favorite line and she used it often. He would not doubt hear it when he went home.

Soon, he would go there, but first he would spend some quality time with Estelle. Sweet Estelle was his only vice. He neither smoked nor drank and only swore in times of extreme duress. Estelle was beautiful, warm and unpretentious. He supposed he loved her too, but as an ethical man, he would never hurt his family. No, he and Estelle simply shared their bodies and enjoyed one another's good company. No complications. No expectations. It was relaxed, open and honest.

If asked, Don would describe himself as a good God-fearing man, a patriot and a model citizen. Of course, no one ever asked. He was a hard worker and dedicated to preserving the greatest country in the world and 'truth, justice and the American way.' He smiled at his habit of interrupting self-praise with self-mockery. Don tried hard not to take himself too seriously. The world was serious enough.

"Nice move, doofus!" Don muttered to himself as a man passed him on the right and then swung over into his lane. The man could have just as easily, and more safely passed him on the left. Don resisted blowing his horn.

He *was*, by most people's standards a very good man. He went to church regularly, was a loving and tolerant husband and father, and strove to be a good and loyal friend. He really hated going to confession. That was when he had to face God and his own imperfections head on. On one hand, he always felt better after confessing his transgressions. On the other, he hated confessing to the same ones every time. He often felt like a hypocrite while saying his 'Hail Mary's', because he knew full well he would be seeing Estelle again. Oh well, nobody is perfect he thought to himself. Don exited onto I-495 toward Alexandria.

His house was in Alexandria and Estelle's was conveniently located along the way in Huntington, just off the interstate.

*   *   *

Estelle Evans was dealing with a severe case of out and out lust and was having a very hard time waiting for Don. She considered masturbating right now just to take the edge off. She decided against it almost before she had thought about it. She wanted nothing to detract from their passion. Don Whitman was the best lover she had ever had or could ever want. She was well aware it would not go on forever, and that was a two-edged sword. She knew when it was over she would miss him terribly, or more to the point, she would miss his love making skills. Yet, ultimately, there was no room in her life for a man until she had reached her career goals and had proven herself to herself.

Estelle saw herself as a single working girl, (all right, working woman) with a very important secretarial position at a very young age. After all, she was just a bit over 30 and she worked for a U.S. Senator in the nation's capital. It was quite an accomplishment for a woman from Racine, Wisconsin who had been born into a working class family.

$$* \qquad * \qquad *$$

Estelle was the oldest of four children. Her father was a tool grinder at Massey Ferguson and her mother worked at Chicken Delight processing the frozen chicken that came in boxes. She had often gone to the restaurant on Saturday mornings to help her mother whose arthritis bothered her terribly from immersing her hands in icy water to clean the chicken.

She loved her family, but she thought of herself as the only one with ambition. Her father was content to put in forty hours a week, drink beer and cheer for the Packers for the rest of his life. Her younger brothers were heading in the same direction as their father. It was not for her. Estelle had made up her mind in ninth grade that she was not going to wind up the wife of some factory worker raising snot-nosed little brats who would also become factory workers. No, she was going to make something of her life. She was going to do important things, meet exciting people, and travel to interesting places.

All it took was two years of Secretarial School after high school. As soon as she graduated, she boarded a Greyhound for Washington D.C. Her family thought she was crazy. They had expected her to get a nice office job in one of the many factories in town and settle down; instead, she had left for a strange city on her own. It was crazy.

With her good looks, excellent school references, beautiful smile and pleasing personality, Estelle had landed an entry-level position with a government agency within her first four days of looking. Her great tits had been the decisive factor.

Estelle's looks, ambition, and willingness to work extra hours were all assets that helped her to find better and better positions within government. Of course, her willingness to provide added benefits for some of her superiors had been helpful too.

✳   ✳   ✳

She landed the secretarial position for the new incoming Senator from Wisconsin almost by accident. She had been delivering papers to the office next to his, and they bumped into each other in the hall. She recognized him immediately from photos she had studied. She smiled and struck a pose.

"I'm so sorry," the Senator said. "I've just been rushing around so much; I guess I had my head up my butt." He found himself trying not to stare. Standing next to him was the most beautiful blonde-haired blue-eyed dazzler he had seen in a long, long time. No take that back; she was the most gorgeous petite blonde beauty he had ever seen. If he wasn't happily married to a gorgeous woman he'd be sorely tempted to pursue this lovely little lady.

"No problem, Senator Franks. Actually, it was my fault," she answered.

"You know who I am?" He asked.

"Oh, I imagine just about everyone knows about the exciting new Senator from Wisconsin. Welcome to DC."

"Why, thank you very much. And who, may I ask are you?"

"I'm your new secretary. Didn't they tell you?" She laughed. Then she explained that she wasn't really his secretary *yet*, but, she would like to be considered. It would be a good career move for her and she was from Wisconsin. As it turned out, she got the job. That was almost a year ago, and she was still happy in her position. The Senator was happily married and never needed any 'benefits', plus he was a hard working dedicated public servant and that suited her just fine.

✳   ✳   ✳

Right now though, the office and her duties were the furthest things from her mind. Just as she felt her lust was going to send her over the edge, her cell phone rang. It was Don. He needed her to raise the garage door for her townhouse. While he was parking his car in her garage, (she did not own a car) Estelle took another P.T.A. bath, and

36

went to her front hall. When Don entered, he took one look at her eyes and they both headed for the bedroom. Don kicked off his shoes as he followed her and laughed when she said, "I hope you're ready to say a shit load of Hail Mary's next week."

CHAPTER 7

FRIDAY

PASTOR (EMERITUS) CHARLES Franks, was not satisfied with how the morning had gone. As he stood at the corner of University Avenue and Ridge Street waiting for his bus, he reflected on the people he had just left. The Horowitz's from Horicon, Wisconsin were a nice young couple facing a very difficult situation. Their four-year old daughter, Anne was battling leukemia and the disease seemed to be winning the battle. Her father, also named Charles, was struggling with his faith. How could God put his innocent little girl through such hell? Why does a merciful God inflict pain and suffering on some of his most loyal followers? His wife, Carol was more concerned with how to heal her daughter and less worried about blaming anyone for her loved one's condition.

Pastor Franks, after so many years of dealing with difficult situations, did not even try to explain God's actions. He knew the 'God works in mysterious ways' platitude would provide no solace. In fact, he still asked the same question himself. Why *does* God allow so much pain and injustice in the world? Of course, that question invariably led to a dead end...and a platitude. He had no answers; however, he did have faith. Yet, this case was going to be especially difficult. The girl's age brought back painful memories of the loss of his granddaughter who was dead before she reached the age of four. He had to put aside the sorrow welling up in his heart and provide comfort to those who were in need. This morning he had prayed alongside Charles and Carol.

They knelt together in front of the altar in one of the small sanctuaries in the hospital. He beseeched God for mercy. He begged God to give the couple the strength to endure His will whatever that might be. Then he prayed for Anne.

"Dear Lord, if it be your will, please let Anne recover from this illness and live to enjoy the many bounties you provide us on this earth; and if that is not to be, please let her pass swiftly." At that point, Charles started to rise and Pastor Franks had to put his hand on his shoulder to restrain him. He then prayed silently and encouraged each of the beleaguered parents to offer their own prayers aloud. They took turns praying and it went on for a remarkably long time. Charles's prayers started out in anger, evolved into frustration, and finally became humble and pleading. Carol prayed quietly and insistently for Anne's recovery. She offered her own life in exchange for her daughter if God would take it.

By the time, they had finished crying and asking for God's help, everyone felt spent. Emotionally wrung out and physically weary from lack of sleep, the couple had embraced Pastor Franks and thanked him profusely.

"Pastor Franks," Carol sobbed. "Thank you so much for being here and for helping us deal with this. Your presence is a god-send. I don't think I could have lasted this long without you." Her husband Charles nodded in agreement and wiped away a tear self-consciously.

Pastor Franks walked with them back to the nearby Ronald McDonald House where they were staying. There, they ate lunch together, which was very good lasagna, a crisp salad with vinegar and oil dressing and garlic toast. Local volunteers donated, prepared, served and cleaned up the meal. Over a dish of spumoni ice cream, he assured them that he would continue to pray for Anne and gave them a blessing.

Now, as his bus approached, he stepped closer to the curb and sighed. At age 79, he knew he would have his questions answered soon enough. He just wished he could put his doubts and challenges to his faith to rest now, instead of after his death. As he stepped up into the bus with some difficulty, he fished in his pocket for the correct change. The fares had increased recently, and he had to dig a little deeper. As he settled into the seat right behind the driver, he acknowledged the nods and smiles of the nearby passengers and then lapsed into thought.

Pastor Franks chided himself for once again letting his depression get the better of him. Whenever he started questioning his worth as a human being, it was a sign that he needed to fight the demon that was taking over his spirit. It had been a lifelong battle. He knew the signs; he also knew what he needed to do. Yet, when the cloud crept over his mind, it was almost like an old friend coming to visit. There was a strong temptation to just relax and let the feeling of helplessness and despair take the helm. When he had done so in the past, surprisingly, it had brought a false sense almost of peace. It was an abdication of responsibility. Poor me; I cannot help being depressed. After all, it is just a chemical imbalance in my brain. It is not my fault. He knew why he was under attack this time. Before meeting with the Horowitz's he had talked with his old friend Doctor Perkins who was treating their daughter. Doctor Perkins had said the child's end was near. The good doctor had exhausted every treatment he knew and the girl was not responding. Armed with this knowledge, he had still gone to see her parents, to comfort them and to convince them to pray. He was a fraud.

"Not only fraud, but also a damn fool," the voice said sneeringly.

At this thought, Pastor Franks sat up straighter in his seat and shook his head. Other passengers smiled knowingly thinking the old man had dozed. No, he recognized the work of the devil. His demon was at him and trying to bring him down. Maybe he had neglected to take his anti-depressant medication this morning. He would check when he got home. Meanwhile, he would concentrate on happy thoughts.

He would put on a positive attitude no matter how he felt. He decided to think about his son, his U.S. Senator son. He was amazed by and incredibly proud of John.

"Yes, the voice said. Think about your son the atheist. That should cheer you up."

"He's not an atheist," Pastor Franks mumbled to himself defying the demon. "He simply has not accepted Jesus Christ as his savior."

*   *   *

The lady seated across the aisle smiled and nodded at him. She observed the clergyman sitting across from her with approval. She had seen him on this bus often, but had never learned his name. He looked and seemed like a very nice man. A little pudgy maybe, but he had a full head of white hair and a cheerful ruddy face. Noah Berry, she thought to herself; that's who he reminds me of; that old time actor Noah Beery. Next time they were both on the bus she would introduce herself.

*   *   *

Pastor Franks continued his musings. When John had come home to him thirteen years ago, he was a wreck. The Air Force had given him an honorable discharge- just barely. John never knew that he had interceded with the base commander on his behalf. John's self-respect had been at low ebb. Let him think he had managed it on his own.

Who could blame John for his despair? Seeing one's wife and daughter slaughtered by terrorists would drive anyone over the edge. He knew John blamed himself for their deaths. He had talked Marcia into accompanying him with their daughter on the trip to his new station in Tel Aviv: when else would they get a chance to see a land so rich in history? Besides, they were only supposed to be there for three days. Charles Franks' greatest burden was his guilt over his failure to set his own son on the path of salvation. It was an unrelenting tortuous feeling of remorse even in his dreams. As a child living alone with his mother, John had simply never accepted the Christian faith. Oh, he gave it lip service and he even went to Sunday school, but he later said he found the Bible stories unbelievable. Later, as a young man he called himself an agnostic. That meant there probably was a God. It was the Christian faith he disdained. Through the years, Pastor Franks had accepted the blame for his son's lack of belief. He felt he had failed him, and he prayed often for the wisdom to overcome his son's stubborn disbelief.

John's best friend since fourth grade was Karim Goldman. Karim had emigrated as a baby from Haifa, Israel to the United States with his mother and father. He knew next to nothing about Israel, but he did know Hebrew because he had to read the Torah.

After his mother's suicide, John took an interest in the Jewish religion. The stories in the Torah were similar to the ones he had heard in the Bible, but somehow they seemed more realistic when read in Hebrew. Pastor Franks had very mixed feelings about that. In the end, he had encouraged his son's interests. He planned to convince John about Christ when the time was right. John's interest in the Torah was getting him to look into the Old Testament at least, so it was a step in the right direction. It was more than he had ever managed.

At Karim's Bar Mitzvah, John had obviously envied his friend's rite of passage. Karim's parents treated him like a second son and even offered to sponsor him. Charles was happy when John declined. His son retained an interest in the language and customs of the Israeli people, so it was no surprise when he majored in Hebrew while in college. He then enlisted in the U.S. Air Force. In his father's footsteps, Charles had said to himself.

After basic training, John had gone to Intelligence School. Upon earning his Second Lieutenant bars, he was assigned to a unit at Wheeling AFB. His job was to listen to conversations from around the world seeking any possible threats to the U.S. There he met, impregnated and married Marcia Dukes (at her request, in a small chapel). Six months later, Brenda had been born. Things seemed to be going well for the new parents over the next three years. John had a promising future, Marcia was thrilled to be a stay-at-home mother and Brenda was a loving and beautiful little girl. At the time, John had indicated he was considering making a career out of the Air Force, so he gladly accepted a transfer to the embassy in Tel Aviv. Being the military liaison was a real plum of an assignment, and he was very excited.

His family never made it to Israel and John never fully recovered from his loss. During the ensuing two years, he drank heavily and performed his duties poorly. His son had to have known that he was skating on thin ice, but he just did not seem to care. Thanks to his intercessions, John managed to get through the period with only a couple of official reprimands and gladly accepted an honorable discharge when his enlistment was up.

Upon his return to Madison, John moved in with him. He remembered how one day, after they had been living together for several months, John had said, "Dad, when I was growing up I looked at you as a not-too-bright man who made a living off other people's superstitions. I think I may have been too harsh in my judgment."

"Which part do you regret son; not too bright or snake oil salesman?" He had laughed.

"The part where you don't take me seriously," He answered and blushed.

"Son, at age 14 every boy thinks his father is old fashioned, out of touch and none too bright. At 21 he is amazed by how much his father has learned in just a few short years."

∗   ∗   ∗

John lived with his father for the next two years. They got along fabulously except when they discussed religion. His father repeatedly urged him to join a Bible study group. John complied twice. Both times he left the group after he found the answers to his questions inadequate and doctrinaire. His father also urged him to join Alcoholics Anonymous, but he said, "Dad, do you know the difference between an alcoholic and a drunk?" His father had replied, "That's an old one, son, but go ahead and tell me."

"Well, we drunks don't have to go to all those damn meetings." John never did go to an AA meeting, but he managed to taper off and then quit drinking. These days he would have a glass of wine or a beer to be sociable, but that was about it.

When John moved out, he became a consultant and taught Hebrew. Through these connections, he began to meet important people in Madison. Over the next few years, he took an interest in local politics and served as an organizer for a state senator's campaign. His father was surprisingly helpful to him during these years, as he seemed to know most of the important people in town. Their relationship had continued to grow. John eventually ran for State Senator and, to many people's surprise, won.

∗   ∗   ∗

Thinking back on these happy days brought an unconscious smile to Pastor Franks' lips. Then he saw the lady, across the aisle from him, was smiling back. She was saying something. He leaned forward and heard, "Pastor, isn't your stop coming up?" He looked out and said, "It certainly is. Thank you so very much."

She smiled again. He managed to get off the bus without too much difficulty and shuffled down the sidewalk to his apartment two blocks away. He was feeling much better and even tried to whistle a little tune. Thinking about his successful son the U.S. Senator had made him feel good for awhile; then, inevitably, the thought that John had not accepted Christ as his savior turned his mood sour. The demon was in charge once again.

CHAPTER 8

FRIDAY

THE TRIP HOME to Madison seemed
inordinately long. John read and re-read the report Don Whitman
had given him. He was torn. There was enough substance to give him
shudders. However, there were also enough unanswered questions to
give him pause. He knew he had to act, but what should his first step
be? The voice of the pilot came over the intercom.

"We are preparing to land in Madison, Wisconsin. Please be sure
your seat belts are fastened and your tray table is in its full upright and
locked position. We will be on the ground momentarily." The captain
continued to talk but John ignored it. He felt the plane decelerate and
nose down for landing. A quick glance out the window confirmed that
they were indeed descending into Dane County Regional Airport.
He decided to think his problem over some more before taking any
action.

He wished he could talk it over with Teri. His wife had a keen
mind and served him well as a sounding board whenever he had critical
decisions facing him. Unfortunately, when they appointed him to serve
on the Homeland Security Committee he had taken yet another oath
of secrecy. He took his oaths seriously.

John worked hard to represent the people of Wisconsin. He
considered himself entrusted by the people, not simply elected. The
committee itself was an amorphous group, still trying to shape itself
into a purposeful body. At first the new Chairman seemed that he was

going to be effective and actually get things done. However, as John had sadly discovered since coming to Washington, it all came down to politics in the end. Ninety-nine percent of what they did was to read and issue reports and appoint more and more committees to investigate more and more areas of concern. In John's opinion, they accomplished little of value.

The Chairwoman of his sub-committee, in particular, had recently disappointed him. He served on the Sub-committee on Intelligence, Information Sharing and Terrorism Risk Assessment. So, how was the Chairwoman of his Sub-committee spending her time lately? She had proudly introduced a Bi-partisan Bill to provide incentives to trade-in inefficient 'clunker' appliances. This bill was to be included in a draft of clean energy legislation. Of course, there were a number of appliance manufacturers in her home state, and they had an active PAC. John did not fault her for the legislation. She was simply doing what was necessary to keep her financial supporters happy. Every legislator had the same burden.

"We're all a bunch of whores," he thought to himself. He was currently working on an extension and revision of dairy subsidies for farmers. He had learned years ago, even long before entering politics that one could never actually just concentrate on doing ones job. Instead, most people had to spend a good deal of their day keeping boss's happy, placating fellow employees and sometimes just looking busy.

John stopped his musings when he felt the aircraft touch ground, bounce once and then settle. Since he was seated in first class, he was one of the first people into the terminal. He particularly enjoyed this little perc American Airlines afforded him. He booked business class, and automatically got bumped up to first class at no cost. Sometimes it was good to be a U.S. Senator.

He found his car and headed home. The weather here was just as gloomy and overcast as it had been out East, only colder. As he rounded the corner to pull into his driveway, he saw that Teri and Maggie had just beaten him home. The garage door was still open. He waited for them to step onto the breezeway before he pulled in alongside Teri's Corolla. John leapt from his car and happily accepted and returned hugs and kisses from both the women in his life. Then he glanced at his watch and, seeing that it was almost 6:00 pm asked, "Who wants pizza?" The ladies laughed and climbed into his car.

As they sat eating slices of the day at Rock's Pizza Extreme at the Hinsdale Plaza near their home, Maggie complained about the problem she was having with Lorna Jorgenson.

"Mom, I understand that Lorna is your and father's honorary niece but, she's really giving me a hard time. Dad maybe you can help." Margaret Stokowski loved John Franks. However, she also felt a loyalty to her biological father. To distinguish between them, she referred to the deceased Tom Stokowski as 'father' and John Franks as 'dad'.

When John met Maggie some five years ago, she was about the same age his daughter Brenda would have been had she lived. They connected almost immediately. Perhaps it had something to do with the fact that she looked and sounded so much like her mother, and he and Teri had formed an instant relationship. Whatever the reason, John considered himself a very lucky man to have both of these beautiful and loving women in his life. He was concerned for his daughter now and wanted to help. Maybe he could intercede for her.

Teri said, "Lorna is in the wedding and that is that."

"But, Mommm," Maggie wailed.

"No buts, Teri said firmly, "we've had this conversation before and I'm sick of it. You know that Cindy Jorgenson and I have been best friends since grade school. On top of that, she and Will were major contributors to your dad's campaign. You know very well that they would be very hurt if we didn't include Lorna in your wedding plans."

"I've called her three times!" Maggie said plaintively.

"Well then, I am going to come to your rescue. I'll call Cindy tonight when we get home and clear this matter up. She's well aware of how Lorna can be. She'll set her daughter straight in a flash."

"Do you really think that's a good idea?" John asked. Teri looked at her daughter and said, "Do you have a better idea?" Maggie cast her eyes down. Teri turned to John and asked how his plane ride home had been.

"Uneventful," he said. He didn't wish to explain what was troubling him, and obviously, he didn't need to get involved where he wasn't wanted. Instead, he looked at Margaret and said, "Magpie, you've barely touched your slice. Still dieting?"

"Endlessly," she answered. "You know I've already ordered my dress. If I don't get down to a size six, I'll have to get married naked."

He laughed and put his arm around her shoulder and said, "You already look and feel like a size four."

"Tell that to my scale," she sighed. They spent the rest of dinner in idle chitchat.

As soon as they were home, John went to his home office and the women retired to the den to make their phone call. During dinner, John had gotten an idea. He quickly checked his cell phone reference guide and looked up Fusion Center D.C. There it was.

Located on Sicard Street, the actual name was Multiple Threat Alert Center (MTAC). It was a component of the Naval Criminal Investigation Service. He hit the call button and the phone dialed. After one and a half rings, a voice on the other end said "M-TAC, Ensign Smith speaking."

John's sense of humor got the best of him and he said, "At least you could have come up with a more believable name; how about Bond?"

"What do you mean, Sir?" The startled voice asked.

"Sorry, Ensign, this is Senator John Franks of Wisconsin."

"YESSIR," Ensign Smith responded, "How can I help you sir?"

"You can tell me about your facility. How long have you been operational? Are you a certified Fusion Center? How many people work there?"

"I'd be more than happy to tell you everything you need to know, sir; but I'll need your code number."

"I assume this is a secure phone line," John questioned.

Yes sir, absolutely sir; but, I see from the signal that you're calling from your cell which can't be secure."

"Very good, Ensign; I'm glad to see you folks are on your toes. I will call you right back, on my office landline."

"Yes sir, thank you, sir." Feeling a bit chagrined, John retrieved the number from his cell and dialed the MTAC on his office phone. Ensign Smith answered again.

"OK, Ensign; this is Senator Franks again."

"Yes sir. I can see that, sir."

"Of course, you have caller ID," John stated. "So, if I'm calling from my office phone which is secure, why do you need my code?" He asked.

"How else can I verify it is you calling, sir? The Ensign replied.

"Yeah, dumb question," John said sheepishly. He decided once again that he really wasn't cut out for intrigue. It was a lesson he had learned while still in the Air Force. He gave Ensign Smith his seven-digit code number.

"Sir, that checks out, sir; what can I do for you?"

"I am in receipt of a very disturbing report from another department. I'm going to fax it to you. I'd like you to get it to the proper people in your office for analysis and get back to me with a plan of action to address the problems."

"Yes sir," Smith said. How soon do you need that report?"

"Ensign, its 7:30 pm where I am, and its Friday night; how soon do you think I want it?" Senator Franks snapped.

John faxed the pages and hung up the phone. He didn't know if what he had done was the proper action at this time, but at least the ball was now in someone else's court. I'm too used to playing the game, he muttered to himself as he set out to find the girls. They were in the den and both were smiling.

"Is your bridesmaid problem solved?" He asked.

"Cindy handled it immediately," Teri answered.

"We even got to overhear Lorna squirming when her mom questioned her about why she hadn't given an answer," Maggie beamed. "It was worth all the crap she gave me just to hear her mom give her hell."

"Well, I'm glad to hear that you were able to resolve the issue; but, Magpie I wouldn't gloat if I were you. You want Lorna to be in a good mood at your wedding."

"The bitch had it coming," Maggie responded. "But, don't worry dad, by the time of my wedding we'll be bosom buddies; even if I have to put roofies in her wine."

"Behave yourself." John chuckled. Then he gave Maggie a peck on the cheek and Teri a nice kiss on the lips before heading to the garage.

"I'm going to get a pint of Hagen Daz, I'll be right back."

"Love you, daddy, Maggie yelled.

"Chocolate," Teri yelled.

CHAPTER 9

FRIDAY

IMAM JAMALI WAS unable to sleep. The night was cool. His bed was comfortable. His wife had performed her marital obligations well. Still, as soon as he closed his eyes, his heart began to race, his breath came in short gasps and his stomach churned. Perhaps, he had had one too any pieces of lamb or one too many onions at dinner. Belching loudly, he struggled out of bed, lit a lamp and looked at himself in the mirror on his abattoir. Staring directly into his black eyes, he recognized that he was lying to himself, and he knew better than to do that. His problem was not one of digestion; his problem was himself. He was not facing up to his worries, and he would not sleep until he did so. The Imam sat up and poured himself a glass of water. Standing, he slipped on his sandals and padded down to the cave entrance.

He felt particularly safe at this location, so that wasn't what was bothering him. It was good to see that the night guards were alert. He nodded at them and strode past them onto the ledge. The guards nervously took defensive positions to either side of him at a discrete distance. The sky was very clear this night. He wished his head were as clear.

Looking up into the vast starlit blackness always gave him perspective on his worries. Allah was showing him how small his problems were in the great scheme of things. Praise Allah. It was true. When he focused on negatives, his problems seemed to magnify. When he concentrated on his achievements, they dwindled. In either case, worry without action was a waste of time. He had formed the habit of taking action before his enemies at a young age. Better to just decide and let Allah guide his hand. With that thought, he turned and strolled back into his sanctuary.

Tomorrow he would sleep in another of his 23 secret locations. He often joked that it was a good thing many of his ancestors had been nomads.

When he reached his secure area, he sat down on the edge of his bed. Overall, things had been going very well recently. The laughable Iraqi National Assembly, whose members were puppets of the Great Satan, had agreed to a cease-fire. The Taliban had again taken control of the SWAT region and were closing all schools for females; some they had burned. Their combined efforts were showing satisfactory progress. Yes, things were going quite well on the home front. That was not what was disturbing his sleep tonight. With a reluctant sigh, Muhammad Jamali decided it was time to deal with it.

He picked up his Sat-Com, verified that the scrambler was on and punched in the number of his second in command. As he waited for the connection, he reflected on the man who was giving him concern. Ammar Ali had come to him at him at a very young age and had shown his devotion to him and to Allah in a unique way. He had cut off his ear and offered it as tribute. It had been an impressive beginning. At that time, he had asked to be called Ammar instead of his given name Ahmad. It was a childish request, which Imam Jamali had granted.

He understood the history behind the request: *Ammar Ibn Yasir was born in the year of the elephant, the same year as Muhammad. He was a freed slave and an early companion of Muhammad. His parents were among the first pagans converted to Islam. They also shared the distinction of being Islam's first martyrs. Both were tortured and crucified for their new beliefs.*

A lifelong friend and follower of Muhammad, Ammar Ibn Yasir lost an ear in the Ridda Wars. To Shiites, Ammar was one of the four pillars of the Sahaba. They mainly admired him as the most loyal supporter of Ali, Muhammad's son-in-law and rightful successor.

By claiming the name Ammar for himself, the boy was making a strong statement of his intentions. He continued to prove himself year after year. Bright and aggressive, young Ammar learned the lessons of

Jihad well. He became an able squad leader and progressed through the ranks until he was participating in the highest-level meetings and conferences. He was the one who conceived of their most ambitious project.

Known as Satan's Head, his bold thinking and careful research had convinced everyone to accept and implement a plan to destroy all or most of the leaders of the United States. It was a plan, which would bring great honor to Islam and great anguish to all infidels. Rightfully, he wished to carry out the plan personally. The Imam put him in charge without hesitation. That had been three years ago. Now, a mere two days from culmination, the once trusted Ammar was giving signals that he may not be the right man to carry out the plan. It was an outrage. This strike against the United States was of paramount importance. Far too much was riding on the success of the mission to allow any one man, even Ammar Abdullah Ali, to jeopardize it.

A voice on the Sat-Com said *"Allahu Akbar."* Imam Jamali replied and said, "I find it necessary to enact safeguard *Azrael;* repeat, initiate safeguard *Azrael.*"

"Yes sir, this is Colonel Habib, acknowledging your order to implement safeguard *Azrael.* Please give me a confirmation number."

"Call it Jamali 666." The Imam had a dark sense of humor and he wondered if Colonel Habib had caught the significance of the number he had chosen. The sign of the beast seemed appropriate for this repugnant action. He hung up the Sat-Com without another word and turned off the lamp. He had resisted doing what he knew was necessary. Now he could relax. He lay back down in his bed and was soon asleep.

CHAPTER 10

FRIDAY

Ammar Ali stood on the corner by the Harrison Hotel shaking his head in amazement. He had never seen so much activity in the area. The ride in had taken almost twice as long as normal due to re-routed traffic and congestion. People were everywhere, and this was Friday, two days before the big event. He made a mental note to allow added time for his plans on Sunday.

An older heavy-set woman carrying a tiny white Yorkshire terrier in the crook of her left arm, tapped Ammar on the shoulder and asked, "Pardon me sir, can you tell me where the Hotel Harrison is located?" He paused for a second and was tempted to point at the front door and say "ten feet that way", but the woman had been polite and so he decided instead to say, "Yes ma'am, its right this way. Please follow me." He then led the woman and her heavier-set perspiring husband to the hotel. He introduced them to Jake the doorman who asked if they had any luggage.

There was an awkward pause as the husband tried to decide whether he needed to tip Ammar. Ammar stood quietly enjoying the man's struggle. He had seen it many times while working at the hotel. If he had been in his bellman's uniform, the decision would have been easier. However, he was just a stranger whom they'd met on the street. Would offering a tip be an insult? Finally, the man reached a decision and stuck out his hand while saying, "Thank you so much. If it had been a snake it would have bitten us." He chuckled at his own wit. Ammar shook his hand briefly and went into the hotel.

As the door was closing behind him, Jake called out, "Hey, Ali, why are you here on a Friday?" Ammar pretended not to have heard him and continued briskly through the lobby. As he walked quickly to the hallway behind the front desk, he smiled about the decision the fat man had made. Travelers, in particular travelers from foreign countries, were often confused about American customs, especially when and how much to tip. He often helped by explaining. He even suggested reasonable amounts. Many people were very thankful when he did this. Some foreigners were absolutely against tipping. A few went so far as to call it barbaric. The French were the worst, followed by the Japanese.

Then it suddenly struck him that he had never examined his own tipping behavior. Thinking back over the tips he'd received for carrying luggage, he estimated that the average tip was probably about $3.00 per bag. Errands netted about $5.00 per twenty minutes. His own tipping practices were considerably lower. He wondered if people classified him as a cheap Arab and ranked him with the French and the Japanese. The thought was disturbing. He began to consider the matter with an eye toward being a bit more generous. While he mulled the idea over, Ammar arrived at the service elevator. He pushed the down button. On the way down he made a decision; he would increase his tips. The decision made him feel good about himself, until he realized that this new behavior would affect very few people in the next day or so. A further thought came: no one he tipped would likely exist beyond Sunday. He changed his mind. Why bother?

Upon reaching sub-basement three, Ammar got off the elevator and took a stroll around the outer halls. There appeared to be no one around, which is exactly what he expected. He took the hotel passkey out of his pocket and opened the storeroom.

Going in, he carefully closed the door behind him and flipped the light switch. Everything looked as he had left it yesterday. That too, was as it should be.

Very few people ever had a reason to come into this room. Occasionally, a janitor needed some cleaning supplies, but that was about it. Ali kept the cleaning supplies handy by the door, so it was not necessary to go into the room any further. Two nearby rooms contained non-perishable foods, which the cooks came down and got on a regular basis. They had no reason to go into this storeroom. Of course, there were the sheets, bedding and towels stored in a closet near the elevator, but again, only the house cleaning staff would have a need for them, and they too, had no reason to go into this room.

Ammar crossed to a metal door marked Authorized Admittance Only. He had used a stencil to paint the sign on the door about six months ago. To his knowledge, no one had ever questioned the door or the contents of the room. He used his other key to open this door. Only he had a copy of this key. The room was about half-full of large cardboard boxes. There were warnings on the boxes that said they contained highly dangerous pesticides, which were only for use by qualified personnel. Ammar particularly liked the red skulls and crossbones he had put on the boxes. He smiled as he lifted away three boxes and then another row of three. Each box was 3 feet, 2 inches high by 14 inches square. Filled with foam packing peanuts, he was able to move them easily. Behind them sat a metal cabinet hidden beneath the other boxes. It was three feet high, sixteen inches wide and fourteen inches deep. This cabinet, with contents, weighed a little over 600 pounds and had a combination lock. The door on the cabinet said Hazardous Materials: Do **Not** Open. There was no need to open this cabinet. Obviously, everything was all right. However, Ammar could not resist checking the combination lock. He quickly spun the dial entering the three-digit code.

The door swung ajar and Ammar quickly closed it and locked it again. His objective for the day completed, Ammar carefully re-stacked the cardboard boxes in place and locked the door. He had gone through this ritual every day since the Friday after Thanksgiving. On that Friday, he had single-handedly put 'Allah's Wrath', as he had personally named it, in place.

Putting 'Allah's Wrath' in place had been remarkably simple. Leaving nothing to chance, he had checked the capacity of the hotel's appliance dolly. It was an Elkay SRT-8 and could handle up to 750 pounds. His package was under this limit. Once he had the load balanced, it was a snap to bring it down stairs on the service elevator and roll it into its resting place. The entire operation had taken less than ten minutes.

Glancing at his watch, he saw it was early afternoon and time for prayer. Since he was by himself and was troubled, it also seemed an excellent opportunity to seek Allah's help. His innate sense of direction allowed him to orient himself, and he turned east to face Mecca. He dropped to his knees on the concrete floor, prostrated himself so his hands and forehead touched the floor and prayed, *"All praise is due to Allah, Lord of the worlds, The Most Gracious, the most Merciful, and sovereign of the Day of Judgment. It is you alone we worship and you alone we ask for help. Guide us to the straight path; the path of those upon whom you have bestowed favor, not of those who have evoked your anger or of those who are astray."*

This prayer he repeated six more times, and then he asked for personal guidance, *"Allah, you are all-wise and all-seeing and I but a most humble servant. I seek only to do your will, but I am unsure of the right path. I ask for your divine guidance. Please give me a sign that I am doing right with this weapon named in your honor even during your sacred month of Rabi-ul-Awwal.* This prayer he also repeated six times. Upon rising, he felt relief. He had placed his fate in the hands of Allah; he could do no more.

CHAPTER 11

FRIDAY

YOU CAN FIND Bear Den Mountain on the
eastern face of the Blue Ridge Mountains. It is one hundred and forty
miles south southwest of Washington D.C. just off Interstate 64 due
east of Waynesboro, Virginia. Skyline drive heads north along the
ridge of the mountain and a small gravel road spurs off of that to
a secret government compound buried deep within Bear Den. The
mountain itself bristles with satellite links, radar antennas, and other
communications equipment as well as air vents and buried water and
gas pipes. Nothing is visible to the casual eye. Everything above ground
is buried, camouflaged or hidden from view. The road leading to this
site has a tall chain link gate with a massive chain and padlock. At the
top is a warning sign which says:

KEEP OUT-AUTHORIZED PERSONNEL ONLY
Security Personnel Instructed to <u>Shoot on Sight</u>
UNITED STATES GOVERNMENT

Off to the side of the gate stands a small one-man guard shack and
a parking lot where some fifteen to twenty cars are usually sitting. Past
the gate a narrow road with a sheer drop off wends its way back and
forth on switchbacks to massive camouflaged metal doors which are
the only access to Reagan Complex 1. The only way into or out of the
complex is by shuttle van.

If you were to ask anyone in Waynesboro what was going on at Bear Den Mountain, they would likely look at you with a knowing expression and say "mum's the word." But, the truth of the matter is, no one from the area has a clue as to what is going on at Bear Den. Everybody has an opinion or a theory. But that is all they are: unproven theories and baseless opinions. When the complex was built, late in the Reagan years, during the Strategic Defense Initiative era, no local contractors or laborers were hired.

The government brought in the Army Corps of Engineers for most of the construction and used out-of-state private civilian sources who had taken oaths of secrecy for everything else. When completed, Complex 1 became the jewel in Reagan's crown. It has a crew of 12 hand-picked administrative people who stay there 24/7 for 90 days at a time.

At staggered intervals each crewmember is given a 30 day furlough with full pay and benefits; then they are back on duty for the next 90 days. In this way the crew is never comprised of the same people all the time. This helps to avoid boredom, maintain sanity and relieve stress. At least, that's what the psychiatrists believe.

In addition to plush offices, comfortable meeting rooms and state-of-the-art communications gear, the underground facility has an Olympic sized swimming pool, a workout gym full of Nautilus equipment, handball court, a surround sound theater, library and a general store. Crew members live in individual apartments with living room, kitchen/dining area, full bath with hot tub and spacious bedroom. Their TVs get every cable channel available.

Eight service personnel are needed to keep the place clean and the equipment running. Their living quarters are much more Spartan, but, they only stay for 30 days at a time. They are paid for every hour on the job, even while they sleep. If you are willing to put up with the thorough investigation of your private life including interviews with your family members, neighbors, friends, former associates and former employers, you can apply for a job. There is always a waiting list. If you manage to get a job cleaning apartments at the Complex, you can probably get a Top Secret classification for government work anywhere.

The 12 member administrative crew's job is to manage the other eighty nine secret complexes that are on constant standby status: Treasury, Transportation, Health & Welfare, Postal Service, Intelligence

Services, Military Command Center, Border Patrol, Social Security / Medicare, etc. In their standby status they monitor and observe virtually everything going on.

In short, each complex is prepared to replace the functions of the management infrastructure should D.C. ever be hit by a nuclear device. Of course, they've been re-configured and re-combined for efficiency. These compounds are located in dozens of below ground bunkers in a big circle around Washington. Reagan Compound 1 is the farthest one out.

Chief Administrator, Kurt Schimler was just finishing up his regular Monday morning staff meeting when Caroline Bechman, Military Liaison Officer, burst in through the doors.

"Sorry I'm late everyone, but I've been on the horn with General Carson, Chief of Staff of the Marine Corps. Earlier I spoke with General Nate Grumwald, Chief of Staff of the Army."

Schimler let her know that he was displeased with her tardiness with a stern look then, he asked what she had determined.

"The situation is still rather fluid. General Carson is not opposed to our command, but he's waiting to see what MacKenzie does."

"And…?" Schimler said impatiently.

"I wish I had a concrete answer for you, but I don't. Grumwald is waffling. I have not been able to reach General Simmons of the Air Force and Admiral MacKenzie will not answer my calls."

"Where the hell are they?" Pete Kendal, Communications Director asked.

"None of them are in D.C. Carson is at Camp LeJeune for a ceremony and a briefing on foreign troop movements. Grumwald was on a hunting trip in Montana. He spoke to me for only a few minutes on a cell phone and said he'd get back to me. Simmons is in flight to Vandenberg Air Force Base. He's doing something with the Joint Space Operations Center and is refusing all calls. Chairman MacKenzie is onboard the U.S.S. Nimitz being briefed on recent developments."

"So essentially you've accomplished nothing as far as solidifying our status with the military," Schimler said with a frown.

"What the hell do you want me to do, Kurt? Order them to talk to me?"

"What you should have done it's now too late to do. You needed to establish control over the military when you first took office here.

Instead, you focused on 'forming relationships'. I told you several times it was the wrong approach, but you wouldn't listen."

"Just because you believe that being a bully is the only way to manage people, doesn't mean a more enlightened method doesn't work," Caroline said adamantly. The rest of the men in the room turned a deaf ear to the dispute. They were used to the two of them going at it. She was second in command and the only female in the compound.

When originally conceived, the Reagan Compounds were strictly all-male enclaves. Over the years women began to assert their rights and a few gained appointments to these strongholds. In most cases it made things more complicated and less efficient, but the political climate was such that our elected representatives felt it was better to live with the consequences than to alienate the female voting public.

"Now, if you'll excuse me," Caroline said, "I'm going to try sending emails and faxes to the known locations of the Chiefs; unless, of course, I've missed something important from the meeting."

"Nothing I can't fill you in on later," Schimler answered. As she exited the room, she acknowledged each of the other administrators.

When the door had closed behind her, Schimler muttered to himself, "If women didn't have cunts they'd be pretty much useless." Three managers overheard him. One of them gave a little chuckle in recognition of Schimler's witticism. One just looked uncomfortable and one suddenly found interesting reading in the briefing papers in front of him. Schimler took his seat at the table in the front of the room and turned on the monitor on the wall.

The screen flickered to life revealing a scene of mass destruction. It was a satellite view of Constitution Avenue in D.C. All that could be seen was rubble. Smoke drifted up from various spots. The camera zoomed in to show close ups of individual mounds. Nothing was recognizable. It was a simulation of what they could expect if a nuclear device were ever triggered in the capitol city.

"Not to linger on it, but this is what Constitution Avenue would look like today if it had been hit yesterday," Kurt said. "You've all been viewing the simulated holocaust in your offices and apartments just as I have, but, I wanted to close this morning's meeting on a note of encouragement. If this were reality instead of just another preparedness exercise, these gruesome images, would allow us to confirm the status of the federal government.

That makes us America's best hope for survival. It would be our responsibility to bring order and the rule of law to our country."

Dick Wren, office of Budget & Economics said, "I understand that you would want us to hit the ground running, Kurt, but why are we having this simulation again? We went through a simulation only six months ago."

"Dick, its Inauguration Week. Every security office is on high alert; we are practically at Defcon 3. It seems pretty damn obvious to me why we're going through this exercise. Do I need to explain it to anyone else?" Dick Wren flushed.

"People," Kurt continued, "I expect each of you to treat this exercise as if it were the real thing. Contact every person in your purview and, please do not assume that they know anything until you have spoken with each and every one of them personally. They have been trained to *courtesy copy* us in the chain of command for getting approvals, but you need to remind them that if this were the real thing they would need to start asking *us* for approvals. There will be some who resent that change. There may even be some who resist it."

"No doubt about that," Craig Fergussen, Intelligence Officer, agreed. Keeping the CIA and the FBI in check is already near impossible. If I were to tell them that they would need to begin reporting to me now, I can just imagine their response."

"Just bend over Craig." Tom Snyder, Federal Reserve Bank called out. Everybody laughed. Not because it was funny, but because they were all pretty much in the same boat and were all very much on edge about the exercise.

"What I want each of you to do this morning is to put together a brief and I emphasize *brief,* report on what you consider your priorities and how you plan to address them. I will do the same and we will meet back here at noon today. It'll be a Pizza Planning Party. No beer allowed." Everyone smiled or laughed.

"What are you waiting for? Let's go gentlemen, let's go." Kurt Schimler stood and watched the administrators file out of the meeting room. It took longer than he would have liked. Once back in his private office, adjacent to the meeting room, he booted up his computer and picked up the simulated satellite images of cities in turmoil. He sent a quick email to Caroline telling her about the report she needed to do and about the meeting at noon.

While the rest of his crew was fretting about the current exercise, he was enjoying it. He even felt a smattering of optimism. He had heard the same rumors that had all the security agencies scrambling: a terrorist group was planning an attack on Inauguration day. Kurt knew it was not just a rumor.

At age 44, he believed he looked younger than he was. He attributed much of that to his crew cut hair style which he kept meticulously trimmed. He reflected on this morning's meeting and he frowned. When he did that the wrinkles in his face were exaggerated so he tried not to frown. It was a losing battle. Most staffers guessed him older than he was. His stand-by position as head of the National Command Authority was beginning to chafe. Even though he knew that change was just around the corner, he still found himself biting his nails. Whenever he became aware of it he would angrily stick his hands in his pockets. Nail biting was a habit he had his entire life despite repeated efforts to break himself. He often wondered why such an unconscious habit provided so much comfort.

*   *   *

Kurt Schimler was born Curt Bronkovic. When people looked at him they saw 'Mr. Joe Blow'. He was of average height and build with a face that had no prominent features. He was neither handsome nor ugly. Kurt was the epitome of non-descript except for his hair. As a boy his father had always cut his hair at home to save money and he always gave him a "butch".

Kurt didn't mind having the short hair; it was easy to take care of and never needed combing.

When he was old enough to be on his own he went to a barber and changed his butch to a crew cut. He never changed it again.

He was the son of a steel worker, born and raised in Pittsburgh, PA. His father Otto was a staunch union man. Otto's enthusiasm for the union grew into a passion for organizing workers and soon he was named a steward. From these humble beginnings, he rose in the ranks of the United Steel Workers of America. At his death, he was second in command. His whole life he lived in a small home on the corner of Sidney Street and Hot Metal Drive. It was a very basic house, but it served the needs of his three person family. It was just him, his wife Emma and Curt. The railroad tracks of the CSX transportation company were a block away.

The house, on the banks of the south side of the Monongahela River overlooked steel mills and factories. It and all the other houses in the area were grey, not because they were painted that color, but because the air was filled with smoke and coal dust.

As an only child, Curt had it easy. Mother did all the cleaning, shopping, cooking and so on. The only bad part of living where he did was that there were very few kids his age. Ronnie Jenkins was a dickhead, but at least he joined Kurt hunting cats with air rifles. Between them, the feral cat population was kept in control and pet cats were practically non-existent. Girls his age were even scarcer. He and Cindy Klatch maintained an ongoing feud and often yelled epithets at each other across the streets on the way home from school.

"You're a filthy disgusting pig, Bronkovic" Cindy would scream.

"Go fuck a watermelon," Curt would yell back. He thought this insult which described the size of Cindy's vagina was the height of cleverness.

"Be proud of who you are and where you live," Otto had said often. "Steel is what makes this country great. Without us there would be no automobile manufacturers, no railroads, and no high-rise buildings. We're the backbone of America, god-dammit." Curt believed him.

Growing up as the son of a union organizer meant Curt had to develop some strong survival skills at an early age. It was particularly tough when the union was on strike and little or no money was being brought home by the striking workers. During these times, the union leaders got almost as much grief as the foundry managers. Young Curt didn't mind. He was proud of his father and defended him against all comers. All that began to change when his dad was elected to be the head of Local 101. That was when he began his rise to fame and fortune.

Unfortunately, much of that fortune was pilfered from the union treasury. When his father was indicted for fraud and malfeasance in office, Curt's world changed forever. After his father was convicted on all charges and sentenced to five years in prison, Curt, who was 19 at the time, moved to Harrisburg. He was so ashamed of his name that he changed it legally. If you were to visit the hall of records in Harrisburg, you could look up the actions taken on February 14 1988,

St. Valentine's Day, and you would see a brief legal document stating that Curt Bronkovic had changed his name to Kurt Schimler.

Ask him where he came up with that name and Kurt would tell you he had no idea. "It just seemed right at the time."

The other thing that seemed right was defending his country. Since doing the right thing had become his credo, protecting one's homeland was a perfect way to live that credo. He enlisted in the Air Force and went to basic training at Lackland Air Force Base in San Antonio, Texas. He was in Texas just long enough to form a prejudice against Mexicans. They were lazy, smelled of stale taco and thought they were really macho. One particularly smarmy asshole had pulled a knife on him during a fight outside a tavern and had actually cut him. He never got the opportunity to right this wrong. All he could do was carry a grudge.

After basic, Kurt was sent to Nellis Air Force Base in Nevada where he attended aircraft maintenance school. He became an expert in maintaining, retro-fitting and modifying F-16 Fighters. He remained at Nellis for nine years, an unheard of tour of duty at one place. But, he was good at what he did and the Major in charge of aircraft maintenance didn't want to lose him. It came as a big surprise to everyone when he was transferred to Barksdale Air Force Base in 1997. It was one year after the U.S. had signed an agreement to sell Pakistan 36 new F-16 Fighters and a long list of weapons and re-fitting kits for their older F-16s. Kurt arrived at Barksdale a short while before the Pakistani pilots began arriving for flight training.

As Chief Master Sergeant, Kurt was the ranking enlisted man on the line and no longer got his hands dirty. He was well-organized and saw to it that the guests were given top-flight service. It was quite by accident that he became close with one of the pilots. He was just doing his job when, during a routine inspection, he spotted a left leading edge flap that looked a little suspect. He ordered a flex test and sure enough, the stabilizer was frozen in position. The LEF on an F-16 is not under pilot control. It is designed to react to aircraft motion and mach speed and to assist in stabilization, especially during take offs and landings. The pilot, Hassan Habib, had been present during the test and witnessed the repair.

He questioned Kurt at length about what might have happened if he had not spotted the malfunctioning part. Kurt hedged because he didn't want to disparage his country's air craft, but, he finally admitted that had the LEF not been functional, there were some situations in which the jet could get in trouble.

"Trouble my ass," the airman who had done the repair said. He had been standing and listening to the interchange between the pilot and his boss. "You could have gone down, my friend; no doubt about it. For instance, if you were in a steep angle of attack, say fifty or sixty degrees and your plane went into a stall, which is exactly what the plane will do at sub sonic speeds, your instinct would be to nose down, but that move could actually send you into a back flip and cause total loss of control. That would be all she wrote, partner."

In that instant Kurt became Hassan's personal hero and frequent associate. Kurt actually was annoyed by the whole thing because he enjoyed a few beers after work and his Muslim 'One-man Fan club' didn't drink. He spent the rest of his time at Barksdale trying to avoid him. As it was, Hassan managed to corral him on occasion and buy him steak dinners at the Blue Yonder dinner club near the base. Despite himself, between bites Kurt learned a lot about Pakistan. When his enlistment was up he reluctantly agreed to keep in touch with the pilot. He never intended to do that and years later, was quite surprised when Habib contacted him.

✳   ✳   ✳

In 2001, after completing his third four-year tour of duty, Kurt decided not to re-up. He loved F-16s and he loved his job maintaining them, but at age 31 it had finally dawned on him that he wasn't going to have much of an impact on the world as an aircraft mechanic in the military.

With his honorable discharge in his pocket Kurt moved back to Harrisburg and got an administrative position at the Capital Building. Eventually he earned a position on the Mayor's re-election committee. Kurt spent the next four years in various capacities in and around city and state government offices. It was a good training ground for a hardworking man with an agile mind and a desire for power.

Kurt had a burning ambition to do the right thing; to make the world a better place.

Mostly he wanted to make restitution for his father's sins. These were admirable traits and politicians were always on the lookout for such comers. What the politicians failed to recognize was Kurt's utter disdain for them.

He considered most politicians to be self-serving deal-making/deal-breaking opportunists who blew with the wind. They were universally adept at one thing: saving their own asses. As a true believer in America and a staunch defender of the *American Dream*, Kurt was often torn by his disdain for our elected officials. It caused him a great deal of cognitive dissonance.

Yet the evidence was in plain view every damn day. It often seemed that all congress did was fight among themselves and spend money needlessly. Hell, our country could save billions every year just by cutting welfare. The politicians knew that but, none of them had the moral courage to bring up a bill attacking such a sacred cow. Of course, Kurt was careful not to express his true feelings within earshot of any of his mentors.

His mentors also would have been disenchanted had they ever heard some of the comments of Kurt's closest friends. His air force buddy Burt Collins had been prone to saying things like "The world would be a much better place without niggers; they're all lazy welfare sucking blights on humanity. The men go around just making babies and the women fuck every black buck that will have them so they can make another baby and get more welfare." Kurt would generally nod his head when Burt expressed such an opinion. It wasn't that he agreed with his friend, but there was an element of truth to the statement. You couldn't deny that.

He never had much success with women. He had pretty much developed his view of the fairer sex while masturbating looking at this month's centerfold. Women seemed to sense his jaded perception and steered clear of him. Eventually Kurt began to dismiss women as "life support systems for cunts". Actually, this had been Burt's definition, but Kurt had adopted it.

"What do women put behind their ears to attract men?" Burt once asked.

"I don't know; what do women put behind their ears to attract men?" Kurt had asked with an expectant smile.

"They put their heels!" Burt answered. Kurt had roared.

To this day Kurt said he'd never met a woman who was his intellectual equal, nor had he ever known any who were self-disciplined or had altruistic goals. No, women were pretty much whiny self-serving and devious. It was the natural order of things that men were in charge.

When he moved to Washington D.C. at age 34, he curried favor with enough politicos from his home state that he found a good job immediately. Eventually, he worked his way into the inner circle of Washington's movers and shakers without ever holding an elective office or contributing a substantial amount of money to any politician's coffers. It was truly a remarkable achievement. Even more remarkably, he managed to retain his comfortable position through three administrations. He was somehow able to simultaneously fly under the radar while at the same time being considered an astute and well-connected addition to one's retinue. He managed to catch the eye of Presidential candidate Adolfus Herman during his campaign and soon was a participant in almost all strategy sessions.

When Herman won the election in 2009, Kurt was rewarded for his intellect and his faithful service. Herman named Kurt Head of the National Command Authority, the group of administrators who were poised to assume the reins of the Federal Government in the event a nuclear attack wiped out all of our elected legislators. Many called it the Shadow Government. It was not a complimentary term.

∗   ∗   ∗

It was in October of 2012 when he had gotten the call from Habib. It started out very awkwardly.

"Is this Kurt Schimler, former United States Air Force F-16 maintenance genius?"

"Well, that might be one description. Who is this?"

"Do you still hate Washington politicians?" The caller continued.

"I need to know who this is now!" Kurt said angrily.

"I'm the man you used to complain to about *those fucking idiots in Washington.*"

∗   ∗   ∗

Kurt checked his watch. Good, he still had plenty of time before the noon planning session. He reached into a locked drawer behind his desk and withdrew a Sat Com phone. He quickly relocked the drawer, stuffed the phone into the left cargo pocket of his pants and headed out of his office to the front gate. When he got there he returned the crisp salute of the sentry and explained he was doing a personal perimeter check. The guard looked at him quizzically but stepped aside without a word.

Kurt proceeded down the road to its first switchback. There he stopped. He was now out of the line of sight of the guards and could only be seen or heard by someone on the road. He was alone. He took out the Sat Com and punched the speed dial button, the phone lit up and in an instant a voice on the other end said "Habib."

"This is Eagle's Nest. The climate here is cool and humid."

"Understood, Eagle's Nest; the weatherman predicts hot and dry."

"Sounds like the ideal time to take a vacation."

"Our travel plans are right on schedule; will you be going?"

"We'll be ready to go when you get here."

"Confirmed and acknowledged. Thank you, Eagle's Nest." The line went dead.

Kurt was ecstatic. The jihadist group had confirmed that their plan to nuke D.C. was on schedule and he had reassured them that he would be withdrawing all U.S. troops from Afghanistan after the attack. It was a win-win situation. The numbskulls in Washington D.C. would finally be out of his way and he would be a hero for bringing home American troops from a very unpopular war. It would be the first of many acts of enlightened leadership by Kurt Schimler, the man who was poised to improve everything about the United States.

He picked up two rocks and carefully reduced the phone to bits and pieces of black plastic, circuit boards and chips. These pieces he scattered randomly off the side of the precipice next to the road. Then he strode smartly back up and into his complex.

CHAPTER 12

SATURDAY JANUARY 19, 2013

THE SECURE LANDLINE phone in Senator Franks' home office rang promptly at 6:55 am. Muttering about unnamed assholes who call so early, the Senator spit toothpaste into the sink in his bathroom, rushed out with tooth brush still in hand and answered with a controlled curt voice, "Franks."

A female voice said, "This call is for U.S. Senator John Franks from Lieutenant General Samuel Birch. Am I speaking to Senator Franks?"

"Yes, yes you are," Franks replied. Before he could continue, a brusque voice came on the line, "Senator Franks, General Sam Birch here; Defense Intelligence Agency."

"What can I do for you General?"

"Well, Senator, maybe you can explain to me why you sent a memorandum about suspected terrorist activity to the MTAC fusion center last night."

"And just how did you get wind of that, General?"

"Damn it, Senator. We're all on the same team here. We have an information exchange agreement with all anti-terrorism agencies."

"Yes, I know that General; which makes me wonder why you're upset that I contacted them for help."

"Senator Franks, with all due respect, you newcomers need to learn the chain of command around here. My office is in the Pentagon and we are a little higher up the pecking order than the local MTAC fusion center. At the very least you should have sent the information to our Defense Joint Intelligence Operations Center first."

"I'm well aware of your status and your command General. When I arrived in D.C. some time ago, I received a thorough briefing on all of the national security offices, and learned the names of all the directors. I also looked up your website among many others. I got a good overview of your operation. If memory serves, I noticed, and it was of particular interest to me, your Wanted Terrorists file had not been updated since 2011." The general hung up abruptly.

John looked at his phone and said "Same to you, you feisty old bastard," then hung up and headed back toward his bathroom. The phone rang again and he picked it up. Before he could say hello, the caller cut him off with "Senator, Sam Birch here. I think we got off on the wrong foot, and I want to apologize. First, let me clear something up. I'm the Deputy Director of the DIA not the director."

"I'm glad you called back, General," John replied. "What specifically are you apologizing for; calling me so damn early in the morning, questioning my right to defend my country or for being so rude?"

"Mea Culpa, mea culpa," the general's voice went from firm to conciliatory. "It's entirely my fault; all of it. Please accept my apology. I'm not in the habit of burning bridges. In fact, I never burn a bridge. I blame the upcoming inauguration. My nerves are frazzled right now."

"That's understandable, general."

"Please, call me Sam, Senator."

"All right, Sam. Apology accepted. I probably owe you an explanation for why I was so bitchy about your website. That was a knee jerk on my part. When someone jumps on me or tries to tell me how to do my job, I get very defensive."

"Don't we all?" The general laughed. He had a nice sounding laugh; not too loud or abrasive. It fit his personae. His merry face had ruddy cheeks and a prominent nose. Even his eyes seemed to be permanently squinted in good humor. General Birch exhibited an air of exuberance tempered with a naughty boy sparkle in his eyes. In reality, his associates and underlings found him to be arrogant and impulsive. His cheerful demeanor however, did help them to tolerate him better.

"I also want to say that I am impressed that you called about the matter personally. That tells me you're a hands-on leader. I like that."

"Well, thanks for the compliment, Senator. You know what they say, if you want a job done right..."

"You hafta do it yourself," the Senator joined the general to complete the old saw.

They both chuckled briefly.

"Senator, I want to assure you I am going to review our website personally and heads will roll if it is as out-of-date as you said."

"It was just one of the links, Sam. It could well be your information was current except for this particular link."

"Senator, I'm a stickler for details. That's why I got my Pentagon post. But, the website is not the reason I called you back. I also wanted to tell you that we have additional information which relates to that report you sent to the MTAC unit."

"Oh?"

"When you read the report, what did you suspect was going on?"

"I'd have to say I wasn't really too sure," John started to hedge.

"Senator, please. I've checked your background. I know you received special training, and served as a strategic listener with Air Force Intelligence. Surely, you have a hunch about what's going on."

"Well, it occurred to me that a terrorist group was planning an attack in the near future, most likely Inauguration day."

"That much was obvious, Senator. Come on, you can trust me. What sort of attack?"

"It wasn't clear, but it seemed to me that a biological/chemical/ nuclear attack made the most sense."

"And if you were a betting man Senator, which would you put your money on?"

"Nuclear."

"Bingo," said the general. And, I'm betting I can tell you what kind."

"You can?" The Senator's jaw fell open.

"Senator, I need to ask you to go online and search for 'Alexander Lebed and Suitcase Nukes'. That's L. E. B. E. D. Read up on it and then we'll talk again. OK?"

"Of course," said John. "Will you call me or should I contact you when I'm ready?"

"I'll call you at precisely 11:00 am Wisconsin time. That's lunchtime here and I always skip lunch."

Before John could respond, the general hung up, leaving him once again looking at the phone in bemusement. The general was obviously a no-nonsense guy, which was good in a way; a bit annoying, but good none-the-less. Once again, he started to head back to his bathroom when he heard his cell phone ring in the bedroom. He heard Teri answer it, "Hello, this is Senator John Franks' cell phone, Teri speaking."

He decided to let Teri handle it while he tried to clean the dried toothpaste from his brush. Then, he stepped into the shower and washed thoroughly. He thought about his morning thus far and wondered again if he was in over his head. Don Whitman seemed to have gotten him involved in a real hornet's nest. As a relative newcomer to the hill and a recent appointee to the Committee on Homeland Security, he wasn't really prepared for this intrigue. It occurred to him that he needed a mentor, someone who could give him some insight on how the D.C. Intelligence Community actually worked. Sam Birch might just be his man.

The shower felt great. It helped to ease the tensions he had felt creeping into his shoulders and neck. As he was drying himself, he wandered back into the bedroom. Teri was sitting on the edge of the bed and glanced coquettishly at his nude body and said, "My, my, Senator. Are you this informal with all of your constituents?"

"Only my closest associates; do you consider yourself a close associate?" He crossed to her and leaned over her.

"Just how close were you thinking?" She asked.

"Oh, very, very close," he said as he kissed her softly at first and then more urgently. She smiled and kissed him back. Then she put her arms around his neck and pulled him to her as she lay back on the bed.

After making love, Teri gasped, "Ooh, I almost forgot to tell you. Estelle called. She said the phone has been ringing off the hook and she has at least eight urgent messages to which you must respond. She's sending them all to your home office."

"Your timing is impeccable, my love. I am so glad you didn't tell me earlier."

"You're welcome, sweetie. So am I."

They enjoyed taking a shower together which almost led to another round of lovemaking. But he had work to do. As he headed back to his office, he wondered why Estelle was working on a Saturday. Then, he answered his question- because she's as dedicated as you are, stupid.

CHAPTER 13

SATURDAY

DON WHITMAN WAS squirming and hating himself for it. Being on the carpet was bad enough, but it was excruciating having to kowtow to his supervisor who was posturing as Grand Master Inquisitor. The ultimate indignity was spending Saturday morning getting his ass chewed. He looked at the room as he waited. The lower parts of the walls were covered with dark oak wainscoting and the upper parts were framed by additional dark oak. The insides of the frames were covered in soft textured ecru colored cloth. Numerous certificates, awards, degrees and photos of Washington notables hung within these framed areas. A large globe on a stand stood in the corner. The end wall consisted of floor to ceiling bookshelves filled almost to capacity.

On that end of the large room were four comfortable looking leather chairs and a huge dark oak coffee table. A set of scales sat on the table. To the right of the desk in front of him stood a massive cloth easel with a detailed map of D.C. pinned on it. Different colored pins could be seen all over the map.

"So, Don, let me see if I understand your reasoning for your actions," said Dennis Ward, Under Secretary of Intelligence & Analysis. He sat behind a large impressive mahogany desk in a large high-backed executive chair. Don found himself seated in an intentionally low armless chair in front of the desk. Don was amused and disdainful, that his boss would resort to such an obvious psychological tactic.

Unfortunately, it worked; even when one is aware of the ploy, having to look up at another person is humbling.

What made it worse was that Under Secretary Dennis Ward was a runt. The running joke in the office was that he had reached his position of power because he was blowjob height. Don's secretary referred to him as Dennis the Menace.

Dennis continued his statement. "You were sending *urgent* memos to damn near the entire D.C. intelligence network for over a week and had not received what you deemed to be a *proper response*, so, *without contacting me*, you decided to accost a United States Senator. This you did, *on your own*, because you decided, *on your own*, that these matters were too important to ignore any longer." Dennis squinted and frowned. "Does that pretty much sum up your actions?"

"Yes sir."

"So, just to be precise and fair; you chose to *ignore* departmental protocol and skip over the chain of command under the rationale that you were the only one who understood the urgency of these matters and needed therefore to take independent action, thereby embarrassing the department and every one of your superiors." Dennis spoke slowly and distinctly, with pauses to let every single word hit home.

"I guess I did, if you say so, sir."

"You've got the balls to say-If I say so?" Undersecretary Ward exploded; "You egotistic asshole! Yes, I say so; and so do my supervisor and the director. Do you have any fucking idea how much egg this department has on its face because of you?" Undersecretary Ward stormed out from behind his desk during his tirade. He was only slightly taller standing than Don sitting. Don turned his face and tried not to smile. Instead, he coughed and said quietly, "Sir, I appreciate my error. I would like to apologize to you and to each of your superiors."

Realizing his mistake in coming out and standing next to this very tall staffer, Undersecretary Ward resumed his seat behind his magnificent desk. Damn it, he thought.

It was not a conscious awareness, but he sensed he had lost the edge.

"Say that again, Whitman," Ward said sternly.

"Sir, my intention was never to embarrass the department. I am profoundly sorry for any and all repercussions from my actions. I regret my decision and I assure you I will not do anything similar in the future."

"You're damn right you'll never do anything similar in the future, *if you have one!* I'm not all that sure you're wanted around here anymore."

"Sir, I recognize that I made an egregious mistake, but threatening my career is going a bit far I believe. I have ten years in and I've received numerous commendations..."

"And your service record is the only thing standing between you and the street or a demotion to second assistant mail room sorter." Ward interrupted. Then he softened his tone. "Please understand your future is not totally in my hands. You pissed off the big guns. All I can do is recommended a proper disciplinary measure."

"I understand, sir." Don Whitman was by now, genuinely contrite and concerned.

"Despite your arrogance in going over everyone's head, I choose to believe that you were, in fact, trying to do your job. Unfortunately, you were also trying to do everyone else's job too."

"Exactly, sir; I mean yes, I was just trying to do my job to the best of my ability."

"Shut up!" Ward stormed. "You certainly don't know when to keep your mouth shut, do you?" Don had enough sense to say nothing.

"I'm recommending an unpaid leave of absence of one week and a letter of reprimand to be put in your file. Keep your nose clean for one year and I'll remove the letter; any questions?" Don paused for a moment and thought.

"I just have one, sir; how soon does my leave of absence begin?"

"Immediately; take the rest of the day off; go fishing or something for the rest of the week. I don't care what you do as long as I don't see your face in town during the next seven days. Am I perfectly clear?"

"Yes sir; am I excused?" Don said meekly.

"Why can I still see your face, Whitson; get the hell out of here, now!" Don almost said "It's Whitman, sir," but caught himself. Instead, with lips firmly closed, he exited the office. Once outside the door, he let out a huge sigh and squared his shoulders.

He hadn't felt so much like a little boy being spanked since he was a pre-teenager. He was abashed and ashamed, but more than that, he was furious. That pompous little ass really knew how to make him steam.

How dare he call *him* arrogant when *he* was the most arrogant little son-of-a-bitch he had ever met? His thoughts more or less continued to run in this vein while he returned to his office.

*   *   *

Under Secretary of Intelligence & Analysis Dennis Ward sat back in his chair and the intercom buzzed immediately. His secretary told him there was an important phone call waiting for him. Who in the hell was it now? He took a deep breath, let it out slowly and answered his phone saying, "Secretary Ward."

"Yes, Secretary Ward; General Sam Birch here."

"Hello Sam, nice to hear your voice. What can I do for you?"

"It's more a matter of what I might be able to do for you, Dennis. Did your office get my memo earlier about the possible nuclear threat in D.C. right now?"

"Yes, Sam. I'm sure we got your memo; just like we've gotten several hundred other memos in the past couple of weeks. Did you have anything concrete for me?"

"No, I just thought it would be a good idea to be extra alert right now. I did review a very comprehensive security memo from one of your own staff recently."

"Jesus Christ. Don't tell me. It was Don Whitson wasn't it?"

"Actually, his name is Whitman, but yeah that's our man."

"And so now you've got the balls to call me and tell me how to do my job, Sam?"

"No, no, no; not at all Dennis..." Secretary Ward cut him off abruptly.

"General I've had several N.E.S.T. teams in D.C. for the past week doing sweeps on every fucking nook and cranny in the city. If there were a nuclear weapon within five miles of this city, we would have found it. Understood?"

"Understood; I'm sorry to have bothered you." The General said meekly.

Dennis hung up his phone and screamed to the room at large, "everybody and their fucking Uncle Charlie thinks they know how to do our jobs better than we do. Well, fuck them all!" Melinda, his secretary in the outer office heard him and decided it was time for a cup of coffee. She flew to the break room; and once inside, laughed like hell.

*　　*　　*

When back at his office, Don briefed his secretary and arranged for his leave of absence. She told him that Senator Franks had returned his call. She gave him the senator's home office number, which he had neglected to get when they met yesterday. He only had the senator's cell number. He would call him later. Right now, he wanted very much to hear Estelle's calming voice. More, he wanted to feel her soothing body. Hell, he had a week of nothing to do.

What might her schedule be like? Even before that, he wanted a good stiff drink. Alcohol was a rarity in his life, but a double martini straight up sounded damn good right now, and he deserved one. There was a nice little Irish Pub not too far from the office, in the Hotel Harrison. Leaving his car parked in the lot, he headed there on foot. He scowled as he walked, not noticing how people were giving him a wide berth. He also didn't notice the clear skies and pleasant temperature in the low fifties which was unusual for this time of year. As he walked off some of his anger, he mulled his next move.

"Hey, watch where you're walking asshole!" The unfriendly barb caught Don off guard and jarred him back into an awareness of his surroundings. Apparently he had stepped off a curb just as a cabbie in a burnoose was turning left. Without a word he raised his finger in the age-old gesture of ill will and stepped back onto the sidewalk. The cabbie blew his horn and returned the gesture as he sped off.

Don continued on and as he walked he savored the sights, sounds and smells of the city he loved. The cherry trees would be in bloom soon. He couldn't wait for glory of their flowers and their scent hanging in the air. The streets were crammed with bumper-to-bumper traffic and no one was giving an inch.

"You really have to be crazy to drive in this town," he said to himself.

As he walked, Don looked with interest at all the new businesses on this block. The only thing certain in D.C. was change. Where he was the sidewalks were wide and perfect for small street vendors. He noted that his favorite hot dog stand was no longer there. Its spot was now occupied by a souvenir stand selling maps of the city and trinkets to the tourists. There were plenty of those. Down the street he saw that his favorite Starbucks was doing its' usual frenzied business. He enjoyed the smell as he walked by, but elected not to get coffee. The cacophony of horns blaring and sirens wailing were music to his ears. In counterpoint there was a group of five black men seated on boxes beating out intriguing rhythms on five different drums /percussion instruments. After listening for a moment he threw a dollar into the collection bucket and continued on. Why would anyone want to work anywhere else?

CHAPTER 14

SATURDAY

TERI, STILL IN her robe, went downstairs to get breakfast. She promised John some toast and coffee. He was dressed in his customary navy blue suit, white long-sleeve shirt and red tie with a double Windsor knot. Well-polished black wingtip oxford shoes completed the ensemble. He sat down at the desk to read the messages Estelle had sent. The first one was from General Sam Birch, and when he saw the time stamp on it, he knew it was from before he and the general had spoken. He hit delete.

Next was a request from the Secretary of the Interior's office. He was to meet with two of the secretary's local speechwriters today to give them some usable quotes that would make the people of Wisconsin respond warmly to the secretary when he visited in May. They needed to change the day for the meeting until next week. He sent a reply and a courtesy copy to Estelle with a note to, please, set up the new meeting time.

The next message got his full attention. It was from Estelle marked "What the hell is this?" There was a link for him to click on. When he did, he wished he hadn't.

What came up was a full-screen image of the front of the Baltimore Falcon bar. There were inset photos plastered all over: him coming out of a door marked Kings, him sitting and talking to a tall man standing at his table. He appeared to be staring directly at the area where the man's penis was. In the background, two men were holding hands and

78

looking lovingly at each other. The last photo showed him leaving the establishment with the tall well-dressed man.

It was a close up photo of him and the taller Don Whitman's chin. A large bold headline introduced the montage: **Senator John Franks coming out of GAY bar and closet?** The photos were obviously taken with a cell phone as their quality was rather poor, especially on the inside shots which were badly lit. Still, he was recognizable in every one of the snaps. Shit. He hit delete and returned to the list sent by Estelle.

Her next message said "It gets worse." There was another link to click. This one was a blog with the headline: **Senator says, "A suck is a suck."** The rest of the article, apparently written by a homophobic gay basher, went on to describe what he purported to have overheard while accidentally eavesdropping on a conversation between the Senator and the bar patron. John saved this one and sent a message to Estelle that she should respond to the author and demand an immediate retraction. Then he changed his mind; to hell with that, he sent her another message saying, tell him we are initiating a ten million dollar lawsuit for defamation of character, slander and libel. Maybe we can get this schmuck to sweat a bit.

The rest of the messages were typical reminders of impending inaugural events and items of specific interest to him. Estelle was a good secretary, he thought. He decided to call her. Just then, Teri walked in carrying a plate with two pieces of buttered whole-wheat toast, a glass of orange juice and a cup of coffee.

She set them down on the desk and sat down opposite him. She took a bite out of one of the pieces of toast and handed it to him. "What's the problem?" She asked.

"Why do you think there's a problem?" He responded.

"Honey, you have three looks of distress: mildly annoyed, pissed off and panic-stricken. Your current expression is somewhere between pissed off and panic-stricken. I repeat, what's the problem?" He proceeded to tell her about the two web postings and the accusations that he was gay. He did not mention the call from Sam Birch.

Teri laughed and said, "If you're gay, you are absolutely the best actor I've ever seen. This morning was wonderful. In fact, I came back up hoping you hadn't dressed yet. She came around the desk, put her arms around his neck and sat on his lap. He brought his arms around her and she nestled into his shoulder. They stayed that way until his mood lightened. For a moment, he even considered undressing. Then, he shifted in his chair and gave Teri a long kiss before standing up and forcing her off his lap.

"Unfortunately, I have a lot on my plate today. I really have to get back to work. Thank you, for calming me down." He smiled and gave her a peck on the cheek. She grabbed his crotch gently as she turned and went back down stairs.

"It's your loss, buster. Try not to think about me as you work." She gave a short giggle.

"You are wicked." John called after her. Well, he thought, at least my wife knows I'm not gay; but, what about the rest of the voting public? He decided to call Estelle.

"Good morning, Senator. How are you doing?" John was briefly taken aback. Try as he might, he was still unable to get used to caller I.D.

"I've been better," he answered. "How are you doing? Has the phone been ringing off the hook?"

"Not really. Except for that web stuff, it's been a pretty typical morning."

*   *   *

Estelle was uncertain of what she should do and had decided to just play it cool until she knew more. She had recognized the chin of the man in the photo with Senator Franks coming out of the gay bar. Actually, it was not so much the chin as the tie. She was certain it was the tie Don was wearing yesterday. She had tied it for him when he left.

What was the Senator doing with her spook? More importantly, why were they in a gay bar! She did not remember ever talking about the Senator to her lover; and, she certainly would never talk about her lover to anyone. So, how had the paths of the only two men in her life crossed? This was just too weird for mere coincidence. She would need to do some checking.

*   *   *

Estelle's suspicion was well founded, but not for the reasons she suspected. She believed that she and Don had met purely by accident.

Actually, Don Whitman had made it his business to find out the name of the secretary to the new Senator from Wisconsin, who now had a seat on the Committee for Homeland Security. He had arranged a chance meeting at the restaurant where she stopped for morning coffee while waiting for the train. He was charming, handsome, and very impressed with how a girl from the Mid-West had accomplished so much at such a young age.

"Hi there," he had said. "Please don't think of this as a pick-up line, but I believe I know you." Estelle looked at the handsome well-dressed man who had spoken to her.

"Really; you do not look familiar to me." She had replied.

"Don't you work for Senator Franks from Wisconsin?" Of course Don knew she did.

"Why, yes I do. How do you know the senator?"

"He toured our officers some months ago. He impressed me." Flattering her boss was exactly the right thing to say to get into Estelle's good graces.

"Thank you. I think he's just marvelous, too. Where is your office?" He explained that he was with the FBI and she was suitably impressed. They talked all the way into the city. To Estelle he was perfect. He was married and so there were no commitment issues. He was intelligent and he recognized her worth as a person.

The next time she saw him, he was again riding the same morning train into D.C. He said his car was in the shop for repairs. They had a nice conversation and wound up exchanging cell phone numbers. She was impressed that he had two cell phones.

As it turned out, she was the one who initiated their next contact. She was adding his number to her speed dial, when she accidentally called him. She was embarrassed when he answered and all she could do was stammer in surprise. He was very gracious while they sorted out what had happened. Then he told her how glad he was that she had called him, even if it was only by accident, and invited her out for a cup of coffee. By now, Estelle had regained her composure and she suggested that she make the coffee and gave him her address. Their first time together was magic.

*   *   *

Senator Franks' voice jarred her back to the present, "Did you get my messages?"

"Yes sir, I'll call to reschedule your meeting with the speechwriters this morning. I already contacted my friend Irma at the Attorney General's Office. She is a secretary for one of the attorneys there and she is going to send an email to the blog author under their logo. That ought to scare the crap out of him."

"Great!" John actually laughed.

"Is there anything else I can do for you this morning," she asked sweetly. John paused, and thought for a moment before responding, "No, no. That's it for now. I'll call again later." He did not want to try to explain the Baltimore Falcon incident right now. Then he thought of something else, "Wait a minute, there is something else you can do for me. Check out the background of a Lieutenant General Sam Birch at the Pentagon."

"He called this morning, right?"

"That's right."

"I'm on it."

"Thanks. Talk to you later." He hung up. Within a couple of minutes, Estelle was dialing the number for Millie, a Pentagon receptionist. If Millie didn't have the low down on General Birch, she'd know who did. She might also be a good place to start researching Don Whitman. She was a little pissed at herself for not having done this sooner. Her image of herself as the consummate executive secretary was tarnished. What had she been thinking; she had initiated a sexual liaison with a man without checking him out first. It was a silly school girl mistake. She hoped she didn't live to regret it.

CHAPTER 1 5

SATURDAY

AMMAR STOOD RESIGNEDLY behind the bellman's desk in the lobby of the hotel. He had been here since 6:00 am and so far had carried only one bag from room 404 down to the lobby and thence to a waiting taxi. He had received a $1.00 tip from the oriental, almost surely Japanese, guest. He had thanked the man and wished him a pleasant day. The man had grunted, frowned and climbed into his cab. Without acknowledging the cabby's greeting, the man said, "Dulles." As the vehicle pulled away, Ammar looked after it and said to himself, "you cheap son of a whore, tomorrow you'll be thanking your pagan gods for your good karma."

He had actually arrived a little after 5:00 am and had checked his locker. Everything was as it should be. Zero hour was just 30 hours from then: Sunday at noon. Ammar shrugged. He was bored. The hotel was at capacity and almost no one was coming or going. Most guests had checked in on Thursday or yesterday and were booked through at least Tuesday. Some would avail themselves of room service, but not enough to keep him busy. He checked his watch for the umpteenth time, 8:06. This was going to be the longest day of his life. He sat down on the nearby cushioned bench and looked at the front page of today's Washington Post. The page contained article after article and picture after picture of preparations for the week's inaugural events. The main photo showed a huge dais in the process of construction on the steps of the White House.

Ammar was not a man of detail and, as he had done several times before, he failed to notice that a re-enactment of the Inauguration ceremony would take place on this dais on Monday January 21.

He had barely started to read when he felt a presence at his right elbow. Ammar looked up at the smiling face of Mr. Dickens, the hotel manager.

"Good Morning, Ghazanfar. How are you doing?" He said. Ammar stood. He had taken the simple precaution of changing his first name. He chose Ghazanfar because it meant 'lion'.

"Good morning, Sir. I am well, thank you. And you?"

"Tip top this morning, tip top. Thank you. Have you been busy this morning?"

"No. Not so busy," he replied.

"I didn't think you would be," the manager agreed. "That's why I came over to ask a favor of you."

"Do a favor for you sir; of course sir." Ammar answered.

"Good. Good. I've called in some extra help for Chez Blanc. I've decided to set up some outdoor tables and catch some of the foot traffic over the next few days." Ammar was not happy. Chez Blanc was the family restaurant off the lobby, and occasionally, if he wasn't busy he was expected to bus tables. The wait staff supposedly shared their tips with table clearers, but in practice, it averaged out to about a dollar an hour for their labors. It amounted to slave wages. It was an ongoing squabble and the people busing tables never won. The next news was even worse.

"I hired a new guy to bus tables. He says he knows you. He goes to the same Mosque as you, over on Massachusetts Street, NW."

"Are you sure Sir?" Ammar responded.

"That is where you go isn't it?"

"Ah...yes sir. Yes it is. The Islamic Center is on Massachusetts. He knows me?"

"Yes, Abdul Anwar is his name. Said he was from Iraq, and he knew you from ESL classes and regular worship schedules. Sound familiar?"

"Oh, of course, Abdul; yes he is familiar." Ammar had never heard of this person, but that was no surprise. It was unlikely that this was the real name of the intruder.

The Islamic Center was a multi-cultural facility with a large membership. Ammar worshipped there rarely. It was one of his contact points. He went there to keep in touch with specific members of his cell and to receive and relay information: oral communication only, never a written message. Orders, which came via Sat Com phones, were transmitted verbally from one cell member to another. Ammar used a Sat Com phone once, then, destroyed it. If this person truly knew him, he would have to be a member of the cell unknown to Ammar. That was possible, but certainly not good.

Why would Imam Jamali have this unknown person contact him? Was there a problem?

As these thoughts were racing through Ammar's mind, he realized that his boss had continued talking... "So if you don't mind, just wait until he gets here and set up."

"Right, Ammar said hesitantly, we'll set up."

"Like I said, just four tables with four chairs each and the sandwich board sign with the specials on it near the curb. You'll be the only waiter for these tables. It should help your tip revenue over the next few days."

"Yes, yes sir. Thank you very much, sir." Ammar said brightly, despite his dour mood brought on by the news of the intruder.

"Think nothing of it," Mr. Dickens replied. "Always try to keep my good workers happy. Just part of my job," he said as he walked back to the front desk. There, he thought, that ought to keep the camel jockey from sitting on his ass the whole weekend.

Ammar wished he had listened more carefully. He may have gotten more clues as to the identity of this new person. Was he friend or was he foe? Of course, Ammar had no knowledge of failsafe measure *Azrael*. It would never occur to him that his resolve or his faithfulness to the cause could be in question. Then, a thought came to him and he wished he had questioned Mr. Dickens some more. Outdoor tables in January did not strike him as being very smart. It also meant he and the stranger would need to go into the storeroom to get tables and chairs. That made him very nervous. He stood watching Mr. Dickens walk away, and was startled when a voice near his left shoulder said, "Peace upon him who follows the teachings of Muhammad."

CHAPTER 1 6

SATURDAY

JOHN FRANKS CHECKED the caller ID on his phone. It was General Birch and he was right on time. It was exactly 11:00 am. He picked up and said, "Hello Sam." The voice on the other end said, "This is General Sam Birches' office calling for Senator John Franks."

Damn, he thought to himself. When am I ever going to get the hang of this?

"This is Senator Franks," he said.

"Sam Birch here, Senator. Have you had a chance to read up on suit case nukes yet?"

"I just finished a few minutes ago. I followed through on several articles starting with:

On 7 September 1997 the CBS newsmagazine News Hour broadcast an alarming story in which former Russian National Security Adviser Aleksandr Lebed claimed that the Russian military had lost track of more than 100 suitcase-sized nuclear bombs any one of which could kill up to 100,000 people" he read slowly and distinctly.

"You went back all the way. That's good. I assume you read all the subsequent arguments and hullabaloo."

"Yeah", John answered reading from his notes,

"State Department spokesman James McArthur gave the official government response:
'We have been assured by the Russian authorities that no such weapons exist and that there is no cause for concern. We believe the assurance we have received' At least that was the initial position."

"Gotta keep the citizens cool, calm and collected right Senator?"

"What else could they do? I remember the panicky reaction at the time. Hell, if I remember right, I was very disturbed."

"So was I, Senator. So was I. Of course, that's when all the second-guessing started. Lebed was called a disgruntled has been. The producer's of the News Hour show were painted as being self-serving as I recollect."

"Exactly; according to an article in the September 27 issue of *TV Guild*, the producer of the story, Brenda Coburn was currently promoting a book she co-wrote with her husband Allan on the dangers of nuclear terrorism called Nuclear Armageddon. They were also co-producers of a just-released film: No Nuclear Deterrent. Of course, neither of these facts proved any disingenuousness of their part, but they certainly didn't help their credibility."

"But, they got a big boost when Yablokov dropped his bomb, no pun intended," Sam added with a wry chuckle.

"That's true. This article says, *Russian scientist Alexi Yablokov, former advisor to President Yeltsin and member of the Russian National Security Council stated that he personally knows individuals who produced these suitcase-size nuclear devices under orders from the KGB in the 1970's specifically for terrorist purposes.*

Then he said, because they were produced for the KGB, they may not have been taken into account in the Soviet general nuclear arsenal and may not be under the control of the Russian Defense Ministry. In other words, don't blame me or my comrades for this shit."

"You got it Senator." Birch replied. "Fortunately, Representative Charles Walton followed up on this. Eventually the Russian government acknowledged production of these weapons."

"According to my notes, Walton spoke on the floor on October 28 and asserted '*a total of 132 devices had been built with yields from 1 to 10 kilotons and that 48 were unaccounted for.*' that's a lot of missing firepower," John said grimly.

"That's for damn sure." Birch agreed.

"I also read some articles saying GRU agents have already planted several of these little blockbusters in strategic places. Other articles say *'no, they only looked for good locations, but no bombs were actually placed'.* It gets very confusing at this point. What was the outcome; what happened to these weapons?"

"Your guess is as good as mine, Senator. But, I'll tell you this, there was a prolonged song and dance on the media with one "expert" after another testifying that such devices do exist and other "experts" saying such weapons would have such a short shelf life that they would be totally impractical. Basically, these arguments went on and on and after enough time passed without a nuclear terrorist attack, the public lost interest and the news media stopped talking about them."

"So what do you think?"

"Senator, in my not-so-humble opinion, we have fully-functional suitcase size nuclear weapons in our Nation's Capitol right now. At the very least, terrorists have them available and ready to place. Why else would we have state-of-the-art radiation detection equipment at virtually every major crossroad in the city?"

"We do?"

"They neglected to tell you that in your briefings? Hah, it doesn't surprise me. I suppose we don't want our new congressional representatives afraid to come to the office, do we?" The general snorted.

"Christ on a crutch. Sam, you've really got me worried now."

"Thank goodness, Senator. Now maybe I won't be alone in my fight to get those idiots in the National Intelligence Office to listen up."

"How can I help you, Sam?"

"I suggest you start by calling the agent who sent you that report."

"That was Don Whitman. He's a good man."

"Well, he seems to be the only one in D.C. with his head not up his ass. Anyway, let's plan on a three-way call in one hour. Get me a number to call for him and I'll call you both at 1:15 my time. I have some additional information to add to his findings. Maybe, between the three of us, we can come up with something."

"OK, I'll get hold of him and alert him to the call. What else can I do?"

"Keep up your history lessons. You may find something I overlooked."

Senator Franks put down his phone. As usual, the general had hung up without saying goodbye. Then it hit him hard: *we may be only a day or two away from a national tragedy that would make September 11, 2001 seem insignificant.*

CHAPTER 17

SATURDAY

BY THE TIME Don Whitman reached Clancy's Pub located on D Street in the Harrison hotel, he had walked off most of his anger. He stood for a moment under the blinking green neon shamrock considering whether he really wanted a drink or not. He was an infrequent drinker, so when he did imbibe, he suffered mammoth hangovers. This thought made the decision for him. He felt bad enough right now; he didn't need a hangover on top of it.

As he was about to walk away, he saw the sandwich board sign advertising 'Today's Specials: grilled Reuben or grilled chicken breast sandwich with chips and a pickle - $5.95.' Checking his watch, he saw it was 11:15. It was a bit early, but he was ready to eat, and he loved Reuben sandwiches. Hell, he had nothing else he had to do, so he sat at one of the little outdoor tables, which were set up on the sidewalk. It was then that he noticed it was a pleasant day: sunny and clear, temp in the mid-fifties, the realization helped lift his sour mood.

Within a couple of minutes a waiter clad in a bellman's uniform brought him a glass of water and silverware wrapped in a paper napkin. He ordered his sandwich and requested a copy of today's Post. As he sat there, Don reviewed this morning's events. Now that he had cooled off, he could admit that his supervisor, although a runty prick, was justified for calling him on the carpet. He had overstepped his bounds by going directly to a senator.

Still how could they continue to dismiss the evidence that was so blatantly smacking them in the face? The waiter, dropping a copy of the Washington Post on his table, interrupted his thoughts. He looked up at the man, nodded a silent thank you, and picked up the front page. As usual, there was a photo and a progress report on the erection of the platform at the White House. A by-line screamed 'Sir Elton John to perform at inauguration.' The rest of the article talked about various and sundry celebrities, who would read poetry, dance and otherwise entertain the mobs attending the historic event.

Based on the front page of the Washington Post, it was a slow news day. Don turned to the second page. North Korea had started up its first nuclear reactor and the rest of the world applauded the isolated little dictatorship's peaceful use of atomic energy. Shit, a few years ago the U.S. was imposing economic sanctions on them because they kept testing nuclear weapons. As always, it was a crazy world; yesterday's enemy was today's champion of peace.

When his food arrived, Don set down the paper. He believed in enjoying his food, not just eating while reading or watching TV, so he concentrated on consuming what turned out to be a better-than-average Reuben sandwich. The chips were even crispy; at least, most of them were. Why restaurants insisted on including a dill pickle with a sandwich he would never understand. The darn juice from the pickle got on the sandwich and almost always turned several of the chips soggy. Taking the pickle off his plate and placing it on his napkin, he was surprised when his waiter showed up immediately with a fresh napkin, asked how his food was tasting, and took the pickle and soiled napkin away. As he watched the waiter stride away, a sense of Déjà Vu struck him.

Had he ever sat at this table before? Had this waiter ever served him before? The sandwich board didn't seem to ring a bell, but the waiter did. Where else had he seen this man before? It was disconcerting, but he had experienced similar feelings in the past and had not been able to explain them away. Now, as before, he simply shrugged his shoulders and dismissed the eerie feeling. Just then, his cell phone rang. By the ring tone, he knew it was a business call.

"Don Whitman," he answered.

"Don, Senator Franks here."

"Yes Senator. What's up?"

*   *   *

As his customer continued to talk on his cell phone, Ammar stood in the hall between the restaurant and the lobby and watched him. The man's eyes had given a momentary glimmer of recognition when he had picked up the unwanted pickle. Ammar, trained to be sensitive to such little signs, knew that awareness was often the difference between success and disaster, the difference between life and death.

His senses, already heightened since the arrival of his old 'friend' and fellow Jihadist, Muhumar, he was now razor sharp. Muhumar was going by the name Abdul. Why, when they were this close to completion of the mission, had Muhumar been sent? He had given some bullshit story that he had come on his own because he was so excited by the project. Ammar knew better than to believe such an obvious lie. No one went anywhere of their own accord. Muhumar had been sent. But who would have sent him?

The man he was watching sat up straighter in his chair. He was speaking to someone important. Unaware that someone was watching him, Don listened intently. Ammar studied him without being obvious. He was a tall, well-dressed person with a good head of hair. Slender of build, he also looked like he kept himself fit. If it came to a fight, he would probably be a worthy opponent. Ammar did not know why that thought had occurred to him. He attributed it to his heightened sense of urgency.

*   *   *

Senator Franks spoke excitedly, "I've been following up on the report you gave me and I've enlisted the help of the Deputy Director of the Defense Intelligence Agency."

"Really, you enlisted the deputy director?" Don was instantly pissed off. His good mood promptly reverted to sullen disappointment. His shitty morning just kept getting shittier.

"May I ask why you did that, sir?" Don tried to keep his voice calm.

"Actually, it wasn't my doing. General Birch contacted me and one thing just led to another."

Jesus fucking Christ! Don thought and immediately logged it in his memory for confession tomorrow. He then realized that he must also have muttered it.

What did you say?" Franks asked. "I didn't catch that."

"Nothing, Senator I was just ordering a cup of coffee after my lunch," Don lied.

"Sorry to interrupt your lunch, Don" Senator Franks said politely. He sensed the tension between them and wanted to find out the problem. "The general was very impressed by your report and suggested we work together." This bit of information somewhat mollified Don's knee-jerk reaction to having another intelligence agency involved in his project. Despite the open sharing mandated by the senate some years ago, the various intelligence agencies continued to jealously guard their secrets and vie for individual supremacy. Loyalty to the corps was still the order of the day.

"That's good to hear," he replied cautiously.

"In fact, the general said you're the only one at the FBI who doesn't have his head up his ass," Franks added with a small chuckle. "He also said he has some additional information we should discuss." The general's compliment went a long way to winning Don over, especially after this morning's event.

"So what's our next move?" Don asked.

"We need to have a conference call on secure phones. I'm calling from mine in my home office and general Birch has one in his, so give me your secure number in your office and the general will set up the call at 1:15 PM your time."

"That's going to be a problem. I don't have access to my office phone right now." Don said sheepishly.

"What? Why, the hell not?" the Senator asked.

"It's a long story, senator. How about I find a public phone and give you that number to call?"

"I guess that'll work. Just make sure it's not so public that people can overhear."

"Hang on a minute" Don replied. He then walked over to the front door of the Harrison Hotel and into the front lobby. Crossing through the lobby, he saw a bank of phone booths against the wall near the front desk. He went into the furthest one back, which appeared to be the least conspicuous and looked at the phone.

"OK. You can call me at 555-335-7605."

"All right, I'll give that number to the general. Just be sure you're at that phone at precisely 1:15. The general is a nut for punctuality."

"That's a common trait among all of us in the intelligence community. We're a very anal bunch," Don said with a smile. "I'll be waiting," he finished and hung up.

Senator Franks looked at his phone and listened to the dial tone. Was everybody in the intelligence community so damned impolite? Was hanging up the phone without saying 'goodbye' a status symbol? With that, he hung up his phone and sighed. Was he doing the right thing? Should he be calling his committee chair and getting her involved? Hell, she got the same reports he did, and she chose to ignore them. Besides, time was too short to try to go through the proper channels. No, this one was very likely to bite him in the ass, but he had to see it through on his own. Whom else could he turn to? He didn't want to scare the hell out of Teri and Maggie. He trusted Estelle, but he couldn't confide in her about something this big. Then it came to him. He picked up the phone and dialed his father's number.

SATURDAY

ESTELLE HUNG UP her phone, pushed her chair back, put her feet up on her desk and her arms behind her head and smiled. What a hell of a productive morning! She had finished the tasks the senator had requested and then had turned to the important stuff. No doubt, the impending inauguration was the reason practically every secretary and Washington staffer was at work this Saturday morning. Whatever the reason, she had managed to talk to almost every resource she had needed. It is a hoot, she thought, how the politicians and military brass were convinced they were the decision makers and the leaders of the free world when actually the secretaries and staffers ran everything.

Oh, the representatives passed bills, gave speeches and sat on important committees, but, without someone to actually do the work and pull the strings, nothing would happen. She had found out a lot this morning and couldn't wait to share it. She now knew that Don was in the doghouse for meeting with her boss and seeking his help on some hush-hush intelligence stuff. Why in hell they were seen coming out of a gay bar, she still didn't understand. She also knew that Don had been given a week off without pay and had a letter of reprimand put in his file. Melinda, secretary to the Under Secretary of Intelligence & Analysis at the National Security Branch of the FBI had typed it. That meant Don was available and in need of some TLC. She had also found out a good deal more about him by talking to his secretary Miriam.

Miriam was aware of the affair going on between them, but she hated Don's whiny wife who called him all the time with her ridiculous 'major problems'.

Miriam liked her boss and felt bad about his dressing down this morning. She also assured Estelle that with Don 'what you saw was what you got'. He was a dedicated public servant and family man. In fact, she had said, "you're his only vice. It's a good thing for you that I approve." Estelle had laughed at that. She knew that Miriam was banging judge Warfield at the Attorney General's office. She and Miriam had never met in person, but they enjoyed a great friendship over the phone and via computer.

Estelle planned to finish out the morning, go home and call Don and set up an afternoon of consolation for him followed by a nice home-cooked dinner. But, first, she had some juicy news about General Birch to share with Senator Franks. This tidbit she got from Lakeesha Smith at Birch's office.

Lakeesha was a civilian who hated military protocol. She considered herself a topnotch executive secretary deserving of respect. She greatly disliked her boss, Lt. General Sam Birch. She described him as snooty, demanding and way too bitchy. As she had summed up, "he's a typical military prick. He absolutely never says thank you. Nor does he ever give a pat on the back. Just do this or do that ASAP. If I hear that asshole say ASAP one more time I'm going to scream."

Estelle had listened attentively and commiserated with Lakeesha's plight. They had talked a couple of times over the months about other matters, but in the past Lakeesha had never opened up to her like this. Estelle guessed she was feeling sorry for herself because she had to work on a Saturday.

"Yeah, I understand completely," Estelle interjected, "I usually hate having to deal with the brass too. Most of them are self-important jerks."

"In this case, 'prick' is the only word to describe the general," Lakeesha stated emphatically.

"How long have you worked for him?" Estelle asked wanting to keep the conversation going.

"Since January 5 2008. I remember the date because I had just been promoted to Executive Secretary and he was my new boss. I had to teach him the ropes, because he had just been transferred to the Defense Intelligence Agency and didn't know shit about our work here."

"Oh my," Estelle commented, "what did you do?"

"I took him under my wing and walked him through all the do's and don'ts. Then I helped him meet the right people who could be of use to him in doing his job. So, in all the five years I've worked for him do you think he's said 'Thank You' even once?"

"My guess is no," Estelle said with empathy.

"Damn right 'NO'," Lakeesha said bitterly. On top of that, now the dipshit thinks he understands the intelligence community better than I do."

"It's bad enough to work for a demanding boss, but a demanding boss who thinks he's always right is impossible, Estelle comforted.

"What's really irritating" said Lakeesha, is that his nickname before he got here was 'General Fuck-Up' or at least that's what his last secretary called him."

Estelle snorted, and said laughingly "General Fuck-Up?"

Lakeesha giggled a bit and said, "You heard me, mama. I guess he damn near lost his commission. The only reason he's here is that he was roommates at WestPoint with some high mucketymuck general who saved his ass." Lakeesha continued her tirade, "I'll never understand the good ol' boy network. How in the hell can you jeopardize national security by appointing some numb nut to an important position just because he was a friend from your school days?"

"That's Washington, my dear," said Estelle. "That's Washington." "I am curious, though. Did you ever find out what he did to earn that nickname?"

"Sure did. It took me a couple of years, but I finally got the low down on him. He was an army advisor to the commanding officer of some air force base in the Dakotas. They pulled a major boner, and he caught the flak for it. Here, let me send you the newspaper clipping." Estelle turned to her computer screen and went to her email. There was Lakeesha's email with an attachment. She opened the attachment and read incredulously:

August 30th 2007 nuclear weapons incident:
 On August 30th, 2007 six cruise missiles armed with W80-1 warheads were mistakenly loaded onto a B-52 and flown from

Minot Air Force Base, N.D. to Barksdale AFB, La. on a mission to transport cruise missiles for decommissioning. It was not discovered that the six missiles had nuclear warheads until the plane landed at Barksdale, leaving the warheads unaccounted for 36 hours. This is the first time since 1968 that nuclear warheads were publicly revealed to have been transported on a U.S. bomber. The munitions crew involved in mistakenly loading the nuclear warheads at Minot were temporarily decertified from performing their duties involving nuclear munitions.

"Wow," Estelle said. "So general fuck-up was in charge of the crew that left nuclear missiles unguarded for 36 hours?"

"You got it, sweetie, what's more, you're reading the air base's PR release which really downplays the significance of the incident."

"Somebody's head had to roll for this one. To be fair, Birch was not directly in charge, but he was the man responsible for nuclear weapons security at this base. Hell, security was his specialty in the army."

"So Birch takes the blame and winds up getting a cushy transfer. Maybe you and I need to figure out some colossal boo-boo so we can get a raise."

"Oh, you ain't heard shit yet," Lakeesha gloated. She was an excellent executive secretary and a graduate of Michigan State. Lakeesha could speak and write perfectly; but when she was dishing the dirt, she often lapsed into old speech patterns learned during her childhood in Detroit.

"His new position here is rated for a three star general, so the prick got an instant promotion too. Dig that shit?"

"Un-be-lieve-able!" Estelle gasped. She accented each syllable.

"And...I saved the best for last," Lakeesha drawled.

"There's more?" Estelle encouraged.

"Hell, that PR release only exposed the tip of the fuckin' iceberg, Honey. It wasn't until later that they discovered that one of the missiles that went on the little joyride was missing its warhead! How's that for some shit?"

"You're putting me on, right? I mean a missing nuclear bomb?" Estelle gasped.

"And they still ain't found that mother, last I heard." Lakeesha said smugly.

"Wow. That is scary." Estelle said slowly. "How the hell do you lose a fucking nuclear weapon? What's more, why isn't everyone aware of it and looking for it? Why isn't the press screaming?"

"Honey, its plain old CYA," Lakeesha said. "Nobody says shit even when they got a mouthful. You know that."

"Well, I want to thank you for ruining the rest of my day, Lakeesha. Shit, I'm not going to sleep a wink tonight thinking about this nuclear weapon floating around god-knows-where."

"No, no, no. Sleep tight honey. It's almost expired by now."

"Expired?" Estelle asked.

"Yes ma'am. This particular kind of warhead had a very powerful, uh" she paused, 'ignition system' is the best way I can describe it. I looked it up on the web. The stuff that set the bomb off has a very short shelf life, like maybe 3 or 4 years. Anyway, by now that bomb should be a dud. It be as useless as my husband." Lakeesha said comfortingly.

"That's good to know," Estelle sighed. I wish you had told me that earlier."

"What? And ruin my fun?" Lakeesha chuckled.

"Well, thanks for all the info, Lakeesha. I really appreciate your help. Tell your boss to keep looking for that bomb."

"Nah, that's Osama/Osaka now."

"What?" Estelle asked quizzically.

"You know, Osama/Osaka." Lakeesha answered shortly.

"I don't get the reference," Estelle replied.

"Oh, that's right. You haven't been in D.C. that long." "Back a few years ago, about 06 or 07, there was a joke going around: what's the difference between Osama and Osaka?"

"The answer was, if you give the FBI and the CIA billions in funding and a map of Japan, they might be able to find Osaka."

"I hadn't heard that one. It's funny. Sadly, it's also true."

"Truth, sister, truth, they couldn't find they own asses if we put superglue on all the toilet seats. They sure as hell ain't gonna find that bum or that bomb."

"You're too much," Estelle laughed. Thanks again. I gotta go."

"Over and out," Lakeesha laughed and hung up.

Estelle took her feet off her desk and sat up straight. She typed up a detailed and concise report about everything she had learned this morning and emailed it to the senator. She included a copy of the Minot

AFB PR release and told him he could reach her by cell phone or her home phone if he needed her later today. With that done, she locked up the office and headed to the train station and home to a hot luxurious bath. She had to get ready to invite Don for his TLC.

CHAPTER 1 9

SATURDAY

THE MESSENGER HAD requested a private audience with Imam Jamali. This was a common practice, as the Imam certainly could not discuss all of his plans in open court. However, this messenger was an unusual case. He was an American from California. He looked to be of Mid Eastern descent and claimed to be a loyal Jihadist. What did he truly want? The American was typically rude and casual. He did not salaam; nor did he address the Imam humbly. Why should he waste his time listening to this infidel? He knew why; because his trusted advisor, Colonel Habib had recommended he do so.

Jamali stood and stretched his shoulders before striding over to the little anteroom used for such meetings. The man stood nervously in the center of the little room. Jamali paced over to him and placing his left hand on the man's shoulder, said "Welcome brother Jihadist. You have information for me?" The stupid American took this as a gesture of respect and friendship instead of the insult it was. The left hand, used only for wiping one's behind or performing other unsavory tasks, was the unclean hand. By ostentatiously placing his left hand on the American's shoulder, the Imam had humiliated and degraded him. The American practically simpered. He was accepted. The others in the room hid their smirks and enjoyed the little interchange.

Imam Jamali turned his back to the man and sat down at a small table. He gestured for the fool to join him. When the man sat, Jamali continued the charade by holding the man's right hand in his left and asked, "So, why have you traveled so far? What important information do you have for me?"

"Your highness," the bumbling Californian mistakenly addressed him, "I know about the Satan's Head project." There was an instant intake of breath in the room and the Imam sat more erectly in his chair. More cautious now, Imam Jamali looked into the eyes of the messenger and said slowly, "tell me what you know of this Satan thing."

"Your highness, I'm a native born American of Arab parents. I am Muslim and an active member of our local group assisting in the fight for righteousness."

Yes, yes. That is good. But, tell me about the Satan project you talked about."

"Well, the rumor is, and it's more than just a rumor as far as I'm concerned, a major attack called Satan's Head is planned on Inauguration day." Jamali dropped the hand.

"And where did you hear this rumor," the Imam asked with a steely tone in his voice.

"I don't know exactly. It's just the scuttlebutt passed around at our meetings. It is true isn't it? I mean, you're the group behind it aren't you?"

"I have never heard of such an activity," the Imam said slowly. "It sounds intriguing. What can you tell me about this plot? Who is involved? What kind of attack?" The American slumped in his chair. He now looked confused and disappointed.

"Damn," he said, I musta got the wrong info. It must be a different group."

"What do you mean?" The Imam coaxed.

"Damn it", the American repeated. I was told that a large Jihadist group called the Sword of Allah was gonna nuke Washington D.C. I came here to help."

"And, just how could you help this Sword of Allah group," the Imam said gently.

"I need to alert them as to which day to do it," the American said defiantly. I was told they were planning to do it on Sunday January 20th."

"Well, isn't January 20th the traditional day for Inauguration? That is what you've done for many years. Your current President, Adolfus

Herman, went through the inauguration ceremony on January 20 2009. We watched it on the news."

"Yeah," the American explained, but in 2009, January 20 was a Tuesday. This year the 20th falls on a Sunday. That means the President and Vice President will be administered the oath of office at a private ceremony that may not even take place in D.C. Then there'll be a re-enactment ceremony in D.C. on Monday. That'll also be the day most of the other celebrations will occur and most of the bigwigs will be in town."

Imam Jamali sat back in his chair. This news was very disturbing. The timing of the enemy's lock step ritual provided the foundation for the entire Satan's Head project; now almost too late, we learn that our information may be incorrect.

"You are sure of this?" The Imam asked earnestly. "You cannot be wrong?"

"Damn right, I'm sure. Why the hell do you think I traveled over 8,000 miles to warn you?" The American sat back with a small smirk on his pimply face. He had made his point. He was due some hospitality, like maybe a young maiden to share his bed tonight.

Jamali nodded and mused for a moment. Then he clapped once. Hassan Habib, his trusted advisor, was at his side immediately. He whispered to Hassan in Urdu, "take the American and get additional information from him. We need to determine how knowledge of our plan reached the United States and how many people know. When you are satisfied you have all the information he can give, slit the arrogant infidel's throat."

Imam Jamali smiled as Hassan led the American away, and thanked him for this important information. He clapped his hands again. A servant appeared with a glass of cool water. The Imam took it and said, "Bring me my Sat- Com immediately." It was imperative that he speak to Ammar at once.

CHAPTER 20

SATURDAY

PASTOR CHARLES FRANKS took a bite of his grilled cheese sandwich and, as if on cue, his phone rang. It never fails he thought, as he got up from his kitchen table and moved to the wall phone, I could sit in this house for a week without a call and the moment I start to eat something, "hello" he said as he took the receiver off the wall unit. It came out sounding like "Howwo".

"Dad, are you there?" His son said. The elder Franks swallowed and said, "Sorry, I was eating." He moved back to the table and set his sandwich on his plate. He would eat it later.

"Oh, Dad I'm sorry. It seems like I'm interrupting everyone's lunch today."

"Don't let it bother you, John. I'd rather talk to you anyway. Who else's lunch did you interrupt and why aren't you having lunch with my lovely daughter-in-law and granddaughter?"

"They're both at the club exercising and I'm home working. I haven't thought about lunch myself." John said, ignoring his father's first question.

"Well, what made you stop working and pick up the phone to call dear old dad?" Charles immediately regretted the flippant question. When would he ever learn to control his mouth? He interrupted while John was trying to respond. "I'm sorry; really. We just haven't spoken in a while and I was being snotty."

"Dad, I'm sorry too, but I don't have time right now for a guilt trip. I need help." After a moment of silence, John said, "Dad, are you there?" The question caused Charles to respond.

"Oh, yes, yes of course. I was just trying to remember the last time you needed my help. I assume you don't need money 'cause you know I don't have any." Pastor Franks gave a little laugh to soften his statement.

"Dad, I'm also operating under a real time crunch; please let me tell you what I'm dealing with and please hold your questions until I'm done." The exasperation in his voice was enough to tell the Pastor it was a serious matter.

"Go ahead, son. I'm listening." Pastor Franks spoke with an apologetic tone as he sat down at his kitchen table. He listened intently and resisted the frequent urges to ask questions or make comments. The longer he listened, the more disturbed he became.

After a while, John began to repeat himself and his father cut him off.

"OK, John. I think I get the picture. I want you to know I'm praying for you."

"Thank you, Dad. I need all the help I can get." His Father knew he was just placating him, but they both kept the game going. Charles continued to hope that his actions would somehow someday inspire an awakening in his son.

"Now, I have some questions for you."

"I hope I have some answers," John said wearily.

"My first question is what do you know about this Whitman? Did you check him out?"

"I'm pretty confident he's on the level. He seemed legitimate, and he spoke with authority. I'm pretty sure I can trust him."

"Check him out, son. I know everything has been happening fast, but that's no excuse for ignoring due diligence."

"You're right Dad, of course. I did have Estelle do some checking on general Birch."

"Estelle is your secretary?" asked Pastor Franks.

"Yes and a damn good one. I trust her completely." The senator replied.

"Good. What has she found out?" the Pastor asked.

"I haven't talked to her yet. Wait a minute; I'm checking my email now, ok, there's a message from her. I'm going to read it."

"John, hold on a second. I don't know what you should do, but I know what you should *not* do. Quit taking this entire burden on yourself. There must be someone you can tell about this threat, someone who can take action or at least give you a recommendation for your next step. Right now you've got a tiger by the tail and its being ridden by these two cowboys."

"OK, Dad. This email is about general Birch. I'm going to read it quick and then I'll get back to you OK?" With that, he hung up. Damn, John thought, I'm starting to act like a spook; hanging up without saying goodbye, gotta watch that.

John read Estelle's memorandum twice. He began to think that his dad's advice was the right thing to do. Yet, whom should he call? Then, the phone rang. John looked at his watch. It was precisely 12:15, 1:15 eastern time. As soon as he answered, he knew by the hollow sound he was on a teleconference call.

"Franks," he answered.

"Birch here, senator." the General, responded.

"Whitman is on line sirs." Don chimed in.

"Where are you, Don?" John asked.

"In the phone booth at the Harrison hotel, Don replied. "There's no one near me." Don Whitman was correct. There was no one near him. However, across the lobby near the main entrance, Ammar stood at his regular bellman post watching Don with interest. The man had answered the public phone when it rang and that made Ammar suspicious. He was obeying his instincts. He glanced to his left and verified that there were no customers at his tables.

With his back turned to the phone booth door, so no one could read his lips, Don concentrated on the conversation. He listened intently.

"General, I assume that you have introduced yourself to agent Whitman." John began.

"Only briefly," the General replied. "Why don't you do the honors?"

"Fine; Don, I wasn't sure what to do with the information you gave me yesterday. Frankly, it scared the shit out of me and I almost called the Chairman of the Homeland Security Committee I'm on; but, I decided instead to try to verify some of the stuff you had put in your report before doing anything else."

"Makes sense to me." Don offered.

"Yeah, I thought so. Anyway, I sent the info to the local MTAC in D.C." John heard a slight chuckle out of Birch, and under his breath the word 'navy', which the General quickly muffled.

"You did what?" Don practically gasped. He also quickly got control of himself and said nothing more.

"Yeah, yeah I know. That may not have been the brightest move; but I needed to start somewhere. I figured a fusion center was a logical place to begin. Anyway, it's done now and that's that; so let's move on shall we?" The Senator was getting a little agitated by their attitudes; especially with Birch's smugness. As if he was infallible, well, John knew better.

"Were they able to verify my findings and suspicions?" Don asked earnestly.

"I'm still waiting to hear from them," John answered with a disgruntled tone.

"They won't be contacting you, Senator." General Birch cut in.

"What; why not?" Franks erupted.

"I put the kibosh on it." General Birch said quietly. "I had some of my connections talk to their connections and told them to take you out of the loop, Senator. I did it for your own good. You should not have been involved in this to begin with. You do realize that don't you?"

"So now you know what's best for me, General? I think that's pretty damn presumptuous, don't you?" He immediately regretted his response. There it was again; that instant anger whenever anyone tried to control him. His father laughingly blamed it on an overactive Y chromosome. Whatever the cause, John was angry with himself for his lack of self-control. However, he was even angrier at Birch.

"John, I repeat, I did it for your own good." Birch continued. "Whatever happens, you do not want to be in the middle of this mess. It's a no-win for you. If there is a terrorist attack and it comes out that you had been warned in advance, you'll be crucified. On the other hand, if you run around blowing the whistle and nothing happens, you'll be ridiculed or worse." Before John could respond, Don Whitman jumped back into the conversation.

"Senator, I'm sorry. I think the General is right. I'm sorry I came to you in the first place. I got my ass reamed for that this morning and I deserved it. I should never have gotten you involved. I am sincerely sorry." There was a brief lull in the conversation as Senator Franks took a breath before he spoke calmly and firmly.

"Whenever the two of you are finished saving my ass, let's discuss what might be about to happen to our beloved country." He paused and took a deep breath. "Now, I believe I was in the middle of introductions."

"Don, General Sam Birch called me early this morning asking why I had contacted the Multiple Threat Alert Center. Lieutenant General Birch is the Deputy Director of the Defense Intelligence Agency."

"That's what I thought." Don responded.

"General, Don Whitman is director of the Joint Terrorist Task Force of the National Security Branch of the FBI. As you well know, he is the man who alerted us to the probable terrorist attack within the next day or so. It was damn fine work in my opinion. What's more, even if his contacting me was unorthodox, god damn it, at least he did something instead of bowing to pressure or kowtowing to rank. As far as I'm concerned Don, you absolutely did the right thing and I'm going to see this through." The Senator spoke deliberately and passionately. The message was clear. Senator John Franks was staying in the loop.

"Actually, I'm the Associate Director of the JTTF, not Director." Don offered.

"And I'm the *junior* senator from Wisconsin." Franks exploded. "Christ! Do we all have our titles down now? Can we finally talk about something of importance?"

"Take it easy, Senator." Birch said in a placating tone. "I think we're all a bit strung out at the moment and getting pissed at each other isn't going to solve anything."

"You're absolutely right General. I am strung out right now. Don I apologize."

"No problem," said Don. "What's your plan, Senator? Do you have any ideas?"

"That's what this conference call is about; figuring out what to do next," said the Senator. "How do we determine the exact nature of the threat?"

"We don't," General Birch said emphatically. "We let the FBI do that."

"I sent a number of memos without a response," Whitman countered. "I also sent out more alerts than I can count to every other agency I could find and no one listened; no one cared. My god damn superiors never even acknowledged receipt of the information."

General Birch fielded this one.

"Don the 'god damn FBI' gets a daily barrage of tips, alerts and downright foolish plots against the nation; everything from Molotov cocktail balloons which are to be lobbed at the president, to aliens planning to zap the Whitehouse with death rays."

"A warning from the Joint Terrorist Task Force is not exactly the same as an alien death ray plot, for pity's sake, Don retorted. I can't believe my memos were lumped in with the loony-toon warnings!"

"They use junior staffers to sort through all the crap that comes in. In fact, one of the first tasks a new trainee gets is just that. It helps train them not to take themselves too seriously. It also teaches them how to discern a real threat from some conspiracy nut's ranting and raving." General Birch explained.

"So our country's first line of defense against terrorism is a group of novice G-man wannabes, who get to decide which threat to take seriously?" John Franks said incredulously.

"Don't be so shocked, Senator." The General said with a little snort. Managers always relegate boring routine tasks to the newest and lowest in the pecking order. It's the way of the world. Don't forget, however, these novices do have supervisors looking over their shoulders."

"That's truly comforting." The Senator said with an edge in his voice.

"Anyway," the General added, "I called my counterpart at the FBI this morning after we talked. They are currently conducting a thorough investigation of Don's findings. He also said the National Nuclear Security Administration has had several Nest Teams sweeping the town all week searching for possible weapons in preparation for the upcoming events. Additional teams are on the way. They should be here by this afternoon."

"What's a Nest team?" John asked.

"Nuclear Emergency Support Team," the General replied. They have the most up-to-date and sensitive radioactivity detection equipment on the planet. The radium dial of a glow-in-the-dark man's wrist watch will set one off. If there are any nukes lurking about, they'll find 'em."

"Well, that much I'm grateful for," the Senator stated. "Did they indicate what they were looking for? Is it a suit case nuke?"

Don exclaimed, "So you think it's probably a Russian suit case bomb, too?"

"It's just a guess, Don. Based on your report, it seemed like the most likely threat, Birch said. "In fact, I'm almost ready to bet the ranch on it," he added.

"Well, General up until a little while ago I'd have said the same thing. Now I'm not so sure. I'm worried about something much bigger," the Senator said cryptically.

"What?" Birch and Whitman said in unison. Franks ignored their question and asked one of his own.

"General, while I've got you on the phone; I'd like you to tell me about your transfer from Minot Air Force Base." There was an awkward pause, before Birch responded.

"That was some years ago, Senator. Damn near ancient history," the General said testily. He hesitated and when the Senator said nothing more, he said, "Give me a minute to think back."

"Take all the time you need." Franks said calmly. Don said nothing. After another minute, the General began his recitation of events.

"It was back in '06'. Strict budgets had caused the army to make cut backs for a number of years. When I got my second star, there was no Fort or Camp in need of someone with my level of security training. I wound up assigned as the security advisor to Minot Air Force base, North Dakota. Minot's main mission is to manage and deploy nuclear weapons. Most of these weapons are in silos located in the surrounding countryside. We also have a number of cruise missiles for delivery by our B-52 bombers."

"And, you were an advisor, not a line officer?" Franks asked.

"That's what the transfer orders said," the General agreed. "God I hated Minot. Indians, cowboys, miners and whores were the main population of the desolate little town stuck out in the middle of nowhere. Worse yet, the winters were endless. I was stuck in this little shithole for over a year and a half. Anyway, the Air Force didn't really want me there, or I should say General Wiggins didn't want me there, and I didn't want to be there, either. It was very cozy. Mostly I did routine reports about the ready status of our base security and conducted occasional surprise inspections.

To say I was bored is a major understatement. That is, I was bored until some jerk-off issues an order to transport six cruise missiles to what we later determined was Barksdale AFB in Louisiana. Remarkably, a copy of this order never crosses my desk. As I understand it, a sentry doing a routine inspection discovers that the missiles aren't where they're supposed to be, and reports that they are gone. Of course, no one contacts me; after all, I'm just some *Army* advisor. The first I knew of the problem was when Wiggins calls me into his office and asks '*how could this happen? Where could they be?*'

Then he informs me that as chief security advisor, the blame for this screw up falls squarely on my shoulders. It's entirely my fault. The whole time he's grinning like a Cheshire cat. It makes no difference that I know nothing about the transfer. In fact, that makes it worse because I had set up the procedures and failsafe mechanisms: '*Why didn't they work?*'

I never did find out why the missiles were sent out; I just got them back ASAP. Anyway, after we got them back, the base PR department issued a statement about the event. They disclosed that the missiles were technically unguarded for 36 hours. Some of the crewmembers got slaps on the wrist and I got my transfer to D.C."

"And this was a mutually agreeable transfer?" The Senator asked.

"Hell yes," the General laughed. Wiggins and I got along like two bulls trying to share one cow. He was my commanding officer, but I had friends in high places. He wanted me gone and I wanted to go. The incident provided the justification for my reassignment."

"Damn, how I love politics," Franks said softly. "The military is as bad as D.C.," he added. "One hand is always washing the other."

"That's the truth," Don agreed rather lamely. He had never liked politics. He preferred 'truth, justice and the American way.' It often bothered him that he was less politically adept than he should be. He knew it would be a detriment to him as he aspired to a higher office.

"Unfortunately, there's more to the story," General Birch spoke again.

"Why do you say 'unfortunately'?" John knew the answer to that question, but he wanted to hear the General's explanation.

"Because two days after I got to D.C. I learned that one of the missiles was missing its warhead. Wiggins presumed it stolen while unguarded; so, that was my fault too. It was total bullshit, but how could I argue? Needless to say, I was extremely worried about the missing nuclear payload and twice as worried about my future."

"What happened?" Don asked excitedly. I never heard anything about this. Did you find the missing weapon? Where was it? Who had it?"

"Slow down, Don," the General said patiently. I'm sorry to say we never have located that rogue nuclear device and we've been searching diligently for 5 years."

"Holy crap," Don said softly.

The General continued, "The reason you've never heard anything about it is we decided it would be in the best interests of the American public not to tell anyone. Actually, to tell the truth, the Joint Chiefs of Staff made the decision. Their rationale was that we'd just gone through a shit storm over Russian nuclear suit case bombs and we didn't need another big scare to further upset the people."

"We politicians call that a cover-up," Franks said disgustedly. "This is the biggest government stonewall I've ever heard of. How did you manage to keep it a secret?"

"There were some consequences," said the General with a sigh. "Some damn fine men lost their jobs over it. I arrived at my new post in early January of 2008. Less than six months later, a newly appointed Defense Secretary, Tom Morton, removed the Secretary of the Air Force and the Chief of Staff from their positions. He used our erroneous transfer of the six missiles and another incident as justification."

"Apparently, in March, the Air Force had also mistakenly shipped some nuclear missile components, nose cones I heard, to Taiwan. Anyway, the new Defense Secretary wanted his own team, so he asked for and received their resignations based on *their pattern of poor performance.*   In turn, he agreed not to bring up the missing warhead. Of course, he also doubled the efforts for locating it, but, so far no luck. Bob Reynolds was the Chief of Staff and an old friend. We met at West Point. He saved my ass and paid with his own. I could always count on Bob to do the right thing."

"You believe that *doing the right thing,* includes covering up the theft of a nuclear warhead?" Franks was astonished. Who the hell had he teamed up with here?

"Senator, you need to put things in perspective. We would gain nothing by causing a nation-wide panic. The people who needed to know the facts, the people who could do something about the problem were on it."

"General, you really amaze me. After five years of fruitless searching, you still have the nerve to say that Americans have no need to know about your major screw-up even though millions of lives are at risk. Birch, how do you sleep at night?"

"Truth be told, quite well these days. I'll admit I lost some sleep in the early going, but, the longer we go on without a nuclear incident the more convinced I am that whoever has it either doesn't know how to use it or..." At this point, Senator Franks cut the General short with an angry shout.

"Oh, that really makes sense," Franks snapped. Someone with the knowledge to open up a cruise missile and successfully remove the warhead, lacks the ability to use it? For crissake General, how stupid do you think we are?"

Don audibly sucked in his breath and held it. He said nothing. The rhetorical question hung in the air for a moment before General Birch spoke again. When he did, his tone was steely.

"As I was about to say, the warhead may no longer be viable. Listen, it has been hard living with this nightmare. You've been dealing with it for 24 hours. I've had five years of this shit. Once again, Franks regretted his harsh remarks. How would he feel if he had been responsible for the theft of a nuclear weapon? What would he do to try to recover it? How well would he sleep? John Franks was quick to anger, but he was also very empathetic. Again, there was a pause in the conversation and then all three began to say something at once. Franks won out by raising his voice.

"What I don't understand General, is why did you say you are sure the threat is from a Russian suit case bomb? Why wouldn't it be our W80-1?"

"It's because I've done my homework, Senator. When that warhead went missing, I set out to learn everything I could about our nuclear arsenal. I went way beyond the tactical training I had received previously. My research has given me a whole new perspective and understanding of our stockpile of weapons, and let me assure you, it is one hell of a stockpile. One thing is certain, if that W80-1 ever were to be used on U.S. territory, I'd never recover. Fortunately, I am quite sure that the time for worrying is long over."

"Why is that?" Franks asked.

"This nuclear warhead uses a mixture of deuterium and a radioactive isotope of hydrogen called tritium in the detonation system. Tritium is highly effective and is stored as a gas. The amount of tritium released determines the power of the explosion."

"You mean the bomb is programmable?" Don asked.

"Yes. The technical term is 'variable yield'. We call it 'dial-a-nuke'. It can be set anywhere from 5 kilotons to 150 kilotons." General Birch answered. "In fact, the yield can be changed while the bomb is in flight."

"Did you say 150 kilotons?" The Senator repeated. "Just how big a blast is that?"

"Senator, the bomb we dropped on Hiroshima has been estimated to be about 15 kilotons. It killed some 80,000 people instantly and with the after effects of radiation over the next five years, maybe as many as 200,000."

"And we're looking for a bomb that is ten times more deadly than the one dropped on Hiroshima. God damn," Don said and immediately made a mental note for confession.

"There is an upside," the General added.

"One of the drawbacks of using tritium is that the warheads have a relatively short shelf life. Unlike uranium, tritium poses less radioactive exposure risk, and it has a half-life of only a bit over twelve years."

"And how old is our warhead?" Whitman asked hopefully.

"I did some real digging on this one," General Birch replied smugly. Officially, this weapon does not exist."

"What do you mean by that?" Franks asked.

"Why?" said Whitman.

"For that we have to go back to the late eighties and early nineties. It was the SALT and START era," Birch explained. Under the Strategic Arms Reduction Treaty, we, and our adversaries were supposed to be getting rid of a large percentage of our nuclear stockpiles. What actually happened, and I can only conjecture that both sides did it, was that we got rid of lots of our older outmoded weapons, but added a few modern ones. Our total nuclear weapon count went down, but our efficiency increased. I gotta believe the Ruskies did the same thing. Production of our warhead's predecessor, the W80 model, ended in September of 1990.

Officially, all nuclear weapon production ended about the same time. I strongly suspect that we continued making Mod 1s. Based on its serial number, I suspect that our particular warhead was built in the mid-nineties."

"So, this warhead is at least fourteen or fifteen years old" Don said, "It should already be expired and non-functional."

"Bingo," said General Birch.

"Not so fast, Guys." Franks said resignedly. "If your suspicions are correct, it might also have been built later meaning it could still be fully functional, right General?"

"Yes. That is true, but I believe..." At this point, Franks again cut him off curtly and asked another question.

"Just how big a package are we looking for, General? I mean, does this thing weigh a couple of tons or is it smaller?

"Much smaller, I'm afraid. The actual warhead weighs less than 300 pounds and will basically fit inside a footlocker." The General sounded almost apologetic.

"Christ! That's not much bigger than a fucking suit case bomb!" Franks raged. How the hell can we pack so much destructive power in such a small package?"

"It's the marvels of science, my friend; the marvels of science." General Birch lamented.

"You know, I've heard all I can stand for now." John Franks spoke with an air of exasperation. "I need to review everything we've talked about before I can do any more."

"That sounds like a good idea, Senator. Let's allow the FBI to do its work and maybe we'll get lucky." The General tried to sound enthusiastic.

"I'll continue to hang around this hotel if you like, so you can reach me on the land line," Don said, hoping it would not be necessary.

"That's probably not needed," Franks assured him. General I want to talk some more. Both of you call me at 7 PM Wisconsin time, earlier if there's any news. OK?" He hung up. Don and the General continued to talk briefly until Don's cell phone rang. It was Estelle. He gladly accepted her invitation and left the phone booth in a better mood.

CHAPTER 21

SATURDAY

TERI FRANKS AND daughter Maggie were side by side on stationary bikes at the Sta-Fit Club, located on Lake Mendota. It was part of their Saturday routine. They both enjoyed sleeping in on Saturdays, getting up around nine and waking up slowly over coffee. It was by mutual agreement that neither of them brought up any controversial topics during this quiet time together. This morning they had talked about how worried and stressed John seemed and had agreed he was working too hard and taking his responsibilities as U.S. Senator too seriously. They had also agreed it was time for them to have Grampa Franks over for dinner. They would call him when they got home from the club. As usual, they had each drunk a large glass of orange juice and grabbed a granola bar to eat on the way to the club. Maggie had driven.

It was now 11:30 and Maggie was enjoying proving that her legs were stronger and had greater endurance than her mother's. Teri, trying to maintain the same pace on her bike, was beginning to get short of breath and to perspire. The moment she realized she was perspiring, the thought popped into her head 'horses sweat, men perspire and ladies glow'; it was a phrase her mother had driven into her head as she was growing up and it invariably came to mind when she was working out. Just as invariably, she thought to herself 'I'm glowing like a race horse'. The witticism never failed to amuse her, and she smiled to herself.

Maggie misread her mother's smile and increased her rate on

the bike. As she grimaced and resolutely pedaled, she stared out the windows in front of them.

"Look at all the sailboats," Teri panted. "I wish I was on one of them right now."

"I hate sailboats," Maggie replied. "They scare the hell out of me."

"If you were a better swimmer, you'd love them," Teri said with her best motherly voice of disapproval. Maggie ignored the remark.

The designers of the club had put this row of stationary bikes and treadmills on the second floor in front of a bank of large windows facing west. The windows overlooked the entranceway parking lot and the lake. Many members came here later in the day and watched the sun go down as they did their daily routines.

Thank god my mother's not one of those people, Maggie thought. She liked to get her exercises done sooner rather than later, so they were not hanging over her head all day. She also liked to watch the various members of all ages, and sizes coming like lemmings to the gym.

It amused her that so many portly or downright obese men and women bothered to come here. Did they really think they could get fit and healthy with a few minutes of exercise in between their jelly donuts? Maggie snorted in laughter and her mother turned to look at her.

Teri misread Maggie's laughter and increased her pace on the bike. Damned if she would be laughed at. The clip was now grueling, but they continued on, both doggedly determined not to let the other outdo her. Maggie saw her mother's surge and decided to just match and maintain. Her younger legs gave her the advantage in the contest; why couldn't her mother just admit it? As she pedaled, she watched an old man making his way gingerly through the parking lot. He shuffled bent over nearly double. No doubt, he was heading for the warm water pool for stretching exercises. She felt a moment of sadness for the old man. His body had betrayed him. It was not a common emotion for her.

She pretty much held most of the old folks that came here in contempt. The women were mostly widows trying to stave off their inevitable demise. They took up space on equipment and always stayed too long. They also spent too much time gossiping and teasing the young men and trainers. Why didn't the old bags just stay home and tend to their knitting?

These mean thoughts were providing the energy needed to continue her break neck pace on the bike. Maggie was glad when her mother finally let up and suggested they head for the pool. Neither of them acknowledged the little contest which had just gone on, but Maggie smiled inwardly. That good feeling left her immediately when she remembered what an excellent swimmer her mother was. Would she now show her up by swimming a lap and a half to her one as usual? Maggie decided to avoid the embarrassment.

"Let's skip the pool today. I'd rather shoot some hoops, take a long hot shower and get lunch. What do you say?" Maggie smiled nicely. Teri groaned and answered.

"Let's also skip the hoops. A long hot shower and lunch sounds perfect to me."

"Fine by me; I don't mind having an easy day for a change," Maggie replied as she changed direction and headed for the women's locker room. She didn't see her mother stick her tongue out behind her.

After showering and dressing, Teri suggested Eve's Garden of Eatin' for lunch. The restaurant located on East Williamson Street, or Willy Street as most of the locals called it, offered a huge salad bar. It did a great eat-in and carryout business from about 10:00 AM to 6:00 PM daily. These hours suited the owner, Eve Magnusson, to a 'T'. Eve was a tall willowy unnatural redhead. She actually had been born a redhead, but the years insisted on turning her hair whitish yellow and she finally quit trying to dye her hair its original color and instead dyed it a bright orange/red. She had a great laugh and greeted all of her customers as they came in and thanked them as they left. If she could have bottled her personality, she might have been able to franchise her successful little shop.

Willy Street begins in the staid downtown area of Madison just two blocks east of the capitol. It runs northward and parallel to East Washington Avenue which is a main drag. The word 'parallel' describes Willy streets lifestyle as well as its location. Tourists consider it a Bohemian breath of fresh air. That air is often laden with smoke from bongs. Locals love the area for its old style stores: you can go into a small hardware store rummage through some small cardboard boxes that are yellow with age and actually buy one bolt, one nut and one washer to re-attach the left side of your license plate. You can stop for an aromatic cup of coffee and read the local happenings in the supply of free flyers lying around or engage in a lively discussion of local bands. Walk one block and you can repeat the experience. One more block and you can see when the next play, most likely written by a local, is on stage at the experimental theatre. Bars, cafes and restaurants abound and if you aren't hungry or thirsty, sit down and watch the weirdo's parade by. Willy Street is always interesting.

Maggie was actually craving a slice of pan pizza with sausage and mushrooms; however, she immediately agreed with Teri's suggestion. After all, she did want to fit into her wedding dress. Thinking of her dress, she decided that lunch might be a good time to raise her other concerns with her mother.

As usual, there was a line of people waiting to get into Eve's. One annoyance was that everyone had to stand in the same line, even those who were getting salads to go. Maggie and Teri both agreed that this was a stupid way to do things. There should be one line for pick-ups and a separate line for people who were eating at the restaurant. They voiced their opinions on this loudly enough for all to hear, but as usual, Eve ignored their comments and greeted them warmly and by their names.

They both ordered medium salads. Teri paid. Both grabbed medium bowls and proceeded to the salad bar. It was always so hard to choose. The bar featured four kinds of lettuce, spinach, every vegetable known to man, chopped boiled eggs, various seeds, and all types of fruits and gelatins. There were eleven types of dressing as well as croutons and rolls. The trick was to maintain self-control. Why bother eating a salad for lunch if you pigged out on salad? Teri, first in line, selected a modest salad of iceberg lettuce, tomatoes, and broccoli florets with shaved carrots and a low-cal ranch dressing.

Maggie followed suit, silently cursing and praising her mother's will power. She skipped the broccoli. It gave her gas.

They found a table for two near the front window and set their salads down. Maggie offered to go get the silverware, ice water and napkins, which pleased Teri. She sat down gratefully. While waiting for Maggie, she lamented how she was losing the battle against age.

It was not that long ago when she finished her routine, she felt refreshed and energized. Now, she just felt whipped. Her legs felt like she was wearing lead weights on them. Hell, she thought wryly, I used to put lead weights on my legs to increase the impact. How long has it been since I've done that? Maggie's arrival back at the table mercifully interrupted Teri's negative self-assessment.

"Did you notice Helen Barnes over in the corner?" Maggie asked as she sat down.

"No. Where did you say she was?" Teri asked.

"She's over by the soda machines, in the corner. You can't miss her. She must weigh over 200 pounds," Maggie replied with a snicker. Teri looked where Maggie had indicated and then spotted poor Helen. They had been on the swim team together in college and now Helen was a blimp. What had happened?

"Isn't she an old friend of yours or something?" Maggie asked innocently.

"Not really," Teri said with a shrug. "I knew her vaguely in college. I haven't seen her in years. She's put on some weight," Teri said kindly. Maggie practically guffawed.

"That's the understatement of the century," she choked out as she took a forkful of her salad. Teri put down her fork and took a slow sip of water. She stole another look at Helen and hoped Helen didn't catch her looking.

"Let's change the subject. Have you had any further contact with Lorna since last night? Do you have everything else under control for your wedding?" Teri picked a floret out of her salad and ate it daintily.

"Based on what I heard last night, I'm done worrying about Lorna. If she doesn't call me by Monday I'll let you know and you can call her mother again; right?" Maggie smiled. Teri frowned.

"I'd much rather you get this handled between the two of you. Leave the mothers out of it. Just call her again and set up a meeting to go over dresses and shoes and so on."

"All right, all right," Maggie said resignedly. "But, since you brought up the subject of dresses, there is something that's been bugging me. May I talk frankly?"

"I've never known you to do otherwise," Teri said cautiously. "What's on your mind? What is 'bugging' you?"

"Well," Maggie said hesitantly, "it's about our dresses." She paused just long enough to swallow and continued. "Actually, it's about your dress." She sat back and squared her shoulders. Teri's eyes narrowed and she looked at her daughter with no emotion on her face and asked in an even tone, "What about my dress?" Maggie had been rehearsing what she was going to say to her mother for days, but now that the time was here, her mind went blank. She sputtered, "Well, it's...it's too..."

"It's too what?" Teri interrupted with a defensive tone in her voice. Maggie groaned. This was going worse than she had feared.

"It's too *sexy!*" Maggie blurted out. She waited for her mother's tirade.

In an instant, Teri had a flood of thoughts and emotions. In her heart of hearts, she knew that the dress she had selected was flattering and daring. Yet, in her opinion, it was not a 'sexy' dress. It was not blatantly provocative, merely alluring. However, Maggie's statement did not surprise her; in fact, she had been expecting something like this. Teri knew Maggie resented her. All of her life Maggie had tried, unsuccessfully, to emulate her. Of course, she would object to a dress that made her look attractive. On the other hand, it was nice to know that Maggie still looked at her as competition.

Then she felt a twinge of guilt. Was she, in fact trying to compete with her daughter on her wedding day? Teri put the thought aside, smiled and said, "Really; too sexy?"

"Yes. It was bad enough for you to choose an off-the-shoulder dress with a low neckline. On top of that the clingy material accentuates everything. What's worse is its off-white with sparking pearl sequins. Damn it, Mother, you dress is prettier than mine. It's my god damn wedding you know!"

"Sweetheart, I'm sorry. I had no idea." Teri looked around to see if anyone had overheard their conversation. No one seemed to be paying them any attention.

"Honey, honestly. I would never try to steal the scene at your wedding. I love you too much for that to happen. You should know that." Teri reached across the table, took her daughter's hands in her own and looked at her lovingly. Maggie pulled her hands away, took her napkin and wiped a tear off her cheek.

"Mom, it's my wedding day. I deserve to be the center of attention."

"And you absolutely will be." Teri assured her. "Your gown is stunning and you look gorgeous in it. Every eye in the room will be on you."

"Except for all the people looking over at you thinking 'oh my, isn't she spectacular?

Isn't it her daughter who's getting married today?'"

"Now you're being silly, sweetheart. No one looks at the mother of the bride," Teri said soothingly

"Mother, can't you just once respect my wishes. Can't you once do what I want?"

Maggie let her exasperation show. Teri was unfazed.

"When we get home, the first thing I'm going to do is try on that dress for you. You'll see that it's nothing special and we can put this silliness aside, OK?" Teri stood to go. Maggie resignedly blew her nose in what remained of her napkin and stood. It had gone just as she expected, but she had had to try, right?

"There, that wasn't so hard was it?" Teri remarked as she opened the door.

"You have no idea, mom," Maggie answered. Once they were outside, Maggie stopped on the sidewalk and said, "Mom, I really do love you."

"Of course, you do dear. What's not to love?" Then she laughed at herself, and gave her daughter a hug and said "And I love you even more."

Maggie smiled and thought, well, the direct approach hasn't solved the problem, so now it's time to work on Dad. She wondered if all daughters resented their mothers as she did.

CHAPTER 22

SATURDAY

HASSAN HABIB HAD learned long ago to rein in his emotions. Self-control and self-discipline were perhaps his greatest assets. Still, it was difficult being patient today.

As the Imam's right hand man, he was privy to the inner workings of their tribal council. He knew all the secrets, big and little and all the intrigues. He also knew all the strengths and weaknesses of their divine leader. On most days, Jamali was a pillar of wisdom, his reasoning impeccable, and his decisions just and accurate. Occasionally, he seemed confused. Today, he appeared to be struggling.

The American had brought them information about Inauguration Day. It would be on the 21st instead of the 20th. When Colonel Habib had determined he knew nothing else of value, he quietly disposed of him. He then went on the web and verified the information. To his mind, it was immaterial; changing the date now was not an option. True, they may miss a few of the leaders by detonating on the original planned date, but there were too many other coordinated strikes already put in motion to make any changes at this point.

On January 20, with the help of the majority of the all-volunteer Pakistani army, there would be a military coup in Islamabad. A coalition of Tribal Districts headed by the Sword of Allah would replace the Pakistan People's Party. On the same day, the United Taliban Front would oust the pro-western government in Kabul, Afghanistan. The new governments of the two countries would work in concert to re-establish fundamental Islamic Shia law and, at last, the people would live in peace and prosperity. The success of these grand plans hinged on the de-stabilization of the United States as a world power.

Too much planning had gone into this new world order; too many risky moves completed over the previous years and too many lives sacrificed to jeopardize the outcome now.

$$* \qquad * \qquad *$$

Hassan had been instrumental in bringing everything to fruition. He had acquired his patriotic fervor as a young man. He remembered May 1998 as being a turning point in his life. Early in the month India, the hated enemy state had detonated nuclear weapons. He and his fellow patriots were shocked and worried. They watched the news and bemoaned this sorry state of affairs; then, two weeks later when Pakistan detonated 5 nuclear devices on the 28th and another on the 29th, they were ecstatic and proud of their country.

Not too long after this, Hassan enlisted in Pakistan's air force. He spent several years working his way up from enlisted man to officer. Eventually, in 2008, he became a pilot of an F-16 Fighter Jet. Pakistan had acquired 36 of the aircraft from the United States. As part of the deal, Pakistani pilots were trained in the U.S. Hassan trained at Barksdale Air Force base, located 3 miles east of Bossier and 10 miles east of Shreveport, Louisiana.

Hassan was lean and wiry. At five feet six inches tall he fit perfectly in the F-16. Those days he was clean-shaven and proudly wore the flashy dress uniform of the Pakistani Air Force. His dark eyes glinted with the look of an intelligent man. What his eyes could not show was his commitment to achieve. He was a man driven by the history of his country.

His broad mouth was usually set in an expression of determination, not a frown but certainly not a happy look either. He kept his jet black hair well-trimmed. His thin face was plain except for a small scar over his right eye. Most people assumed it was a battle wound. Actually, he had fallen down a flight of stairs at around age three and cut his forehead on the lid of a tin can. His mother had held the blade of a knife to the cut to stop the bleeding. Stitches were out of the question. Now he had the permanent scar.

While at Barksdale, he made friends with several air force officers as well as with a number of civilian employees who worked in various capacities at the base. One of these friends was Pablo Hernandez.

*   *   *

Pablo was a physicist. He monitored nuclear warheads. Born in Mexico, he had never married. He came from a large family and had many relatives still living in his native country. He had come to the United States at age 12 to live with his aunt and uncle in Enid Oklahoma. His family had chosen him to go because he had shown the most promise. He was smart and worked hard. The day he arrived he managed to say in English, "Uncle Jesus and Aunt Maria thank you for bringing me here. I love you." Within a year, he was fluent in the language. He listened and he learned.

"Hey, Spic," Larry the schoolyard bully would say, "give me some of that grease in your hair for my bike chain." Then he would laugh and the others would join him. Pablo listened and learned that he belonged to a lower class. He was born unworthy. In school they taught that in America all men were created equal. He knew better.

His progress in school was remarkable and his Tio and Tia were very proud of him. Upon graduating from high school, he received several grants, arranged with the help of two influential Latino self-betterment groups. He graduated Summa Cum Laude from MIT at age 22. On his 23rd birthday, he became an American citizen. The world was his for the taking. He soon learned that it made little difference what he did for a living; he could pick fruit in an apple orchard or design nuclear weaponry, he was still a Mexican and many if not most Americans referred to him as a 'greaser' or a 'spic'. Either term put him in a sub-category of humanity.   Pablo managed to find good jobs. Yet, he consistently earned less than his white constituents did. Passed over for promotion after promotion, He cursed the civilian hierarchy at Barksdale and grumbled about revenge. Hassan empathized with the man and lamented that he too experienced prejudice every day.

*   *   *

Hassan did not drink; he was a good Muslim, however he did sit and commiserate on a number of occasions while Pablo imbibed. On one particular occasion, when he was very inebriated, but not so drunk he would forget the conversation, Pablo had boasted that he would soon exact his revenge, and be well rewarded for it.

"Yes, amigo; the time will come soon when I will be able to return home a wealthy man. I will be magnanimous and loved by all."

Hassan took in this information without comment and waited patiently for Pablo to bring up the subject again. Then, on a hot and sweltering day in late August, Pablo called him at home. It was obvious Pablo was drinking, but he was quite coherent. By this time, his alcohol consumption had become a daily event. His co-workers regarded him with contempt. Pablo did not admit, even to himself, that he had slid into a self-destructive routine. He just knew he was desperately unhappy and he welcomed Hassan's empathy and understanding. More importantly, Hassan shared his disdain for Americans.

"It's good to hear from you my friend," Hassan said. Pablo listened with the sincere rapt attention only a drunk will display, as Hassan complained about the civilian cliques and the closed-rank military hierarchy at the base. He boasted that he had attended Harvard some years ago, and he said that he learned a great deal while in college, but the most important thing he had learned was how Americans think.

"Most Americans have had little or no contact with people of other nations, and that insulated life style makes them naive." Pablo nodded his head somberly in agreement. Of course, Habib could not see this because they were talking on the phone.

Hassan continued, "Americans believe that everyone thinks as they do. They not only cherish their freedom, they think everybody wants to live like them. This simplistic view of the world is their greatest weakness."

"So true," Pablo slurred, "Americans are so weak." He was longing for the simple carefree days of his youth in his beloved homeland. Now, all he had to do was complete a simple task, then, $500,000 richer, he could return to Guadalajara. He would live like a king. He would be a philanthropist to all of his kin. His success would garner him respect and he would be a local hero. He wanted to ask his very best friend in the world for help with this simple task. Hassan asked what the task was and when Pablo told him, he did not believe him.

A few days later, Pablo again approached him and requested his assistance. Pablo was sober. The item he needed the help with weighed almost four hundred pounds, but the two of them could handle it with a portable lift. It would be here on August 30th. He needed help storing it in a warehouse on base. This is when Hassan made his decision.

*   *   *

In early September a couple of days after the cruise missiles were flown back to Minot AFB, two local fishermen found Pablo Hernandez' body floating in a bayou. It appeared to be an accidental drowning. The local coroner, under-staffed and over-worked, ruled it as such without an autopsy.

Hassan personally took the warhead to the nearby town of Longview, Texas where a small privately owned company constructed lead products. He had them make a lead-lined case. Pablo had explained to him that this warhead gave off very little radiation, so the shielding was able to be quite thin. With the warhead inside, the entire package weighed less than 600 lbs. He then rented a storage unit in the same town and moved the weapon in with the dolly. He arranged to pay the rental fee annually.

The last thing he did was to fill up the rest of the little storage shed with miscellaneous items he found at a local dump. Anyone who broke into the shed would find nothing worth stealing.

*   *   *

In early 2009 Hassan completed his training and flew his assigned jet back home. He had never been as proud as that day he landed the fighter jet in Karachi and stepped out of the aircraft to the strains of patriotic music being played by the Pakistan Military Band. The pilots had been personally greeted by the General of the Air Force and the Mayor of the city. They were then honored with a parade. Later they reciprocated by performing a low fly-over of the city in the classic V for victory formation. Those had been heady days.

When his enlistment was up Hassan decided that he could achieve more in the civilian sector and he knew how he was going to do it. As a local hero, it was relatively easy for him to secure an invitation to a function of the most powerful jihadist group in Pakistan, the Sword of Allah. As an honored guest, he sat and ate beside the Imam. Toward the end of the meal he casually let it be known that he was moving to Peshawar soon and hoped to find suitable work for his abilities. It was enough to open the door without being obvious and within six weeks he was an accepted member of the Sword.

For the next two years Hassan Habib was like a shirt tail relative: tolerated but not a close member of the family. Eventually he was given some routine assignments which he completed without complaint. He was used as a messenger for many local functions and within a reasonable time was given the responsibility of keeping shirt tail groups in line. His willingness to do as told and his ability to always complete his tasks successfully made him a man to rely on. The real question was "Could he be trusted?"

Hassan proved his trustworthiness the Jihadist way. The Imam mentioned how one of the council members seemed to be unnecessarily disagreeing with him lately. He was not certain what to do about it because the man had been a long term member, almost from the formation of the group. By the unwritten laws of the area, Jamali could not address the problem directly without getting a severe backlash from other members. Indeed, it was a problem only Allah could solve.

The very next day the trouble maker died when a suicide jacket he was preparing accidentally blew up. The blast destroyed an important bunker and took out three other workers and several pounds of explosives. It was a tragedy. People shook their heads and said he must have gotten too cocky. He had performed this task without incident hundreds of times. Others voiced the opinion that Allah had called him to his reward. Still others thought, but did not say aloud, that it was not a good idea to disagree with the Imam.

Soon after, Hassan was introduced as a trusted member of the group and not long after that he met Ammar. Before long they became a duo to be reckoned with. They often attended prayer together, they backed each other up on missions and they both had the ear of Imam Jamali. Hassan considered Ammar to be an ally which was as close as he allowed anyone. He considered friends to be liabilities and had none. Hassan also preferred to remain out of the spotlight. He chose a day when he and Ammar were performing routine duties, loading C2 explosive into canisters to make IED's, to innocently muse aloud, "hmm, I wonder, if it would be feasible to send several suicide bombers to D.C. at the same time to cause a real setback?"

At the next high level meeting of the Sword Ammar voiced his idea of sending a squad of suicide bombers on Inauguration Day. Hassan had mentioned the Inauguration Day idea on a different occasion and let Ammar put the two together. He congratulated Ammar for his brilliant idea and complimented the Imam for his acceptance of it. When the naysayers seemed to be stifling the project from moving forward, he revealed his access to a nuclear weapon. This revelation brought him great stature and truly lit the fuse on the project. He let Ammar have all the credit. It was only right, since Ammar would be the one to detonate the weapon.

In February 2010, all his careful planning suddenly looked like it was a monumental waste of time. Hassan learned that the weapon he had stolen was a deuterium-tritium warhead and tritium had a half life of only 12.32 years. He had been on line and came across this vital piece of information by accident. His device had to be older than that because the U.S. had discontinued its nuclear armaments program in the nineties. In order for his weapon to detonate it would have had to been made in 2001. He had stolen the weapon in 1998. The damn thing was worthless.

SATURDAY

AMMAR ALI WATCHED as the man left the phone booth. He had kept his back facing out so no one could see him talking. This in itself was suspicious. Still, when the stranger exited the phone booth he was smiling and had a bounce in his step, much like a man on his way to a lover's rendezvous. Well, whatever the man's destination, he was leaving the hotel and so, for now at least, Ammar could put him out of his mind. As soon as he did, the Muhumar problem took over the space.

Ammar made a decision. Regardless of why he was here, Muhumar was an unnecessary distraction and a potentially significant danger. The choice was clear; the intruder must be eliminated. His mind kicked into high gear and a plan formed quickly. He left the bellman's post, went over to the outdoor table 'Abdul' was busing, and stood for a moment. Abdul looked up at him with a questioning expression.

"Abdul, I have a favor I must ask of you," Ammar said casually. "I have an important errand to run and I need you to cover for me while I'm gone." Naturally, they both referred to each other by their aliases when speaking in public.

"An errand; what sort of errand?" Abdul inquired.

"I don't have time to explain things right now," Ammar replied. "I'll tell you when I get back. Also, when I am back I'll show you what you have asked to see." Abdul was surprised and wondered about this sudden change of heart in Ammar, still he was not going to jeopardize the opportunity and agreed to cover for him.

Ammar ducked back into the hotel and put on the light spring jacket he always kept there. He then left the hotel and walked around the corner where he hailed a cab.

It was a much faster ride back to his apartment by cab than by bus. Even with a stop at a drugstore to pick up some nail polish remover, a bottle of hydrogen peroxide and a can of scentless shaving cream, he was home in less than twenty minutes. Once there, Ammar wasted no time. He took a 950 ml bottle of hydrochloric/muriatic acid out of the kitchen cupboard. The label said it had cost him $8.50. Plus, shipping, he thought to himself and chuckled. The nail polish remover and peroxide together had cost less than $7.00. A five-pound bag of Pillsbury's Best flour completed the list of ingredients needed to build a powerful IED, or Improvised Explosive Device as American soldiers in Iraq and Afghanistan called it.

Ammar simply called it a bomb. He carefully blended these components in the proper proportion and put them in a glass storage container with an electronic ignition device. He set the container on the kitchen table near the door and went into his bedroom closet to get the travel bag he had saved after his *Hadj* many years ago. It contained pretty much everything he would need to complete his plan for the day. He added his toothbrush, razor, a fresh bar of unscented soap, and the shaving cream to the bag. He then stopped for one last look around to make sure he had forgotten nothing.

He took two cell phones from the closet, one a standard type and the other one a 'no-hands' phone you wore on your ear. He put them on the table and checked his Sat-Com. There were no messages. He had not really expected any messages as Imam Jamali would be the only one to call him on the Sat-Com, and he never left messages. It was against his philosophy.

Ammar then turned on the little Motorola radio on the table and found a music station. He did not want the music on so loud it would disturb the neighbors, but loud enough so he would be sure to hear it on the ear-bud phone he put in his right ear. He used the regular cell phone to call the ear-bud phone and then set it back down by the radio. He answered the ear-bud phone and he could hear the music from the radio coming out of it. He could also hear the music from the radio in his left ear, but it sounded different. It was an eerie effect. He set his travel bag out in the hall.

The last thing he did was to arm the ignition switch and point it precisely at the edge of the door to his apartment. A red laser beam flicked on and showed on the door. He then took his remote switch and turned the ignition switch off. The beam affirmed that it was indeed off. He then stepped out into the hall and hit the button on his remote again. The bomb was now armed. There was little to no chance of a premature detonation, but when someone opened the door a few inches interrupting the beam, the device would go off. He expected that the explosion would destroy this floor and severely damage the floors immediately above and below. In any case, 'Abdul' would no longer be a concern.

Ammar left his apartment building and immediately cursed his stupidity. He had forgotten to call a cab before leaving the apartment. Reluctantly, he walked over to Chet's Diner, went in and sat at the counter. The 'bitch-waitress' came over to him and asked what she could get him. Ammar politely requested a telephone to call for a cab. The waitress looked at him and shrugged her shoulders. She then replied, "I can see that you have an ear-bud cell phone; why don't you just use that?"

"It is unusable at this time," Ammar practically stammered.

"Then why in the hell do you have it in your ear?" She snapped back. Ammar wanted to throttle her. Was every American waitress a bitch? Instead, he calmly asked if there was a pay phone nearby. She pointed at the front entryway and walked off.

Ammar rose from his stool and went to the pay phone. When he got there, he realized he had no change. He also saw that there was no phone book.

He did not know the number of any cab companies, so this was yet another problem. By now, he was getting truly irritated. Allah was testing him. Ammar returned to his stool and in his most gracious voice explained his need for both a phone book and some change. The waitress, who knew she had the upper hand, smiled and said, "Buy something. You'll get change when you pay." Ammar tensed and almost stood up, but there were more important issues at stake here than the insolence of this particular female. He smiled and ordered a cup of coffee and a piece of raisin pie.

"All outa raisin, honey," the waitress said when she returned with the coffee. "Would you like apple pie instead?"

"Apple would be wonderful," Ammar replied. "And the phone book, please."

"Oh yeah, I forgot; you wanted a phone book didn't you?" She smiled slyly. Ammar bit the inside of his cheek and looked away to the nearby wall. What he saw there made him smile. Some enterprising cabbie had stapled his business card to the poster board on the wall. Ammar grabbed the card and ostentatiously set it on the counter in front of him so the waitress could see it. When she brought his apple pie and fork, she pretended not to notice it. She set the pie down harder than necessary and went back in the kitchen.

Ammar ate the pie quickly and sipped his coffee once. It was stale. The waitress returned and asked if he wanted anything else. She looked boldly and directly into his face. When Ammar declined, she set the bill down in front of him, covering the card. The total came to $5.75 including tax. Ammar laid a ten-dollar bill on the counter. The waitress picked it up and came back with four one-dollar bills and a quarter.

Ammar picked up the quarter and made a production out of folding the dollar bills and tucking all of them into his wallet. He then held the quarter up in his fingers as he turned and went out to the entryway to use the phone.

"Damn camel jockeys are all alike," the waitress muttered to herself. "They're arrogant as hell, and cheaper than Scrooge McDuck." Her reading level had never progressed much beyond comic books.

Ammar waited outside the diner for his cab, which was there remarkably quickly. He was back at the hotel twenty minutes later. All in all, he had been gone about an hour and fifteen minutes. He was pleased. He went into the hotel via the Chez Blanc entryway and stashed his travel bag and jacket behind the stand at his bellman's post.

As Ammar looked for Abdul, he listened to the music in his right ear. He would be glad when this distraction was over. He found Abdul standing at a table taking a customer's order. He waited until Abdul was free and asked him how things had gone while he was away.

"I had no problems, none at all," Abdul responded proudly. "What's that thing in your ear?" He reached out to touch it and Ammar backed away.

"It's just an ear-bud, a type of cell phone that leaves your hands free. I find it quite useful." Ammar replied. "I am sorry to say I must impose on you one more time."

"What do you mean?" Abdul asked.

"Stupid me; I left the key to the storeroom in my apartment this morning when I came to work. The item you have wanted to see is in this storeroom."

"Can't you go to your apartment and get the key?" Abdul suggested.

"I've already been gone too much today. I can't risk leaving again. Won't you please go get it?" Ammar cajoled. "I will cover for you just as you did for me. It'll be fine. You know where I live right?"

"Yes, yes, I know where you live; but you'll have to cover the taxi both ways!" Abdul said resignedly.

"Of course, my friend; of course," Ammar said. "Here's fifty dollars which will be enough for both ways with generous tips. You will find the key on the little table next to my bed." Abdul accepted the cash without a word, turned and left without looking back. He hated being an errand boy. The only good thing was that he planned to keep the tip money for himself.

*   *   *

Peter Bogdasian had been a cab driver/philosopher for almost ten years. When he dropped off his fare at the address given, he turned his cab around and parked on the other side of the street to await his return. This was to be a round trip and he wanted to be going in the right direction when the man came out. As he sat and waited, Peter reflected on the vagaries of the cab driver's life. These days, if you saw an Arab or an Indian in a taxi he would usually be behind the wheel not riding in the back seat. He wondered what this one was doing.

Then, a loud explosion and shock wave blew out his left eardrum. He turned his head just in time to take in a scene of horror as the building he had dropped his client at expanded and erupted, then crashed down. Debris flew outward in all directions and the shock wave pummeled the cab. Peter didn't realize it at the time, but his decision to move his cab to the other side of the street had saved his life. No, all Peter could think about, once the dust had settled, was that he was not going to be paid for this trip and his ear hurt like hell.

Ammar, suddenly aware that the music had just stopped playing in his ear, paused on his way to the table with a coffee pot and removed the ear bud cell phone, turned it off and put it in his pocket. He sighed, shrugged his shoulders and continued on with his duties waiting tables.

CHAPTER 24

SATURDAY

AFTER HIS CONVERSATION with Birch and Whitman, John Franks hung up the phone and immediately sent a message to Estelle asking her to run a background check on Associate Director of the Joint Terrorist Task Force Donald Whitman. Right after he sent the message, it occurred to him that Estelle was probably gone from the office by now and would not be back until Monday morning; after all, today was Saturday. His next thought was for Estelle. With this terrorist threat hanging, he did not want her in the office on Monday. To his mind, if terrorists were planning to detonate a bomb in D.C., Monday would be the optimum day.

He decided he would call her at home and tell her to take Monday off. He would do the same. He was supposed to attend a number of Inauguration events, but t his presence was not of paramount importance; after all, he was just the junior Senator from Wisconsin. His absence would hurt him more than anyone else. Then, his conscience started in. Here he was ditching his duties as a U. S. Senator because he had advance warning of a possible nuclear attack; shouldn't he be doing something to warn the President and all the other government officials who stood to be annihilated?

Of course, he should! But what could he do? Call the President directly? He did not have a direct number. If he were to find a number and try to call the President, he would most likely not be able to get through. If he contacted the FBI directly, they would probably just tell him they were already on it. Hell, no matter whom he called just convincing them he was a U. S. Senator over the phone would take time and time was too damn short!

He considered going to the media and then discarded that as not feasible. Chances were the panic created by a media alert would be almost as devastating as an attack. In the midst of these cascading thoughts, he heard the garage door open and close. The girls were home from their morning workouts. He decided to call Estelle before going downstairs. She answered on the second ring; she brightened when she saw it was him and asked if he had read her report on General Birch.

"Yes, I certainly did, Estelle. That was excellent work. You really helped me out with that information." The Senator was always sure to compliment work well done. He complimented Estelle frequently.

"I was amazed by what the General's secretary told me about him," Estelle said. "Did you also get my message that the Attorney General's Office sent a "cease and desist" letter to our blogger?" Her tone indicated she really would like more information from him regarding his presence in a gay bar, but he chose to ignore the implied query.

"Yes, and that's great too." The Senator said hurriedly. "Listen, Estelle, I first want to thank you for all your help already today. It's just like you to come in on a Saturday and not make a big deal about it."

"It's not a problem, Senator. You know that," Estelle said warmly.

"Thank you, anyway. Now, I'm embarrassed to ask for one more favor." Senator Franks said in his most winning voice.

"How can I be of help to you?" Estelle responded.

"Just one more task for the day, and then I promise I'm done. I need you to find out whatever you can about a man named Don Whitman." Was that a quick intake of breath he heard? The Senator continued to give her the details she needed to complete her research.

He ended by saying, "I would appreciate any information you can find by sometime today if at all possible." Estelle said nothing. She had too many mixed feelings. He then told her the "good news" that she was to take Monday off. Estelle was now too stunned to say anything and only listened with partial attention. She finally responded when she realized that the Senator had asked her if she had heard him.

"Uh, yeah I heard you," Estelle said vaguely. "I'm not to go to the office on Monday. I have the entire day off, right?" She did not think she was right.

"That's absolutely right. I'm taking the day off too. We've both been working too hard lately. We deserve a holiday." The Senator's words rang hollow to both of them. They were both workaholics; it was the main reason why they got along so well and respected each other so much. Working through a weekend was like a trip to Disneyworld to them.

"Well, thank you very much, Senator," Estelle said doubtfully. "If you're really sure we don't need to be in Washington on Inauguration Day, I guess you know what you're doing." Estelle's tone implied that she obviously did not think he knew what he was doing and she needed an explanation right now. When people work together or live together for a long time, an inflection or tone can say more than the words they speak. Again, Franks chose to ignore her implied question.

"No need to thank me, Estelle. Just take care of this last errand for me and then enjoy a couple of days of rest, OK?" Just then, Teri called from the front hall to see if he were home.

"Coming, honey!" he yelled and abruptly hung up. Damn, he thought, I did it again.

Teri and Margaret were in the front hall hanging up their jackets in the closet. John came down the stairs and gave Teri a kiss and then a peck on the cheek for Maggie.

"How are Madison's most beautiful women doing today?" He asked cheerfully.

"If you see two continuous tracks in the snow behind me, those are from my ass dragging," Teri lamented with a groan.

"I'm just great, Dad," Maggie chirped as she went into the living room. John watched Teri's disgusted look at Maggie's back and gave her a questioning look. Teri cocked her head and gave a grimace in Maggie's direction. John, unsure of what was going on between them, responded to Maggie's reply, "Glad to hear that Magpie." He followed her into the living room.

"Have you had lunch?" He asked no one in particular. They both answered, that they had "eaten at Eve's...had a salad", then Teri joined them. John paused, thought for a moment about sitting down, considered the chilly atmosphere in the room and decided to get a sandwich. As he walked into the kitchen, he called out, "How was the club today, crowded?"

"About normal," Teri answered. Then she continued, "While you're in the kitchen would you please call your father and invite him to dinner tonight? Tell him I'm roasting a chicken and making his favorite gravy for the potatoes. Ask him if he'd also like roasted carrots." The phone rang and John answered it. It was his father.

"Speak of the devil; we were just talking about you." John said.

"Speak of the devil?" Pastor Franks chuckled.

"It's just an expression, Dad; just an expression."

We were wondering if you would be available for dinner tonight. Teri's fixing your favorite, roast chicken and potatoes with gravy. Would roast carrots be ok, or would you prefer something else?"

"Well, I was going to go back to the hospital tonight, but I haven't had Teri's roast chicken in ages."

"Great." John said, covered the mouthpiece of the phone and called into the living room, "What time's dinner?"

"Let's plan on six thirty," Teri called back.

"We'll be eating around six thirty. I'll ask Maggie to pick you up about five." Again, he covered the mouthpiece and called, "OK by you Magpie?"

"Yeah, I suppose." Margaret seemed a bit reluctant, but, John didn't notice.

"It's all set then. Maggie will pick you up at five and after dinner you and I can discuss my little problem."

"That's what I was calling about," the elder Franks responded. "Have you learned anything more?"

"I've found out a lot. But, I don't want to try to tell you about it over the phone. I've got a lot to think about this afternoon and then we can talk about it later, OK?"

"That's fine. Any way I can help. You know that." His dad reassured him.

"All, right. We'll see you at five, then." He hung up and started for the refrigerator. Maggie, listening to this conversation, realized that if she were going to get her dad to help her with her dilemma; she would need to get to him before dinner. She quickly stood and called, "Have you had lunch yet, dad?"

"No, I was just going to fix a sandwich right now," he answered.

"Have a seat. I'll make you a ham sandwich with lettuce and mayo. Want some chips?" Maggie came into the kitchen and steered her father toward a chair. Her dad, surprised by her solicitousness, sat and gladly let her take over his lunch preparation.

"Do you want a glass of milk too?" Maggie asked as she began removing items from the refrigerator.

"Yes, please," John, said as he glanced out into the living room. He couldn't see Teri and then he heard the TV. It was one of her favorite judge shows. She would be busy for the next half hour, so he turned to watch his daughter as she made his lunch. Maggie poured a glass of milk and brought it to the table. She then started making the sandwich. Her father frowned. He preferred his milk as cold as possible. He would have liked her to serve it after she had made the sandwich. He decided not to say anything.

"Damn, the lettuce is moldy," Maggie, said. "How's a plain ham sandwich sound?"

"Just fine, Honey." The Senator smiled. She finished putting the ham on the bread, cut the sandwich in half, and grabbed a small bag of potato chips out of a cupboard, brought them to the table and sat down next to her dad. She had forgotten the mayo. Her dad thanked her, bit into the dry sandwich and said nothing about the missing mayo.

"So, how go the wedding plans?" He asked absently. Maggie paused for a moment. Was now the time? Should she let him finish his lunch first? Should she wait until her mother was totally out of earshot? No! It was time to grab the bull by his cajones. She smirked at her private joke.

"Actually, dad I'm glad you asked. I do have a small problem which has been bothering me for some time."

"Anything I can help with?" John asked. He dreaded her answer.

"I certainly hope you can, because if you can't help me, no one can," Maggie replied almost, but not quite, tearfully.

"What's the matter, baby?" He was instantly concerned.

"It's kind of a delicate matter," Maggie said sniffling just a little.

"Just tell me," her father said gently.

"Well, it concerns mother," Maggie said with a touch of defiance in her voice.

"It concerns your mother? What about your mother?" He asked. "I thought the two of you had this wedding totally under control. Except for that little flap with Lorna, of course and I thought that was all settled."

"Mom's not the actual problem," Maggie said tactfully. "It's her dress."

"What's wrong with her dress? I thought it was gorgeous."

"It is gorgeous!" Maggie stated emphatically. "But, it's more than gorgeous; it's too damn revealing, much too form-fitting and way the hell too sparkly." The sentence came out in a rush and then Maggie sat back waiting for her dad's reaction. Her dad glanced over his shoulder to see if Teri had heard. He heard Judge Joe Brown hammering on a teenager in his court about becoming a man. Apparently, Teri was absorbed in her program.

"You mean she looks too good in that dress?" Her father asked in a low voice.

"I know it sounds silly, dad," Maggie picked up his napkin and dabbed at a tear.

"No, no, not silly at all, sweetheart; I understand." John was perplexed. He knew that his wife and daughter were both knockouts and that they enjoyed going out together dressed to the nines and turning heads.

So why was Maggie reacting like this? Then it hit him. Of course, it was her wedding day! She wanted to be the only star!

"Well, damn it, she deserved to have her own special day and he would make sure she got it!" He expressed the last thought aloud. Maggie threw her arms around his neck crying and saying "Thank you, Thank you. I knew you'd understand." Her Father hugged her back and thought, how in hell am I going to do this? Maggie settled down and sat back in her chair.

"When the time is right, I'll talk to your mother. I don't have a clue as to what I'll say, but I will address the problem, I promise."

"Dad, you're the best." He nodded and picked up his dry sandwich and ate it without tasting it. He poured the now warm milk into the sink and grabbed a handful of chips before heading up to his office.

"Are you working some more?" Maggie called after him as he started up the stairs.

"Yes, I have some serious issues to deal with at the moment."

"When will you be back down?" Teri called after him.

"Tell me when my dad is here," he answered. Once back in his office, the Senator sat down in his comfortable chair and grabbed a yellow pad. He began to make notes to himself about what issues he needed to address and what questions he needed to ask. He had long ago formed the habit of preparing a daily 'to do' list and planning his day. Of course, his overriding question was *what should I do now?* The answer to that would have to wait until he had more pieces of the puzzle. He began to run a mental checklist of things that had happened today. Then the secure phone in his office rang.

"This is Senator Franks," he said into the phone.

"Birch, here. I have some news."

"What is it, General?" Franks asked expectantly. He hoped it was good news.

"The FBI called me. They have a line on a possible terrorist suspect. He has been on the watch list for years, but until now, no one knew where he was. Apparently, he is in the D.C. area. He was born Ahmad Abdullah Ali. He changed his name to Ammar Ali, like that makes a big difference the General snorted. Now he's going by Ghazanfar Ali. He is an important member of a terrorist group that calls itself The Sword of Allah. How is that for a bullshit name?"

"Any identifying marks or scars?" the Senator asked suspiciously. That name had sounded familiar.

"Funny you should ask; he's missing his left ear. Dossier says he cut it off himself. God knows why," the General replied with another snort. John was shocked into a momentary silence. Could this actually be the murdering son-of-a-bitch who killed his family?

"Do we have a recent photo?" Franks asked.

"As a matter of fact we do. Wears his hair long: probably to cover up his missing ear. I'll fax you a copy."

"As soon as possible, General, please. I want to see what he looks like today."

"What do you mean 'today'? Do you know this asshole?"

"There's a chance this is the son-of-a-bitch who killed my family twenty years ago," the Senator said tersely. "If it is him, I'm on the next plane to D.C."

"Holy shit," said General Birch softly. "He killed your family?"

"He and a bunch of crazy Jihadists blew them apart with M-15's at the airport in Rome. I was the only 'lucky' one. I thought our paths would never cross again. If they have, I'm going to find him and kill him...very slowly." The Senator spoke deliberately.

"I can understand how you feel, Senator. But, let's remember, we have a bigger problem on our hands than your personal revenge. We're going to find this s.o.b. and put him behind bars before he can do any damage. We have a current address and agents are on the way there right now."

"Just send me his photo and let me know where he is after you arrest him, OK?"

"The photo you can have. The rest of it I'll have to think about, Senator." He hung up abruptly. Soon the fax machine rang and began receiving and printing the image of the most hated man in Senator Franks' world. As he sat waiting for the Fax machine to spit out the photo, he heard Teri and Maggie come up the stairs. Teri stopped by his door and said, "Maggie and I are going to try on our dresses for the wedding. If you want to see them, come in the bedroom."

"Will do," he answered. Then he removed the photo from the fax and looked at the face of the longhaired man who had probably butchered his family all those years ago. When he saw the face and compared it to the one seared in his memory, his blood ran cold. It was him. He studied the photo for several minutes. It was a touch out of focus, but it had to be him. If he could see the side of his face where the ear was missing, he could be 100% positive.

"Hon, we're ready. Come see your gorgeous girls," Teri called out with a giggle. His mood shifted abruptly. He forcefully put the image of the hated Jihadist out of his mind. He now focused on his daughter's needs. He knew exactly what he had to do. It had occurred to him the moment that Teri had told him they were trying on their wedding dresses. It was a stroke of genius, he said to himself. John came into his and Teri's bedroom where they were standing. With barely a glance at Maggie, he gave Teri a long look and said, "Wow, you are stunning. That dress is you!"

"Really..." Teri said with a bit of hesitation.

"Absolutely breathtaking," John assured her. Turn around so I can see the full glory." As Teri turned in a slow circle, John caught Maggie's eye and winked. She understood immediately. She played her part to the hilt by sitting down and looking hurt. Upon finishing her turn, Teri said "Isn't Maggie's dress lovely?"

"Oh, absolutely; it's gorgeous too." John said much too quickly and loudly. Teri looked at her daughter seated on the bench by her dressing table and walked over to her. She looked at herself in the mirror and said, "Well, that decides it. John, I'm sorry you like this dress so much because I'm taking it back."

"What, but why?" John cried.

"Oh, Mother no. You love that dress." Maggie added.

"Now that I've seen it in my full length mirror, I've changed my mind. It's too tight and it shows too much of my boobs," Teri said firmly. "I'm taking it back and that is that. Maggie, can you come with me tomorrow to find a new mother-of-the-bride dress?"

"I'd love to mom," Maggie stood and hugged her mother. John came over and put his arms around both of them. He wished all of his problems could be resolved so easily.

CHAPTER 2 5

SATURDAY

JOHN WAS SITTING in the high-backed leather side chair in his home office. The girls had changed out of their bridal dresses and gone downstairs to watch TV. He had his COG manual in his hands but so far had been unable to concentrate. He put the book down and briefly considered calling his Father to bring him up to date on developments. This got him thinking about his Dad.

The old man was really starting to show his age. His mind was still clear, but he had started to shuffle instead of walk and his shoulders were more and more stooped. Worse, it seemed recently that the worry lines in his face had become more pronounced. Lord knows, I've been responsible for many of those lines, he said to himself. Scattered images flitted through his mind-his Father frowning when he took the Lord's name in vain, his father shedding tears over his inability to instill the Word of God in his son, his Father battling severe bouts of depression.

He tried picking up the manual again and almost immediately he found himself mentally reviewing The Conversation. He and Teri both referred to it as The Conversation. It was a long talk about religion that Teri had initiated a few weeks after they met. She had pulled no punches.

*   *   *

145

"John, I need to know-do you believe in God?"

"Whoa, where did that one come from?" He had responded. She had really caught him off guard.

"You know how I'm starting to feel about you, don't you? I mean I think we're both having special feelings right?"

"Teri, I think my feelings are pretty evident. Haven't I said I love you?"

"That was during sex sweetie. It doesn't count. Although I meant it when I said I love you too."

"Well before sex, during sex and after sex I love you with all my heart. I can't believe you question that."

"It's not that I question it Honey. In fact, because I believe we do love each other we need to discuss some issues."

"And that includes the God issue?" He asked.

"It especially means the God issue." She replied.

"OK, where should we begin?"

"How about by answering my question; do you believe in God?"

"Well, the short answer is 'yes', however I need to qualify that answer by telling you that I do not believe in the Bible."

"What are you saying, John; are you a Buddhist or something?" She was very perplexed by his answer.

"It means I am not a member of any organized religion and that includes Christianity."

"Oh no, that's what I was afraid you'd say." Teri was on the verge of tears. John hugged her and said *"Please understand, this has been a very long journey for me and I am still on it."* She pushed away from him slightly and looked into his eyes.

"What does that mean?" She asked as she wiped away a tear.

"I've come a long way in my beliefs Teri." John paused. *"When I was a kid, I had doubts and a lot of questions. I guess I was what most people call agnostic.* John paused again and took a deep breath. In a moment, a tear appeared in the corner of his eye and he said in a husky voice,

"When my Mother killed herself, I was devastated. I loved my Father but his beliefs made it even worse. He was telling me that my Mother had gone to hell. Not too long after that I became an atheist. How could I accept a deity that was burning my Mother for eternity? It was unacceptable. How could my Father worship such an evil entity? He was just as evil.

It took me many years to reconcile my Father's beliefs and to forgive him."

Teri wrapped her arms around his neck and cried openly; as his tears began to flow harder he clung to her. Soon they were both sobbing. He had never told anyone about this time in his life before. It was a heavy burden and he finally had someone to share it. He had never confided in Marcia, his first wife. He instinctively had known she would not understand.

"I can identify with your anger at God and your Father. You were going through hell yourself. I'm so sorry!"

"God; How I do love you!" John said as he kissed the side of her neck and continued to cling to her. *"Thank you for understanding."* John then took another deep breath and dried the tears on his face as he stepped back from Teri. He had a sheepish grin on his face. She leaned in and kissed it away. John continued his explanation.

"As I grew older and discovered how complex the universe really was, it became impossible for me to explain even my own existence. The human body is an absolute wonder and there I was taking for granted all the interconnected systems that must function in complete harmony just for us to live. I could not be just an accident of nature. Eventually, the only conclusion that made sense was that there had to be some super-intelligence behind my existence. In other words, there must be a God."

"It makes me so happy to hear you say that," Teri said gratefully. I was so afraid that you and I wouldn't be able to be together, because I am a Christian."

"If you can tolerate my beliefs, I can tolerate yours. It's as simple as that," John said.

"Tell me about them," Teri said with a brave smile. "I want to know all about you."

John took her hand and led her to the worn old sofa in his apartment. She had asked her initial question while they had been standing in the living room. They had remained standing during the entire conversation. When they were seated, he continued to hold her hand.

"Once I came to the conclusion that God does exist, I had a new problem. I could not accept the God described in the Bible. Mainly, I could not accept the Bible itself. Now, I know I'm going to offend you, but I also

do not believe in religion; any religion. As far as I'm can see, Religion is simply a great way to control people.

"What are you talking about? Why do you say that?"Teri asked.

"Look at your ancient rulers. Every king, emperor, pharaoh or whatever claimed that they had been chosen by their God or Gods and had the divine right to rule. Some went so far as to claim they were God incarnate. They were infallible because the local religion said so.

To some extent, most religions were similar in that they used the old 'carrot and stick' method.

The 'carrots' were rewards for good behavior: bountiful crops, successful child birth and even good health. Incidentally, animal or human sacrifices were often defined as 'good behavior'.

'Sticks' were everything from a bad crop to burning in hell for eternity. Guess where that last one came from."

"John, you sound like an arrogant cynic." Teri was angry.

"I'm sorry if I'm hurting your feelings, but I think I am the complete opposite of arrogant. I am still searching for the truth. I think it's the people who claim their religion is the one and only true path to God who are the arrogant ones."

"How can you say that?"

"Let me clarify that. I do not fault anyone for believing in God or for the related beliefs of their religion. What I absolutely cannot stand is the believer who declares all other faiths to be wrong. To me that is the height of arrogance."

"I guess I kind of feel the same way." She murmured.

"Just think about it. Within the Christian religion alone there are numerous conflicting beliefs and sects. There's Catholicism and its many subdivisions, Protestantism and its many divisions…"

"OK. I get the point." Teri said resentfully.

"Sorry, I guess I am my Father's son. I was starting to preach," he said with a grin.

"All right, if I understand you correctly, you're not a Christian because you don't like the Bible and you can't decide which branch of Christianity is the right one."

"That's not completely on target, but it'll do for now if you're satisfied with that explanation." John stated.

"Well, I can't say that I'm actually satisfied." She paused for a moment. "But, I think I can live with it as long as you can tolerate my beliefs."

"That's no problem for me. I ask only one thing: don't try to convert me."
"All right, I'll agree to that; if you'll agree to come to church with on special occasions like Christmas and Easter or weddings."
"I can live with that" he said as he pulled her to him for a long, long hug.

*   *   *

Once again John picked up his COG manual and then set it on his desk. He and Teri had an occasional dispute over religious items but mostly they got along without problems. He had often wished his Father had been present during The Conversation. Maybe they would have a better understanding of each other. Then, as always, he would think, 'no, if Dad had been there the discussion would not have gone anywhere near as well- its better he wasn't there.' Still, he did wish that He and his Dad could have a similar talk. Whatever the reason, the time just never seemed right for it. And time was getting short, he lamented. His Father was getting old.

Then the thought struck him, time was getting short for his current problem too. Resignedly, he picked up the manual again and opened it.

CHAPTER 2 6

SATURDAY

IMAM JAMALI RESISTED the urge to throw his Sat-Com phone across the room. He had tried repeatedly to reach Ammar Ali without success. The last time he called, he almost broke his own code of discipline by leaving a message, but he resisted. Then he tried to reach Muhumar, his project Azrael safeguard, also without success. Now when he tried either number the lines were dead. Neither phone would work. He calculated the time difference and determined it was late afternoon in Washington D.C. They were both probably still at work. Still, that did not explain why their phones were not functioning. Of course, he had no way of knowing that Azrael was dead and that his cell phone and Ammar's Sat-Com phone were in little pieces.

Then, Hassan and the other members of the council came in and, after properly greeting Jamali, sat in their assigned areas. It was time for the daily progress review of Project Satan's Head. Imam Jamali began by reminded everyone of the American's warning that January 21st would be the best day to detonate the nuclear weapon as it would kill the most American leaders. He then explained the problems he was having getting in touch with Ammar. Only he and Colonel Hassan Habib knew about Azrael.

A discussion ensued and, as the Imam had come to expect, the usual hand wringing and wailing about imminent failure began. The council members were all loyal and dedicated followers who would gladly give their lives in his defense, but he could never expect to get any useful advice from them. Hassan was the sole exception. He had a clear head and an agile mind; however, he was too dogmatic and inflexible.

He also, at times, made the Imam nervous with his strong opinions, which he never hesitated to voice. At their last meeting, Hassan had actually disagreed openly with him. Afterwards Jamali took him aside and counseled him. Had another member been so disrespectful, his response would have been much more severe, but he valued Hassan's ideas and so he had been magnanimous. After letting the conversation continue among the council members for a few moments, Jamali cleared his throat and spoke briefly.

"My friends, as you know, we are on the brink of a world changing event. This is not the time to panic, or to deter our course. We will be victorious. Allah has been lighting our way. Surely, he will continue to be our champion." At the mention of Allah, the council members all chanted, "Allahu Akbar. Allahu Akbar." The Imam continued.

"Allahu Akbar, indeed; with his blessing and his protection we cannot fail. Now, Hassan where do we stand with our compatriots?"

"I spoke only moments ago with General Rashad, head of the Pakistani army and all of the top Leaders of the Taliban United Front. They all have assured me that they are ready to proceed as planned. I also spoke recently with our American confederate and he has assured me that the order to withdraw all American troops from Afghanistan will be given top priority as agreed." Hassan spoke with authority.

"And, did you apprise them of the information the American visitor gave us, and if so, what was their reaction?" The Imam spoke slowly. Hassan answered immediately.

"I did not discuss this issue with the American, as his input is unnecessary. The Taliban leaders and General Rashad had the same reaction I did. The date of the detonation is of little or no importance. They will proceed with the plan as scheduled, unless you tell them differently."

"So, you think we should not attempt to change the detonation date to Monday?"

"I believe we will be equally effective on either date. It is true there may be more government officials in and around D.C. on Monday, but most of them will also be participating in preliminary events and preparing for the week's events on Sunday. Should the detonation occur on Sunday, as originally planned, we have what the Americans call 'a double whammy'. If we wait and detonate on Monday, it would be what the Americans call a 'one-two punch'. Either way, we strike a major blow. At this time, all the military arrangements for the double coups are in motion. I think we should proceed as originally planned."

The Imam looked at Hassan with approval and said, "Your time spent in the United States has been of great value." He then turned to his council and said, "Are there any suggestions or disagreements?" He paused and resumed, "Hearing none I hereby approve Colonel Habib's remarks. It will be so. Allahu Akbar! Allahu Akbar!

The council members joined in and the shouting continued for some time. When he had had enough, the Imam retired to his private chambers to worry in private about his inability to reach Ammar or Muhumar.

Colonel Hassan Habib had accepted the compliment from the Imam without reaction. He knew his own value and did not need the praise of others. Actually, he regarded most of his co-conspirators beneath him in intellect and ambition. Their opinions were not important. It was good that Jamali looked upon him with favor as this helped him with his plans. The first major action was now so close. Habib reflected on all the events leading to this moment.

*   *   *

In 2010, when he had discovered the problem with his warhead, he had been devastated. As was typical of him, he told no one else of his dilemma, not even Ammar who was scheduled to leave for America soon to be in position to detonate the weapon on Inauguration Day 2013.

Fortunately, Habib was a resourceful man and had many connections. One such connection was a fellow pilot who had remained in the military and achieved the rank of Lt. Colonel. Today the man was in charge of one of Pakistan's nuclear weapons caches where he did testing and readiness exercises for underground and air borne warheads. Most of these were smaller payloads in the sub-kiloton range. Checking systems was the important thing at that time. While touring the plant, Hassan was introduced to a civilian engineer named Abu Hashim. He was in charge of weapons development and had designed ignition systems for the larger warheads the Pakistan military was developing.

These were modeled after the smaller packages they had purchased from the United States, France and Russia.

Abu was quite proud of his accomplishments at the plant. Hassan made sure that Abu Hashim knew that he was very impressed. As they talked about Abu's work, it struck Hassan that he may have found just the man to help him. He turned on his considerable charm. He invited Abu and his wife Fatima to dinner at a local club famous for its desserts.

His father had always said "the best way to establish a relationship with someone was to feed him." It was good advice and he had used it often. Over dinner Abu explained,

"I am of Afghan descent, but I was born and raised in Ottawa, Canada." Fatima was a Pakistani girl from Peshawar. He had met her through a matchmaking service.

"I flew from Ottawa to Peshawar. It was love at first sight." As he was telling this to Hassan, Fatima shyly held his hand and smiled. This had been three years ago and they were still like newly-weds.

They shared an excellent dinner of Lamb Pasanday, Tarka dal and rice. The half inch thick lamb chops had been expertly fried and boiled to perfect tenderness with onions, green chilies, cumin, garlic and coriander seeds then covered with yogurt and savory onion rings. The Tarka dal was made with yellow lentils mashed into a thick puree with an amazing blend of spices, including the chef's 'secret' spice, then liberally dolloped onto the hot rice. Dessert was Suji Halva: feather light layers of dough covered with almonds and raisins and honey as well as sugar and cinnamon. It was a meal fit for an Imam.

"This Halva was made in heaven," Fatima said as she licked the sweet glaze from her fingers. Hassan learned things of great importance. Abu had no love for his neighbors to the south. He often referred to them as "Those goddam bullies." He had many reasons for his dislike, everything from pollution that drifted northward, to inequitable trade agreements to 'superior attitudes shown by American tourists.' His main reason for resenting America, and the one he never mentioned or even admitted, was that upon graduating from college at the top of his class he sent numerous resumes to American nuclear energy firms and had never gotten a nibble.

He finally landed an entry-level position at a Candu Plant in

Canada near Ontario. Once he was settled, he took advantage of an on-line service to meet foreign women of his ethnicity.

Although he had never been to Afghanistan, he knew how the women were raised by what his father had taught him. He too wanted a woman whose prime objective in life was to please her husband. He soon met the lovely Fatima and happily brought her home. They were married within two months and within another two months Fatima was so homesick their marriage was in jeopardy. Abu was an easy going man and wanted his wife to be happy so he applied for a position in Pakistan at the Karachi Nuclear Power Plant (Kanupp). This power plant had been sold to Pakistan in 1972 and had been operating ever since. It was a modified Candu design that Pakistan had purchased from Canadian Power. Abu was exactly the kind of person they were looking for, he was a recent graduate, so he knew about current designs, he had experience working at a Candu plant, and he was of middle-eastern descent.

Soon, they had moved to Pakistan and Fatima was happy once again, so Abu was happy. After a year and a half at the power plant, Abu was promoted and transferred to the weapons development operation where Hassan met him.

Hassan made a concerted effort to win the friendship of Abu and Fatima. He and Abu often went to mosque together for prayers. Whenever Hassan came by their house he brought a bag of goodies for Fatima's sweet tooth, of course Abu also loved his desserts. Hassan was disappointed when he invited Abu to a meeting of the Sword and was turned down.

"I am sorry my friend, but I am just not a joiner. I do not wish to be involved in any organization. I do not fault you for your zealous concerns, but it is not for me." Hassan astutely chose not to pursue the subject any further. He wanted Abu to see him as someone he agreed with, not a pest. There was one subject they could discuss and be in complete agreement: those goddam Americans. This was a subject they compared notes on and discussed often. Fatima almost always joined in the diatribes. She had lost family to errant U.S. missiles and stray bullets from American forays into her neighborhood. She despised the arrogant killers.

After some months of such wooing, Hassan was ready to attempt to enlist Abu in his plans. He needed Abu to re-arm his weapon of mass destruction. He believed that the man would be amenable to his desires. If not, then regrettably Abu would have to pay with his life.

With great caution he broached the subject of nuclear weapons. Over dinner at their home one night he asked a question.

"Abu, maybe you know the answer to this. I have been told that the Americans have nuclear weapons that are programmable. Is this true?"

"Oh yes, yes that is true. They have a number of such deadly devices."

"How much do you know about them?" Hassan probed.

"I am quite familiar with them, my friend," Abu said with a grin. "I am working on just such a warhead for us right now."

"This is true?" Hassan gasped. He had had no idea that Abu was working on such a project. Since Abu's work was classified he never volunteered information on what he was doing. The fact that he told Hassan that he was working on this project meant that he considered Hassan completely trustworthy. Of course, Abu did need to caution his friend.

"Obviously, that is not for passing on. My work is top secret and I could get in big trouble..."

"Abu, you have nothing to worry about." Hassan interrupted. "I will never repeat this information to anyone. I promise you."

"I know, Hassan; I know. I just wanted to be sure you understood."

"What can you tell me about this weapon that won't get you in trouble?" Hassan asked.

"Not a damn thing," Abu replied. Then he burst into laughter. Hassan sat back and Fatima left the table; she was not interested in such topics. Abu turned serious.

"We are working on a Variable Yield nuclear device. Our current goal is to achieve a small portable package that will deliver from 1 kiloton of explosive force to 5 kilotons."

"Incredible." Hassan said. "That is outstanding. How do they work?" Abu was somewhat taken back by his friend's curiosity. Why did he need specifics? He decided to answer anyway.

"We are copying the American design for a deuterium tritium device. We can control the power of the explosion by altering the amount of tritium used. The principle is really quite simple: the more tritium, the greater the reaction."

"Where does the tritium come from? Do you have to import it? Hassan asked anxiously.

"No, no, no" Abu said with amusement. "We get our tritium from our Kanupp plant. It's a Pressurized Heavy Water Uranium Reactor. Tritium is a bi-product of its operation."

"Outstanding," Hassan said trying to keep from appearing too excited. Nonetheless, Abu saw the eagerness in his friend's posture.

"Why is this news so 'outstanding' to you?" Abu asked as he lit a cigarette. Hassan decided then and there to tell Abu the whole story. During his explanation Abu asked many questions and Hassan could see the excitement growing in Abu's demeanor.

"So, my friend, you need your weapon re-armed with a new batch of tritium. Allow me to ask you a simple question: do you have funds to achieve this?" Hassan was taken aback at this. He had felt like he was talking with a fellow conspirator; now the issue of money had come up. It put him on edge. Was this his friend he was talking to or someone he must hire? He answered cautiously.

"We have funds. What amounts are we talking about?"

"Well, buying the tritium would not be too expensive. I would estimate that $8,000 to $10,000 U.S. dollars would be sufficient."

"We have that much. I can assure you of that." Hassan responded and waited.

"What we would need to do is fabricate an order for that much tritium to be used for a peaceful purpose. Perhaps we can fake a large order of self-illuminated 'exit' signs. I know my cousin's sign company combines tritium with phosphor to make a paint that glows. Such glow-in-the-dark signs are very popular because they solve the problem of staying visible during a power outage. We have them in our plant."

"Would you cousin do this for us?"

"No, I wouldn't want him involved. I only mentioned him because I was talking about signs. No, you would need to have one of you own people pose as the customer."

"You tell us what to ask for and we'll take care of the rest." Hassan assured Abu.

"Of course, there is the matter of getting the tritium to America and installing it in the device. That could present a problem. It would require someone who knows what he is doing."

"Let us not talk in circles Abu." Hassan spoke crisply but not in anger. "This mission will be very risky. How much do you want?" Abu paused, took a drag from his cigarette, blew the smoke out without inhaling and set the cigarette down on a dessert plate.

"Please understand, Hassan if it were anyone else asking I would not even consider this dangerous undertaking. However, since it is you, I will consider it."

"You do understand that this will be a major strike against your hated 'bullies' don't you? It's not just for the benefit of the Sword." Hassan bargained.

"Certainly that is part of my consideration, my friend." He looked up at the ceiling as if calculating in his head. Hassan wanted to strangle him.

"All right, I will do it. I will do it for you, Hassan and I will ask only a token gift of $50,000 for my efforts." Hassan was pleasantly surprised. He had expected a much higher asking price and was prepared to continue bargaining until they arrived at the mutually agreeable amount of $100,000.

"Thank you, Abu. Your generosity is appreciated. $50,000 U.S. it is." Abu winced. He knew he had sold himself too cheaply.

As it turned out, Hassan's uncle had posed as the sign maker. He presented an order for 4,000 glow-in-the-dark exit signs from the Wal-Mart Corporation. His tritium purchase was approved and the die was cast. There was one snag. Fatima insisted on coming along on the mission. She had never been to America and had always wanted to visit. As usual, Abu could not say 'no' to her.

Hassan objected to no avail. Finally it was decided that Fatima would travel with them. Since Abu was a Canadian citizen and his wife a citizen by marriage, the little group flew into Winnipeg, rented a van and entered the U.S. on I-29. They got to the border at sunrise and waited impatiently as the small Canadian Crew processed other cars in order. The border guards were in no hurry. Eventually it was their turn. Abu did all the talking except when each was asked where they were from. Everyone answered honestly. He and Fatima were vacationing in the U.S. and their friend Hassan had been promised a temporary job in

Minneapolis. He showed his work visa and they were waved through without further inspection.

The trio continued on down I-29 through North Dakota, South Dakota, Iowa and Kansas until they hit Kansas City. Hassan and Abu shared the driving. Fatima had no license. They stopped only to re-fuel, use a bathroom or hit a MacDonald's; most of the time they did all three in a single stop. Fatima complained all the way. Why couldn't they see some of the sights? She wanted to go to Mall of America. At least they should eat one meal a day sitting at a table in a nice restaurant instead of choking down a hamburger and fries in the car.

Out of Kansas City they picked up I-35 and continued their marathon journey through the rest of Kansas, Oklahoma, and the upper part of Texas to Dallas. Fatima continued her griping except she got more strident and more insistent. Why did they have to drive through the night?

She couldn't see a thing. Americans really were stupid. They expected you to pay an exorbitant price for water in a bottle. The ladies restrooms were filthy. Her bottom hurt. Could they stop and get out of the car and walk around? Why didn't they go to one of the other restaurants instead of MacDonald's? Even Abu, began to shush her. This just made her angrier.

After Dallas they picked up I-20 and soon they were in Longview, Texas. They arrived at sunrise. It had been almost exactly 24 hours and Hassan calculated they had come 1,361 miles. All Fatima cared about was that they were finally at their destination and she expected to stay here for at least a day and see the sights.

Hassan pulled the van to the side of his storage unit. Fortunately it faced east so when he opened the garage door, the sun coming over the horizon illuminated the inside. He enlisted the aid of Abu and Fatima to remove some of the trash he had put inside to hide the metal case.

Fatima complained about having to work so soon after such a long trip. When enough trash was out and the case was accessible, Hassan told the couple to wait outside on the side of the unit while he opened the case with the combination. When he was done, he came out and asked Abu to fetch the tritium from the vehicle. Abu did so and came back.

"I think Fatima and I should wait outside while you take care of your business." He put his arm around Fatima's shoulder and steered her to the side of the building as her husband moved into the storage unit. Fatima accepted the gesture and started to ask, "Can we go see..." Hassan quickly covered her mouth and nose with his right hand; with his left he brought his field knife deeply across her throat. He severed both carotid arteries and her voice box. She was able to gasp only a little and then bled out very quietly and quickly as Hassan held her. He then deposited her quietly on the ground out of sight. He waited for Abu.

In a few minutes Abu said "OK. It's done." As Abu stepped near the front of the storage unit Hassan swiftly and expertly thrust his knife upward through Abu's rib cage piercing his heart. It stopped beating immediately and Abu dropped to the floor of the unit. Hassan had liked Abu and so had made his death as painless as possible. Poor fool, Hassan thought; he never suspected a thing.

Hassan used the dolly he had left on site to quickly move the lead-lined box and its precious cargo into the van. He then dragged both bodies into the storage unit and covered them with the trash from outside. After gathering up sand and dust from the area to cover the blood stains, he closed the garage door and padlocked the unit. He washed up at a nearby gas station, filled his tank and purchased a large cup of coffee. Then he drove north east toward Richmond, Virginia where he had rented another locker. With any luck, the smell of decaying bodies coming from the storage unit would not attract any attention for at least a couple of weeks. By then he would be back home.

CHAPTER 27

SATURDAY

DON WHITMAN ROLLED over in bed and stretched. He was exhausted and drained. Literally and figuratively, he thought as he smiled and reflected over the past two hours of intense sex he and Estelle had shared. God, she was good and, insatiable. He wished his wife could even come close to meeting her passion. If she did, he would not be in another woman's bed. Then he chided himself. Nice try Romeo; put the blame for your sins on your wife. You strayed and it is her fault. What kind of an asshole are you?

Before he could answer this question, Estelle came back in the room. She was wearing a see-through negligee and carrying two glasses of red wine. Estelle put one glass on the nightstand on her side of the bed and crossed over to Don. She reached over, and put her hand on the back of his neck and gently raised him to a sitting position while cooing softly, "Poor baby, is he all tuckered out? Does he need nourishment?" She carefully tipped the glass to his lips. Dutifully, he drank. While doing so, he casually caressed her right breast, which hung near his hand.

"Ooh, not all that tuckered." Estelle giggled and stepped back. She handed him the glass and went around to her side of the bed. She snuggled up to him and sighed. There was no doubt about it; Don was the best bed partner she had ever had. It was almost enough to make her consider trying to break up his marriage. No, that was against her ethics. Besides, if she had to do his dirty laundry and pick up after him on a daily basis, he might not be as sensual or exciting. No, it was better to leave things just as they were.

She sighed again and stretched. Don leaned over and gave her a kiss on her neck. She enjoyed that, then set her glass down, took his face in her hands and kissed him gently. The next kiss was a bit more urgent, and in a moment, Don was putting down his glass. Soon he was inside her again. In less than a minute he came, for the third time that day. This time, Estelle did not climax, but she did not care. She had lost count of her orgasms in their earlier lovemaking. Usually, after making love, Don was happy to cuddle and make small talk. It was one of his best traits. This time he simply withdrew, rolled over on his side and promptly fell asleep. This did not bother her at all. Estelle got out of bed, walked over to his sleeping form, kissed his shoulder, smiled and went to take a hot bath.

Don slept for almost an hour. He awoke when he heard Estelle clattering around in the kitchen. She was dressed and called out, "Hi sleepy head." Don was still in bed and suddenly, inexplicably, he felt naked and exposed. When she turned her back to him, he jumped up and ran to the bathroom, which was next to the bed. He took a brisk hot shower and dried himself thoroughly. He did not want to put the clothes he had worn earlier back on, but he had no choice. He had come here without a change of clothes. They had not yet reached the point in their relationship where he would keep clothes and toiletries at her condominium. He dressed in his office attire, but left his coat and tie off. He then wandered out into the kitchen.

"What time is it?" He asked. His watch was on the nightstand in Estelle's bedroom. He had wound up undressing hurriedly after he arrived three hours ago.

"Five thirty." Estelle answered.

"Holy cow," Don said, surprised. "I guess time really does fly when you're having fun." He laughed and came over to Estelle and gave her a hug. She kissed his cheek and resumed her cooking duties.

"I'm making scampi with pasta and red sauce. We need some carbohydrates," she said over her shoulder. Why don't you fetch our glasses and pour in a bit more red wine? Dinner will be ready in two shakes." Don retreated to the bedroom, and as he was picking up the glasses, glanced at the princess phone on the nightstand. He decided a quick phone call from here would be secure. He quickly searched his wallet for the Senator's home office number, sat on the edge of the bed and dialed.

"This is John." The casual greeting took Don by surprise.

"It's Don Whitman, Senator. I'm just calling to see if there have been any new developments or if you've made any decisions yet." The Senator stammered for a moment as he replied, "Don, it's you. Yes, yes. I'm glad you called. Actually, there has been some progress. We have a line on a possible terrorist who might be our man right in D.C. His name is Ghanzafar Ali. Birch faxed me a rather blurry photo of him. Are you near a fax machine?"

"Ah, no Senator, no I'm not. But, there is a Kinko's around the corner from here, I've used it a number of times. I have their fax number right here, it is 555-636-0101. Why don't you send it 'attention: Don W.'. They know my name and they'll hold it for me."

"That probably isn't really necessary, Don. There are agents on their way over to his apartment already. In fact, they probably already have him in custody. You can see what he looks like later."

"Senator, I'd really like to get a look at this guy. I'd appreciate it if you'd just send me his picture," Don said. He was feeling that the conspiracy he had uncovered was no longer his. He was now becoming just an observer. That rankled.

"OK, Don, OK. I'm punching in the number now. The last digits were 0101, right?"

"That's correct. Thank you very much Senator." As Senator Franks finished the number, the location came up on his caller I.D. screen. It was a Kinkos in Huntington, where Estelle lived. The Senator grimaced. It re-confirmed what he already knew: Estelle's name had come up on his caller ID when he answered the phone a few moments ago.

As he transferred the photo, the Senator said, "Don, I have another call coming in, can I call you back?"

"Ah no, not really; I'm at a public phone on a street corner and I can't stand around here waiting for a call without raising some eyebrows. How about I call you back in about half an hour?"

"That sounds good. Bye, Don." The Senator hung up and sat there with a puzzled expression. Estelle's name had come up on his caller I.D. The Kinkos Don was using was near her home. What was going on? Had he been too naive in trusting Estelle so completely? He needed to look into this matter.

Something in the back of Don's mind seemed to be niggling at him. Was it that the Senator had sounded a little strange? He couldn't quite put his finger on it. "Ach, just nerves, I guess," he said to himself as he picked up the glasses. He emerged from the bedroom and while crossing to the kitchen area, drained his glass and re-filled both. It was not like him, but he was feeling reckless. Remarkably, he was also feeling freer than he had in ages. Earlier, he had called his wife on his cell phone and told her that he had a last second assignment and would be out of country for the next few days. This was not a regular occurrence, but it did happen enough that she no longer questioned it or complained.

This left him free to spend time with Estelle and he wouldn't have to explain why he wasn't going to the office. The prospect of several days without accountability and in the arms of Estelle was actually intoxicating in and of itself. He did not need wine. Yet, he took another sip as he sat down and hungrily dug into the plateful of pasta Estelle had served him. She took a sip of her wine and delicately ate a shrimp. They passed the next half hour in pleasant conversation while dining graciously and finishing their wine. When done, Estelle turned on her TV and told Don to watch the news while she cleaned up the kitchen.

Don protested and offered to help clean up, but she said no, he was a very special guest. After tidying up and putting the dishes in the dishwasher, Estelle passed by Don on her way to the bedroom saying, "I have a call to make. Why don't you find a movie and I'll join you in a few minutes."

"Actually, I need to run a quick errand," Don replied. He got up and headed for the Kinkos around the corner. She crossed the room and closed the door after her when she entered her bedroom. Hmm, she thought. The room still smells of sex. Estelle pulled a Glade air freshener out of a dresser drawer and sprayed it around before dialing her boss.

"Senator Franks," John answered brusquely without looking at his caller I.D.

"Hi Senator; It's Estelle. How are you doing?"

"Well, ah, Estelle. I'm fine. More importantly, how are *you* doing?"

"What do you mean, Senator? You sound a bit cranky."

"That could be. It's been a rough day. Did you get that information I asked for?"

"Yes, and that's why I'm calling you. I checked out this Don Whitman as you requested, and it appears he is legit. He's been with the FBI for about ten years and he has the position of Associate Director of the Joint Terrorist Task Force in the National Security Branch. Prior to that, he was with Naval Intelligence for six years. He's married with two children. He graduated with distinction from Rutgers. The only negative I found was that they disciplined him recently for an infraction of procedure. Apparently, he over-stepped his authority somehow and got a week off without pay and a letter of reprimand in his file."

"What did the letter of reprimand say?" The Senator knew, but chose to play dumb.

"I couldn't get any details, the secretary I spoke with would only tell me that she had typed it and that she thought it was B.S. office politics and he didn't deserve it. He is apparently quite well liked in the office, and also known as a straight shooter."

"And what is your opinion of him, Estelle?" He hoped to catch her off guard.

"Why, why, I don't have an opinion of him, Senator. Only what I just told you."

She was dying to ask Senator Franks if Don had been at the gay bar with him; however, she kept her curiosity in check and simply waited for the Senator to respond.

As she waited, Estelle began to ask herself how much she really knew about Don. Her train of thought ended abruptly when the Senator spoke.

"Of course; why *would* you have an opinion of him?" Senator Franks said with a slight questioning tone. Estelle said nothing. His implied question was going to go unanswered. Well, we can let it be for now; he would find out some other time.

"Do you have anything to add to what you've already told me?" The Senator gave it one last shot.

"No. That's all I found out," Estelle said. "I'm sorry if it wasn't what you were looking for."

"Not at all, dear. You did exactly what I asked. Again, thank you for your efforts and thank you, once again, for working on a Saturday."

He had no sooner hung up than the phone rang again. It was Birch.

"Senator Franks speaking," he said as he brought the phone back to his ear.

"Birch, here. There's been a new development and for the life of me, I don't know if it's good news or bad news."

"Well, don't keep me waiting. What's the news?" Senator Franks had always hated it when people prefaced important information with a "good news/bad news" statement. It was trite and wasted his time. He took a deep breath and waited.

"Little testy there aren't we?" General Birch said stiffly. "The news is our terrorist is dead. When agents showed up at his apartment, they were too late. Apparently, the fucker accidentally blew himself up while making a goddamn bomb. He took out most of the apartment building."

"Are they sure it was him?" The Senator, stunned by this obviously good news, almost wanted to clap his hands in delight.

"Who else would it be? The signature of the blast still needs to be verified by forensics, but, the agents have seen enough home-made I.E.D.s to know one just from the smell of the chemicals used. I believe our immediate threat is over."

"I think I agree. Christ, what a relief!"

"Well, I would rather have had the opportunity to question this son-of-a-bitch. We could have learned a lot about their operations within our borders. But, I guess, all in all, I'd have to call it good news too." The General let out a short nasty chuckle and said, "Sure woulda liked to have had that bastard in my control for a few days though."

"How long will it take forensics?" Franks asked curtly. The news of the Jihadist's death caught him totally by surprise. Things just continued to move at a breakneck pace. Now he wondered whether he should bother going to D.C. No need to go, just to look at pieces of a corpse. The prudent decision was to wait for the forensics report.

"Hell, Senator. I don't know. Forensics will poke around until forensics decides it has done enough research. Could be hours; could be days." The General was getting a bit tired of the Senator's curt tone. John Franks recognized this in Birches tone and spoke in his most conciliatory manner.

"I'm sure you're right, Sam. Do me a favor please; see if there is any way you can speed up the process and then get me any findings ASAP." He intentionally used the acronym he had heard the General use in an earlier conversation. He had learned this little trick of persuasion long ago. People liked you more when you spoke their language.

"You got it, Senator." General Birch said as he hung up his phone and reached for a bottle of Jack Daniels in the bottom drawer of his desk. It was time to celebrate.

SATURDAY

AMMAR FINISHED CLEARING the table from his last diners and stacked the chairs neatly upside-down on all the tables. He then checked for any messages at his bell stand and, finding none, quit for the day.

He turned and went into a side room at Chez Blanc and sat at a corner table. Without a word, one of the waiters brought him a bowl of the soup of the day and a glass of ice water. Most of the hotel employees took advantage of the free dinner or lunch benefit provided by the hotel. The soup was chicken gumbo, one of his favorites. Half way through his soup, the waiter returned with a roast beef sandwich, another of his favorites.

"You seem happy today, Ghanzafar; Any particular reason?" Derek asked.

"You've brought me one of my favorite dinners," Ammar hedged.

"Thank the cook. I only serve what they give me." Derek said.

"Thank you both and may Allah smile on you." Ammar replied. When he finished, Ammar was in a good mood and left a five-dollar tip. It was his charitable contribution for the day. He laughed quietly to himself as he envisioned how stunned the waiter would be by his uncommon generosity. Then his mood turned somber. Chances were Derek would not live to spend it.

He crossed back to the bell stand, picked up the travel bag he had brought from home, and casually strolled over to the counter in the lobby. The front desk clerk was busy on the phone handling an obviously irate client. A quick peek at the registration log showed the entire ninth floor available as well as half of the eighth. He logged onto the check-in section and quickly listed room 959 as occupied by Robert Smith. No one would know that he was the occupant until tomorrow, and by then it would be too late.

As he turned to go, Ben, the near-sighted night clerk called after him, "Have a nice evening, Ghanzafar," he said.

"Thank you, Ben. You have a good night also."

They smiled at each other. Ammar felt that Allah was smiling on him. He proceeded to the service elevator in the hallway behind the front desk, and took it to the ninth floor. He got off the elevator, turned the corner and used his passkey to enter room 959. The entire floor was non-smoking, which he preferred.

He set his travel bag down on the table next to the television and plopped onto the nearest bed. There were two king size beds, a recliner, a mini-bar, and a large flat screen digital TV. None of them interested Ammar. He just wanted some rest. He took off his hat and threw it on the other bed. Then he kicked off his shoes and let them drop off the end of his bed. In a matter of moments, he was asleep. He dreamt of home.

* * *

As Ammar was falling asleep, two FBI agents came into the Chez Blanc restaurant and asked to speak to the manager. They showed their ID's to him and asked whether a Pakistani named Ali worked there. The manager explained that Ali only subbed in the restaurant. Actually he was the head bellman and they needed to talk to the hotel manager. The agents handed the restaurant manager the blurry photo of Ali and asked if that was him. The restaurant manager said he believed it was, but he couldn't be sure. He called Derek over and asked him to look at the photo. Derek suspected these guys meant no good for Ghanzafar.

"Can't say he looks familiar," he said as he handed the photo back. They thanked him and crossed over to the hotel lobby front desk and asked for the manager.

Ben explained that the General Manager Mr. Dickens had gone for the day but he would be happy to assist them. They showed him the photo and asked if this man worked there. The near-sighted night clerk squinted at the fuzzy picture through his coke bottle lenses for a number of minutes before finally telling the agents he couldn't tell for certain. He recommended that they come back in the morning and talk to Mr. Dickens. As the agents turned to leave, he remembered that Ghanzafar always came in first thing in the morning and that he was scheduled to work the next day. The agents thanked the clerk and said they'd be back bright and early in the morning.

*   *   *

Ammar slept peacefully until almost midnight, and then his dreams turned bad. He was on an Umrah. It had to be an Umrah, he reasoned in his dream, because it was not during the Muslim month of *Dhu-al-Hijjah*. He did not know how he knew that, but he did. He was running desperately between the hills of *Safa and Marwah*, re-enacting *Hagar's* frantic search for water for her son *Ismael*; however, on each step forward other pilgrims pushed him back. The harder he tried, the more the others would get in his way. He screamed at the mob of worshippers and began to pummel those near him. Then he found himself falling; soon, the angry crowd trampled him under their feet. He woke up in a sweat.

Ammar sat on the edge of the bed and shook his head. He did not recall what he had been dreaming, but he knew it had not been pleasant. He stood and drew a hot bath. He then fetched his scentless soap from his travel bag, disrobed and sank into the hot water with a sigh. As he soaked, he thought back to his *Hajj-* his once-in-a-lifetime journey to Mecca. He had gone in 1994, when he was 30.

*   *   *

Ammar was disappointed by some aspects of his arduous trip and inspired by other things. His first impression was that the powers-that-be had commercialized the sacred pilgrimage. You could buy complete packages in different price ranges. You could stay at five star hotels and eat *haute cuisine*, or you could stay at cheap inns and eat sandwiches. You could purchase complete travel kits that included everything you would need including unscented soap, a visa with your photo, Ihram to wear, a map and instructions on how to do your Hajj properly, and much more. Ammar had balked at these deals.

He blamed the western leaning Saudis for this almost blasphemous transformation of every Muslim's holiest act. To Ammar, it was a shame that Mecca, the home of Islam's holiest shrine, was located in Saudi Arabia. The Saudis were in cahoots with the Americans to control oil flow in all countries. Nonetheless, Mecca was indeed in Saudi Arabia and he had to do his Islamic duty. He chose to do the sublime deed the *Sunnah* way.

Ammar assembled the items he would require himself and studied with locals who had already gone on the blessed journey. He rode with other members of The Sword of Allah on a bus, and arrived on the sixth day of the twelfth month. They slept in the bus. Ammar reveled in the feeling of unity, not only with his fellow travelers on the bus, but also with every *Hajji*. The aura of comradeship and the feeling of belonging were so powerful he wept.

He did not weep alone. The group spent much of the night in prayer and did not sleep until exhaustion forced them individually to rest.

At sunrise, on the seventh day of *Dhu al Hajji*, the pilgrims on the bus were up and in *Ihram*. They used a public bathing facility to cleanse them using unscented soap.

Each wore a plain hem-less sheet draped across their torso, another secured around their waist by a white sash and plain sandals. It symbolized that all men were equal, a pauper being no less than a king in the eyes of Allah. They neither ate nor drank and proceeded as a group to the *Sacred Mosque (Masjid Al Haram)*.

Ammar was awestruck by the splendor and grandeur of the magnificent structure. Minarets and holy buildings surrounded the white Mosque. The group merged with others as they entered, and each recited, "*Here I am for Hajj. Here I am, oh Allah, here I am. Here I am. You have no equal. Here I am. Surely, all praise, grace and dominion are yours, and you have no equal.*"

Once inside, the little group had to crane to see the *Kaaba*. Ammar peered over the heads of tens of thousands of other pilgrims. This holiest of temples, was a simple large black cube in the center of the immense courtyard. Made of granite, it stood 15 meters high and 12 meters wide on each side. Originally dating back some 2,000 years to the days of Ibrahim (Abraham to Christians), it had repeatedly been demolished and rebuilt.

In 632 A.D., Muhammad returned to Mecca and reclaimed it from the heathens who had stored their pagan idols and false gods inside of it. He then dedicated it to Islam. Secured to one wall near a corner, was the *Black Stone*. Said by many to be a meteor, most believed it to be the cornerstone of the original temple, put in place by *Ibrahim* himself. The group, as planned, formed a single line and began their first *Tawaf*, walking briskly counter-clockwise around the *Kaaba* while reciting the same prayer over and over: "*In the name of God, God is great, God is great and praise be to God"(Bism Allah Allahu Akbar, Allahu Akbar, Allahu Akbar wa lil lahi Alhamd)*.

This they did seven times, while pointing their right hand toward the holy *Black Stone*. During each circuit, the pilgrim in front continually edged his way leftward toward the holy shrine and the pilgrim behind him did the same. Picture a worm going round and round an apple gradually eating its way toward the core.

The maneuver required much pushing and shoving and incurred the anger of many other worshippers, yet they continued on, determined to work their way into the closest file of *Hajji*. Their aggressive plan worked. By their seventh and final circuit, and despite the angry shouts of those they had jostled and crowded out, they had managed to get close enough to the *Black Stone* to kiss or at least touch it.

Ammar had been somewhat surprised by how small it was and even more taken aback by the silver frame which attached it to the wall. He thought the frame resembled nothing so much as a woman's labia. He immediately chastised himself for this irreverent thought and added another recitation of the prayer. Ammar was proud to kiss the stone and again immediately chastised himself for his arrogance. His small group then offered two *Rakaat* prayers at the *Muqaam Ibrahim* (the place of Ibrahim). Ammar prayed fervently to atone for his lapses.

Upon the completion of their prayers, the group returned to the bus to sit and rest up for the ritual of *sa'i*. As they sat and rested Ammar grew tired of the complaints of thirst made by many of his fellow pilgrims. He resolved to maintain his demeanor of peace and goodwill as required by the teachings of the *Qu'ran*. After awhile, his resolve began to weaken and he stood and shouted "My beloved fellow *Hajji*, let us thank Allah for this opportunity to be nearer to him and praise his mercy. Allahu Akbar!"

He led the group in three choruses of 'Allahu Akbar' and then said, "let us go now and perform *sa'i* with love in our hearts." The

171

men shouted in unison and followed Ammar off the bus laughing and hugging each other. All thoughts of their thirst were gone.

Try as they might, the group was unable to stay together during *sa'i*. Running back and forth between the two hills of *Safa* and *Marwah* seven times was not only physically tiring, it was chaotic since there were tens of thousands of other pilgrims doing the same thing. The ritual resembled a mad relay race between several armies of frantic runners. The ritual was a re-enactment of *Ibrahim's* wife *Hagar's* desperate search for water for her son *Ishmael*. During her search, an angel had appeared and hit the ground with his heel (or brushed the ground with his wing) and the water of the *Zamzam* had gushed forth.

Upon completing the seven trips between the two hills, pilgrims are required to drink from the *Zamzam* well. Ammar still marveled at his disappointment with the 'well'.

In his mind's eye, he had envisioned an oasis with green foliage standing alone in the hot desert and pilgrims kneeling around it scooping up handfuls of water to drink. There was no actual well, just jugs of water strategically placed to serve as many pilgrims at a time as possible. Although disappointed, Ammar had drunk deeply finally admitting to his own great thirst.

$$*\qquad*\qquad*$$

Ammar paused in his reminiscing and turned on the faucet to add more hot water to the tub. Then he chuckled when he remembered that today the back and forth circuits were all enclosed and air-conditioned. This is what some call progress, he lamented. His mind returned to his hajj.

$$*\qquad*\qquad*$$

The following morning, after spending the night in the bus, the group walked about five miles east to the town of *Mina*. There they stayed in tents furnished by the Saudi Arabian government.

"Today has been everything I had hoped for and more," Ammar yelled to the group. A chorus of agreements came from his fellow Hajjis. They spent the night in prayer.

The morning of the ninth day, they left *Mina* for *Arafat,* a hill near the mount where Muhammad had given his last sermon. They arrived mid-morning and proceeded to the designated holy area on the plain of Arafat. There, as required, they each stood in silent contemplation. Some, like Ammar prayed and reflected on their lives in the service of Allah. Others simply stood and fidgeted. All felt their resolve tested as the day wore on and the heat of the sun beat down upon them.

At last, the sun did set and the pilgrims happily left for *Muzdalifah* where they gathered pebbles for the next day's ritual stoning of the Devil *(Shaitan)*. That night they huddled together and slept on the ground. By this time, the grueling routine and meager rations had sapped the strength of everyone and they slept deeply.

The next afternoon they returned to *Mina* to perform the ritual of *Ramy al- Jamarat*, the throwing of stones to signify their defiance of the devil. This symbolized the trials experienced by *Ibrahim* while he decided whether to sacrifice his son, as Allah had demanded. Three times the Devil challenged him and three times, he refused. Three pillars represent these challenges. First, they stood on the *Jamarat* bridge and each threw seven pebbles at the largest of the pillars, *Jamrat' al Aqabah*. They then proceeded to the next pillar and threw seven more pebbles. Lastly, they gathered around a long low wall, which circled a pit and threw seven pebbles at the pillar there. As the pebbles bounced harmlessly off the pillar, they fell into the hole which surrounded it and disappeared.

Later, groundskeepers would quietly go into an underground tunnel, shovel the pebbles into wheelbarrows and scatter them on the grounds of *Mina* for the next batch of pilgrims to gather. Of course, Ammar and his comrades were unaware of this expediency. With the completion of the first *Ramy al-Jamarat*, it was time to rejoice.

Eid al-Adha was an important Islamic festival celebrated around the globe every year on the tenth day of *Dhu-al-Hijjah* in commemoration of Allah having mercy on Ibrahim, and allowing him to sacrifice a ram instead of his son. Each true believer slaughtered a sheep (one cow could be substituted for seven Muslims). Ammar's group had purchased vouchers for the slaughtering of one cow and two sheep in their names. Certified butchers would do this, and the meat would be packaged and distributed to the needy as an act of charity.

The little group then returned to the public baths and assisted each other in the careful shaving of their heads. This act of submission served to re-enforce the concept of equality among men. The participants, exuberant from the exercise of throwing the stones, and laughing at each other's baldness, piled onto the bus, which had been driven to Mina to pick them up. There was a cacophony of conversations and shouting during the ride back to Mecca.

"Adlar, keep your arms at your side. You're stinking up the bus," one of the young newcomers to the group shouted with a laugh.

"And you remain seated," Adlar responded. Everyone laughed.

Upon arrival, they quit talking and walked purposefully and quietly to the sacred mosque. Once inside, they completed their *Tawaf az-Ziyarah*. This was a repetition of their previous *Tawaf,* and they walked briskly around the *Kaaba*. This time, however, they were content to point their right hands at the *Black Stone* and were careful not to jostle any other Hajji. They then climbed wearily back onto the bus and returned to Mina, where they purchased a ram, sacrificed it themselves, and then butchered, roasted and ate it. It was a very long day.

On the eleventh day, they again gathered and threw pebbles at the three *Jamarat* of the Devil. This was a much-needed day of light activity. It gave the pilgrims a chance to rest up from their previous days of physical activity.

On the twelfth day, they returned to Mecca to perform the *Tawaf al- Wada*. This was the farewell circumambulation around the *Kaaba*, and many members of the group were in tears as they completed the seventh circle. At Imam Jamali's prior insistence, the bus did not immediately turn for home. Instead, they rode to *Medina* where they visited the *Mosque of the Prophet*, which contains *Muhammad's* tomb. For Ammar, it was the most memorable part of his most memorable journey.

*   *   *

As Ammar fondly reflected on his visit to Medina, he drained some water from the tub and again replaced it with hot water. He then reached to the floor beside the tub and picked up his razor and a can of unscented shaving cream. He began by lathering his legs and shaving them. Next, he stepped out of the tub and stood in front of the mirror over the sink. He used a scissors to cut off most of the hair on his head and face, and then finished the job with his razor. Finally, he shaved the rest of his body as well as he could. He regretted that he was unable to reach most of his back, but he had known that would be a problem before he had even started.   He was not able to ask someone to assist him, since his actions would have been certain to arouse suspicion. He observed himself in the full-length mirror on the wall by the TV and decided he was as clean and as pure as he could be. He was ready to go to paradise and to face his Creator. He was at peace with himself. He went back to bed and finally fell into a fitful sleep around three AM.

CHAPTER 29

SATURDAY

MAGGIE PULLED THE car into the garage slowly and carefully, put it in park and removed the keys. She then helped her Grampa out of the car and up the step into the kitchen. He was her grandfather only because her mother had married his son, but you'd never know that. They regarded themselves as grandfather and granddaughter and loved each other completely. As she took his arm, he placed his hand gently over hers and gratefully accepted her assistance up the step. Maggie shut the door, kissed him on the cheek and sat him down at a kitchen chair. "We're home," she yelled. Teri, who had been setting the dining room table, came into the kitchen, kissed her father-in-law on the cheek and gave him a big hug.

"I'm so glad you could make it," she said. "We've missed you."

"Thank you; I'm happy to be here," he replied. "My son's schedule and mine don't mesh very well, I'm afraid."

"John," Teri shouted up the stairs, "your father is here. Come down for dinner."

"Be there in a sec, Hon," John yelled back, just as his phone rang. "Damn it," he muttered and answered, "Senator Franks."

"Yes, Senator, Don Whitman here," the urgent sound of his voice caught the Senator's instant attention.

"What is it, Don?" Franks asked.

"That fax you sent me, the terrorist that could be our man?" Don started.

"Yes?" Franks encouraged.

"I'm almost positive that he served me a sandwich at lunch today."

"He did what?" Franks said in disbelief. "You think he served you a sandwich? Where? When was this?"

"I ate lunch at a sidewalk cafe at the Harrison Hotel, in front of the Chez Blanc restaurant. I knew there was something about this waiter. Something kept telling me that I had seen him before, but, I couldn't for the life of me; remember where I had seen him." The words tumbled out in a rush and the Senator needed a moment to absorb what Don was telling him.

"You're sure that this is the man? The one in the photo I faxed you."

"Well, he looked a few years older than in the photo and the picture was a bit out of focus…" Whitman said as his old CYA training kicked in.

"Was it him or not?" The Senator asked sternly.

"It was him." Dan replied resolutely. "It had to be him."

"And what time was it that you saw him?" Franks continued.

"It was about noon our time. Right before you and I and General Birch talked. In fact, I think I noticed him watching me while I was in the phone booth at the hotel talking to you." It was clear from the surprised sound of Don's voice that he was just now realizing the last part of his statement.

"Where are you now?" Franks asked. He knew that he was calling from Estelle's home. He was looking right at the caller I.D. screen.

"Uh, I'm calling from the Kinkos," Don lied.

"Don, it could well be that our problem has already been solved." He then told Don about General Birch's earlier call and concluded with, "chances are our terrorist is dead and no longer a threat. We'll know more after forensics has had time to do its job."

"I certainly hope you're right, Senator. I'll rest a lot easier when his death is confirmed by the forensics team." On one hand, Don was thrilled that the major conspiracy he had detected was over. On the other, he wished he had had more to do with the resolution. On the third hand, he felt that it had been too easy. Nothing was ever this easy.

"Meanwhile," Franks continued, "I want you to go back to the

Harrison Hotel and talk to the manager and look around to see if our man is anywhere to be found. Obviously, you should take his photo along. Are you armed?"

"Yes sir. I didn't have to turn my weapon in."

"Why would you have had to turn in your gun?" The Senator knew why, but he wanted to hear Don's explanation.

"That's a long story, sir. Let's just say I stepped a little out of line and pissed off some of my superiors. I'm technically on vacation at the moment."

"Don, let's be honest with each other here. You got your hand slapped for talking to me, right?"

"Yes"

"I'm sorry to hear that. Is there any way I could be of help?"

"Oh, I don't think so sir. It'll all be over in a week. Let's just make sure that our big problem is actually handled."

"All right, I'll call Birch and tell him your news. Don't be surprised if the search team winds up at the hotel at the same time as you. If they don't already have a copy of the photo, make a copy of yours for them. If you find out anything of value, call me immediately. OK?"

"Absolutely sir, Thank you." Don felt he was back in the saddle and it felt good.

"No thank you Don. This has been your baby from the get go. I'm just along for the ride."

The Senator understood exactly how Don was feeling and he played to those feelings with the polish of a consummate politician. Getting things done through other people was his forte. "Let me know when you know something." Then he hung up.

"You got..." Don started to say and realized he was talking to himself.

Senator Franks yelled downstairs that he would be down in a moment and called General Birch. He quickly filled the General in on Don's sighting and hung up when he started to demand more details. He didn't have any details. The General would find out when he did. John hurried down the stairs into the dining room, while saying, "sorry for taking so long everybody, last minute crisis." The elder Franks looked at his son questioningly and he gave his father a reassuring look and a hug in return. "Let's eat everybody. It smells delicious," he said.

Dinner was delicious and everyone enjoyed the quiet meal with three generations present. The talk was almost painfully banal for the Pastor. He was bursting with curiosity and they were discussing the weather, the Packers and the play Jesus Christ Super Star that Teri and Maggie had seen. The subject of the impending wedding never arose and neither John nor his father opted to bring it up.

At last, dinner was over and the men retired to John's upstairs office while Teri and Maggie cleaned up. The men promised to be down in no more than an hour so they could play Monopoly.

"How about a brandy," John asked his father who was heading for the easy chair next to his desk.

"That's an excellent idea, son. Thank you," the Pastor said as he sank into the chair. John poured two snifter glasses of Korbel, each about a third full and handed one to his father. John sat at his desk and took a sip of brandy before he spoke. His father was leaning forward in his chair with the brandy snifter cupped in his hands. He waited for his son to start.

"Well, Dad, in a nutshell, the terrorist plot was probably real, but the crisis is almost certainly over, because we believe the terrorist accidentally blew himself up this afternoon." He sat back in his chair and took another sip. His father did the same. They sat in silence for about two minutes.

"When you say, 'you believe' the terrorist blew himself up, when will you know for certain?" His father finally asked.

"When the forensics team tells us," Don answered flatly. "Meanwhile I've got Whitman checking out the hotel restaurant where the terrorist worked and the search team will most likely be joining him as soon as they're done at the site of the explosion. At this point, all we can do is wait. But I truly think the problem is over." John spoke with a certainty he did not feel.

"So, what do you do now?' The elder Franks asked.

"I have some arrangements to make. I was going to take Inauguration Day off, but now I think I should go. That means I have to tell my secretary she won't have Monday off after all, and I need to book a flight and a room for tomorrow. Meanwhile, I'm going to stop studying my C.O.G. manual."

"Studying your what?" His father asked. "What's a C.O.G.?"

"It stands for Continuity of Government," John explained.

"You've lost me, son," his father replied.

"Well, the details are top secret, but, I can tell you it's a disaster response plan. As I had it explained to me, it all started with Winston Churchill during World War II. The ongoing bombing of England by the Germans worried Churchill. His main concern was the possibility that an attack during a high-level meeting could kill all or most of the country's leadership at once. This would leave the country without direction and the resulting chaos could mean losing the war. He assembled his best minds and they put together a plan covering every possibility.

When Eisenhower became president of the U.S., he implemented a similar plan. That was why we built Camp David. As I understand it, every president since has had his own C.O.G. plan designed to his personal specifications. President Herman's disaster program is very thorough. I'd let you thumb through it but, as I said it is top secret."

"That's fine, son. I don't require details. It's comforting enough just to know that such a plan exists." The Pastor took another little sip appreciatively, and continued, "Did you know that Wisconsinites drink more brandy per capita than any other state?"

"I think I heard 'in the whole world'," John said as he took another sniff and then a sip. The brandy was doing its work and both were feeling a warm glow.

"So you're heading back to Washington in the morning?" It was a statement, not a question.

"Yes, I'll call my travel agent in a few minutes. He's a whiz and I'm sure he'll get me there at a reasonable time. My first function is a luncheon with the Daughters of the American Revolution and another luncheon with some members of my re-election committee."

"Really," His father said. "You have a re-election committee already?"

"Dad, I formed that the day I was elected. No better time to get the ball rolling than when it is already going full steam."

"I suppose you're right," the elder Franks said with a little shake of his head. "I guess I've just never been that organized, myself. Good for you. I'm glad to see my son so on top of things."

"Dad, false modesty isn't necessary. You know darn well that you taught me my organizational skills. You also taught me how to persevere. Without your help, I'd never have been elected U.S. Senator."

"Nonsense, you did that on your own," his father said while

finishing his brandy. He deflected his son's compliment, but enjoyed the recognition. He didn't know if it was the brandy or his humility, but he found himself getting red in the face. John looked away and deliberately set his own glass down unfinished.

"Shall we head downstairs? I know the girls are looking forward to beating us in Monopoly."

"I can play for a couple of hours, but I'll need a ride to the hospital later. There's a little girl there I'm ministering to. She has leukemia."

"I remember you telling us about her, but I can't recall her name. How is she doing?"

"Her name is Anne Horowitz and she isn't doing well at all; not at all." John picked up his phone and dialed his travel agent. He would have to leave a message on the answering machine but it did not concern him. The agent checked his messages frequently. Don would have a flight for tomorrow. As it turned out, the agent answered in the middle of his message and managed to book him an early morning flight immediately. Things were going right for a change. John stood and offered his father his arm. The Pastor accepted his son's arm and allowed him to escort him down the stairs.

SUNDAY, JANUARY 20 2013

IMAM JAMALI COMPLETED afternoon prayers and waited patiently for his followers to finish theirs. He then stood, raised his arms in victory and shouted "Allahu Akbar." The response was a deafening roar as tens of thousands of fellow Jihadists answered with fervor, "Allahu Akbar, Allahu Akbar, Allahu Akbar." The day had gone exactly as planned. Thus far the coup was a complete success. He and his allies were now in control of Pakistan, or at least in control of the country's parliament. He had received word only moments ago that the United Taliban Front was having less success in Afghanistan. The news troubled him. On the Islamic calendar, it was now 4:00 PM on the 8th day of *Rabi-ul-Awwal,* 1434. It was a day that would long be remembered in Pakistani history and in Shiite lore. In Washington D.C. it was 6:00 AM on January 20th, 2013.

*   *   *

Teri Franks groped bleary-eyed for the raucous alarm clock blaring in her ear. It was one of her marital concessions that the alarm clock was on her side of the bed, even though John was the one who got up early most often. She pushed the off button and glared at the face of the noisy little device that had awoken her. "Five fucking AM," she moaned. She used a knee to deliver a kidney blow into John's back. He awoke with a painful grunt and she immediately regretted her spiteful action. "Sweetheart, it's time to rise and shine," she said, cuddling him.

∗   ∗   ∗

At precisely 6:00 AM EST, Don Whitman strode into the front lobby of the Harrison hotel, crossed to the front desk and asked for the hotel manager. The front desk clerk smiled and explained that Mr. Dickens normally didn't come in until seven, but he would be more than happy to assist him in any way he could. Don flashed his identification and explained that he was looking for someone whom he believed worked in the hotel restaurant. He pulled out the photo of Ammar Ali and showed it to the clerk. The genial man behind the counter pushed his glasses further back on his nose and held them so he could look at the picture without them falling off. "Why yes, I do believe that's Ghanzafar our bellman. He's a bit younger in this photo, but it certainly does look like him."

"You're sure?" Don asked.

"Well, it's an old photo and it's quite blurry, but I definitely think it's him. Of course, I couldn't swear to that in a court of law," the clerk hedged.

"That won't be necessary. What time does he come in?" Don replied.

"He's usually here before me. I come on at six and so does he, but I don't see him at his bellman's post. Perhaps he already had a call."

"Is that the bellman's post over there by the front door?" Don didn't wait for a reply, but walked over to the bench next to the podium and sat down. Almost immediately, two men in suits came in and repeated his session with the front desk clerk. He watched as they showed IDs and a photo. Eventually, the clerk pointed to him and the agents came over to confront him. After a brief discussion, Don and one of the agents headed into the Chez Blanc for breakfast. The lowest man on the totem pole stood watch at the bellman's post.

∗   ∗   ∗

Ammar was sleeping fitfully. He had gone back to bed after his ablutions and had tossed and turned ever since. He had awoken several times. He finally gave up trying. The alarm clock next to his bed said 6:35. Ammar yawned and stretched and sat on the edge of the bed. He then stood, dropped to his knees on the carpeted floor facing east and brought his forehead to touch the carpet with his hands placed to each side.

183

Rising up on his knees, he prayed, "O Allah! Praise to thee, thou art the guardian of the heavens and the earth and of those that are therein. Thou art the king of the heavens and the earth, and those that are therein. Thou art true, true is thy promise. True is our meeting with thee; true is thy word as are the prophets. True is Muhammad, and true is the hour of judgment. O Allah! Unto thee I do surrender. Unto thee do I seek judgment. So forgive me for that which I expedite, and that which I defer and which I conceal; and for that which I reveal. And also for my sins whereof thou art better aware than I. Thou art the expediter and thou art the deferrer. There is no god other than thee."

Ammar repeated this prayer six times as he repeatedly supplicated himself on the carpeted floor. Then he rose, stepped into the shower and cleansed his body one final time.

∗   ∗   ∗

Don Whitman and agent Gordon Perkins sat at a small table and ordered breakfast. Don asked for oatmeal with skim milk, raisins and brown sugar. Perkins ordered two eggs over easy, bacon fried crisp and whole wheat toast. Neither knew they would not live to enjoy this last meal. Don excused himself and crossed the hallway behind the front desk to the last phone booth; the same one he had used the day before. He put in his calling card and dialed. Senator Franks answered on the third ring.

"This is Senator Franks."

"Good morning Senator, Don Whitman reporting in."

"Good morning, Don. Where are you?" The senator was finishing combing his hair, a job which required two hands, so he put the phone on speaker.

"I'm in the same phone booth as before, at the Harrison Hotel. Our man isn't here."

"The Harrison Hotel, is that where you had lunch and our suspect served you?"

"Yes, this is the place.

"And he's not there, you say?"

"Correct. I'm here with two other FBI agents and we've got the lobby covered. The desk clerk confirmed that he works here and that he's normally in promptly at six each morning."

"And what time is it now?" The senator yawned.

"6:45 Eastern Standard Time," Don dutifully replied.

"Well, I consider that very encouraging. I think General Birch was right and our terrorist accidently blew himself up yesterday." Don heard the relief in the senator's voice. He wasn't so sure. Nothing was ever this easy. Nonetheless, he agreed with the senator.

"Yes sir, I guess sometimes we get lucky. I'm just going to hang around a little longer in case he comes in yet. Should I tell General Birch?"

"No, that's ok. I'll call him. Thank you, Don. Have a good one." He hung up. Don replaced the receiver in the cradle and crossed over to the bellman's post.

"How do you like your coffee?" Don asked the agent sitting there.

"Black, thank you," the agent replied with a smile.

"I'll send our waiter out with a pot for you," Don said as he crossed back into the restaurant.

*   *   *

After drying himself off, Ammar retrieved his items from his overnight bag and got dressed. Wearing the same Ihram he had worn on his Hajj so many years ago made him feel holy. Today would be the most blessed day of his entire life. Today he would stand before Allah. He picked up the pass key and storeroom key, then wrapped a towel over his head and stepped into the hallway. To a casual observer he would look like someone headed to the hotel pool area.

He quickly went around the corner next to his room and pushed the down button for the elevator. He was in luck, the door opened immediately. Allah was favoring him. He could feel it. A glance over his shoulder as he entered the elevator assured him that he had not been seen.   When the elevator doors opened on the lobby floor Ammar peeked out and, seeing no one nearby, hastily exited and immediately turned right to the service elevator around that corner. He pushed the down button and again the elevator opened at once. Almost gleefully, he entered the elevator and pushed the B3 button. Indeed, Allah was at his side.

The FBI agent sitting at the bellman's post glanced up from reading yesterday's <u>Washington Post</u>. He had seen something out of the corner of his eye. Did someone dressed all in white just get out of the main elevator? Nah, must be just his nerves. Anyone getting off the elevator would certainly have headed out toward him. He resumed reading yesterday's news. A moment later a waiter brought him a tray with a pot of coffee, a cup, sugar, creamer, spoon, and a plate with two Danish, two pats of butter, a knife and a white linen napkin. He forgot all about the person dressed in white getting off the elevator.

*   *   *

Senator Franks finished the double Windsor knot in his tie and looked at his watch. He was on the 7:10 flight to D.C. via Detroit. He saw that he had time to call Birch. As he sat down in his office he called out, "Teri, sweetheart, is my bag ready and my briefcase in the front hall?" "Both all set. I packed enough for you for three nights. Is that good?" Teri was carrying the bags down the steps as she called back to her husband. She enjoyed helping him out by taking care of menial chores like packing so John didn't have to be concerned with them. Besides, this way she could be sure his shirts and ties matched.

"You're an angel. I'll be down as soon as I make this call." John picked up the phone and dialed the secure number for General Birch. The phone rang four times and then a voice said, "You have reached the office of Lieutenant General Samuel Birch of the Defense Intelligence Agency. Our offices are closed. Our regular office hours are…" John hung up and headed for the stairs. He would talk with Birch later. Teri was waiting for him in the front hall. She had used the downstairs bathroom earlier to touch up her make-up and brush her hair. As usual, she looked gorgeous even standing there in her bulky robe.

"You're sure you don't need a ride to the airport?" Teri asked as she helped him on with his overcoat.

"No thank you. I can't be 100% sure how long I'll have to stay. Most likely I'll be back in three days." He finished buttoning his coat and took Teri in his arms for a long goodbye kiss. When it was over she said, "Well, I have to send you on your way more often."

"I love you Mrs. Franks, and tell Maggie I love her too." With that he hugged her one more time and picked up his bags before crossing to the garage. Teri called out to him as he walked, "I'm sure she knows you love her, honey. Especially after that little drama the two of you put on in our bedroom." John stopped and turned to her.

"What little drama do you mean?" He asked.

"The scene in which my dress was so, so gorgeous and Maggie's didn't measure up."

"Were we that obvious?" John said with a smile.

"No, just you were obvious John. Maggie was fine. Don't worry; it's one of the things I love about you and so does Maggie." She blew him a kiss. He shrugged and turned to go.

*   *   *

At 6:50 AM, Ammar stepped out of the service elevator into the main entryway of the hotel maintenance and storage area on basement level 3. It was deserted, just as he had expected. He walked deliberately over to the main storage room door, inserted his pass key, entered and closed the door behind him as he flipped the light switch. Everything he did seemed somehow surreal. It was almost like he was floating above himself and observing the actions of a stranger.   Every action was in slow motion and worthy of notice. In the back of his mind a separate little voice was decrying the fact that no historian was present to accurately record this momentous event. He continued into the room and opened the door marked Authorized Admittance Only. He stepped in and began lifting the cardboard boxes away from the front door of the metal case which securely held Allah's Wrath. He quickly spun the dial and pulled on the handle. The metal door swung wide revealing the W80-1 warhead.

Now on his knees, Ammar stared in awe at the metallic device which would catapult him into the history books and into Allah's favor.   He glanced at his watch. It was 6:57. The original plan was to detonate at noon, but as he looked at the powerful weapon in front of him, he saw no reason to delay. He took a deep breath and began to enter the instant detonation code.

When his finger touched the final number there was a small click, then a beep and one nano-second later, the temperature in the room went from a comfortable 68 degrees Fahrenheit to 540,000 degrees (approximately the temperature of the face of the sun.) Ammar and the surrounding area did not merely vaporize. Absolutely everything was reduced to sub-atomic particles which became one with the universe.

CHAPTER 31

SUNDAY

A⊤ 6:57 AM the entire Reagan Complex One crew was instantly awakened by the raucous alarm system blaring all over the compound. As they stumbled out of their beds, the six sleeping members blinked the sleep out of their eyes. Caroline Beckman covered her ears and quickly threw on her emergency uniform. Then she touched up her make-up and headed for the control room. Dick Wren shot out of bed and decided the first order of business was to pee. This he did by sitting on his toilet. He didn't want to waste time washing his hands.

Kurt Schimler was the only one to wake up with a smile. His smile changed to a grin as he hurriedly donned his commander's uniform. These special outfits had been designed for one purpose and one purpose only: to designate the absolute authority of the handful of people who wore them. Except for the original fittings, they had never been worn. They simply hung in the closets of the people who had been hand-picked to guide our nation through what was presumed would be a chaotic and horrible chapter in our history.

"Where the hell is everybody?" Schimler yelled as he strode into the control/conference room. The only one there was Bob Eden, Homeland Security officer and a member of the morning crew.

"I don't know, sir." Eden responded. "Of course, the alarm has only been ringing for a couple of minutes," he added. With that, Kurt took a step to the wall and switched the alarm off.

The sudden silence was deafening. A second later Caroline and Dick burst into the room followed by the rest of the emergency management team.

"Everyone please take a seat," Schimler ordered brusquely. "Caroline not you; please get some coffee going, OK?" Caroline grimaced but said nothing. As she left for the kitchen in the next room, he took his seat.

"Bob, please turn on all of the monitors. Bob rose and went to the control panel and began moving levers and flipping switches. The room, which had been in semi-darkness, came to life as large wall-mounted screens lit up and computers booted up. There was no sound, but the images on screen told them all they needed to know. One satellite image showed a huge mushroom cloud forming and rising to the heavens as they watched.

"Jesus Christ," Craig Fergussen exclaimed. "Will you look at that?"

"Jesus Christ," Caroline echoed as she glanced back over her shoulder from the counter where she was making coffee.

"This is for real, isn't it?" Dick Wren's voice betrayed the fact that he was crying.

"Abso-fucking-lutely, Dick," Schimler said softly. "Abso-fucking-lutely."

"Oh my God," Fergussen cried as he watched the billowing cloud grow. "I never thought it would really happen. Never in a million years!"

"Me either," agreed three others in unison.

Kurt rose and strode to the front of the room under the main monitor.

"Well, you better believe it. You all better believe it. The shit has actually hit the fan and we are all that stands between the citizens of our nation and utter chaos. Aren't you all glad we had that drill yesterday?"

"Glad?" Two people shouted in unison.

"You know what the hell I mean," Schimler barked back. "It is now incumbent upon us gentlemen…and lady, to do our jobs to the best of our abilities. With that thought in mind, did any of you think to grab your plan and bring it here?" Bob Eden raised his hand.

"Just, Bob?" He exploded. "What are all of you…"Then he caught himself and forced himself to calm down. The excitement of finally getting his chance at the helm was causing his adrenaline to flow and he quickly realized that what he needed now was a cool head. With an effort, he slowed his breathing and stopped in mid-sentence.

"What I meant to say is that we will all stay in this room long enough to assess the impact of the event and then we'll adjourn to our offices to take the appropriate actions. Be sure to refer to the disaster plan you brought to yesterday's meeting." No one said anything.

The scene on the monitor shifted. This was a different view from a different satellite. The camera zoomed out and the devastation was clear. Washington D.C. no longer existed. The mushroom cloud just kept getting wider. It began to obscure the view. Everyone watched the screen in silent awe. Caroline sniffled.

"Here's a ground view," Bob said as he switched to a security camera mounted on a high pole on the outskirts of the city. All that could be seen was dense smoke. He tried another ground camera and got the same result.

"Get back to the satellite image," Schimler ordered.

"God," Bob said softly. They all sat and watched the grisly scene without saying a word for the next five minutes. The air was so thick that little could be seen except for fires everywhere. As the camera began to zoom in for a closer look, Schimler thought, enough if enough.

"OK, everybody," he said. "Let's get to work." To emphasize his point he stood and walked rapidly into his adjoining office. "Caroline, please bring me my coffee when it's ready.

Make it black with two sugars." He said.

"I'll get my own, Caroline," Craig said as he rose and headed for the kitchen area.

"Thank you, Craig. At least one person around here realizes that I'm not a secretary or a waitress." She cast a glare in the direction of Schimler but he was already in his office and didn't know it or hear her. That frustrated her even more.

Schimler wasted no time in releasing the DVD which had been prepared to announce the transition of authority from the oval office to him. He began sending a feed to every satellite with the capabilities and to every television network and radio station in the United States. Later, after the actual succession he would release the foreign language versions around the world. It was tedious work but he didn't trust anyone else to do it right.

Everyone else went to their offices and began contacting the departments they were in charge of to confirm the day's event. The other eighty-nine underground bunkers that surrounded our nation's capitol in a huge looping circle all had their own early warning alert systems. The entire National Command Group was already in full motion and scurrying to fulfill their emergency requirements. Most of them resented the phone calls, faxes and emails from Compound I. How in the hell were they supposed to do their jobs if the god damn honchos kept bothering them for reports and updates. In a way, it was "business as usual".

CHAPTER 32

SUNDAY

DON WHITMAN WAS patiently chatting with agent Carlton while waiting for his oatmeal. He was explaining why he was not convinced that the terrorist was dead. Don was right for one more nano-second, and was about to take a sip of coffee when he and everything else in a three mile radius from ground zero ceased to exist.

A molten circle of impossibly hot gasses with a diameter of six miles had formed instantly and Don was at the epicenter. Within this circle all life was extinguished. Every human being, dog, cat, rat, every tree, shrub, flower and blade of grass as well as every insect, including the nearly indestructible cockroach died. The heart of the city simply vanished. A blinding flash seen for many miles was followed by a blast of such extraordinary power that it pulverized everything for another three miles in every direction. All this occurred in the first second of the horrific explosion of the device named Allah's Wrath.

* * *

For over 200 years the White House, residence of America's president, stood proudly at 1600 Pennsylvania Avenue. This icon of power was virtually destroyed in 1814 when the British and their Canadian allies burned it almost to the ground along with the rest of Washington DC. On Christmas Eve 1929, a conflagration destroyed the west wing. In 2007, a small fire in the Eisenhower Executive Office

Building, next to the White House, damaged two offices. After each event, the damage was repaired and the building emerged grander than before. This time there would be nothing left to repair. The incredible vaporizing temperature struck as the president and vice president and several foreign dignitaries, congressmen and senators were being seated, along with their spouses, for breakfast in the East Wing.

The White House kitchen staff had prepared a varied menu to suit each diner's individual palate. President Herman was from the south and preferred a slab of ham, eggs over easy, biscuits & gravy and grits. The First Lady was expecting her usual: a bowl of fruit and dry whole wheat toast. Menachem Sulie, the Israeli Ambassador would have bagels and lox. Senator Wilforest (Rep) Maine planned to settle for an English muffin. He was on a diet. The elegant table was draped in a damask tablecloth and set with Limoges china, Paul Revere silver ware and linen napkins. President Herman complimented the staff. He and his wife and their guests never got to sit down.

*   *   *

The U.S. Capitol Building also stood for over two centuries. A proud monument to the American people and their representative form of government, it housed the meeting chambers of the House of Representatives and the Senate. The cornerstone was laid by President Washington on September 18th, 1793. Located on Capitol Hill at the east end of what is now the National Mall, it also was severely damaged by fire in 1814. Afterwards, it was rebuilt and expanded several times to where it now had a floor area of 16.5 acres. Surprisingly, when the hellfire struck, there were several thousand tourists lined up to visit.

Everyone would have been disappointed because the Capitol is closed on Sundays. Among those in line was Billy Peterson from Redwing Minnesota. He and fellow eagle scouts were working on their American Civics badges. Their deaths were instantaneous and painless. The Capitol Building itself resisted destruction for only about one-half second and then the marble walls and concrete steps melted.

*   *   *

An unknown number of dedicated workers at the nearby J. Edgar Hoover FBI Building were on duty at this early hour on a Sunday morning. Named after a former FBI Director, the building was done in the Brutalist architectural style with all poured-concrete outer walls. The Washingtonian Magazine deemed it and the Kennedy Center as "the buildings we would most like to see torn down".

These workers and every other worker in every other office building within the circle disappeared. Included were the Departments of the Treasury, Education, Energy, Interior, Labor, Agriculture, Justice, Commerce, State, Transportation and Housing & Urban Development, along with congressional and senate office buildings: the Rayburn House, Longworth House, Cannon Building, Russell Senate Office Building, Dirksen Senate Office Building, Hart Senate Office Building, the Federal Emergency Management Administration Headquarters, the Internal Revenue Service Home Office and the Federal Reserve Building. In short, every cog that turned every wheel in the great complexity of our nation's hub had turned into smoking ash.

*   *   *

Of course, the National Mall was a victim; all nine buildings of the Smithsonian Museum were wiped off the map along with the National Museum of Natural History, National Museum of American History, National Gallery, Government Services Administration, Library of Congress, U.S. Supreme Court and National Archives. Ford's theater, where President Lincoln was assassinated, was a wood building, so it went even faster than the others. The World Bank, International Monetary Fund, DAR Museum, Washington Post, Constitution Hall, Kennedy Center, Union Station and 143 foreign embassies were destroyed.

*   *   *

Christian churches were not immune to the destructive power of Allah's Wrath. The Washington National Cathedral and the Basilica of the National Shrine of the Immaculate Conception disappeared along with dozens of other sacred places of worship frequented by Muslims, Buddhists, Judaists, and every other religion known to man.

*   *   *

Gone was the Washington Monument; the white marble edifice which honored the man who, after winning the revolutionary war, refused to be named king. He chose instead to serve as the first President and thereby confirmed the establishment of a democratic government of the people, for the people and by the people. Standing over 555 feet tall, the classic Egyptian obelisk honoring him had dominated the horizon and could be seen from thirty miles away. Now it was melted into a shapeless mound.

*   *   *

The nearby Jefferson Memorial suffered the same fate. Directly south of the White House, it had been built to honor the principle author of the *Declaration of Independence* and America's third President Thomas Jefferson. It had consisted of circular marble steps leading up to a circular colonnade of Ionic order columns which supported a shallow dome. Inside the open air rotunda had stood a nineteen foot tall bronze statue of the great man. The bronze had succumbed to the heat a fraction of a second sooner than the surrounding rotunda.

*   *   *

Opposite the Washington Monument; at the far west end of the reflecting pool stood the Lincoln Memorial. Its neoclassic design was modeled after an ancient Greek Temple. A series of wide steps led up to a magnificent marble building with thirty-eight Doric Columns, each forty-four foot tall, leading to an open air Pavilion. Inside was a nineteen foot high marble statue of Abraham Lincoln seated in contemplation. On one wall was his Gettysburg Address; on another his 2nd Inaugural Address. In 1963 the Reverend Martin Luther King had chosen to deliver his "I have a Dream" speech standing at the foot of this memorial which honored the man who had preserved the union and signed the Emancipation Proclamation. This memorial too was now a shapeless mass.

*   *   *

In front of the Lincoln Memorial had stood the reflective black granite walls of the Vietnam Veteran's Memorial. These two walls reached a height of just over ten feet at the center where they joined and tapered off to about eight inches at both ends. One wall pointed at the Washington Monument the other at the Lincoln Memorial. Inscribed in the black granite were the names of over 58,000 American military men and women listed as killed or missing in action in that disastrous debacle of a war. Now their names were lost forever.

*   *   *

The Marine Corps War Memorial had stood near the entryway to Arlington National Cemetery. This inspiring tableau memorialized the raising of the American flag on Mount Suribachi on the tiny island of Iwo Jima in 1945. It was a sight that had given heart to the thousands of marines of the fourth and fifth divisions who had fought valiantly to take this strategically vital dot of land in the Pacific. The image of four marines and one naval corpsman lifting the flag into position on Suribachi also inspired a nation that had grown weary of the prolonged war. Visitors to Arlington often would have a chill go down their spine when that scene loomed into view. Five 32 foot tall bronze soldiers lifting a sixty foot pole with a huge cotton flag was a sight to behold. Now, the flag that had flown 24 hours a day was a wisp of ash in a pile of scrap metal.

*   *   *

On the grounds of Arlington National Cemetery was the Memorial Amphitheater and in front of that had stood the Tomb of the Unknowns. Inscribed on one end of the white marble sarcophagus were the words: *"Here rests in honored glory an American soldier known but to God."* This memorial was guarded 24 hours a day year 'round in *all* weather by volunteers from the 3rd U.S. Infantry (The Old Guard).

Every year thousands of visitors watched the elaborate ritual of the hourly changing of the guard. The relief man would come to attention; surrender his rifle for inspection, then join the corporal of the guard and the man he was replacing in saluting the tomb. He would then regain and shoulder his rifle and solemnly pace twenty-one steps to the end of the black mat on the ground by the tomb. At the end of the mat he would turn smartly and pause twenty-one seconds before turning again and then pacing twenty-one steps. Back and forth the Sentinel marched until relieved by the next man. Now, for the first time since its dedication in 1937, there was no one honoring those who had given their lives in defense of our nation.

*   *   *

In years to come many would say that America lost its history that day. Others would shake their heads and say, worse than that we lost our power. In addition to erasing every trace of the American Federal Government, the blast radius had reached the Pentagon building and totally demolished it.

*   *   *

Equally horrendous was the loss of artifacts and memorabilia which lived in our hearts.

Gone was every copy of the Declaration of Independence.

Gone was every copy of the Constitution of the United States of America.

The original airplane built and flown by Wilbur and Orville Wright was black ash.

The first jet airplane to break the sound barrier flown by Chuck Yeager had vanished.

Gone were the ruby slippers worn by Judy Garland in The Wizard of Oz.

The Hope Diamond had become a deformed lump of carbon.

*   *   *

Some five million people lived in or near Washington D.C. The impending Inauguration events had drawn enough tourists and students to increase that number to seven million. In the days to come, experts would estimate that some two to two and a half million people died in the initial blast. Another million were seriously burned or traumatized by flying debris and collapsing structures.

The blinding flash which accompanied the super-inferno reached a height of some three thousand feet. Those unfortunate individuals who looked at it were literally blinded. Some, the lucky ones, were only temporarily without sight; many others lost their ability to see permanently. This instant loss of vision resulted in chaos on the roads and in the air.

Eight airplanes which had been circling Dulles, Reagan and even the further away Baltimore Washington Airport, were suddenly being flown by pilots and co-pilots who were blind. All eight wound up crashing; four of them in the city of Washington D.C. from electrical failure. Nearby Bolling Air Force Base suffered the same devastation as Ronald Reagan airport. In a rare bit of good luck, the air force had transferred the Global Strike Command from Bolling to Barksdale AFB in July of 2009 or the country would have also lost its' nuclear response and deterrence capabilities.

Had the control towers remained operational, airport personnel may have been able to communicate with a seeing person on each remaining aircraft to keep them aloft and guide them into safe landings. However, the EMF wave which followed the blinding flash knocked out all radios and computers. The hurricane force winds created by the blast finished the job of disabling ground equipment. The control towers were blind and deaf.

Flight 234 out of Memphis and Flight A19 from Scranton were involved in a mid-air collision and rained fire and debris all over the already destroyed Georgetown. Both had been in holding patterns, but the pilots of flight A19, a small turbo-prop, unknowingly allowed their altitude to decrease to where they were in the direct path of the L1011 from Memphis. The pilots on the Memphis flight barely had enough time to scream "pull up, pull…"

Months later, the little battery-operated cockpit recorder on American Flight 767, a red eye out of Los Angeles, provided an ominous and inspiring record of courage as the pilot and co-pilot discussed their options and their duties. They had repeatedly radioed the tower, "Reagan tower May Day, repeat May Day. We are American Flight 767 heavy. We have lost power and are descending blind." When they continued to get no answer they decided that the moral thing to do was to try to reach the Atlantic so as to not kill people on the ground. It was evident on the recording that they had tried to use the intercom to calm the passengers.

"Ladies and gentlemen, this is your captain speaking. We are encountering a slight problem and will be diverting from our original destination. Instead of landing at Reagan airport in Washington D.C. we will instead be landing in Baltimore. There is no cause for alarm. All passengers will be bused to their destinations. Connecting flights will be held for you." Had the passengers been able to hear this message they would no doubt have accepted this as an all too common annoyance and probably gone back to their conversation, newspaper or lap-top. Unfortunately, the intercom electronics were also fried. Instead, they watched out the side windows in terror as the plane plummeted. The pilots managed to ditch just offshore. There were no survivors.

Southwest's Flight 354 out of Albuquerque impacted so hard in a field that one of the engines flew off, traveled another 900 feet in the air and hit a gas storage tank which erupted in flames that shot up into the air over 500 feet. Everyone, including the workers at the gas storage facility died. Some died slowly, horribly burned and in excruciating pain. The airline passengers, who had died upon impact, never knew how lucky they had been.

*   *   *

Some twelve thousand motorists, passengers and pedestrians on the streets, highways and Inter-States surrounding Washington D.C. were also blinded. Pandemonium ensued as cars ran off the roads and crashed into each other in multi-car pile-ups. Within a few seconds almost every route in and near the city became impassable blocked by vehicles contorted into twisted scrap heaps. The cries and moans of the injured filled the air. Many mortally wounded individuals were so close to death they couldn't call out. It would have made no difference if they had. The screams of pain and calls for help went unheard. There was almost no one left alive to hear them.

The SUV of the Morrison family, Dave and wife Judy, daughter Kimberly and son Jacob was crushed under an overturned semi. Judy was killed outright by the weight of the behemoth. Dave had serious injuries and was pinned in place. He was going in and out of consciousness and hated waking up to listen helplessly to the screams of his maimed children.

The only survivors were people who had been indoors and far enough from the blast that their buildings remained at least mostly intact. Most survivors were not anxious to venture outdoors.

Although it had been a ground-level detonation, rather than a mid-air explosion, the EMF wave spread out in a radius of thirty miles from ground zero. Virtually every electronic device within this zone was 'fried'. Telephones, cell phones, computers, automobiles, watches and all other electrical technology had become useless.

Television stations within the radius were unable to receive or transmit signals. Radio stations were mute. The airwaves consisted of bands of static. Cell phone towers were disabled and all land line communications equipment was knocked out. Washington D.C. and immediate environs had gone silent. In the proverbial blink of an eye, the most connected, most wired, most powerful city on earth had reverted to the communication system it had had when founded. The sole exceptions were battery -operated Ham radios.

Within seconds the tell-tale mushroom cloud began to form. The worst was yet to come. At ground level it appeared as an impenetrable thick veil of dust. Denser than any pea soup fog ever seen in the area, it obscured everything. Everyone not dead, disabled or blinded by the flash of light soon discovered that they too were all but blind. But, not being able to see was merely an inconvenience. The real problem was that they were too close to the epicenter and were taking in radioactive material with every breath.

"Cover your mouth and your nose with your hanky," Burt Lymon choked to his wife as he did the same.

"I don't have a hanky," his wife Julia cried. "Oh God, oh God I'm going to die aren't I?"   "We survived the blast. We're gonna be OK." He answered. "Now shut up and find a cloth to breathe through. And for God's sake, don't go outside." Burt and Julia lived just outside the blast zone. Eventually they managed to get away from the devastation without ingesting too much radioactive material through their mouth or nose. They lived to tell about their brush with death. Others were not so fortunate.

Twenty minutes after detonation the mushroom cloud reached its' maximum height of some thirty six thousand feet and spread slowly and grimly ever outward until it had a diameter of almost twenty miles. The radioactivity of a tritium based nuclear device is not as deadly as other nuclear materials such as Uranium 238; however it is still lethal if inhaled or swallowed in quantity. Radioactive fallout rained down steadily.

Over the next few days a million and a half more people would die; most from injuries sustained during the original blast, some from accidents following the blast, and a few from radioactive poisoning. The death toll continued to climb to where the news media eventually all started to use a final 'lump sum' number of 4.5 million.

The total could have been higher if Mother Nature had not interceded. The deadly cloud traveled in a slow north-easterly direction passing over Annapolis, Maryland where it contaminated and eventually killed some of the student body of the Naval Academy as well as a fair number of townspeople.

From there it drifted toward Dover, Delaware dropping its lethal mixture of radioactive debris and particles on the unsuspecting population of rural Delaware before contaminating and eventually killing just under one and a half percent of the thirty six thousand residents of the city and a few of the personnel at Dover AFB.

The winds then eased it out into Delaware Bay where it veered slightly south just touching the southern tip of New Jersey where it contaminated the few thousand people who lived in the Cape May area year around. It made a few people sick but, by this time the radioactivity had declined to where it was no longer lethal unless someone ingested gallons of contaminated water.

Forty eight miles north of Cape May, the gamblers in Atlantic City's casinos continued to pull the levers on their slot machines, roll the dice at the craps tables and take hits at the black jack tables, totally unaware that anything of importance was going on outside their isolated clockless little worlds. Eventually the airborne grim reaper headed out into the Atlantic Ocean where it dissipated and was neutralized by dilution in trillions of gallons of salt water.

CHAPTER 33

SUNDAY

SENATOR FRANKS PULLED into his reserved parking space on the ground floor level of the Dane County Regional Airport. He quickly glanced at his watch as he grabbed his suitcase and briefcase from the trunk. Good. It was only 6:28. He should have no trouble being on time. Immediately inside the terminal were the arrival and departure kiosks. He walked briskly over to the nearest one and looked to see if his flight was on time. What he saw was very disturbing. His flight had been delayed. What in the hell was going on? He crossed quickly over to one of the ticket windows, handed the agent there his e-ticket and asked about the delay. The agent accepted the ticket with a smile and said, "Good morning, sir. I'm sorry to tell you that your flight has been delayed."

"Can you tell me why?" John asked politely.

"No, I really can't" the agent replied. "Dulles and Reagan just suddenly both went dark."

"Went dark?" John said quizzically.

"Well, that's what I call it. Just all of a sudden we couldn't communicate with either one of them. We've tried computers, fax machines, land line phones and cell phones. No answer."

"How long ago did this happen? Have you contacted the FAA?"

"About a half hour ago and that's another weird thing. We couldn't get through to the home office of the FAA in D.C. so we called the regional office in Chicago. They don't know what's going on either."

"Damn," said Senator Franks with an anguished look, "do you have a radio or television handy?"

"There's a TV in the Crossroads Bar, about halfway down the terminal, but..."

"Thanks for your help," John said quickly and turned to leave. The ticket agent thought he was being sarcastic and called after him, "Hey man, the bar doesn't open until ten", under his breath he added "jerk".

Senator Franks had picked up his luggage and brief case and raced down the hallway. Before he arrived at the bar he could see it was not open and instead exited through the nearest doors out to the parking ramp.

He started his car and turned on the radio to AM station 99.9 WIRD. *"...all we have at this time. We repeat, News Radio 99.9 WIRD all news all the time, has learned that our nation's capitol may have been the victim of a nuclear attack. Again, we have not yet confirmed this report and all efforts to obtain further details have been unsuccessful. We urge our listeners to stay tuned for further developments which we will pass...just one moment, I've been handed an update. An unidentified news station in Baltimore is reporting numerous sightings of an ominous black mushroom shaped cloud moving eastward..."*

John changed stations. *"...our network stations in the D.C. area remain unresponsive leading us to fear the worst..."* He switched to the next station on the dial, *"...confirmed reports of mass casualties in and around the greater metropolitan area of Washington D.C."*

Senator John Franks had tears in his eyes as he pulled away from the airport and headed for his home. He continued to flip back and forth between radio stations trying to get a feel for the one that had the latest and most complete information. Two blocks from home he almost ran a red light and stopped in the intersection where he endured the angry stares, horns and raised middle fingers of fellow motorists. At last, he pulled into his driveway, pressed the garage door opener, then proceeded cautiously into his garage, put his car in park, turned off the engine and fell forward on the steering wheel and sobbed. He sat there for several minutes. When he finally looked up he became aware that Teri's car was not in the garage.

Then he remembered that it was Sunday. As he entered the house he called out, "Anybody home?" There was no answer. John concluded that

Maggie had gone to church with her mother. It was a concession she made on occasion to appease Teri's disapproval. Teri attended church regularly. While not particularly religious herself, Teri understood the importance of appearances and the social benefits of being a member of an established religion. She, and daughter Maggie, whenever Maggie could be shamed into it, went to Saint Luke's Episcopal Church which had the advantage of being only four blocks away.

For her part, Maggie accepted the social importance of church; she was going to be married in this very edifice in a few weeks, but like her stepfather, she felt that it was actually a boring waste of her time. John and Teri had established an uneasy truce early in their marriage regarding church. Except for Maggie's confirmation, John could honestly say he had never seen the St. Luke's altar without poinsettias or Easter lilies.

No doubt, that was where they were, which meant they wouldn't be home until about 9:30. That was good. He needed time to think. He hung up his overcoat in the front hall closet, grabbed his suitcase and briefcase and took the steps up to his bedroom two at a time. He dropped the suitcase on the floor in the bedroom, took off his jacket and tie, and carried the briefcase into his office. He turned on his computer and went online.

The headlines screamed from the screen: *"Nation's Capitol decimated...Millions feared dead...no word on the whereabouts of the President or Vice President...unconfirmed rumors of Russian nuclear attack, further rumors of Al Qaida or other terrorist group involvement, America held hostage..."* Disgusted by the typical hysterical reporting technique of the American news media, John turned down the volume on the computer and pulled out his Continuity of Government manual.

He shook his head and tried to calm himself. Remarkably, he had just read this manual recently, was it just yesterday? Yet it seemed to him like this was his first time looking at it. The more he read the worse he began to feel. The manual seemed woefully inadequate. The scenario it laid out was based on a ten kiloton nuclear weapon, like one of the Russian suitcase nukes or some home-made nuke put together by a terrorist group.

Based on the early news reports, the device detonated in D.C. was way bigger than that. Christ, just how big? John looked back at his computer screen just in time to see an aerial view taken by satellite of the devastation in Washington. All he could see was the top of the lethal mushroom cloud which appeared to cover an area at least thirty to forty miles in diameter. He would have to wait for recon photos from an airplane to see exactly how badly the city had been hit. Then he read a crawler going along the bottom of the screen: *The Atlanta, Georgia regional headquarters of the Federal Aviation Administration has issued an order to ground all aircraft immediately No one has been able to confirm whether this order is legal or not. Personnel at the Boston headquarters of the FAA, which is actually closer to the impacted area of Washington D.C. have refused to comment, although one employee who wishes to remain anonymous has stated, "we think Atlanta has breached protocol and overstepped its' authority."*

"Well Johnny boy, it doesn't look like you'll be seeing aircraft reconnaissance photos any time soon," John said to himself. Then he turned his attention back to his manual. He laughed when he read that the military run Operation Scatana was charged with shutting down all U.S. airspace in event of enemy attack. It appeared that the FAA folks in Atlanta had beaten them to the punch. He re-read the initial priorities in the COG plan. Right now, according to plan several first response helicopters and limousines would be en-route to locate the President and Vice President to squire them to safety in a secret location. One glance at the images on TV made it clear that there were no survivors needing rescue, nor anyone to do the rescuing.

Another thought struck suddenly, Holy shit! How have the military branches responded? Christ, he thought, we've probably got nuclear missiles pointed in every possible direction by now just waiting for the order. Quickly he dialed General Birch's secure phone. A recorded voice said, "We're sorry. The number you have dialed is no longer in service. If you would like to dial another number, please hang..." John hung up his phone and cursed himself for only having the one means to contact Birch.

His thoughts continued to race and questions came at him pell-mell in no discernable order of importance. How could he contact someone in authority? Who was still alive to be in authority? What were his specific and primary responsibilities? Mercifully, just then his phone rang. He grabbed it hoping for a friendly voice. It was his father.

"Hello, John. Is this you?"

"Yes Dad, God I'm so glad you called."

"John, please don't use God's name as an exclamation point. It offends me."

"Sorry Dad. Really; it just slipped out."

OK John. I believe you. I'm just calling to find out how you were. I was worried you had made it to Washington early this morning.

"No, no. As near as I can figure the bomb went off while I was still on my way to the airport. Except for the fact that I'm damn near a basket case right now, I'm fine." John winced when he realized he had inserted an expletive in his remark and considered apologizing, but decided against it. What would he say, sorry for saying 'damn' Dad? Pastor Franks ignored it.

"So what do we do now, son? I mean 'we' as a nation. Do we just hunker down and wait for the next one to fall? Should I start duct taping my windows?"

"Dad, I really don't need your sarcasm right now. You always do that. Every time there's a crisis of any kind you downplay it by making ridiculous remarks."

"I'm sorry, John. You're right. I am guilty of doing that. I think it's my way of dealing with stress. Anyway, I apologize. Seriously, though what are we going to do? More importantly, what are you going to do?"

"I wish to hell I knew," John sighed. Again he considered apologizing for his language, but his father cut him off before he could talk.

"That's not what I had hoped to hear. Are Teri and Maggie there?"

"No, I expect they'll be returning from church in a little while, though."

"Good woman, that wife of yours. I've always hoped that some of her belief would rub off on you, you know."

"Yes Dad, I know," John's tone made it clear that now was not the time.

"Well, would you mind if I called Teri on her cell and asked them to drop by and pick me up on their way home? I may be of some assistance to you in sorting through this mess."

"You know, that sounds like a great idea, Dad. Right now I feel very much in need of an older and wiser viewpoint."

"Thank you, Son. I love you. See you soon."

"I love you too, Dad." John put down the phone and pickled up the COG manual. As he paged through it he realized how much thought had gone into its preparation and how thoroughly the authors had worked out various scenarios and the proper responses to each.

Unfortunately, the responses too often seemed to be closing the barn doors after the horses were long gone. Everything was laid out as to what to do *after* a nuclear attack. Nothing was said about measures to prevent one. When he got to the last page and started to read his blood literally ran cold.

IN SUMMARY

This manual has been researched and prepared to assist our nation's elected representatives in the unlikely event of a sudden and unexpected nuclear attack. The mechanisms and guidelines the authors deem necessary for our country to continue functioning have all been implemented. The fact that you have this manual in your hands means that you are in a position to be a facilitator in this process. If you have carefully read this manual, you should know what priorities you must address and what actions you must take.

Lastly, should the unthinkable have happened and all elected representatives are thought to be deceased, refer to Chapter 9, Section G. This section outlines the powers and duties of the National Command Authority. The NCA consists of hundreds of well-trained dedicated men and women who are ready to assume the reins of leadership and provide continuity of operations for our country. You are urged to contact them as soon as possible and to assist them in their efforts. Refer to Executive Order H-2.

John found Executive Order H-2 on page 76. Based on its date, Herman had executed this order early in his presidency. It stipulated that in the event of a nuclear attack a waiting period of 48 hours would ensue. At the end of that time, if it was reasonably believed that the President, Vice-President and Speaker of the House were all deceased, the Authority of the Executive Branch would transfer to the head of the National Command Authority. Secondly, if a quorum could not be achieved in either the Senate or the House of Representatives these bodies would be suspended until such time as a proper election could be held.

"Bullshit!" John said aloud; "No way no how Mr. President. In the first place I do not believe that you have the authority to name your own successor. And I know for a fact that you do not have the authority to suspend the Senate or the House."

John Franks was a constitutional scholar and he dearly loved the thoughtful way the founders of our great nation had instilled a system of checks and balances to prevent any legislative branch from becoming so powerful that it stood alone and ran the country.

"No sir; this is not going to happen. Not as long as I'm alive." He said with finality.

CHAPTER 3 4

SUNDAY

GENERAL HASSAN HABIB sat forward in the high-backed executive chair and stared fixedly into the television camera. He was prepared to recite the speech he had rehearsed several times last night. His new uniform was uncomfortably tight, but it was necessary to lend credence to his words. He was accustomed to his comfortable shalvar kameez but his new position required a western style uniform as worn by officers of the Pakistan Army. As he had suggested, Imam Jamali had recently promoted him to General of the Provisional Army. This clearly made him a person of power and someone to take seriously.

By the Gregorian calendar it was 7:00 AM on Monday in Islamabad, which made it 9:00 PM in Washington D.C. That city would still be reeling from the nuclear strike he had engineered. Their overthrow of the incumbent Pakistani government had gone about as expected. He was seated in the office adjacent to President's office with the official government seal and the national flag of Pakistan behind him. At first Imam Jamali had planned to deliver this upcoming proclamation to the nation himself, but Hassan had convinced him that as the new President, it would seem below his station to be seen as a mere messenger.

"Consider, Mr. President," Hassan had rolled the words deliciously on his tongue; "which would you be more receptive to: a man declaring himself king, or a King who was announced as such by a high military official?"

Eventually Jamali agreed that someone else needed to break the ice and that he would appear later to put the official stamp on the changes.

When Hassan volunteered to be the messenger, Jamali hesitated and then agreed, but only if Hassan would accept a field promotion to General of the Armed Forces. Thus he would have sufficient authority to speak for President Jamali. Of course, Hassan had planted the seeds of this idea in the Imam's mind weeks ago, but Jamali had so many details going on in his head, he was unaware that this idea had not originated with him.

In fact, he was quite pleased with himself that he had come up with such a clever way to help secure his new power as President of Pakistan.

Hassan congratulated Jamali for his astute move and humbly accepted the call to duty. However, he suggested that perhaps his rank should be General of the *Provisional* Army, a designation he made up on the spot, so as not to anger the leadership of the standing Pakistani military forces who were their allies.

As the *General of the Provisional Army*, Hassan had equal rank with other military commanders which gave him sufficient clout. As chief advisor to President Jamali, he also occupied a position of power greater than that of the Prime Minister. As always, the Imam was pleased by the political adroitness of his trusted advisor and he implemented the idea without further discussion.

General Habib straightened his uniform one last time just as the cameras started to roll. A voice off screen said, "Attention people of Pakistan. Seated before you is General of the Pakistan Provisional Army Hassan Habib with an important message."

As Hassan spoke clearly and distinctly in English, his words appeared below him in a crawl written in Urdu, Punjabi and Pashto. It was immediately evident that this was a quality production using up-to-date technology; not some home video recorded on a hand held camera in some obscure location.

"My fellow Pakistanis and Afghan neighbors, Allah grants you peace and good fortune this day and in all days to come. Allahu Akbar. Allahu Akbar. Allahu Akbar. Today I have a message of great importance for you. Rejoice for you are now truly free. At last *Shar'ia* has come to both of our countries. Yesterday the Sword of Allah led by Imam Jamali and in concert with the Pakistan military forces, seized control of the government in Islamabad while our allies, the United Taliban Front staged a similar coup in Kabul. Both countries are now in control of true Islamic leaders."

The last statement was not true, but Hassan felt that only a total victory would provide the momentum they needed for drastic change. Besides, he was confident that the Taliban forces would eventually be victorious, so his statement was merely an eager anticipation of that event.

"This morning, in a special emergency session, the Pakistan Senate and National Assembly instituted charges of malfeasance in office against President Afir Ali Mahdari. He was impeached by acclamation and summarily removed from office. This action was initiated by the Muttahida Majlis-e-Amal party and was unanimously backed by a majority of every party's representatives including the PPP and both factions of the PML." He paused a moment for the importance of his declaration to sink in.

"In further action, Imam Muhammad Jamali of the MMA party was elected by acclamation to the office of President. Prime Minister Sura Malani has retained his office and has pledged to work with the new regime to establish true Islamic Shar-ia in our beloved country. Lastly, I am proud to announce the Sword of Allah has detonated a nuclear weapon in the United States capitol city of Washington D.C. Later in this video we will show satellite images of the destructive power unleashed by this weapon. Now, it is my great honor to introduce our new President Muhammad Jamali."

The image changed to a head and shoulders shot of the Imam seated in the executive office. He had a warm friendly look on his face and he spoke softly, "My dear people of Islam and fellow countrymen, today you are witnessing the greatest step forward in all of Pakistan's glorious history. Today we begin our journey to become a true nation of Islam as decreed in the *Qur'an*. Today at last, we can look forward to living in true *Shar'ia*. Our beloved country and our good friends and neighbors in Afghanistan will live in harmony and unity and in accordance with Allah's wishes.

To accomplish this tremendous goal we, the Sword of Allah have taken *Jihad* to a new level. Even now as I speak, the city of Washington D.C. lies in ruins and is burning to the ground, devastated by the nuclear weapon we detonated. We have cut off Satan's Head.

If any leaders of the United States are still alive, I urge you to heed my words: we have five more such devices hidden in large American cities. We demand that you immediately withdraw all military forces from Pakistan and Afghanistan. If you do not act on my warning immediately, I personally will order the detonation of these weapons.

Finally, my Pakistani brothers and sisters I urge you to spread the word of the momentous events going on in your country and to celebrate with family, friends and neighbors. Allahu Akbar. Allahu Akbar. Allahu Akbar."

With these final words President Jamali's face was replaced with satellite images of the city of Washington D.C. in flames. The images remained on screen for several minutes without sound. It created an awesome and eerily disturbing effect. Then, without warning the screen went blank. Every viewer sat in stunned silence for several moments. After a while some erupted in joyful cheers; many looked about at other viewers to assess their reactions before reacting themselves, a few wept, but most just tried to control their fear and anger.

CHAPTER 3 5

SUNDAY

THE D.C. FIRE fighters who survived the initial blast were simply overwhelmed. The city boasted 33 fire stations with 33 engines, 39 EMS units, two fire boats, two emergency aircraft and a staff of over 2,000 dedicated individuals who were ready to put their lives on the line at a moment's notice day in and day out. Two thirds of this force was wiped out by the destructive force of the largest nuclear weapon ever detonated on U.S. soil.

The remaining 600 plus brave men and women were hampered by their lack of functional radios and electrical equipment; still they jumped into their ambulances and engines and responded as well as possible to the chaos that surrounded them. Their vehicles had been turned off when the bomb went off so the EMF wave did not affect the electrical systems of the engines, but their radios, phones and computers were on 24/7. Radio silence was maintained not by choice but by necessity.

There was no way for them to assess the boundaries of the 'no go' zone; the area closest to the epicenter of the blast within which no survivors would be expected. In the early minutes these first responders where not even aware of what they were dealing with. They knew something immense had happened and many suspected a nuclear attack, but no one knew for sure. Their job was to save as many lives and buildings as possible.

Watch Commander Harold Putz surveyed the futile efforts of his men as they struggled to put out fires. Despite his unfortunate name, he was well respected and had risen in the ranks quickly. He actually enjoyed the "putz" jibes. Everywhere they went electrical fires were springing up and ruptured gas lines were exploding while their efforts to contain the hundreds of fires around them were thwarted because water lines also were broken.

"Listen up everybody," Commander Putz yelled at the top of his deep voice, "Stop trying to save the buildings. Concentrate on assisting victims and turning off ruptured gas lines." He sent runners in all directions to pass the order on to other firefighters.

After awhile, the firemen even gave up trying to contain the fires; instead they started setting up Incident Command Posts. After some confusion and exchange of information via runners, they managed to coordinate their efforts well enough to establish four ICPs situated at roughly equal intervals all around the perimeter of the main devastation.

From these outposts they frantically searched for survivors and began treating the tens of thousands of victims. The dead were left where they were found. There was no time for the identification and body bagging of the corpses. That would have to wait for later when the graves registration crew arrived.

The dead outnumbered the survivors two to one; yet there were still too many survivors to handle. The firemen were forced to streamline the triage system because of the sheer number of casualties. Anyone seriously burned or wounded was considered 'beyond saving' and segregated in separate areas from survivors who had a chance of recovering. The workers soon dubbed the serious injury area the 'BS', ward because the people in it were given virtually no treatment. At best they were given a relatively comfortable place to lie down to await their demise. The cries of pain in the'BS'ward seriously demoralized the rescue teams.

Fireman Henry Cummins couldn't stand it. Maybe he was too sensitive over human suffering, or perhaps he put his own discomfort ahead of the needs of others.

Which explanation you believed depended on whether you agreed with the defense attorney or the prosecutor.

*   *   *

In any case, Henry had stood among the dead and dying and he made a decision. He took the Adz-Maul Pro Set hanging from a belt over his shoulder and disconnected the adz from the 8 pound maul. This tool was used for tearing into the side of a burning building for venting or to gain entry. It was a 'must tool' for any professional firefighter. The adz itself consisted of a metal handle with a pry bar on one end and a chisel and spike on the other. The spike was about 3 inches long and looked like an eagle's talon. It was sharp.

Henry casually roamed about the "BS' area seeking out those in the greatest pain. When he found one, and it seemed no one was looking, he quickly drove the adz into the skull of the suffering person, thus ending his or her unbearable pain in an instant. He then wiped the gore off the spike and sought out his next 'mercy mission'.

∗   ∗   ∗

At his murder trial the prosecutor stipulated that there were 84 confirmed dead from his efforts and another 14 possible.

∗   ∗   ∗

Henry might even have gotten away with it, but he began to see that he couldn't keep up with the need by himself. There were simply too many serious casualties for one man to dispatch in a timely manner. His mistake was in thinking that his fellow firefighter and good friend Jim Burdick would agree with his actions.

"Jim, have you ever experienced anything as horrible as this?" Henry asked him with tears in his eyes.

"I've seen some shit, but this one takes the cake." Burdick replied. He was bending over a man whose right leg was missing below the knee. He had used the man's belt as a tourniquet.

The man grimaced in pain as Jim helped him up and started to lead him to the critical care site where he would be transported to a hospital or other emergency unit. Henry quickly jumped to the man's other side to assist. As they walked, they talked. The man was in too much pain to join in the conversation.

"I've never seen so much pain in one location," Henry ventured.

"Yeah, the B.S. area is the worst," Jim agreed.

"I just can't stand listening to all the crying and screaming," Henry continued. They stepped around a burned out car and turned down what remained of a decimated street toward the critical care site.

"It's hard. That's for sure." Jim said. "But, what can we do about it? We ran out of pain management drugs in ten minutes."

"Well, maybe we can do something," Henry said. He waited for a response. After they deposited the man at the critical care site, Jim and Henry turned to go back to the area they had just come from.

"What the hell could we do?" Jim asked Henry. Henry paused and looked into the eyes of his long time friend and fellow fire fighter. He made another decision.

"Follow me," he said.

"What the hell; where are we going, Hank?" Jim followed him into the B.S. zone. Without a word Cummins took out his adz and headed for a woman who looked like a corpse. She was lying on the street. She was burned over most of her body including her face and scalp. Her eyelids were burned off and she whimpered in pain. He stood out of range of her vision, looked at Jim and then drove his adz into her skull. She stopped whimpering immediately.

"Jesus Christ, Hank!" Burdick yelled. "What in the hell do you think you're doing?"

"I am showing compassion, Jim." Henry said quietly. "I was hoping you'd help me."

"You're out of your fucking mind!" Jim exclaimed. He was horrified and immediately went in search of the watch commander who placed Henry under arrest.

*   *   *

Six months after the bombing, Henry went on trial. He explained his reasoning and his compassion for the victims. The jury deliberated only six hours before finding him guilty of 84 counts of first degree murder. Henry was sentenced to 84 consecutive life terms in prison without chance of parole.

Most of the first responder crew did not learn of Henry's actions until days later. It became the subject of much discussion; many were simply dumbstruck and could not understand what had gotten into the seasoned veteran. Some, the pragmatists, thought it was just the stress of the situation; maybe even Post-Traumatic-Stress-Disorder. A few said they understood what prompted Henry to do as he did and they wished they had had the compassion to do the same. Three even wrote letters to that effect which were read aloud by the defense attorney at Henry's trial. The jury dismissed them as 'examples of cronyism'.

Henry's story received national attention in the news and became a symbol of the entire horrible experience perpetrated by the cold blooded terrorists. Newspaper polls showed that about forty-five percent of Americans considered him a sociopathic killer. Another forty-five percent deemed him to be a humanitarian they would want as a neighbor. Eight percent were 'undecided' and the final two percent said "Huh?"

*   *   *

The wounded and burned citizens who were able to walk were lead on foot to the nearest hospital, clinic, emergency center or critical care center. Within thirty to forty minutes there wasn't a free bed in any of the facilities within walking distance of any of the ICPs.

The more seriously wounded victims were transported by ambulance, truck or engine to care units that were further away. These too were soon filled to capacity. Just when the first responders were tearing their hair out trying to come up with a solution to this dilemma, volunteers from the small fire departments and independent rescue squads in the local communities began to arrive.

They took over the immediate care and transportation of the victims to the care units and hospitals in their communities. These too were soon forced to turn away all but the most critically injured.

With much of the initial burden of caring for the wounded off their shoulders, the first responders turned their attention to setting up a Radiation Triage and Treatment System. There was actually not all that much help they could provide. Each of them wore protective clothing and gas masks as well as dosimeters which told them how many rads their bodies had absorbed. By the time they had established the RTTS, their alarms were going off which meant they had to abandon their efforts and get out of the radioactive zone before it killed them too.

"All right everybody," Putz yelled. It's time to get out of here. I am ordering all of you to leave with me. We will be heading as a group further away from the epicenter."

Many wanted to stay "at least a little longer." The commander tried to convince the dedicated rescue workers to grab as many victims as possible and to get into their vehicles and go. He had to remind them that hundreds of Disaster Management Assistance Teams (specially trained volunteers from emergency rooms and rescue squads from around the country) were no doubt on their way as he spoke.

Finally, he drew his revolver and fired a shot into the air.

"God damn it, I'm getting out of here and you're coming with me now!" He said sternly. They agreed to leave, but had they been aware that all aircraft were grounded and therefore the DMATs were driving and would not begin to arrive for hours, many would have stayed.

They left behind as many bottles of Potassium Iodide Tablets as they could at each ICP. It would be like putting a band aid on someone missing an arm, but they reasoned that some hope for surviving radiation poisoning was better than none. It wouldn't hurt and it may help ease the minds of some casualties. It made many of the rescue workers feel like hypocrites.

*   *   *

The Homeland Security Administration was wiped out along with all the other federal departments in the city. The Transportation Security Commission which oversaw all trucking and shipping also was gone. To the credit of hundreds of mid-management personnel around the country, the correct actions were taken even without orders from above.

The Port Authorities in every major port city shut down. All incoming cargo ships were subject to thorough room by room searches to locate anything that might appear suspicious or illegal. Likewise, the Coast Guard went on full alert and began patrolling all along America's vulnerable coastlines, boarding ships and conducting searches before they were allowed to enter the ports.

The Border Protection crews placed the entire country under lockdown. No one was allowed in. Within less than an hour after detonation, the bomb had resulted in the entire country being sealed off.

*   *   *

The Inter-agency Modeling Atmospheric & Assessment Center was charged with providing critical weather data during national emergencies. They were directly connected to 37 Primary Entry Point radio stations around the country. These PEP stations would broadcast information and updates that could impact on people's survival chances. Right now the most critical need was for the IMAAC to track the speed and direction of the radioactive mushroom cloud. Of course, the EMF wave had fried their computers and phones just like everywhere else within a twenty mile radius of the epicenter. The experts sat helplessly by and watched the cloud drift north and east and they could do nothing to warn anyone.

*   *   *

If you were to ask whether any good came out of this devastating attack, perhaps two things could be said.

This was the wake-up call America needed. Every single citizen now recognized the threat posed by terrorist organizations. A cold shiver went down America's collective spine and galvanized awareness and protective measures in ways that the attack of September 11 2001 never had.

More importantly, people questioned why we had been so stupid in the first place. Why had we located every single federal office, every elected official and our primary military headquarters all in one convenient place where one bomb could take them all out? No one seemed able to provide a plausible answer to this question. With today's advanced communication options there was simply no reason that a senator needed to be in the same room with every other senator to discuss, debate and vote on a bill. By logical extension, the same thing applied to congressmen, the president and every head of every federal department. But, these were future considerations to be dealt with at a future time. Right now, America was still reeling from the deadly blow dealt to its collective smugness.

CHAPTER 36

SUNDAY

JOHN FRANKS DESCENDED the stairs in his home to where his wife, daughter and father were sitting in the living/dining room and announced that he had made a decision. They all looked at him expectantly and no one said a word. Teri muted the sound on the TV. Every channel was broadcasting the same thing: updates on the devastation in D.C.

"Based on the information on TV, I think we can all agree that our country is for all intents and purposes without leadership. Already we're beginning to see looters and gang activities as well as ordinary citizens breaking the law and raiding stores. I believe it is necessary for martial law to be declared to bring order. However, I do not know who is left alive that has the authority to do that. I also fear that, if and when martial law is instituted, we may not be able to undo it.

They all began to speak at once and John shushed them. They all quit talking.

"I've decided that my most important task at this time is to let people know that I am alive and to find out how many other elected officials have survived. So, I'm going to go to Channel 4 and request that I am allowed to broadcast to as many people as possible that I am here and that any other Congressmen, Senators and federal department heads should get in touch with me as soon as possible."

"Excellent idea," Pastor Franks said almost to himself.

"Way to go, Dad," Maggie loudly agreed.

"All right, John…if you say so," Teri said.

"Why did you say, if I say so?" John asked.

"I was just wondering where you would have them contact you. We're not equipped here to handle thousands of phone calls or emails. It could be a disaster."

"That's my Teri," John said with a smile, "always the smart and practical one. OK, I'll go to the phone company first and set up a call room with multiple phones and computers. Thanks, sweet heart." Just then the doorbell rang. It startled everyone. It seemed unlikely that anyone would be out and about during this national crisis. John started toward the door but Maggie headed him off. "I'll get it, Dad. You're too important to risk answering a door when we don't know who it is." John allowed her to get past him and to the door. "Who is it?" She called out.

It's Randy Quinn" a young voice answered. "You don't know me, but I'm a neighbor of yours from four doors down." Maggie opened the door a crack and saw a freckle-faced teenager standing on the porch. "What do you want, Randy?" She asked cautiously.

"I have an important message for the Senator," Randy answered. "I'm a Ham Radio operator and I am in contact with someone named General Birch. He needs to talk to the senator." Maggie stepped back and swung the door wide, "Please come in, she said. Then she called out "Dad, it's for you."

Within minutes, John was at his neighbor's house and on the radio with General Birch. He picked up the microphone and depressed the send key. John knew radio protocol.

"Hello, General Birch. Are you there, over?"

"Yes, Senator, I'm here, over."

"Where are you, over?"

"I'm at my house in Camp Springs, Maryland. I own a little place next to the eighth hole on the Andrews Air Force base golf course. How are you doing, over?"

"I'm just fine. A little rattled but, OK. It's good to hear your voice, over."

"Well, that's one I don't hear very often," the general chuckled. What are your plans, over?"

"Not too much yet; I'm still trying to get organized. So Camp

Springs is far enough away from DC to avoid the EMF wave that knocked out communications, over?

"Hardly," Birch said. "I'm sitting here in the dark and it looks like every electrical device in the area has been fried. The only reason I'm able to talk to you is that I own a battery-operated Ham Radio set, over."

"Thank God, you do," John said and was glad his father wasn't there to hear it. Sam, this was the big one, right? The one we feared, over?"

"God help me, I'm afraid so, Senator. The blast was so huge it had to be the W80-1. I don't know how after all these years, but I don't have any other answer, over."

"General, I could use your help. Can you get to Wisconsin, over?"

"You know that all aircraft are sitting on tarmacs at airports and air force bases, right? Fortunately my car was turned off and sitting in my garage when the wave hit, so I could drive. But it's at least nine hundred miles and I don't know what condition the 'I' system is in, over."

"Sam, I don't care if you have to bike here. Just get your ass to Madison ASAP, over."

"Yes sir, Senator Franks, sir. Lighten up. I'll be there as soon as I can, over."

"Thanks, Sam. I really do need help here. Along that line, how close are you to Huntington, Virginia, over?"

"Huntington? It's right off I-95. I go past it whenever I'm heading west why, over?"

"My secretary lives there. I need you to find her and bring her with you. I don't know her address but her name is Estelle Evans, over."

"Estelle Evans in Huntington got it. Anything else you want? Should I pick up a gallon of milk or a loaf of bread on the way, over?"

"Just get here as soon as you can. Oh, and Sam? Thank you, over and out."

General Birch stared at his radio and listened to the static for a moment, then, he grinned, picked it up and began packing for his trip. John thanked Randy and his parents for the use of the ham radio and assured them that their son had done his country a great service today. Then he returned home to find his father, wife and daughter in the midst of a heated discussion. It soon became apparent that Teri was worried because he was going to go on television and people were bound to start showing up at their door or calling them on the phone. His father and daughter felt he had no choice.

John halted the squabble by shouting out over everyone else, "OK, OK, everyone. That's enough; its family council time right now." He waited until everyone was seated and stood in front of them.

"First, let me tell you something you do not know. I've been reading my COG manual, Dad, you already know what that is, but let me explain to Teri and Maggie. It's a Continuity of Government plan for times of national emergency. It contains plans and explanations on how things will function to keep our country from being leaderless in the event of a major attack such as what happened today. Based on the news it seems pretty reasonable to assume the worst in our nation's capitol. I don't know if anyone in the city survived and I'm guessing that virtually every elected official and every appointed administrator is dead or disabled." Maggie gasped. She had suspected this already, but it was hard to hear her father confirm her suspicions aloud. Teri started to cry softly and the senior Franks looked down at his shoes.

"The good news is we have been preparing for this for many years." He gave them the brief history of how it started with Churchill and Eisenhower. "President Ronald Reagan took it another step further. He put together an entire crew of appointed administrators who were ready to step in and take over if our government should fall. Conspiracy theorists had a field day with this. Some called it the 'Shadow Government'. I vaguely remember something in the news at the time. Some group, I think it was the American Freedom Foundation, challenged the constitutionality of his action. I don't remember the result. Now I don't have any details, but from what I've read and been told, this process has been more or less continued by every president since. Today we have some 90 Continuity of Government sites within a 300 mile radius of D.C. If my information is accurate, they are fully staffed and run by 12 man teams. If this is true, and I believe it is, we don't have to worry about day to day operations of the country. The mail will continue to be delivered, banks will stay open, Social Security checks and Medicare benefits will be paid, etc."

"Well, John I for one am glad to hear that," his father stated. Teri and Maggie agreed. Then Maggie asked, "Dad, does this mean you're out of a job?" John gave a short laugh.

"No Magpie. My job is guaranteed by the constitution. But, you do raise an interesting issue, one I've been wrestling with since early this morning. The constitution provides a system to maintain an orderly transition of power. Should the president die, or be unable to perform the duties of his office, the vice president steps in. If the vice president cannot or will not accept the office, the speaker of the house is next in succession. That was about as far as the constitution ever went. Apparently, none of the founding fathers could envision the need for a longer system of succession. Through the years Congress and the White House managed to pass some laws which dealt with that issue and provided for transition beyond the speaker of the house. However, nobody was prepared for the entire federal government to be wiped out."

"My God," Teri exclaimed and looked sheepishly at her father-in-law, "you mean you might be the only one left?"

"I certainly hope not," John said with a sigh. "But, until I hear otherwise, I need to operate as if that is the situation."

"Wow," Maggie said and stared unseeing into the room. Finally, she looked at her father and said, "Dad, if this succession thing is what you say it is you might be President now."

"Good lord," Teri said and this time looked away from Pastor Franks.

"Technically, you might be right, honey. The question is, President of what?"

"Well, that settles it," Teri stated with finality in her voice. "You absolutely need to let everyone know you're alive. You need to get to that TV station now. Don't you agree, Dad?"

"Yes, yes I do." Pastor Franks said with just a hint of doubt in his voice.

"You do agree, don't you?" Teri was surprised by how he now seemed hesitant, where earlier he was all for it. Truth be told, the Pastor was having some second thoughts spurred by his son's remark: 'the question is, president of what?' Indeed, what kind of democracy did America have today? Did it even have a democratic form of government now? What would his son be up against? He decided it was time for a prayer. Quietly he started the Lord's Prayer; soon Teri and Maggie were reciting it along with him. When they got to "…give us this day our daily bread" John joined them.

CHAPTER 37

SUNDAY

GENERAL SAMUEL BIRCH packed for a lengthy road trip. He dressed in civilian clothes, and hung his dress uniform carefully in his travel bag along with several well-pressed shirts on a bar across his back seat. His underwear and toiletries were in a small overnight bag on the rear seat. His holstered .45 caliber hand gun lay next to it. His ham radio sat next to that. He believed in being prepared for any eventuality. He turned off the water and the gas in his house and drained the toilets to prevent freezing in the event of a cold snap. He elected not to bring his golf clubs. He locked the house up securely and gave it one last look over his shoulder while climbing into his 2011 4-wheel drive Hummer. He loved this vehicle.

It was almost noon by the time he actually got started and he felt like an adventurer because he had no idea what he was facing. Information from ham radio operators was spotty. Some had not even been aware of the attack on Washington. Others had heard varying accounts of how extensive the damage was. One thing was clear almost immediately, the EMF wave that had hit his area had to have been huge. Within half a mile of leaving his driveway he began to encounter stalled and wrecked cars and trucks. Fortunately, they were scattered along the road and he was able to maneuver around them without much difficulty. Remarkably, they all seemed to be abandoned. He was alone.

As he headed north on Branch Avenue toward I-95, the number of wrecked vehicles began to increase and he had to stop twice to provide first Aid. In a fourth car he found a baby crying in a car seat. The car had apparently slammed full speed into a bridge abutment under an overpass. The parents, who had not been wearing seat-belts, were dead. The baby, a little girl, seemed unhurt. He grabbed the child and the carrier she was in and gave her some water. After strapping her into his back seat in her car carrier, he continued on.

He figured he could drop her at a hospital or something. When he got within eyesight of the I-95 on-ramp he saw that there was no way he was going to get onto the Interstate. The little girl started to cry louder. It was no longer an adventure. He turned the car around and headed back the way he had come. At last, here was Andrews Air Force base. He pulled up to the gate which was down. Two Air Police sentries came to a parade rest on either side of his car.

"Halt and state your business," the Staff Sergeant said.

"Personal business," he answered. "I need to drop off a survivor for medical attention."

"Sorry sir, no one is allowed on base without prior authorization. We are on Defcon 3 alert status."

"God damn it, I am Lieutenant General Samuel Birch from the fucking pentagon. Let me talk to your base commander." The two men snapped to attention and smartly saluted. The General returned their salute.

"Sorry sir, your rank is not indicated on your vehicle," the sergeant said as he handed the General a phone. "I punched in the number for our commanding officer's phone. He is General Oliver Sturtz, sir." Birch took the phone.

"This is my private vehicle sergeant," he said. "I don't want to have my rank on it."

"No sir." The sergeant replied. "I was just…"

"Hello Ollie," the General said loudly cutting him off. It's Sam Birch."

"Sam, how are you doing, long time no see." General Sturtz answered.

"Too long, Ollie; too long and I'm not going to be able to stop for a visit. I'm just dropping off a package then I have to head out again immediately."

"Sorry to hear that. Well, just show the sentries an ID and do what you need to do. Does it have to do with our current crisis, Sam?"

"I'm afraid that's classified, Ollie." Birch did not want to tell him he was dropping off a baby. At the current alert status everything was top secret and filled with red tape. He wanted to get in and get out fast.

"Have you heard about Pakistan and Afghanistan?" Sturtz asked.

"No. What are those assholes up to now?" Birch shot back.

"It's looking like the D.C. attack was coordinated with a coup in Pakistan and an attempted one by the Taliban in Afghanistan. The only reason the Afghan take over has not been successful so far is because our troops are fighting on behalf of the current government."

"Have you heard anything from above, Ollie?"

"Sorry Sam, that's classified."

"Touche', Ollie. Thanks for the info."

"Good luck, Sam."

After speaking with their commanding officer, the sentries fell over themselves trying to be of help to Birch. They gave him explicit directions to the nearest infirmary and offered to escort him. He found it by himself and promptly dropped his problem off on the first nurse he saw when he entered the building. There were some perks to being a general.

Since he couldn't get to Huntington on I-95, he would need to find a back route. He headed south on Highway 5 to Highway 301 along the Potomac. Then he turned right on 218 and crossed the river into Virginia where he picked up Highway 1 and headed north again. This became the Richmond Highway and he followed that into Huntington.

He figured the detour had cost him at least an hour and a half. Except for people milling in the streets, Huntington was at a standstill. Traffic lights were inoperable and cars were stalled or crashed everywhere he looked. He finally found a phone book at an outside kiosk and looked up the address for Estelle Evans. He was in luck; she lived at 211 Peach Tree Street and it was a main drag. He found it on the map in the phone book and determined where he was. It was a snap to get to her house.

As he drove up, General Birch found himself wondering how a secretary could afford such a nice apartment in such an upper middle class neighborhood. I guess typing letters pays better than I realized, he thought. When he found out later that it was actually a two story town house which she owned, it gave him pause to think some more. Maybe it had been a mistake to make a career out of the military.

He rang the doorbell and stepped back to the edge of the little concrete stoop. He stood there for a few moments and then rang the bell again, a little longer this time. In a little while he heard a sleepy voice behind the door, "who is it?"

"It's Lieutenant General Samuel Birch," he answered. "Are you Estelle Evans?"

General Birch? Estelle wiped the sleep out of her left eye and asked herself where she had heard that name before. Then it hit her, it was general fuck-up!

"Uh, just a second sir," she said. Then she ran her fingers through her hair and straightened up her robe as best she could. She put on a nice smile and opened the door about half way. "How can I help you general?"

"You can start by inviting me in," he said impatiently. Didn't this dumb blonde secretary understand that she was talking to a superior officer?

"Can I see some ID, please?" Estelle did not respond well to being ordered around. She took longer than necessary to verify that he was who he said he was, and asked, "What do you want?"

Exasperated, he said "I don't want a god dam thing, but your boss, Senator Franks wants you in Wisconsin." At the mention of her boss, her attitude changed and she let the general in.

She explained that she had slept in because she and her boyfriend had been up late the night before. He had left around 5 am and she had gone back to sleep. Over the next couple of hours, Estelle learned that Washington D.C. was no more and that it was almost a certainty that Don had been killed. It was a lot to absorb and General Birch actually treated her with compassion.

It didn't hurt that once Estelle had cleaned herself up and put on fresh make-up, along with a cute but professional dress she was a knockout. She enjoyed the effect she was having on the old goat. Sam wished he had worn his uniform. Women were impressed by rank.

They finally got going around 5 pm. General Birch was appalled by the number of suitcases Estelle required. She had one bag just for shoes. They managed to get everything loaded into the back of the Hummer and headed west on Highway 644. They decided to take turns driving, after Estelle convinced Sam that she was capable of handling the massive vehicle. Sam picked up I-64 which he said they would take all the way to Louisville, Kentucky. There they would turn onto I-65 north to Chicago. Lastly they'd get on I-90 west to Madison, Wisconsin. Stopping only to gas up, use a bathroom and grab a bite to eat, they should make the trip in 20 hours. Estelle listened half-heartedly to his itinerary and stared straight ahead trying to ignore the stalled and wrecked vehicles they were going by.

Once they were about twenty miles west of Huntington, the highway started to clear and they began to pick up radio stations. The dismal news updates about Washington helped to keep them both awake for the first six hours. Neither of them spoke much. Estelle was prone to breaking out in tears periodically. She tried not to do it when the general was awake.

General Birch tried to tune in a PEP station without success. They flipped back and forth between radio stations. Most were concentrating on the D.C. disaster and providing such news updates as were available. One station in Charleston, WV was constantly re-broadcasting a taped speech which had been simul-cast nationally on both TV and radio. This they listened to in its entirety twice: *"My fellow Americans, this is Senator John Franks in Wisconsin. I am broadcasting to you live from the studios of channel 4, WMAX in Madison. It is difficult to find the words to express my sorrow and my horror at today's events.*

In the unlikely case that you have not heard, I regret to inform you that our nation's capitol came under attack early this morning. A large nuclear weapon of undetermined size and origin was detonated in the center of the city. The number of people killed and injured is still mounting and the city and surrounding areas lay in ruins.

He paused to chide himself. He was starting to sound like a news reporter sensationalizing the event. He needed to watch his tone.

"Initial reports from people outside the blast zone indicate that it is likely that all federal offices and government buildings including the White House and the Capitol have been destroyed. Because tomorrow was the scheduled day for the Inauguration of our new President and Vice President, we must assume that most if not all government representatives were within the greater metropolitan area at the time of detonation.

As he listened to himself he regretted that there hadn't been time to put his remarks on a teleprompter.

Let me re-phrase that. Since I was here in Madison, obviously not all representatives were in D.C. This brings me to the main purpose of this broadcast. Please pass the word that I am indeed alive and still functioning as a United States Senator. I urge all other senators, congressmen and government administrators to contact me as soon as possible. I have set up a complete call center with phones, fax machines and computers here in Madison. Contact information will be provided at the conclusion of this message.

My family and I offer each and every viewer or listener our sincere condolences and our promise to stand beside you as we weather this atrocious attack on our nation. I will now pass on some information about recent developments. Please bear with me as I read from the notes being handed to me. Apparently a terrorist group in Pakistan has claimed responsibility for the strike. Oh my god, er…excuse me a second."

The senator could be heard talking off camera to someone. Then he returned to his place in front of the camera. To those watching on TV, he looked shaken. Sam and Estelle could hear it in his voice.

Fox News has just reported, and I just verified it with station management, that the terrorist group has demanded that we and all of our United Nations allies withdraw all military personnel and equipment from Afghanistan and Pakistan. They have threatened that if we do not comply, they will detonate five more bombs in five large American cities.

He dropped the paper and looked into the camera.

"I don't know what to say to that."

He paused for a moment and looked out at the television crew. A couple of them were shaking their heads "no". Apparently, they agreed with him.

"Actually I do know what to say. I do not believe them. I think if these murdering savages had more nuclear weapons they would have used them. I will be seeking counsel as to what response we should initiate.

On a similar vein, a word to our military forces; I assume we are at Defcon 2 or 3. Please, remain on Defcon stable for now. Do not, I repeat do not *initiate any reprisals. We will deal with the criminals who did this when the time is right. Please continue to use discretion.*

I am proud of how our military leaders have responded so far, and I urge continued cool heads and self control. A further message to all nuclear armed nations, I am sure you have been on alert and have your missiles poised awaiting America's response to this cowardly and deadly attack on our homeland. Please rest assured that the United States is committed to a peaceful resolution. It is inconceivable to me that anyone in our great nation would even consider a nuclear response against even a confirmed enemy. We have been grievously wounded, but we will not strike out blindly to exact retribution. You have my word on that.

Finally, to my fellow Americans, in this, your hour of loss, remember the strength of our great country. Born of revolution, we were founded under the principles and ideals that all men are created free and equal. We have endured numerous conflicts as well as lengthy wars, both civil and world-wide. We have always emerged victorious and stronger. Most importantly let us remember-our democratic government does not consist of buildings and officials in Washington D.C. Our democratic way of life lives in the hearts and minds of our citizens. It lives in your belief and your resolve. Because of this, "we the people" will never be defeated. This is Senator John Franks bidding you goodbye and god speed. Please stay tuned for the phone numbers and email addresses to contact me.

After a brief pause the message was repeated.

Estelle was the first to comment, "That is so typical of the Senator. Always thinking of others first. Always ready to step up and take the lead. I'm so proud of him."

"Yeah, he definitely stepped up," general Birch agreed. I just hope he hasn't also stepped into the crosshairs."

"What do you mean?" Estelle said abruptly. "What crosshairs?"

"Miss Evans," the general said condescendingly, "your boss has just told the world where to find him. He practically drew a map and put out a welcome mat. Apparently, he didn't stop to think that he has a world full of people who would like to see him dead.

I would be surprised if there wasn't already a Fatwa put on his head by the terrorists, not to mention your normal run-of-the-mill nut cases who would love to be in the history books as one of the world's greatest assassins. Of course, there are also the non-elected people who will soon be running the country. They won't want to lose their jobs because the duly elected representatives have shown up again.

Lastly, any self-styled leader of some survivalist group or subversive force will see him as a hindrance to their plans of empire. Get the picture?"

"Holy shit," Estelle said with a look of panic on her face.

"Holy shit is right," the general said. "I hope we get to him before someone else does."

Unconsciously he stepped a little harder on the gas pedal and began passing other cars. Now that he had said it out loud, he was even more worried for the Senator than he had been.

CHAPTER 3 8

MONDAY, JANUARY 21, 2013

AROUND 6:00 PM Sunday night the phones in the Franks household had started ringing. At first the closest family member would answer. Most callers fell into one of three categories: fearful citizens asking what they should do or what was the senator going to do now, news reporters asking what people should do now or what was the senator going to do next, and angry nutcases telling the senator what he had to do now and threatening physical harm if he didn't do it. After awhile the family stopped picking up and let the answering machine take over. Finally they just unplugged all the phones in the house. Without thinking, Teri accidentally unplugged the phone in John's upstairs office along with all the others.

*   *   *

At 6:05 AM Senator John Franks stumbled down the stairs into his living room. He was only half awake after a very restless night. He found his father sitting in his robe watching TV. His father said, "Good morning. Take a look at this." On the screen was a news reporter talking about 'the last bastion of democracy'. Behind him was the front of their house. This woke John up completely and now he could hear the sounds of a crowd outside. He went over to the front bay window and pulled the drape aside just enough to peek out. The crowd went wild, yelling and waving and asking him to come out. There were 3 mobile TV units and 4 mobile radio units. Cameras and reporters were everywhere. Behind them was an anxious crowd of gawkers. The doorbell was ringing continually. John closed the drape, stepped back into the room and said, "Holy shit."

"Pretty much my sentiments too," Pastor Franks said. John went into the kitchen and made a pot of coffee in his instant brew machine.

He brought a cup out for both of them and sat next to his dad on the sofa. His father had stayed with them throughout the long Sunday, and had accepted their offer to stay the night in their guest room.

"Son, do you truly believe that there are no further bombs? What makes you so sure you're right?"

"All I have is gut instinct, dad. I have just never known a terrorist to use discretion. If this group had more bombs, they would have used them."

"God knows I hope you're right," Pastor Franks said as he took a sip of coffee.

"God help me. I better be." John said.

"I didn't even know you believed in God," the Pastor retorted.

"Dad, how many times do I have to tell you; I believe in God. It's religion I can't swallow." His father turned away and concentrated on his coffee.

∗　　　∗　　　∗

John had come directly home after his TV announcement yesterday and asked how he had done. They all told him he had been marvelous. He didn't believe them. Eventually, after they unplugged the phones, the entire family had sat watching the news until midnight.

The threat of five more nuclear bombs in five large American cities had created an unprecedented panic. The freeway systems near the cities of New York, Baltimore, Miami, Atlanta, Pittsburgh, Detroit, Chicago, Denver, Kansas City, Houston, Los Angeles, San Francisco and Seattle became parking lots. Many smaller cities were paralyzed in a similar manner. It was the largest mass exodus in U.S. history. Hundreds of lives were lost.

The Senator cringed as he watched the televised scenes of traffic jams and listened to the incessant honking of horns. Other enterprising TV camera crews were covering the looting and burning going on in the cities. For the most part city police forces, already short-handed because many of their officers were part of the exodus, had quit trying to halt the looters and concentrated instead on controlling the vandalism. The term used frequently by the media was 'mass hysteria'. It was an understatement. By 7:00 PM, both Canada and Mexico had closed their borders. No one was being allowed into either country. Smugglers, who knew the back routes, started offering their services openly on the streets of border towns and were doing a booming and lucrative business.

The worst impact was on the towns and states bordering the large cities as literally hundreds of thousands of refugees descended on them.

Madison, Wisconsin like the cities of Kenosha, Racine, Janesville and several little towns along the Illinois border were inundated with people fleeing from Chicago. It taxed every system to the limit and beyond. Imagine sitting quietly in your home and fifty relatives suddenly show up asking for room and board, not just for the night, but for the next few weeks. The resulting logistic problems aggravated the chaos.

*   *   *

The smell of coffee had awoken Teri and Margaret. They came out of the kitchen in their robes with cups of coffee and sat in the recliners by the sofa. Neither said anything at first, then

Maggie yawned and said, "Man, I hope this mess is all over in time for my wedding." John, Teri, and Charles just looked at her in disbelief and said nothing. Maggie, adjusted her robe and squared her shoulders and said, "What?" Everyone turned their attention back to the TV.

John changed channels with the remote and there was the front of their house again. "...the revelation yesterday that a U.S. Senator from Wisconsin was alive, we've been trying to get a live interview. Channel 6, WIRK has obtained word from the Senator's call center that no other elected officials have tried to contact him. The phone company has refused to give details but company spokesman Ralph Meyers said that all contacts have been from private citizens and/or the news media. He did admit there were several crank calls and threats, but would not give details. Meanwhile, we continue to wait outside the senator's home hoping to learn what his plans are for the future." John muted the sound and said, "Well, that's the $64 question, isn't it?" The doorbell rang again.

"Do you want me to get that and stall them?" Teri said. Then she remembered she was still in her robe and was glad when John didn't accept her offer.

"No, I'm afraid we're in for another long day," He answered with a sigh. "I'm going to shower and get dressed. I suggest everyone else do so too." With that he set his cup on an end table and bounded up the stairs to the bathroom off his and Teri's bedroom. After peeing he took a fast shower, brushed his teeth, combed his hair and dressed in his customary navy blue sport coat, long sleeved white shirt and red tie. He was ready to face the citizens of America and the rest of the world. Unfortunately, he had no idea what he would say to them. As he descended the stairs he passed Teri who was on the way up to use their bathroom.

Margaret was using the main bathroom on the first floor to take her shower. Halfway down the stairs he heard his father call, "John, get down here; hurry." He came into the living room and saw a printed document on the TV screen. A voice was solemnly reading the document aloud. His father had turned the sound back on and he spoke excitedly over the voice and the doorbell which continued to ring.

"This came on just seconds ago, right after the girls left for their showers. Apparently, President Herman issued this special Executive Order in 2009. It deals with the Continuity of Government plan."

The voice on the TV continued: "… should no elected official in this line of succession be found within two days, I hereby execute this document to provide an orderly transition of administration. First in line I name the head of the National Command Authority and his/her staff members to assume the administrative duties of my office. Specific and detailed instructions on what to do in the event of a national emergency have been given to this agency."

The announcement went on to cite a series of laws passed by congress which dealt with the orderly transition of power, beyond what the constitution had specified. This apparently was done to give credence to President Herman's executive order.

The TV camera then zoomed in and focused on the bottom line of the document showing President Herman's signature above his name and title and the official seal of office. The image of Ron Nelson, morning anchor of The Waking Hour news program replaced the document. "Ladies and gentlemen, remember you heard it first on Channel 4, WMAX your source for breaking news in the greater Madison area. We will be repeating this story momentarily. For those who just tuned in, we have received an email of international importance from the National Command Authority located near Washington D.C. Apparently, in 2009 President Herman issued Executive Order H-2 which deals with the potential problem that could result from his death and the deaths of all possible successors. He also prepared a written pre-amble which explains his action. It appears that, in the event a disaster should leave the United States without leadership, this document stipulates that a group known as the National Command Authority will assume the powers of the Oval office. A panel of constitutional experts is being assembled for a discussion of this momentous proclamation in our studio as soon as feasible. Without further ado, here again is the document. Please stay tuned for further developments."

As his image and voice faded, a hastily designed logo appeared with 'America: A new Beginning' superimposed on the presidential seal and the first few bars of 'Hail to the Chief' playing. This was replaced by the document and voice over. John muted the sound again. He was disgusted.

"Well, everything nice neat and tidy," John said. "Dad, we have just witnessed a bloodless coup. I never would have dreamt it possible."

"Son, what are you talking about? This is just a very intelligent way to keep the country from falling into anarchy. We need a strong central government and the President gave it to us."

"Dad, we do need a strong central government of *elected representatives*. Democracy is government of the people; by the people and for the people, remember? Under this executive order we have government by an appointed individual. Who will name his successor, him?"

"Whoa, I see what you mean, son. I always knew you were quicker than me. But, what can we do about it. Should we do anything? What are you going to do?"

"If I were as quick as you give me credit for being, I'd have an idea. Right now I'm at a loss." The ringing of the doorbell was now joined by a vigorous pounding on the door. John decided to get it over with. He flung the door wide and boldly stepped outside almost colliding with the television reporter who had been banging insistently on the door.

The reporter quickly regained his composure and said, "Senator, senator may we ask you some questions?" Other reporters in the back were also yelling for his attention, "Senator we're from Channel 4 WMAX, do you have any updates on your remarks made at our studio yesterday?" Playing the "our studio" card only served to annoy senator Franks and he spoke instead to the nearest reporter who happened to be from radio station WAKY, "radio's early morning news leader in Madison".

The reporter asked, "Senator, what new developments are you aware of?" He then thrust his mike into John's face. It was a reasonable question and the Senator managed a smile as he said, "That's a good question mister..?"

"Bob Newsome of radio station WAKY 109.5 FM. All news all…" The senator interrupted.

"Thank you, Bob. Please, step back everyone and I'll do my best to handle any questions for which I have answers. The crowd surged forward a step. Senator Franks stepped back against the door and put his hands out with a pushing back motion. Reluctantly, most of the mob took a small step backward.

"I have no more recent information than anyone else who has been watching television regularly." The Senator continued. "The devastation in Washington has exceeded all expectations. The threat of five more nuclear attacks on American cities has created a panic and a mass flight from our larger cities which has caused unprecedented traffic jams all over our great country. Canada and Mexico have closed their borders indefinitely. Communication from the D.C. area is non-existent. As like everyone else, my family and I are appalled. For those of you standing here, you probably missed the most recent announcement of importance.

"What's that Senator?" Bob Newsome asked.

"President Herman, in his desire to protect the country in the event of a cataclysm such as we experienced yesterday, issued an executive order bestowing the authority of the executive office on an administrative group hidden in a bunker somewhere near the Capitol. If you will return to your homes and studios, I urge you to read and listen to this proclamation. I must also state that I unequivocally disagree with the legality of this executive order. It goes against the Constitution and cannot be implemented. I believe an informed citizenry will support me on this.

The reporter from Channel 4 pushed forward again while yelling out, "Senator, do you plan on issuing any more statements from our studio? Will you be continuing to keep your constituents informed?" Franks looked at the reporter and made a decision.

"As a matter of fact, I do intend to make another statement later today. However, I am not ready to disclose the content of this message just yet. I will be asking for a 1:00 PM broadcast. Please ask your station management to air messages advising viewers of the broadcast time. Thank you. Are there any more questions?"

"Yes Senator, Ted Reynolds of Channel 8, WITD here. How much is channel 4 paying you for this exclusive?"

John was caught off guard and stammered a denial as he prepared to go back inside.

Finally, he just called out as he was closing the door of his home, "I'm sorry Ted. I'll try to do a better job of being fair to the media in the future."

Once inside, he picked up his coffee cup from earlier, filled it and plugged in the phone in the kitchen again. It rang immediately. He picked it up and said, "Senator Fran..." a guttural voice cut him off saying, "you useless piece of shit...come out of your house and face the people you've ignored..." He quickly hung up and pushed the talk button again and said, "Hello, you've reached Senator John..."then he was interrupted.

"Jesus Christ I finally got ahold of you." It was general Birch.

"Sam?" The senator asked. "Is that you? Where the hell are you?"

"We're in Bumfuck, Indiana; about 30 miles south of Indianapolis. Senator, we were going to keep heading north through Chicago, but you wouldn't believe the traffic headed south out of Indianapolis. We're going to have to change our plan and take back routes to Madison."

"You're saying 'we', does that mean you have Estelle with you?"

"Of course, want to talk to her?"

"Yes, please put her on." The general handed her his cell phone.

"Hello, senator Franks," she said.

"Estelle, thank god. It's so good to hear your voice," the senator gushed. Birch shrugged his shoulders and thought the senator sounded a little too relieved to hear his secretary. Oh well, couldn't say as he blamed Franks. She was a tasty morsel. Estelle saw the little smirk on Birch's face and responded in a completely businesslike manner.

"Thank you for your concern, senator. It's good to hear that you're all right too. How is your family doing?"

"They're fine, thank you, fine. Have you two been able to keep up on the news?

"Yes, we've been listening almost non-stop. We caught your message and I want to compliment you. I think it was exactly what America needed to hear.

"Thank you. I'm kind of playing it by ear at this point. I'm going to deliver another message at 1:00 today. I'll request a TV/radio simulcast as before."

"Do you need any help with the writing?" Estelle asked.

"I'm not 100 percent sure what I'm going to say. If I have time, I'll try to get your input on my speech. What is the cell phone number you're calling from?

Estelle gave him the number. Then she explained that they had been calling his office phone without success all night and during the morning. They had left two messages at the call center but, had not heard back from him. He apologized for the problem and assured Estelle he would fix it ASAP. He said the last words loud enough for Birch to hear. Then he said, "Thank you, sweet cakes." The pet name was their little inside joke. She and the senator had a strictly professional relationship, but he enjoyed teasing her about her good looks. "Would you put the general back on, please?"

"Sho' nuff," Estelle said with an exaggerated southern drawl, before she handed the phone over. Birch gave her a strange look and returned his attention to the road.

"Birch here," he said a bit more gruffly than intended.

"General, have you and Estelle heard about President Herman's executive order passing on the reins of power to some administrative group near D.C.?"

"Shit. That would be the National Command Authority. It's a bunch of non-elected non-military know-it-alls. No, I hadn't heard about it."

"Well, I'm not trying to pass myself off as a constitutional scholar, but it seems highly unlikely to me that the founding fathers would have condoned this power play. I cannot accept that America is now being run by an appointed committee.

"Have you heard about the Afghanistan/Pakistan fiasco?" Birch asked.

"What are you talking about?" Franks said with concern.

"Apparently the nuke attack was timed to coincide with a joint Coup. Some Pakistani group has taken over the parliament in that country and our troops are barely managing to fight off a similar take-over by the Taliban in Afghanistan.

"Shit." Senator Franks' one word response seemed eloquent.

"Sir, I believe it has hit the fan." General Birch agreed.

"That settles it. I'm declaring Martial Law. What do you think our military leaders will do? Will they accept me as their Commander-In-Chief?"

"My first reaction is 'hell yes', but then I gotta admit, I really don't know. It depends on who is still alive. The Chairman of the Joint Chiefs of Staff is Admiral MacKenzie and I know for a fact that he's a staunch defender of the constitution. I can't see him taking orders from some appointed clerk."

"Then he's our starting point. Let's hope that he's still alive and let's make a concentrated effort to contact him."

"If I still had my office, I'd be better able to help you there. Unfortunately, the Pentagon no longer exists."

"Sam, what are your thoughts about Pakistan and Afghanistan?"

"Now's not a good time to ask me Senator. I'd probably just nuke the fuckers." Then he chuckled.

"Well, Sam that's a bit drastic. But, I do think we cannot stand by and allow this to go uncontested."

"You're right, of course John. What do you have in mind?"

"First see if you can locate MacKenzie. I need to know where he stands."

"Let me make some calls to a few old friends and I'll see what I can find out."

"Thanks, Sam. Please do it as quickly as possible and then get back to me, OK?"

"You got it Senator. Do you have a plan?"

"Maybe, Sam maybe I do. According to my COG manual, the actual transfer of power does not occur until two full days after a disaster. That means we have a window of opportunity to pre-empt it today."

"Good thinking, Senator. What are you going to do?

"Just get that info on the admiral to me and listen to my simulcast today at 1:00 Central Standard Time. When do you think you'll be here?"

"I'm not sure. We need to take the back roads and it depends on traffic. I'm hoping for late this afternoon. I'm giving the wheel to Estelle so I can concentrate on making contacts."

"That sounds good, General. Keep me advised and drive safely." He hung up and went into the living room and said, "Dad, things may be looking up." Then the phone started ringing again.

CHAPTER   3 9

MONDAY

AFTER HIS IMPROMPTU press conference
Senator Franks retired to his office to continue reviewing the COG
manual and to think about his 1:00 broadcast. His family knew not
to bother him and they all stayed downstairs watching the scenes of
turmoil across the country. Unknown to them, incredibly important
events were occurring above their heads.

At 9:15 AM the senator's computer beeped letting him know he
had an email. It was from the call center. They had forwarded an email
received from the Chairman of the Joint Chiefs of Staff, Admiral Leon
Mackenzie.

*   *   *

He was aboard the U.S.S. Nimitz. Mac had his choice of ships
to sail on; but he preferred one that had some miles on her. He also
liked being aboard the only super carrier named after a real navy hero.
Chester W. Nimitz was the Fleet Admiral who led the United States to
victory in the Pacific during WWII. This floating airport was the first
of ten Nimitz class Aircraft Carriers built by the United States. The last
and final one was the U.S.S. George H.W. Bush launched in 2010. Most
of them had been named after presidents. The only exceptions were a
long term senator and a Secretary of the Navy. Mac had often said,
"Why in the hell should a warship be named after a politician?" It was

just another 'burr under his saddle'. Mac had left a call back number and a request that the Senator contact him at his earliest convenience.

*   *   *

After reading the email, John picked up his phone and put it to his ear. It was dead. "Shit," he said. Then he saw that it was unplugged and he plugged it in. He called immediately. The phone was answered on the first ring.

"Admiral MacKenzie, here; Thank you for calling Senator." Hah, John thought: caller ID.

"Thank you for getting in touch with me Admiral."

"You can call me Mac, Senator. I prefer that."

"OK, Mac. I think we have a number of items to discuss."

"Well, let's begin with our alert status. We are currently at DEFCON 3. From what I've been able to learn so far, there aren't any other immediate threats. The D.C. nuke appears to have been an isolated incident. I think we could safely back off to Defcon 4."

"That's great news, Admiral, er, Mac. I agree that it was an isolated event."

"OK, good. Then I'll plan on ordering a stand down as soon as you announce it." Things were going even better than he had hoped with the Chairman of the Joint Chiefs.

"That would be perfect, Mac. I'm planning to address the nation at 1:00 PM Central Standard Time today."

"All right; I'll plan on issuing the stand down order at 1:05 CST so you can announce it. You can also tell the world that there are no plans to take any action unless provoked. I am in constant communication with the other Joint Chiefs and we are all in agreement about this."

What a relief! It sounded like he and Mac were on the same wave length. Of course, there still might be some sticking points.

"So tell me, Senator, what are your plans? Do you know what you are going to do?

John was caught off guard for a moment. He had not anticipated the question coming from the admiral; at least not so soon.

"To be honest, sir I'm wrestling with the answer to that question right now. I think my status is undetermined at this time. It might be that I'm the only elected federal government servant left, but I'm still hoping that's not the case. By the way, please call me John."

"To start with, Senator you don't call me 'sir', I call you 'sir'. You do understand that, right?"

"Yes, uh…I do understand Admiral. And, thank you."

"There's no need to thank me, sir. Whether or not you are the only living elected official is immaterial. At this time, you are the only *known* living official and therefore by the rules of military chain of command, you are the ranking officer. You understand that too, right?"

"I understand," John said softly. He felt a shiver run through his body.

Mackenzie continued, "General Birch spoke very highly of you, and he and I are in complete agreement; the shadow government President Herman created should never be in control of the U.S. military forces."

"Do all the joint chiefs agree?" John asked.

"Don't you worry about that," the admiral reassured him, "they'll follow my lead. Now what is your first action as Commander in Chief?" John took a deep breath and let it out slowly. The admiral waited a moment and then said, "If I may make a suggestion, I have an idea."

"Please do, Admiral."

"At this time it is of utmost importance that the citizens of the United States and the leaders of all the countries in the world understand that America still has a leader and that he is in control of the most powerful military force on earth."

The admiral let the implications of his remark sink in and then continued, "I suggest two things: one, order me to surface three of our nuclear submarines in three different locations. This will confirm that you are in charge. The satellite images of three submarines coming to the surface should convince even the hard core skeptics that you mean business.

Second, order the immediate withdrawal of all troops from Afghanistan and Pakistan. This will quiet the fear in the cities that more nuclear bombs may be set off. In addition, it will save American lives by bringing home the troops who are engaged in a war which, in my opinion, cannot be won."

"Thank you for your ideas, admiral. Please let me think on them for a bit and I'll get back to you," John said cautiously.

"As you wish, sir" John recognized a trace of irritation in his voice.

"Hang on a second, Mac." John took the phone from his ear and looked at the continued chaos being shown on his TV. Then the image changed to the Herman document and the somber voice reading it. All of his life John had been a procrastinator. He abhorred making "rash" decisions, even when they seemed perfectly plausible. Better to mull over what the admiral had said, at least for awhile. He took a deep breath and suddenly said, "Bullshit!" Then he realized he had said it aloud. Then it hit him. He had reached a decision. He picked up the phone and put it back to his ear.

"Admiral MacKenzie, I've made my decision. First, I hereby order you to surface three nuclear submarines; locations to be at your discretion. These events are to be coordinated with my television appearance."

"Yes sir," Mac said crisply. The tone of his voice changed completely.

"Second, I will be declaring Martial Law. Please advise the other Chiefs.

"Yes sir," Mac said respectfully.

"Lastly, Mac, I disagree with your suggestion of withdrawing our troops from Afghanistan."

"But, I think…"

"Bear with me a moment while I explain, Mac. OK?" John interrupted.

"Yes, Senator," Mac said hesitantly. Then he asked himself: Have I created a monster?

"First, Mac I do not believe for one second that there are five more nukes. If these Jihadists had them they would have used them yesterday. I am convinced that they are just using this bogus threat to gain a strategic advantage in Afghanistan."

"I guess that is possible," Mac said.

"Secondly, I assume you are aware of what's been going on in those two countries?"

"I was briefed just moments ago," Mac answered sheepishly. He had been furious when he found out that the coup and the attack in Afghanistan had been going on for several hours before he heard about it.

"I think it is imperative that the Jihadists who attacked us not get away unpunished. I also think that we cannot allow Afghanistan to fall under the rule of the Taliban. I need an assessment of how many additional troops I could send to these troubled areas."

"I will pass your message on to Grumwell and Carson." Mac said tersely.

"Admiral, I strongly believe that we cannot allow this assault on our nation to go unpunished. I'm not talking about retaliating with nukes. I'm talking about rooting out these sons-of-bitches where they live and stringing them up in a public hanging just like Saddam Hussein. Do you read me Mac?"

"I read you loud and clear sir; loud and clear." Admiral MacKenzie was inspired by the Senator's posture. He was still not happy about the war in Afghanistan, but maybe; just maybe, it could actually be won if a new leader was at the helm.

"Good. Can I count on your support then?"

"I will give you my conditional support, Senator. I'll have to see how things progress."

"That's fine by me, Mac. I too am not sure how things will go; I just know that yesterday my country took one on the chin worse than Pearl Harbor. We all know what a mistake Japan made. I intend to convince the Jihadists that this attack was the biggest mistake of their lives."

"Your submarines will surface at 1:05 CST this afternoon. And, I'll be passing your plans on to my chiefs. Thank you, sir."

"Please pass something else on to your chiefs for me. I want to put a Fatwa on the head of the son-of-a-bitch behind this attack. I want him found at all costs. I want to see him standing on a gallows and hanged."

"We'll do our best, sir." MacKenzie said.

"Thank you, Mac." John sat back in his desk chair and tried to calm his nerves.

CHAPTER 40

MONDAY

KURT SCHIMLER PUSHED his chair back and put his feet up on his desktop. His wall mounted television was tuned to the channel he had been watching on and off since early this morning. It was almost 2:00, time for that arrogant junior cadet from Wisconsin to come on.

Suddenly the image of Senator John Franks filled the screen. Schimler turned up the sound.

Franks was seated in a swivel chair at a small desk. There was a vase of daffodils on it. An American flag hung on a brass pole to his right and the flag of Wisconsin to his left. A WMAX logo was on the front of the desk.

"...for tuning in my fellow Americans." The image said. *"As you probably know, I am Senator John Franks from Wisconsin. Yesterday, I addressed the nation on a radio/TV simulcast. That message has been run almost continuously today throughout the country. There have been a number of important developments since that message."*

"You bet your sweet ass there have been," Kurt said to the TV set.

"First, let me inform you that while the Pentagon was destroyed yesterday, all five Joint Chiefs of Staff are alive and well. I spoke with the Chairman of the Joint Chiefs, Admiral Leon MacKenzie this morning."

Schimler barely had time to react before the next shoe dropped.

"Admiral MacKenzie and I agreed that yesterday's criminal attack on our nation's capitol was an isolated incident and that it was highly

248

unlikely that the Jihadist group behind it is capable of further nuclear mayhem. If they had more bombs in more cities, they would have set them off yesterday. Accordingly, three minutes from now the Joint Chiefs are ordering a reduction in the military's alert status from Defcon 3 to Defcon 4. For those of you unfamiliar with military jargon, that means we have taken our first step toward returning to normal. Franks paused for a moment and deliberately looked at his wrist watch.

"At the same time, I have ordered three of our nation's nuclear submarines to surface. Continue to watch your television or listen to your radio to see or hear confirmation of this event. The sole purpose of surfacing these vessels is to affirm to other world leaders that I am in charge of our military. As I said in my earlier message, there are no plans for nuclear retaliation."

"SON OF A BITCH" Schimler screamed loud enough for everyone in the compound to hear.

"You're a miserable political know-nothing!" He added. Then he stopped ranting in order to hear what the Senator was saying.

"...does not mean I intend to let the perpetrators off the hook. We will seek out the leaders of these evil Jihadist criminals and see that justice is done. I swear that this will happen.

I swear it on the graves of my fellow elected representatives and on the graves of our nation's murdered citizens." Franks rose and came out from behind the desk; he then moved slowly to a pre-determined spot in front of it and looked directly and sincerely into the camera.

I regret to inform you that due to the mass migrations from our cities and the resulting chaos, I have found it necessary to declare Martial Law. All citizens are advised to remain indoors as much as possible. In addition, there will be a mandatory curfew beginning at 6:00 PM across the nation. Anyone seen outside after that hour will be considered a looter and subject to arrest.

The curfew will be lifted at 8:00 AM each day. Martial Law will remain in place until I am convinced that order has been restored in our country. He took two more steps closer to the camera. It was now a tight head and shoulders shot. The American flag, soft focus but recognizable, was directly behind him.

"And now I have a special message for the leader of the group known as the National Command Authority. I want to praise you for your patriotism and your willingness to endure long hours and separation from your family

and friends in order to fulfill your mission. I know that you have only the best intentions for our country. However, after discussions with a number of constitutional experts and after re-reading the document myself, I have come to the inevitable conclusion that President Herman overstepped the authority of the oval office in turning over the executive power of the Presidency to your organization. Accordingly, I have temporarily assumed the duties and powers of the nation's highest office until such time as elections can be held and a joint session of Congress can name a new President, Vice-President and Speaker of the House."

Schimler went ballistic. He began throwing objects from his desk at the screen. He was literally foaming at the mouth as he spit out a stream of expletives. None of his colleagues dared enter his office. Some had been watching the TV in the conference room and could hear him going crazy. The rest had watched in their offices and were spared most of his diatribe until he started calling them on their phones. At this point none of them were completely sure how Senator Franks' statement would affect them. However, Dick Wren and Caroline Bechman didn't fly into rages, so they actually heard the next remarks made by the Senator.

"I believe it would be in the best interests of our country for the National Command Authority and I to work in concert during this turbulent and unsettled point in our nation's history. In pursuit of that cooperation I invite the leader or leaders of that organization to contact me for a discussion on how we can best implement a team approach."

By this time Schimler had cooled down just enough to pick up his phone and dial the number of Craig Fergussen, Intelligence Officer. Kurt had been so busy cursing he never heard Senator Franks' request.

"This is Fergussen, sir. How can I help you?" Craig answered in a business-like manner.

"You can get me the number of that private security organization that is under the wing of the CIA."

"Which one do you want sir?" Craig knew there were a number of private security groups on the payroll of the CIA. It depended on what he wanted done.

"God damn it Craig. The one that is fighting in Afghanistan, Pakistan, Iran, and everywhere else our so called military can't handle the heat. The

one that goes where we tell them and does whatever we ask without a bunch of fucking questions." Craig knew who he meant.

"Well sir, I believe you mean PaxCorp."

"That sounds right. They're the ones that started out as arms dealers and evolved into a private army with contracts for paramilitary divisions, security forces and clandestine operations squads, right?"

"That sounds like PaxCorp alright."

"Give me their number and the name of a top contact over there." Fergussen didn't like the sound of this, but it wasn't his decision.

"Their secure number is 313-555-1000. The man to talk to is Gerald Fox. Our code is 444-1670."

"Thank you, Fergussen. Oh, and this conversation never happened, understand?"

"Yes sir; understood, sir." This also troubled him, but he said nothing more.

While Schimler was on the phone, Franks had been urging all Americans who had fled the cities to return home as soon as possible. The sooner this would happen the sooner America could return to normal. During his final remarks the soft strains of 'America the Beautiful' were playing under his words.

And, in conclusion a special appeal to all governors of all states. I want each of you to arrange and hold national elections for the Senate and the House of Representatives. The election date is to be Tuesday, April 2. These bodies will meet in joint session at a place and date yet to be determined to elect a new President, Vice President and Speaker of the House. Lastly, I am designating next Sunday to be a national day of mourning to honor all those who lost their lives during this great tragedy. I call upon each mayor of each city, village or township in our great nation to arrange a suitable ceremony.

Let me bid you goodbye now and God bless America!" 'America the Beautiful' cross faded into 'The Battle Hymn of the Republic,' which played over the contact information which was crawling on the bottom of the screen.

All of this was lost on Kurt Schimler who was busy establishing contact with the Covert Operations Wing of PaxCorp.

MONDAY

A FOUR CAR POLICE escort, two in front and two behind, managed to deliver the Senator home. They also were able to disperse the crowd of citizens and news reporters camped on his lawn. John entered his sanctuary and thankfully collapsed. So much had happened in the last 24 hours and he needed time to reflect. Teri and Maggie ran and gave him hugs. Pastor Franks remained sitting in a recliner.

Teri had her arms around his neck and said, "John, I can't tell you how proud I am of you. I've never seen you so decisive and proactive. Your speech thrilled me."

"Dad, you were awesome." Maggie agreed.

"Thanks to both of you; that means a lot to me." John responded.

"Son, I'm really proud of you too," his father said from his chair. John gave each of his ladies big hugs and kisses then he went over to his father and gave him a hug.

"Thank you, Dad. I appreciate it. His father stood and hugged him back. As he looked over his father's shoulder, John saw the wall clock said 2:37. Where had the time gone?

"I know it's beside the point, but unless you can arrange a police escort for Maggie and me, we won't be going shopping for a mother-of-the-bride dress today." Teri laughed to let him know she was just teasing. Maggie's laugh was delayed and not as convincing.

"I'm going to my bedroom; let me know if anything important happens." Maggie said.

She wanted to call her fiancé, but when she plugged the phone in her bedroom back in it rang immediately and continually. She unplugged it again and went on-line instead.

John went into the kitchen and grabbed a Pabst from the refrigerator. "Anyone want a beer?" He yelled.

"I'd love one," Teri answered.

"None for me, thank you," his father said. John came back into the living room, handed an open bottle of beer to his wife and sat down next to his Dad who was now on the sofa. He turned to his father and said, "I seem to remember you saying something about having a tiger by the tail." They both laughed.

"I did indeed, son. I did indeed. Looks like you may have tamed this one."

"I hope so, Dad. I sincerely hope so." With that he took a sip of beer. He no sooner swallowed when the doorbell rang.

"I'll get it," Teri said as she set her beer down. As she got up to answer the door, Maggie came out of her bedroom.

"Who's at the door," she asked. Seeing her mother was heading to the door, she followed. Teri opened the door cautiously and looked out at the most stunning blonde she could ever remember seeing.

"Hi." The blonde said with a bright smile. "I'm Estelle Evans and this is General Sam Birch. Is this the home of Senator Franks?" Maggie, who was looking over her mother's shoulder, gasped.

"Estelle, Sam is that you?" John yelled excitedly from his chair. Teri and Maggie exchanged looks that were not lost on Estelle. She sensed trouble on the horizon. It wouldn't be the first time.

"Yeah, we finally made it," Birch yelled back.

"Oh God, where are my manners?" Teri said. "Please come in." She cast a guilty glance at her father-in-law who was rising to greet the newcomers. He had not noticed her gaffe. John rushed to the door and gave Estelle a big hug. Teri tried to keep her expression non-committal.

Estelle hugged him back. Teri and Maggie squirmed. Neither said a word.

"Sam, thank you so much for coming," the Senator said as he shook the General's hand firmly and sincerely.

"Orders are orders," Birch said with a laugh. "Besides, I couldn't let you face everything alone. You need my help."

"That is for certain, Sam. That is for certain. Please, both of you come in and sit down.

Could I get anyone a beer or a cup of coffee?"

"Not for me," Estelle said. She sat on one end of the sofa. Pastor Franks nodded and said, "Hello, young lady. I'm John's Father."

"A beer sounds good, Birch replied as he sat on a recliner.

"I'll get it," Teri yelled and she headed to the kitchen.

"I'll help you mom," Maggie yelled as she followed her into the kitchen. Once there, they began a silent pantomime that was unmistakable. It could be summarized in four words: *Who is this bitch?*

In the living room, General Birch had the floor. John was glad that he finally had the chance to meet the General in person. He was pretty much like the mental image he had had of him. Birch was clean shaven, stocky, but not portly and of average height. John estimated him to be 5'10". His craggy face was weathered, but his eyes were cheerful and seemed to always be smiling. He sported a fringe of hair from just above his ears all the way around his head. His bald pate gleamed. His hands seemed too big, or his arms were too short for them. John couldn't decide which it was.

"We listened to your speech today, Senator. Or should I call you Mr. President?" The General said. John gave a short chuckle.

"That's not necessary, Sam. You know that. Although, I suspect a lot of people will wonder what to call me." He said.

"Well, to some folks, your name is Mud." Birch waited for a response. Franks just looked at him in bemusement. Finally he said, "What do you mean by that?"

"Senator, you are the number one target in the country right now. Not only would the terrorists like to see you dead, every disgruntled crackpot in America sees you as the enemy and worst of all, when you announced that you had taken control of the military, that "shadow government" on the east coast has no doubt made you their number one priority. You might as well have a bull's eye painted on your forehead."

The Senator sat back in silence. He had known that his actions would make him more vulnerable, but he had accepted that as the price he had to pay. Now hearing the words from Sam's mouth awakened him to the urgency of his predicament.

"Sam, I think you're over reacting…" as he was answering, Estelle cut him off, "Senator, please listen to the general. He's right. You're in grave danger right now."

"You really believe there are people out there who want to kill me, Estelle?"

"I'm sure of it," she said. "You don't know what a skitzy place the U.S. is right now. Everybody is running scared and all manner of folks are carrying guns. The general and I agreed we need to get you someplace safe as soon as possible."

"But, but what about my wife and daughter and my father?" John stammered.

"They can come too," Birch answered.

"Come where?" Teri asked as she and Maggie came into the room. She handed him his beer and crossed over to her husband.

"We're heading to Cheyenne Mountain Colorado. I've made arrangements to secure the Senator and his family and as many assistants as necessary in the NORAD complex."

"Colorado?" It was too much information coming in too fast. The Senator was stunned. He looked at his father and said, "Dad, have you been listening to this?"

"Well, it would be pretty hard not to. But, that's not really your question is it? If you want my opinion, I think these folks are right. You probably are in danger, or at least it would be prudent to act like you are."

"That's it then," the general said. "Let's plan on your whole family coming.

"How can we get to Colorado?" the Senator asked. All planes have been grounded."

"In times of imminent threat, the military can override such orders." Birch explained. "Air Force Chief of Staff Simmons has issued a non-compliance directive. I have a C-130 transport plane being readied at Truax field. Tell everybody to pack lightly. They have stores in Colorado Springs." He cast a look at Estelle who pretended not to notice.

"Thank you, Sam," the Senator answered. "But, we need to talk about this."

"Talk all you want, Senator. Just be ready to go in an hour." Birch took a swig of his beer and headed for the kitchen.

"Got anything to eat in here?" He asked.

Estelle sat uncomfortably as the four family members looked at each other in dismay. She had had time during the journey to get used to the idea. This was all new to the Franks family. Maggie was the first to speak.

"I'm going to my bedroom to email Ed and see what he says." Ed Matzke Jr. was her fiancé. Teri thought John was feeling paranoid and blindly following these two strangers in her living room, but she said nothing. Pastor Franks spoke up next.

"John, I don't think you'll really need me where you're going. But, there are people who need me here. I won't be going."

"OK, Dad. I understand how you feel. It's all right by me." Teri excused herself and went into the kitchen.

"General, we're pretty much out of everything right now. I haven't been able to get to the market. Can I fix you some eggs?"

"Thank you, that would be great," Birch replied. "I practically live on em."

"How should I fix 'em?" Teri asked. She had learned that little device from her husband.

"Scrambled; please." The General responded.

"General, can you tell me about this Cheyenne Mountain place?" This she asked while retrieving eggs from the refrigerator.

"NORAD is a practically impregnable fortress built into the mountain. It's a cooperative venture between Canada and us. NORAD stands for North American Aerospace Defense. It was built in the early sixties. I've never been there myself, so this will be an adventure for me too." Teri started a pan heating up and broke three eggs into a bowl. She sprayed the pan with Pam and stirred the eggs vigorously with a fork.

"What will my husband be able to accomplish there that he couldn't do here? She asked pointedly.

"Well, number one, he can stay alive." General Birch replied sardonically. "Just as importantly, he'll have the most up-to-date and sophisticated communications equipment in the world at his disposal. He'll be able to maintain contact with everyone and he'll be able to direct the military." Teri plopped the eggs into the pan and began stirring with a wooden spoon.

"And we'll have our own apartment or whatever? Will he have an office?

"Like I said, I've never been there but, I have to believe they have all the amenities. There are staff members who live there virtually 24/7." Teri put the General's eggs on a plate and set them down in front of him with a salt shaker and pepper shaker. Then she fetched a fork and a napkin.

"These look perfect," the General said.

"Are you OK with your beer?" She asked.

"Breakfast of champions," the General smiled.

"Excuse me," Teri said. "Enjoy your eggs." She came into the living room and saw John sitting on the sofa with Estelle. They were on either end, but it still bothered her. John saw the look on her face and said, "My dad is in the guest room packing his overnight bag. We'll need to give him a ride home."

"OK," Teri said as she sat in the recliner by John. Maggie then walked into the room and announced that she would not be going to Colorado.

"Ed has it all set up," she said. "I'm going to stay with the Matzkes until the wedding."

"Who are the Matzkes?" Estelle asked.

"My future in-laws," Maggie answered. They're wonderful people. They helped my dad get elected."

"John," Teri said. "I've decided that it makes sense to go to the mountain. I guess it'll just be the two of us, though."

"Don't you mean the four of us?" John said with surprise.

"Oh, of course," Teri said. I assumed that General Birch and Miss Evans would also be going. I was only referring to family members."

"Please feel free to call me Estelle, Estelle interjected. Teri nodded with a tight smile.

John rose and gave Teri a kiss.

"All right," He said. "It's settled then. I'm glad you came around. We'd better get packing." He then headed for their upstairs bedroom with Teri right behind him.

$$*\qquad*\qquad*$$

Estelle sat alone in the living room and contemplated what life was going to be like living in an underground fortress with the Senator and his jealous wife. Oh well, I always wanted to go to exciting places and meet interesting people, she thought.

*   *   *

Within an hour everyone had left the house. The travelers went to Truax and Maggie took her grandfather home, before continuing on to the Matzke's house. There she was greeted literally with open arms.

*   *   *

Sometime in the wee hours that night the Franks home was blown up. No one was aware of it until the next morning.

CHAPTER 4 2

TUESDAY, JANUARY 22, 2013

JOHN AND HIS entourage arrived at Peterson Air Force Base near Colorado Springs late Monday evening. Upon arrival they were escorted to guest quarters at the base where they stayed the night. Everyone was exhausted and everyone slept deeply.

*   *   *

NORAD headquarters was originally established at Ent Air Force Base; a six square block compound right in the heart of Colorado Springs. President John F. Kennedy toured the facility not long before he was assassinated. When the Cheyenne mountain compound was ready in 1965, the operation was moved there. In late 2008, amidst a great deal of controversy, the operations of NORAD and the U.S. Northern Command were moved to Building 1 at Peterson Air Force Base. The commander of the facility had by-passed the normal protocol for such an expensive and extreme action when ordering the construction and transfer of the facility.

The House Committee on Military oversight was flabbergasted and caught totally unaware. By the time Senator Rothschild raised a major stink in the media and in congress, it was too late. Building 1 was complete and the mission moved to its new up-to-date facility.

Critics pointed out that the new complex was extremely vulnerable. One study revealed that the building had only a six percent chance of remaining operational from a moderate attack and '0' percent from a serious attack. In addition, the Electro Magnetic Force from any air detonated Nuclear weapon would disable all the electronics in the building.

Nonetheless, the transfer was made. The Cheyenne Mountain Complex was kept 'warm' and used primarily for training and other support functions.

Base scuttlebutt said the commanding officer was borderline claustrophobic and ordered the re-location to get out of the confines of the mountain. For proof of their assertions, gossipers would point out all the windows in the new facility.

∗   ∗   ∗

After breakfast at the base mess hall, The Senator and his group were given a tour of Building 1.

"Senator, General, ladies welcome to NORAD/USNORTHCOM," said the spiffy Staff Sergeant/Tour guide. My name is Sergeant Olsen and I'll be showing you around." He saluted.

Birch returned the salute.

"Here at NORAD we continuously monitor the air and space above three major regions, Alaska, Canada and the continental United States." As he spoke, he walked across a large atrium in the entryway and the group followed him. During the next twenty minutes he kept up a steady fount of information. The Senator learned that there was a huge network of satellites, ground based radar and airborne radar monitoring our skies at all times. The center kept track of some forty thousand flights worldwide daily. Any inbound aircraft without radio contact was met by a jet escort. This happened almost daily. There were over 100 fighter jets on alert at all times.

Birch was surprised to learn that, as a result of September 11th, the commander of the base was authorized to bring down a hi-jacked commercial plane deemed a threat without prior approval from the President.

The monitoring room in the basement of the building was a complex of colorful wall- mounted screens and banks of computers and control consoles. The FAA and its Canadian counterpart NAV had a crew on duty at all times. They claimed final control of the airways in both countries.

"We also monitor maritime airspace," Sergeant Olsen proclaimed proudly. "We help detect possible drug smuggling into the U.S."

Just then the Senator's cell phone rang. He answered it and put his hand up to silence the tour guide for a moment.

"Hello?" He heard nothing. "Hello, is anyone there?"

"John?" It was his father.

"Dad, it's good to hear you. How are you?"

"I'm fine John, but I have some bad news."

"Bad news, Dad; what is it?"

"Yes. First let me say that Maggie is fine and so am I."

"Yes, well I'm glad to hear that. What's your news?"

"Somebody blew up your house last night. It's all over TV this morning. I just told Maggie about it. I've been getting calls from the media since 5:00 AM. They woke me up and told me about it. I had to assure them that you and Teri were not in the house when it went."

"Sergeant, can you switch one of these monitors to a news channel?" Franks asked.

"Of course, sir" the Sergeant responded and made a gesture. An operator flipped a switch and Channel KBTA from Denver came on the screen. They were giving local news and promised to report on the local weather next. Apparently the destruction of the Senator's house was big news in Madison, but not in Colorado. Then the music changed suddenly and the sound of a teletype machine clacking came on while a reporter's face filled the screen.

"This just in," the reporter said excitedly. "KBTA has received confirmation that the home of Wisconsin Senator John Franks was bombed in the early morning hours last night.

The status of the family is not known at this moment." He paused and held his earphone tighter to his head. "I have just gotten an update. Apparently TV channel WMAX in Madison, Wisconsin has spoken with the Senator's father and he said that no one was home at the time of the explosion. Well, that's good news."

"Did I hear right?" Teri said. "Someone blew up out house? Jesus Christ!"

"The Senator used one hand to keep the phone to his ear and put his other arm around his wife's shoulder. She started to cry and burrowed into his comfort. Estelle wandered off a bit and stood watching the news.

"The whereabouts of the Franks family is unknown at this time. Stay tuned for further details and updates as they occur. This is Brad Corby, Channel KB…" The Senator had given the signal to turn the TV off. He turned to the Sergeant and said, "I thought we came here to be at the Cheyenne Mountain Complex. Has that changed?"

"No sir, it has not." A full-bird Colonel answered from the pit where he had been viewing a console. The mountain complex has been kept on 'active but reduced use' status. We fired it up as soon as we heard that you were coming. I believe you will find it to be comfortable and well suited to your needs."

He stepped up out of the pit and offered his hand, "I'm Colonel Sparks, sir. Welcome to NORAD. They shook. Then he saluted General Birch. Birch returned the gesture and put out his hand. The Colonel took it in both hands as a warm gesture. He was a P.R. man, and his job was to make the guests comfortable and to keep questions down to a minimum.

"Dad, thank you for calling," John said. "It's being reported on the news out here, so we'll be able to keep up on developments. I love you." Pastor Franks assured him he loved him and to pass his love on to Teri.

"I'll do that Dad; Good bye." He said. Then he hung up and put his cell in his pocket. "My Father says he loves you," He said to Teri.

Teri sniffled and said, "Tell him I love him, very much." John let it pass. Then he turned back to the Colonel.

"Muhhamad is ready to go to the mountain." He said smilingly.

"By all means, Senator; I'll make arrangements immediately."

"Teri, do you remember the name of our home owner insurance company?" John asked as they went back outside. Teri didn't remember.

*　　*　　*

It was about a twenty minute drive to the north entrance. A U-shaped metal roof led to the opening of the granite tunnel. Four lanes of well-lit road took them to the entry point 1/3 mile into the cave. John stared up at the walls and ceiling which were covered in white ceramic. He was told that the sixty foot high ceiling concealed a man-made steel reinforced concrete dome. On top of that was 2,000 feet of solid granite. The tunnel itself continued on another 2/3's of a mile to the South portal. The design was such to allow the force of a nuclear detonation to pass through the mountain with little or no damage to the compound.

At the 1/3rd mile drop-off point they came to two 25-ton blast doors. Teri and Estelle were dwarfed by the mammoth portals. From here on in, it was travel by foot past numerous sentries with M-16 rifles, down eerie tunnels with metal lined walls. It was almost as bright as day inside.

The first open space was at section 2212. The entire complex occupied 4.5 acres. There were a number of intersecting chambers 45 feet wide and with 60 foot ceilings. Within these chambers 15 steel buildings stood like fortresses. The outer walls were continuously welded 3/8" carbon steel attached to structural steel frames. Twelve of these buildings were three stories high. Three were two stories. Each building sat on a cluster of eighty-eight enormous ½ ton steel springs. The springs allowed the buildings to move up to 12 inches in any direction when an earthquake occurred, or should a nuclear attack ever happen.

Of course, the main control room, farthest back in the complex, housed the sophisticated equipment still being used to track objects in space as well as in the skies and on the seas. The wall mounted screens and the bevy on consoles and computers were like a mirror image of those at Building 1.

"I'm very impressed," Senator Franks said.

"Well, you're seeing what very few people have ever seen, Senator." Colonel Lawrence Smithers had elected to escort the newcomers personally. Next I'll take you all to your quarters and then we'll take a look at the amenities available.

"Thank you, Colonel." General Birch said.

"Please follow me," the Colonel said. You living quarters are just down this hallway. He continued to point out features of the facility as they walked. "The air in here goes through special chemical, biological, radiological and nuclear filters that are also designed to equalize the pressure in the event of a nuclear detonation. In addition, there is a reservoir with over one and one half million gallons of water inside the mountain. Should power go out, we would run for twelve hours on large batteries and then six 1750 Kilowatt generators would kick in. Ah, here we are."

The newcomers were ushered through a steel fire door into an anteroom. Off this room were private rooms, each with its own full bath. Estelle got a room here. The Senator and his wife were escorted a little further down the hallway to the VIP quarters. This had the added luxury of a small kitchen and living room area. General Birch rated a "ranking officer" apartment which was like the Franks' quarters, minus the kitchen.

"Are you feeling claustrophobic yet?" John said to Teri as they set down their luggage in their new home.

"Like a goddam mole." Teri said with a shudder. "I now know how a prisoner must feel, surrounded by clanging metal."

"Oh, it's not that bad," John said as he hugged her. "We'll get used to it, soon enough."

"John, my love you are a total optimist, and a goddam Pollyanna. It's one of the things I like most about you; except right now it's irritating as hell." John laughed and pinched her on the bottom. She giggled and gave him a big kiss. A few moments later they were engaged in a 'house warming' at their new home.

$$* \quad * \quad *$$

General Birch was feeling restless, so he went over to Estelle's apartment and asked her if she wanted to join him as he reconnoitered. She obliged and between them they discovered the dining room, medical facility, pharmacy, dental office, barber shop, sauna, two fitness rooms and a small base exchange (military market). Birch bought a fifth of bourbon. Estelle agreed to share it with him.

CHAPTER 43

THURSDAY, JANUARY 24, 2013

IT HAD NOW been two days since their arrival at NORAD and Senator Franks was settling in. He had a private office and access to all manner of information and communications equipment. He would have felt he was at the helm of the 'ship of state', except one thing that was really bothering him. Yesterday he had contacted the call center in Madison and asked if there were any messages. There were a number of them. However, none were from any surviving elected representatives and none were from the National Command Authority. He had just tried again and again there was no response from the NCA.

He was turning this bit of news over in his mind when Estelle came into his office.

"Why so glum, chum?" She said.

"Hi sweet cakes," he said with a frown. "I think we have a problem."

"What kind of problem?" Estelle asked. She wondered if Teri had said something to upset him. She seemed like that kind.

"Well, I believe it's only a matter of time before we capture the perpetrators of the attack. But, we're going to have to do more than that. Soon, we'll be engaged in a full-scale war in the Middle-East."

"Yeah, that's a bitch." Estelle sympathized.

"That's only half the story, Estelle."

"Oh?"

"I have not had a response as yet from the National Command Authority. I offered them an olive branch and they have just ignored it. Damn it!"

"Well, Mister President Pro-Tem," Estelle said with a firm resolve in her voice, "our nation's eagle has an olive branch in one claw and arrows in the other. The symbolism is there: we offer peace, but we are prepared to fight."

John laughed at her use of his honorary title. The title was originally created by a journalist writing for the Wisconsin State Journal on Tuesday. He had suggested that John Franks be afforded the designation President Pro Tem. It made sense as he was temporarily performing the duties of the executive office. The news media glommed onto the phrase and by that evening he was being called PPT across the nation. Wednesday morning a press release from the Governors of America, a hastily formed bi-partisan group comprised of every Governor of every state made the title official. The motion had passed unanimously.

"I know you're right, Estelle. It's just that I do not look forward to fighting two wars at the same time; one in the Mid-East and one civil."

"I don't think you'll have a choice." Estelle said as she sat down at her desk.

"You know, you may well be right," he said. He paused for a moment considering her remark; the he decided he did have a choice and reached for his phone. He punched in the speed dial for Admiral MacKenzie, who answered on the second ring.

"Mac, do you know the name of the person who is in charge at the National Command Authority and where he or she is?"

"Of course," Mac said. "Why do you want to know?"

"Well, Mac," the Senator motioned for Estelle to leave and waited until she was gone;

"The following discussion is top secret and just between you and me."

CHAPTER 44

MONDAY, JANUARY 28, 2013

CRAIG FERGUSSEN, INTELLIGENCE Officer at Compound One put down his phone and sat staring into space. The call had to have been legit; but he was just stunned by the request. As an ex-navy seal, Fergussen was used to covert assignments and not squeamish about 'wet work', but this one was momentous. It had to have been Admiral MacKenzie on the phone; he had heard the man speak on numerous occasions and the voice sounded right. What was most convincing was that the man claiming to be MacKenzie had read Craig's service number to him as proof of who he was. Who the hell else would have access to that?

His computer beeped indicating a message. Craig went into his mail box. There was a coded message. He enacted his decoder and the unscrambled message contained two pages of gibberish with the following words—recent request confirmed; repeat, recent request confirmed inserted midway through it. Damn it. That was just like the brass. Issue an order to kill a man and confirm the order with a non-committal statement. Still, the message said it came from the U.S.S. Nimitz. Fergussen looked up the name of the Executive Officer of the Nimitz and dialed his sat-com number. "Captain Connelly," a brusque voice answered.

"Captain, I have an urgent request." Craig said. "My service number is USN16706332. If Admiral MacKenzie is aboard please tell him this number and ask him to speak to me."

"What makes you think the Admiral is on my ship, son?" The Captain replied cautiously.

"Please just do it, sir!" Fergussen spat back. A moment went by and the next voice on the sat-com was that of Admiral MacKenzie.

"I'm glad to see you are thorough, Fergussen. Your orders are re-confirmed."

"Yes sir, Admiral. Thank you, sir." Craig said as he slowly set the phone back in its cradle. Well, that was that.

Craig Fergussen was a man of action. He was also cautious and deliberate. These traits made him a dangerous and effective killer. This mission was not one to rush into, yet the Admiral had stressed the need for haste. Yeah, Admiral, Craig thought, that's because it's not your ass on the line.

How does one kill a person in a locked down community and not get caught? That was the problem. Killing was easy. There was any number of ways it could be done. Not getting caught? That was not so easy. It can't look like a murder. There would only be eleven suspects. Could it seem to be a disappearance? What does one do with the body? There were no hiding places in this little compound. He considered the trash compactor but ruled it out as too small to accommodate a human body, even a dismembered human body.

Suddenly he remembered something Bernie Schwartz the Chief Medical Officer had said to him a few years back when pop star Michael Jackson had died. Schwartz had said the doctor who had been treating him wasn't a killer, he was just sloppy. Michael was on several different drugs at the time because he had difficulty sleeping. The doctor had given him too much of one of them. What was the name of it? He had to find out and he had to find out now.

Luck was with him. When he went to the cafeteria for lunch, Bernie was there. They ate together and chatted casually for twenty minutes. When they were done Craig suggested a game of cribbage. Bernie was amenable; after all they had only had a quick lunch. He invited Craig to his office where he kept cards and a board.

"Man, you really got a cut that time." Bernie remarked. It had been Craig's first crib and he had held two fours and two sixes. He had put a ten in the crib and saw a five cut.

"I guess I can't complain," Craig said with a snicker.

"Can't complain, my ass," Bernie said as he counted his run of three.

During the game Craig casually brought up their prior conversation about Jackson. Bernie didn't remember it.

"Yeah, you said Michael's doctor was sloppy. He had accidently overdosed him with what was the name of it?" Craig said.

"You mean propofol." Bernie said immediately. Yes, that's right; I remember reading how Jackson was on a cocktail of drugs to help him sleep. He had to have gotten too much propofol."

"So, is this a sleep agent?" Fergussen asked innocently.

"Actually, it's been used and abused by many people for many purposes. It's an excellent short term anesthetic. Works quickly and the patient comes out of it just as quickly with no real after effects. I've heard of many interns using it to get an intense nap between grueling shifts. I've also heard of people using it for recreational purposes."

Bernie was one of those people who, once you got him talking about a subject he knew, it was hard to shut him up. That suited Craig just fine. He listened intently as Schwartz rambled.

"Unfortunately, several interns and other medical people have been known to overdose on it. Most of these were presumed to be accidental. A few were thought to be suicides. I guess it would be a great way to go; insert needle, go to sleep, not wake up."

"Sounds like a 'must have' for any Medic's arsenal."

"Oh yes," Bernie agreed. "I have several bottles on hand for emergency procedures and even for major surgeries. Two cc's and I can quickly and painlessly remove a boil and ten minutes later send you on your way."

Craig now knew everything he needed to know and changed the subject. Bernie made a great comeback and won the game by pegging out when it was Craig's crib. Craig went back to his office and thought.

That evening he went back to Bernie's office and picked the lock, a handy little trick the Seals had taught him. He easily picked the lock on the drug cabinet as well and quickly found the propofol. He carefully filled a syringe with what had to be an overdose and put it in a plastic carrying case. This went into his pocket and the bottle of propofol went back into the cabinet.

Unless Bernie kept an accurate count of his syringes, no one would ever know.

Two other bits of information entered into Craig's plan. He knew that Director Schimler was on heart medication for an arrhythmia and he often was out of breath in the hallways. Pretty much everyone in the complex was aware that he had 'a bad heart'.

Craig also knew that Kurt followed a strict exercise regimen and ate sparingly. He was determined to live a long time. Every morning from 6:15 to 6:45 you could find him doing laps in the pool. Today was no exception. Craig entered the pool area and without preamble dove in. As usual, Kurt ignored him and continued his laps. He was caught totally by surprise when Craig, an excellent swimmer came up to him from behind and quickly inserted the hypodermic needle up his rectum and pushed the plunger.

Kurt barely had time to feel the needle before he was out. Fergussen never knew it but he actually had been very lucky. In order to work, propofol needs to be administered intravenously. There are a number of perianal veins in the rectum and he had managed to hit one.

Kurt lived only long enough to take two deep breaths, but his face was in the water. The autopsy confirmed water in his lungs and there were no signs of trauma anywhere on the body.

Bernie ruled it an accidental drowning, possibly due to a heart attack.

Later that morning Craig called Gerald Fox at PaxCorp. He informed him that Kurt was dead and he should terminate any actions recently ordered by Schimler. Their bills would not be honored. Fox thanked him for the heads up and immediately called off Operation Cheyenne.

That afternoon, Caroline Bechman, Military Liaison and Second in Command at the National Command Authority complex dialed Senator Franks' call center and left him a message to call her. By 3:45 Mountain Standard Time, she and the Senator had established how they would work together to capture and punish any and all Jihadists in Afghanistan and how they would expedite the reformation of our system of government. John Franks was too busy to procrastinate and he loved it.

The End

EPILOGUE

On WEDNESDAY JANUARY 3rd little Anne Horowitz passed away in her sleep. Pastor Franks thanked God for his mercy. This he did in private. At the hospital, he simply tried to console her parents with reminders that she was in a better place. It didn't help.

Maggie and her fiancé were too absorbed in their upcoming nuptials to pay attention to world events. They were not even aware that on April 1st, newly-proclaimed President of Pakistan Muhhamad Jamali was accused of 'war crimes which endangered the Republic.' He was deposed and arrested that same day. He claimed it was a covert action of America's CIA and vowed he would be back.

Senator Franks worked hard and, as the days passed with no further nuclear attacks despite the escalation of conflict in the Middle East most people felt that America's "President Pro-Tem" was a capable leader and a Godsend to the nation. His popularity escalated after he teamed up with the NCA and the country got back to normal.

On April 2nd the United States held an unprecedented national election and replaced all Senators and Congressmen from all fifty states. Several Governors moved up which precipitated a round of state elections. The new government, under the direction of PPT Franks, operated out of buildings in each state and met electronically. One of their first actions was to hold an election of officers. John Franks and

Caroline Bechman were unanimously elected as President and Vice-President. It was politics as usual

Estelle met a Major who was in charge of supplies for the compound which meant he got out of the complex on a regular basis. They hit it off pretty well and occasionally she accompanied him on his errands. When she did, they got a motel room. He wasn't the lover Don had been, but he was better than nothing. At least she didn't have to settle for sharing Jack Daniels with the old goat. Meanwhile she had reached her ultimate goal: secretary to the President of the United States. The only negative in her life was Teri Franks.

General Birch was bored. He also hated living in a steel casket as he called it. Eventually he managed to get re-assigned as head of security at Fort Carson. He knew it was a demotion but at least he was back in a job he felt comfortable doing. He and John kept in touch by email.

Experts from Virginia measured the crater that was once Washington D.C. It was almost three miles across, and the average depth was sixty feet. Most of the material inside looked like glazed rock, except for occasional twisted chunks of metal and some stains which may have been from living things.